Praise for Tim Waggoner

'Tim Waggoner has a knack for taking conventional horror tropes and giving them a deliciously bizarre spin.'
Horror Fiction Review

'His ability to weave the surreal with the hyper-real is his greatest talent.'
Signal Horizon

'Waggoner is literally the blueprint for horror writers.'
Cemetery Dance

'An excellent read.'
The Literary License Podcast on *Your Turn To Suffer*

'Often macabre and sometimes terrifying, *The Forever House* is a ghastly and grim adventure.'
Grimdark Magazine

'A wild trip, an amazing experience, a highly entertaining read.'
Sci-Fi & Scary on *The Mouth of the Dark*

'*They Kill* plunges readers deep into the heart of pulse pounding supernatural horror with a story that could only come from the mind of Tim Waggoner.'
This is Horror

TIM WAGGONER

LORD OF THE FEAST

FLAME TREE PRESS
6 Melbray Mews, London, SW6 3NS, UK
flametreepress.com

US sales, distribution and warehouse:
Simon & Schuster
simonandschuster.biz

UK distribution and warehouse:
Hachette UK Distribution
hukdcustomerservice@hachette.co.uk

Thanks to the Flame Tree Press team.

The cover is created by Flame Tree Studio with
thanks to Shutterstock.com.
The font families used are Avenir and Bembo.

Flame Tree Press is an imprint of Flame Tree Publishing Ltd
flametreepublishing.com

A copy of the CIP data for this book is available from the British Library
and the Library of Congress.

PB ISBN: 978-1-78758-636-9
ebook ISBN: 978-1-78758-639-0

Printed and bound in Great Britain by Clays Ltd, Elcograf S.p.A.

TIM WAGGONER

LORD OF THE FEAST

FLAME TREE PRESS
London & New York

This one's for two amazing men: Joe Lansdale and Michael Knost. I skipped a panel I was supposed to be on at StokerCon to have coffee with them, and it was one of the best decisions I've ever made.

CHAPTER ONE

NOW

Give in. You know you want to.

Kate is lying on a rough stone floor, and she presses her hands to her ears to shut out the cold, mocking voice, although she knows it won't do any good. You can't shut out what's inside you. The world around her is a riot of noise and motion, and her mind struggles to make sense of what's happening. She catches only fleeting impressions – a maelstrom of wraith-like forms swirling around her, Ethan chanting in an alien language. Even with her ears covered, the foul words stab into them like ice picks. She draws in a shuddering gasp of air so frigid it sears her lungs, and she's grateful for the pain. It centers her, focuses her. Above her, on the ceiling…no, where the ceiling *should* be is…is…. She doesn't want to think about that, doesn't want to look up and see, afraid that if she does, she'll lose what's left of her mind.

There's no need to fear. The Gyre loves all – especially you.

"Go fuck yourself," she says, maybe out loud, maybe not. Inside her head, the voice laughs.

You first.

Her vision swims with tears of terror, pain, and sorrow, and through them, she sees Lee kneeling on the floor, head bowed, wrists and ankles bound with leather restraints, a ball gag in their mouth. Great-Aunt Caprice stands next to Lee, and she grips their curly black hair and yanks their head up, forcing them to watch the completion of the rite. *I'm so sorry, love,* Kate thinks. Lee doesn't look at her, stares blankly forward, and Kate wonders how much of their mind is left. An older man, bearded and disheveled, kneels next to a rusted shopping cart, hands clasped in front of him as if he is praying, on his face an expression of almost childlike wonder.

Ethan stands in the center of the chamber, wild eyed, brown hair blowing in a sourceless wind. In his hands he grips the *Liber Pravitas Itineribus — The Book of Depravity*: cover fashioned from fragments of fused bone, pages formed from desiccated, discolored flesh, letters written using the dark blood of the greatest sinners to ever walk the face of the Earth. On the floor in front of Ethan is a collection of unclothed body parts. Arms, legs, torso, head. Each part comes from a separate individual. Men, women, different races, different ages… and the parts look fresh, as if harvested within the hour. There's no blood at the junctures where cuts were made to separate the pieces from their original bodies. The top of the skull has been removed, exposing only emptiness within. The parts begin to move with life of their own, writhing as Ethan reads from the book, his mouth speaking blasphemous words, each syllable causing micro-tears in reality. The wraith-things swirl around him like a miniature ethereal cyclone, making him difficult to see, and Kate can't read the expression on his face. Does he feel joyful? Apprehensive? Triumphant? Maybe all three, she decides. He is, after all, creating a god.

The longer Ethan reads aloud, the more damage reality takes. The air is brittle now, sharp, burning, and breathing feels like inhaling white-hot metal razors. The wraith-cyclone bends away from Ethan, arcs toward the collection of body parts, separating as it rushes toward them. The wraiths vanish as they enter the pieces of the god-to-be, and Kate knows that it's game over for her, for Lee, for everyone.

You can make sure Lee survives this, the voice in Kate's head says. *And you know how.*

She does, and she's tempted, sweet Oblivion how she's tempted. All she has to do is think one simple word — all she has to do is *surrender* — and she could save Lee, save the world, maybe even the whole damn universe. Her mouth starts to form the first letter of *Yes,* but before she can say it, or even fully think it, she sucks her lower lip between her teeth and bites down hard. Warm-wet floods her mouth, and the pain

– sharp, piercing – is so welcome she laughs with delight, spraying the air red.

You think that's funny? The voice shouts in her head, furious. *Try laughing at this, bitch.*

Agony tears through her skull, more intense than anything she's ever experienced or imagined. It feels like something with large sharp claws is inside her head, furiously trying to dig its way out. The pain is so great, it drives her to her knees. She grits her teeth, presses her hands to her head and pushes inward as hard as she can, as if trying to squash the pain, make it smaller, contain it, but this only makes it hurt worse.

LET…. ME…. OUT!

No!

As she lies there, an endless series of explosions going off in her head, she hears Caprice laughing.

And laughing….

And laughing….

Then Kate hears the Lord's first footsteps, and she knows the rite is complete. The Lord is whole – or nearly so – and it's coming for her, for what's inside her. She would rise to her feet and run, but she's in too much agony to twitch a finger, let alone stand.

The voice inside her head giggles like a mad child as the Lord draws closer.

CHAPTER TWO

THEN

Caprice Linton's office was luxurious to the point of decadence – which was exactly the way she liked it: coffered ceiling, built-in shelving and cabinetry, custom-built executive desk, wood flooring, all obscenely expensive, of course. No windows, though. Caprice sometimes needed to do things in here that she didn't want the world witnessing. Misshapen globs of light hung from the ceiling on thin metal rods. The globs pulsed slowly, as if they were breathing, and they made soft humming sounds that Caprice found relaxing – as long as they were fed regularly, that is. If a meal was so much as fifteen minutes late, they'd scream like infants being torn limb from limb. The walls were painted a rich red – the precise color of arterial spray – and the shelves were filled with skeletons of small creatures that had no counterparts on Earth. Caprice loved collecting the remains of exotic animals, and they didn't come more exotic than these. From time to time, the skeletons' empty eye sockets would glow with pinpricks of light, and when this happened, Clarice turned off the chandelier so she could admire the illumination of the spirits trapped inside the skeletons.

She sat at the desk in a high-backed black leather chair, laptop open in front of her, going over outstanding accounts, as she did every month. She'd send a reminder to those clients who had yet to settle their bills, and if they had not done so within two weeks after receipt, they'd lose their privileges at the House of Red Tears. If they still had not paid after an additional two weeks, she'd send one of the freelance operatives she contracted with to have a 'talk' with them. And if the bastards *still* didn't cough up the cash after that, they would be brought back to the House, not as guests this time, but as playthings. Everyone paid in the end, one way or another.

Caprice was sixty-four, but she looked a good decade younger. She kept her blond hair cut short, and she wore a white business jacket, blouse, skirt, and high-heeled shoes. She always dressed in white, regardless of what she was doing. She prided herself on being able to perform the messiest tasks without getting so much as a speck of dirt – or drop of blood – on her. She never wore makeup, saw it as a meaningless affectation. Her eyes were a striking crystalline blue, and her thin lips were perpetually pressed together, as if she were in a permanent state of disapproval. Those lips compressed even more tightly when there was a single sharp knock at the door. Only one person ever knocked like that, and she almost shouted for him to fuck off. Once she started a task, she wanted to keeping working at it until it was finished. She *loathed* being interrupted. Ten years ago, the most important project she'd ever been part of had been interrupted and left unfinished, and it still galled her now, a decade later.

"Come in," she called out.

With a single exception, none of the doors in the House of Red Tears had locks – including her office. The door opened smoothly on freshly oiled hinges, and Axton entered. He was fifty-nine, with a round face, silver-black hair, and thick black mustache. His chin came to a point, a feature Caprice disliked. She wished he'd grow a beard to cover it, had even suggested it once or twice, but he'd never done so. At Clarice's insistence, he also dressed entirely in white – white suit, white shirt, white tie, white slacks, white shoes. She noted that his shoes were speckled red, and she sighed softly. The man could be a real slob sometimes. *Good thing he has a huge cock,* she thought. *And can still get it up*.

"I hate to bother you, Ms. Linton."

"Bullshit. You live to bother me."

Axton didn't dispute this.

"I've just finished making my daily check on the Repository. I believe we have some new activity."

Caprice felt a zing of excitement at Axton's words, but she forced herself to respond calmly. "When you say *activity*...."

Axton – who normally was the epitome of emotionless composure – allowed himself a small smile. "I think this may well be the moment we've been waiting for."

Caprice drew in a breath and closed her eyes. After ten long years, could it finally be happening? *We've had false alarms before,* she cautioned herself, *and this might well be another.* Still, her pulse quickened, and she experienced the first faint stirrings of what might have been hope.

She opened her eyes, closed her laptop, and stood.

"Let's go find Ethan."

★   ★   ★

Ethan stood in front of a long metal table set against a tiled wall. Upon its surface rested a number of implements – gleaming stainless-steel surgical tools, an assortment of knives (carving and hunting), glass containers filled with pins, needles, and nails (various sizes and lengths), tools such as handsaws, pliers, and hammers, drills, hatchets and axes, and several chainsaws, smaller ones with eight-inch blades up to monsters of twenty inches, depending on how much meat and bone you wanted to cut and how fast you wanted to do it. There were lengths of rope – hemp, nylon, and satin – as well as scarves of different types and sizes, and garottes made with regular wire or, if you were looking for something with more bite to it, barbed wire. No guns, though. Caprice used to supply them, but then one of her clients decided to continue the party after he finished with his plaything and rampaged through the house, shooting anyone unlucky enough to find themselves in his path. Since then, guns were strictly forbidden in the House of Red Tears – at least for clients. There were bottles of chemicals on the table, acids and poisons mostly, along with plastic containers filled with common household cleaners. There were plastic goggles to keep fluids from getting in your eyes, rolls of silver duct tape for clients who preferred their playthings to remain silent, and a stack of towels and cleansing wipes, should clients feel the need to tidy up during their session. The only fire-related equipment on the table was a lone gas-fueled blowtorch. Over the years, a number of the House's clients had petitioned Ethan's grandmother to include cans of gasoline and kerosene in the rooms' setup, but she always refused. *The last thing I need is for some lunatic to burn down the place,* she'd say. A sensible precaution, Ethan thought, but he could see how some clients would find it a disappointment. There was nothing quite like burning another human alive. The sound of bubbling skin and fat, the screams, the smell of cooking flesh....

Like all the client rooms in the House of Red Tears, the floor, walls, and ceiling were covered with white tile. Recessed lights in the ceiling could be set to whatever level of illumination a client preferred. Some liked to work in near-blinding light while others preferred dim shadow. A metal cabinet contained space for clients to store their clothes, should they wish to disrobe before getting to work. Caprice wanted Ethan to follow in her footsteps and learn how to kill without getting any mess on himself, so he always kept his clothes on when playing. The cabinet also contained leather aprons and rubber gloves, along with an assortment of masks, whips, dildos, and restraints. Ethan never bothered with the masks. He thought they were childish and more than a little cowardly. As far as he was concerned, if you were going to kill someone, you should be willing to show your face to them. Each room had three workstations: a steel autopsy table with gutters to catch and funnel blood, a steel chair with leather restraints, and a steel X-cross with manacles for wrists and ankles. There was a large drain in the middle of the floor, a hose attached to one wall, and a sink and a shower in the corner for clients to clean themselves when they were finished. The walls were soundproofed as well, but sometimes you could still hear cries of agony coming from adjoining rooms when someone was assigned a really good screamer.

Ethan picked up a hatchet, considered it, then put it back down. He sighed, picked up a wickedly sharp filleting knife, turned away from the table, and started walking toward the chair. An elderly man sat there, naked, arms and legs bound, duct tape covering his mouth. He was bearded and so skinny you could see the outline of his bones, a skeleton wrapped in parchment-thin flesh. His eyes were wide with terror as Ethan approached.

Ethan stopped within reach of the man and regarded him for a moment. Caprice wanted Ethan to take over the business when she retired, and so she'd started teaching him the trade when he was a child, not long after he'd come to live with her. At first, she'd bring him into rooms to finish off playthings that clients, for one reason or another, had left alive when their session was concluded. These days, he cleaned rooms and restocked equipment, but every once in a while, he got a plaything of his own to practice on. Unlike the majority of his grandmother's clients, Ethan didn't have a specific type of plaything that he favored, and he didn't get a sexual charge from torturing and killing humans, so he was happy to take whatever leftovers Caprice gave him. The best specimens should go to paying clients anyway; that was just smart business.

"Sorry, but I'm not really into this today," Ethan said to the man. "It's not you, it's me. I know that sounds like a lame excuse, but it's true. Don't get me wrong. I like killing people well enough. But it just feels…empty unless there's meaning to it, you know? Some kind of *reason* for doing it."

Ethan searched the man's eyes for any indication that he understood, but he saw only fear. The man's gaze kept darting to the knife Ethan held, and beads of sweat gathered on his forehead.

Ethan's grandmother procured playthings for the House of Red Tears from a variety of suppliers. All the people in the world who disappeared every year had to go somewhere, and more than a few of them ended up here. Sometimes Ethan wondered if anyone really vanished, or if there were hundreds of places like the House of Red Tears located across the world, all in need of a constant supply of material. As an extra touch, Caprice made sure that each of the playthings she bought came with biographical data for those clients who preferred to know some personal details about their toys.

The old man's name was Luke Riley, retired high-school history teacher from Racine, Wisconsin, divorced, with two adult children and three grandchildren. He was a type 2 diabetic, had sleep apnea, and he'd started running marathons in his thirties, but had to quit when his knees couldn't take anymore punishment. He'd had a hip replacement in October, and while the incision had healed nicely, it was still quite visible.

Ethan wondered what Luke thought of him. Twenty-two, shaggy brown hair, meager mustache and beard, thin, medium height, wearing a long-sleeved olive-green top, jeans, and sneakers. His most striking feature – so he'd been told – was eyes so dark they looked almost black. He supposed Luke didn't find him particularly intimidating, and he could see why some clients liked to wear masks when they played. They wanted to make themselves into monsters to intensify their playthings' terror. It was a little late for him to don a mask now, though. Maybe next time.

Ethan looked at Luke's scar. He'd never seen an artificial hip before. It might be interesting to open Luke up and take a look at it. But no. If he wanted to, he could find a video of the medical procedure on YouTube to watch. It would be easier and less messy.

"Unfortunately, I can't let you go, and since no clients want you…." Ethan gave an apologetic shrug.

Luke made muffled sounds of alarm behind the tape and shook his head rapidly back and forth. As he did so, Ethan swiped the filleting knife through the air and laid open the man's left carotid. He took a quick step back – just as his grandmother had taught him – and watched as Luke's blood jetted out. The old man thrashed in the chair, struggling uselessly against the restraints, but his exertions quickly grew weaker as his blood pressure dropped. Soon the jet of blood become a trickling fountain, then stopped altogether. Luke went still, eyes wide and unblinking.

It was so easy to kill people when you knew how, Ethan thought. Not much more difficult than flipping an off switch on a machine, really.

He looked up. A shiny-smooth obsidian half-globe protruded from the ceiling, roughly the size of a basketball…well, *half* a basketball.

Clients, if they noticed it at all, assumed it contained a hidden security camera. They were wrong.

"Hope you have a good trip, Luke," Ethan said.

He walked to the sink, rinsed off the filleting knife, then returned it to the table and cleaned it with an alcohol wipe. He then headed for the door. He was happy to keep his regular clothes on when killing, but when it came to clean-up, he always donned coveralls. Each floor of the House had a maintenance/janitorial office, and Ethan kept a pair of coveralls in each one, his name stitched on the front to keep any of the regular staff from stealing them. He intended to get his coveralls, along with a bucket, mop, and some bleach, and return to clean up the mess left by Luke's dying. He'd also have to call someone down in the crematorium to come up and get Luke's body. He scowled as he stepped into the hallway. He liked the idea of running the entire House one day, but he was sick of all the scutwork Caprice had him doing. How much longer was she going to make him clean up blood, organs, piss, and shit?

If you want to really learn a business, she'd once told him, *you've got to learn it from the bottom up.*

He'd spent more than enough time at the bottom as far as he was concerned, and when he next saw his grandmother, he'd tell her so.

The elevator dinged as he drew near it. The door slid open and Caprice and Axton stepped out, both wearing their ubiquitous white outfits. Caprice kept urging Ethan to wear white too – *It's a branding thing,* she'd say – but there was no fucking way he was going to do that. The two of them looked ridiculous.

He was surprised to see his grandmother here on the third floor. She usually didn't leave her first-floor office during business hours – and *every* hour was a business hour at the House of Red Tears. But now that she was here, he figured this was as good a time as any to let her know how he felt about being little more than another member of the cleaning staff. He stopped, opened his mouth to speak, but then Caprice broke into a wide grin and rushed to embrace him. He couldn't remember the last time he'd seen his grandmother smile – or the last time she'd touched him – and in his shock he forgot all about his determination to better his status in the House.

She held him tight for several moments, and when she released him, he said, "Is everything all right?"

Caprice laughed and then actually reached out and tousled his hair, something she'd never done before.

"It looks like the day is here, sweetie," she said.

At first, Ethan didn't know what she was talking about, but then it hit him.

"You mean *the* day?"

She nodded.

The news stunned him. Caprice had been talking about The Day since he'd been a child, but he'd never actually believed it would happen – and maybe it wasn't. This might be merely another in a series of false alarms that had occurred over the years. But he'd never seen Caprice so excited before, and that made him think that maybe, just maybe, this time was different.

"Come with us to the Repository," Caprice said.

Ethan glanced back in the direction he'd come.

"I need to do clean-up in 319," he said.

"Finished with Mr. Riley already?" Caprice asked.

Ethan wasn't surprised that his grandmother had known who he'd been playing with. She knew the name and stats of each plaything that was brought into the House, and she knew everything that happened to them while they were under its roof.

"We ended early," Ethan said. "I guess I wasn't really feeling it today, you know?"

Axton's brow furrowed as if he was displeased by Ethan's statement.

"If you're going to do a job, you need to take the time to do it right," the man said.

Ethan hated it when Axton got judgy. Sometimes the guy acted as if he thought he was Ethan's father.

Without taking her gaze off Ethan, Caprice laid a hand on Axton's shoulder to silence him. The man bristled, but he shut up. Ethan couldn't help smiling. He loved it when Caprice did her *Hush, doggy* thing with him.

"Axton will call one of the regular staff to take care of the room — and Mr. Riley. Won't you, dear?"

Without replying, Axton removed his phone from his pocket and stepped away to make the call.

Ethan smiled. "It's good to be the queen, isn't it?"

Caprice smiled back. "Yes, it is."

★   ★   ★

Ethan got on the elevator with Caprice and Axton. The House of Red Tears had three main levels — most of which were reserved for playrooms — as well as a basement and subbasement. The basement was where Caprice's and Ethan's rooms were, as well as Axton's. It was off limits to all guests, of course, and staff were only allowed in to clean once a week. The subbasement was where the Repository was located, and only Caprice and Axton had access to it. Caprice had taken Ethan to the Repository several times over the years — *To get you used to it*, she'd told him — but it had been a while since his last trip. A special key was required to allow the elevator to reach the subbasement, and Axton removed his from a pocket, inserted it next to the lowest button on the elevator's control panel, turned it, then pressed the button. The door slid closed and the elevator began to descend. There were mirrors on the walls of the elevator car — to give an illusion of more space, Ethan assumed — and he watched his grandmother's reflection as they headed toward the subbasement. There was color in her normally wan cheeks and she couldn't stop smiling. She always looked younger than her age, but right now she appeared twenty, even thirty years younger. Ethan had always wondered if his grandmother's youthful appearance had some magical basis, and right now he was certain of it. She might not wear makeup, but that didn't mean she wasn't vain about her appearance in her own way. *What a trivial use of power*, Ethan thought. Then again, maybe he'd feel different when he was in his sixties.

The elevator came to a smooth stop as it reached the subbasement. The door slid open, and Axton removed his key. Caprice was the first to step out of the elevator car, and ceiling lights activated, tripped by motion sensors. Ethan followed and Axton brought up the rear. Overhead fluorescent lights illuminated an antechamber of rough-hewn rock barely larger than the elevator car itself. The air was cool here, but stale, and breathing it was like trying to swallow a handful of chalk. Opposite the elevator, built into the stone wall, was an iron door. Etched symbols covered the entirety of its surface — letters, pictographs, ideograms, and shapes for which no human language had a name. Ethan understood most of them...well, okay, about half, thanks to Caprice's tutelage, but he didn't like looking at them. They made his eyes hurt, and if he stared at them too long, he'd get a killer headache. Some of the symbols were designed to keep anyone who shouldn't be here from getting in, but most were to prevent the things inside from getting out.

There was a single lock on the door, and just as with the elevator, there were only two keys: one for Caprice and one for Axton. Ethan resented not having his own pair of keys that would permit him access to the Repository. Not because he necessarily wanted to come here alone — the damn place creeped him out — but because it was his birthright, and because he wanted his grandmother to trust him. Whenever he brought up the subject, she'd tell him that *of course* she trusted him, and *of course* he would get his own keys...someday. So far, someday hadn't come, and he was beginning to doubt it ever would.

I'm going to run things differently when the House is mine, he thought. Although, truthfully, he had no idea what exactly he'd do. He supposed he'd figure it out.

Caprice used her key this time instead of Axton. She stepped forward, slid it into the lock, and whispered a series of noises that sounded more animal than human. Then she turned the key with an authoritative *click*, took hold of the knob, and pulled the door open. Ethan had never opened the Repository door himself. It looked heavy as hell, but Caprice seemed to have no trouble with it, and she stepped inside without hesitation. Ethan looked at Axton. The man smiled and made an after-you gesture.

Fucker, Ethan thought, then followed after his grandmother. Axton came in after him, leaving the door open so they could leave in a hurry if need be. Ethan wasn't certain how the wards on the door worked, but Caprice had once assured him that they continued operating for a short time after the door was opened, emphasis on *short*. With each passing moment that the door was open, the wards grew weaker, and if you didn't close the door in time, the things inside would escape – but only after they had their fun with you.

How long before the wards fail? Ethan had asked.

Caprice had given him a sly, dark smile. *I don't know. I've always managed to make it out before that happened.*

The fluorescent light from the outer chamber couldn't cross the Repository's threshold for reasons Ethan was unclear on. This meant that it was absolutely pitch-black inside, but only at first. Soon a faint white glow began to appear, manifesting as small, dim pieces of light, like a midnight snowfall. The pieces expanded, growing brighter as they did so, and began to take on human shape. They floated around the chamber, slowly at first, then with increasing speed, arcing, dipping, diving, and circling. They possessed no discernible features, not even separate fingers or toes, and their forms fluctuated, expanding and contracting, lengthening and shortening as they soared through the air. It was impossible to tell how many there were. Hundreds surely, perhaps thousands. On the rocky ceiling above was a black half-globe that resembled the ones installed in the playrooms, except this was much larger. The small half-globes were called Conveyers, while this one was the Receiver. Ethan didn't know exactly how the process worked, but the Conveyers captured the spirits of those who lost their lives in the playrooms and – as their name suggested – sent them down to the Receiver, which then released them into the Repository. Luke was somewhere in this maelstrom of swirling wraiths, along with every other person Ethan had killed since coming to live with his grandmother. Not for the first time, he wondered how self-aware these spirits were. Were they merely life energy, no more sentient than electricity freed from batteries? Or did they retain the personalities they'd had in life, either partly or in full? The few times he'd been down here, he'd tried to sense if the wraiths – or as Caprice liked to call them, the Gathered – were reaching out to him, attempting to communicate telepathically. But he hadn't felt anything then, and he didn't feel anything now. As far as he could tell, the Gathered were no more intelligent than a school of fish. He supposed it was a mercy. Who'd want to be confined down here in the dark, moments after being tortured and murdered in the most horrendous ways imaginable, along with hundreds of other victims who'd experienced the same thing? It did *not* sound like a good time.

One of the things he'd always found most eerie about the spirits was their absolute silence. They didn't moan, wail, or shriek like ghosts in movies or cartoons. They were voiceless, another reason he thought – or maybe hoped – they were also mindless.

"I know it's been a while since I've been down here," Ethan said, "but I don't see anything different about these ghosts."

"The Gathered," Caprice corrected. "It's important to have a sense of style about these things."

Ethan shrugged.

"And as for what's different about them…" Caprice said.

"Just wait," Axton finished.

Christ, they're completing each other's sentences, Ethan thought. He knew they screwed – neither was particularly quiet when they did it, whether it was in Caprice's office or her basement bedroom – and that was gross enough, but the idea that they were an actual *couple*? That was as disgusting as any mess he'd ever mopped up in a playroom.

The three of them watched the wraiths flit around for several moments, and then Ethan saw that the ghosts – the *Gathered* – were beginning to group together. They soon formed a funnel, like a glowing ectoplasmic tornado, and began spinning around so fast that they appeared to become a solid object. Now *this* he'd never seen before.

He turned to Caprice. "What does it mean?"

She gazed upon the whirling Gathered with an expression Ethan could only think of as worshipful. To his surprise, tears started sliding down her cheeks.

"It means that after ten long years, enough fuckers have died in this shithole to give us the power we need."

She turned away from the Gathered and walked toward two recessed areas carved into the wall near the doorway, one above the other. The bottom area was empty. The top, however, was not. Axton followed Caprice, and after a second, Ethan joined them. The top hollow space was roughly eye level, and the Gathered put off enough light to illuminate the object displayed within – a human head, eyeless and missing the top part of its skull. Not only were the eyes gone, there was no brain, either. Ethan didn't know who the man had been, nor did he know exactly how he'd met his end, although he doubted it was peacefully. Ethan hated the thing. There was no blood on it, and despite the many years it had resided here, it showed no sign of decay – no rotting flesh, no stench of spoiled meat. The damn thing looked so fresh, in fact, that Ethan almost expected it to open its mouth and begin speaking at any moment. But as unsettling as the head's appearance was, what really bothered Ethan was the way it made him feel when he was near it. His temperature began to rise, pressure built on the right side of his head, and his stomach roiled with incipient nausea. When he'd been a child, he put these symptoms down to not being used to seeing such a grisly artifact, but now that he was an adult – not to mention an experienced killer – he was at a loss to explain why he should react so strongly to the head. He did his best to conceal how he felt, but Axton gave him a sideways glance, as if he was fully aware of how uncomfortable Ethan was. Caprice paid no attention to him, though. Her attention was focused entirely on the head.

She reached up and gently, almost lovingly, stroked a cheek. Ethan shuddered and felt hot bile splash the back of his throat.

"It won't be much longer now. Soon you'll be with us once more, and the world shall cry out in despair."

Caprice leaned slightly forward, and for a horrible moment, Ethan feared she was going to kiss the fucking thing, but then Axton said, "We should go. The Gathered are getting restless."

Ethan looked back to the whirling column of spirits and saw sparks of blue-white energy shooting off them. The column itself was beginning to wobble, like a gigantic top that was losing momentum, and once it fell, what would happen? Would the spirits break apart and attack them? Or would they rush toward the open doorway and fly outward, heading to wherever the ghosts of murdered men, women, and children go?

Caprice turned away from the head – reluctantly, Ethan thought – and examined the Gathered. The column had now slowed to the point where the outlines of individual spirits could be made out.

"You're right, Axton. We must leave. Besides, we have much planning to do. Let's go, Ethan."

Caprice started toward the door, Axton at her side. Ethan gave the head a last look, and was startled when one of the empty eye sockets winked at him. He turned away quickly and hurried after Axton and his grandmother, mouth clamped shut tight to keep himself from vomiting.

INTERLUDE

Head

Nelson Young was late for a meeting with new clients — not that he gave a shit. He'd spent the last couple hours in his favorite bar enjoying an extended liquid lunch, and he was feeling no pain. He sat behind the wheel of his cherry-red Corvette, blazing down the street, whipping past slower vehicles, rock music blasting from the sound system, windows down, air on his face. Life was *good*. On paper, at least. In reality, his life was on the shitty side these days.

At forty-three, Nelson was a successful lawyer by any standard, but especially a criminal one. He first started blackmailing people in law school, finding out who was cheating on exams and threatening to expose them if they didn't pay up. After law school, he joined a small firm, and it didn't take him long to learn the other lawyers' secrets — one thing you could always count on is that *everyone* has secrets of some kind — and he began blackmailing them too. He soon extended his blackmailing operation to those clients who were well off and could afford to funnel a bit of extra money to their lawyer on a monthly basis. One thing he never did, though, was take advantage of a client who was of modest means. Nelson had grown up poor — *really* poor. People thought they knew what poor meant, but people didn't know shit. Unless you grew up in actual fighting-rats-for-food poverty, you had no fucking conception of how being poor ate away at you, body and soul, how it ground you down until you had almost no sense of self left, how you'd vow to do whatever it took to claw your way to a better life so you would never again know bone-chilling cold and gut-gnawing hunger. That was why Nelson had studied his ass off in school, gotten scholarships to college and law school, and eventually started his blackmail side hustle. He might've made himself into a predator – although he supposed the people he blackmailed probably viewed him more as a parasite, not that he gave a fuck what any of them thought – but he refused to prey on anyone who was even close to being poor.

He had his own practice now, and his clients were all wealthy, or at least wealthy-*ish*, which meant he was too. He had a hot wife who was ten years younger than he was, and an even hotter girlfriend who was twenty years younger. At least, he'd *had* a girlfriend. Tonya had gotten knocked up and had wanted him to leave his wife and marry her. He'd wanted her to get an abortion, was happy to pay for it, but she refused. She wanted his baby and she wanted him. No one gave *him* ultimatums, so he told her to get lost and if she tried to make contact with him again or tried to cause trouble for him in any way, he'd destroy her and the little fucker growing inside her. So what did the bitch do? She went back to her apartment – which *he* paid for, for Christ's sake – undressed, got in a tub of warm water, and slit her goddamn wrists.

Talk about a drama queen.

Her funeral had been this morning. He hadn't intended on going, didn't see the point, really, but he went anyway. *Must be getting sentimental in my old age*, he thought. Tonya had kept their relationship secret – that was the deal – so no one at the service knew who he was, which was fine by him. He sat in the back of the small room at the funeral home on a rickety wooden chair. The scent of fresh flowers hung in the air, heavy and cloying, along with the sounds of muffled sobs and hushed whispers. Most of the mourners were Tonya's age – friends, most likely, along with co-workers at the restaurant where she'd been a server – but there was a contingent of older people who he assumed were relatives. Parents, grandparents, aunts and uncles…. Nelson ignored the various speakers who stepped up to a wooden podium at the front of the room to talk about Tonya and what a tragedy it was that she died so young. He focused on the open casket surrounded by floral arrangements, on Tonya's still body lying within, and wondered whether the mortician had used makeup to conceal the cuts on her wrists or just sewn them up.

Tonya was garbed in a long-sleeved blouse, so there was no way to tell.

By the time the service concluded, Nelson felt irritable and out of sorts. He hadn't loved Tonya, of course, but he had *enjoyed* her, and the realization that he was never going to get to fuck her again depressed him. He left without giving his condolences to Tonya's parents. What would he say? *Too bad she's gone. I really liked the way she used to squirt during orgasm. She made a real mess, you know what I mean?* He'd gotten in his car and turned on the engine when he got a text from Roy Dennison, a fellow lawyer he saw at the casino now and again. Roy was a gambling addict, and Nelson had floated him a couple loans over the last couple years in hopes of being able to make use of the man someday. The text repaid Nelson's investment. Roy was a divorce attorney, and his text was to give Nelson a heads-up that his wife, Audrey, had met with him to explore the possibility of getting divorced.

I don't think she's ready to pull the trigger yet, Roy had texted. *But she's close. FYI.*

Christ, Nelson had thought. *What the fuck is it with these goddamn women?*

After that, he was depressed *and* pissed off, so he drove straight to a bar, had a few drinks, then a few more, and before he knew it, he was late for his afternoon appointment. He'd almost called his assistant to cancel, but he didn't have anything else to do, and he didn't want to sit around brooding. Better to be busy and keep his mind off Tonya and Audrey. Besides, this new client ran a horse farm – a big one – and he might be a good candidate to join his off-the-books income stream, depending on whether he could find any information to leverage against the man. He relied on a private investigator who was just as amoral as he was to dig up that kind of dirt. If the horse guy seemed promising, he'd give the PI a call after the meeting and—

The speed limit in this part of town was thirty-five, but Nelson was doing over fifty as he approached the intersection. He was drunk, the light was red, and four vehicles were lined up, their drivers waiting in various states of impatience for the light to turn green. Nelson slammed into the rear of the last car in the line – a blue Miata – and his world exploded into deafening noise and vertiginous motion. When the sound and movement ended, he sat for a moment, listening to the hiss of the Corvette's air bag deflating. He didn't know what had happened, where he was, or even his fucking name. He heard the ticking of his hot engine and people yelling, although he couldn't make out what any of them were saying. He wasn't sure they were speaking English.

His driver's side door opened then, and hands reached in, unlatched his seat belt, and gently helped him out of the car. His chest hurt, and he thought he'd cracked some ribs, maybe even broken them. He looked into the face of the man guiding him toward the sidewalk. His vision was wonky, and the man's features were a confused blur.

"It's going to be okay," the man said.

Good to hear, Nelson thought.

He looked back over his shoulder as they walked, and saw that his beloved Vette – which had spun out after the accident and now sat in the left lane – was totaled, the entire front end smashed in, making it one damn expensive accordion. He started to laugh, but that set off a burst of pain in his head, and he clamped his mouth shut. The Miata had been crushed between his Vette and the vehicle in front of it – a Ford pickup – and someone inside, a woman from the sound of the voice, was screaming like a fucking banshee.

"My baby! Oh god, my baby!"

What was the bitch whining about? She was still alive, wasn't she? She could always squeeze out another pup.

Nelson's benefactor had one arm wrapped around his waist to steady him, which Nelson appreciated. His legs felt weak and limp as an old man's cock. The man helped him onto the sidewalk and then into an alley between a car parts business – ironic, huh? – and a title agency. A woman was waiting in the alley. Her face was no clearer than that of the man helping him, but Nelson didn't think he recognized her. The man lowered him to the ground, and Nelson sat with his back against a brick wall. Sharp pain shot through his chest whenever he breathed, and his head felt like it might split open any moment. He was beginning to think the man should've left him in the Vette until paramedics arrived. After all, you weren't supposed to move an accident victim, were you?

Hadn't he read that somewhere?

Now that he was sitting, his vision cleared a little, and he could make out more details about the man and woman in the alley with him. Neither was particularly remarkable. They were both middle-aged, the man wore a suit and the woman a dress. The woman held something Nelson didn't recognize at first, and then it came to him – it was a bowling ball bag. The man bent down, picked up an object off the ground, and stood. He now held an ax.

The man looked at the woman.

"You were right, Tressa. He was just where you'd said he'd be."

"Told you," the woman said, smiling.

The man turned back to Nelson.

"We appreciate your sacrifice."

Before Nelson could ask what he was talking about, the man drew the ax back, swung it sideways, and Nelson felt thick, sharp metal bite into his neck. It took several more strikes before his head came off, but Nelson was already dead by that point, and unlike Tonya, no one in the world would mourn his departure from it.

CHAPTER THREE

Kate, sweetie, I need to go to the bank. Would you mind checking on your grandpa while I'm gone?

When Tressa Shardlow had spoken these words – less than an hour ago now – Kate hadn't been able to suppress a shudder. She'd hoped her grandmother hadn't noticed, but she knew she most likely had. The woman might be in her seventies, but her mind was still sharp as ever. Still, Tressa hadn't remarked on Kate's reaction, and Kate was grateful.

Sure, Grandma. No problem.

Then again, Tressa had seemed distracted, as if she had something on her mind, although Kate couldn't guess what it might be. Tressa was an absolute master when it came to concealing her emotions, and Kate knew from experience that nothing could get her grandmother to talk about her feelings until she was ready. So Kate had kissed Tressa on the cheek, and her grandmother gave her a wan smile then turned and left the house. Kate went to the front window and watched Tressa get in their ancient Mazda, back out of the driveway, and head off, the car's engine complaining the entire way. Kate found it odd that her grandmother was going to the bank. They usually did their banking online. And although it was mid-May, the day was a gloomy one, the air Autumn-chilly, the sky filled with purple-bruise rain clouds, and Tressa had left without a jacket or umbrella. Kate felt sad as she turned away from the window, but she couldn't say why. Maybe the overcast day was getting to her, too.

Now Kate was lying on the couch in the living room, TV on, sound low, while she texted Lee. On the screen a pair of drag queens were talking about the longest times they'd stayed tucked, and Kate tried to imagine how uncomfortable it must be to conceal your penis and testicles like that. Talk about dedication to one's art.

Her phone buzzed as a text from Lee appeared on her screen.

lunch?

Kate glanced at the time displayed in the upper left-hand corner of her phone. It was 11:17.

gram went out on an errand she's not back yet

She waited for Lee to respond. The drag queens had moved on to comparing their most embarrassing moments on stage and were laughing uproariously. Kate's mouth formed a token smile, but she wasn't paying much attention to them.

She was listening for Grandpa Delmar.

Her phone buzzed again, startling her. She looked at the screen.

want me to come over and wait with you?

Kate's gut twisted into a sudden knot. She typed *NO!* but stopped before she could hit send. She and Lee had been dating for close to six months, and in that time, Lee hadn't set foot inside Kate's home. Tressa and Delmar's house might've been modest — a three-bedroom, two-bathroom ranch — but it was nothing to be ashamed of. And even if the house had been a run-down piece of shit, Lee wasn't the sort of person to judge by appearances. No, the reason Kate hadn't let Lee come here had nothing to do with the house itself. It was Delmar.

She was trying to think of a good excuse for why Lee couldn't come over when she heard a choking-hacking sound issue from the other end of the house, a noise like a cat straining to bring up a large wet hairball crossed with someone trying to literally cough up a lung. She put her phone on the coffee table, rose from the couch, and stepped to the hallway entrance. She listened but heard nothing more. She hoped Delmar would stay quiet, maybe settle down and go to sleep — or better yet, finally die. She felt like a shit for thinking this, but she couldn't help it. Tressa would be grief-stricken to lose her husband, but Kate knew that on some level, she'd be relieved too. Tressa had taken care of Delmar every day for the last decade, and the woman was emotionally and physically exhausted. Kate would be relieved too. Delmar was the reason she couldn't let Lee come over, but he was also why she hadn't gone away to college after high school, despite Tressa's urging. How could she go off and leave Tressa to care for Delmar alone? She couldn't, so she'd put her education on hold to stay and help. And while she had chosen to do this, knew she shouldn't resent Delmar for it, she still did sometimes, and that made her feel like even more of a shit.

Kate was nineteen, medium height, slender, with short red hair. She usually dressed down, and today she wore a T-shirt with Mario and Luigi on the front and jeans with the knees nearly worn out. She didn't have any tattoos yet – Lee had been encouraging her to get one – but she did wear a hoop nose ring. Not especially daring as body modifications went, but that was as far as she cared to go for now.

A minute went by. Two. She started to relax, thinking Grandpa had drifted off, but then that horrible hacking sound came again, far worse this time. She hesitated another second, wishing Tressa was here to deal with this, and she felt a momentary flash of anger at her grandmother for going to the goddamned bank and leaving her in this position. Then she was running down the hall toward Delmar's room.

Halfway there, the stink hit her. She knew it suffused the house – yet another reason she didn't want Lee to come over – but she was so accustomed to it that she mostly didn't notice it anymore. But the stench intensified the closer she got to her grandfather's room, to the point where it could no longer be ignored. When she'd been in second grade, her class had gone on a field trip to a farm in the spring. She'd loved seeing the baby chicks and lambs, and she looked forward to seeing the baby piggies. But she was appalled to see that the pigs' pen was filled with a soupy mixture of mud, piss, and shit, and the animals were covered in the foul muck. The smell had revolted her so much that to this day she couldn't eat ham or pork, couldn't even be in the same room with it. Delmar's stink was like that, only a hundred times worse.

When she reached his bedroom door – Tressa's room was across the hall; as much as she loved her husband, she couldn't sleep in the same room as him – Kate stopped and knocked three times.

"Grandpa? It's Kate. Is it all right if I come in?"

She performed this absurd ritual every time she needed to go into Delmar's room. With as much noise as he was making, she could swing a sledgehammer into the door and he wouldn't hear her. But even if he was quiet and did hear her, he couldn't reply – at least, not in any way that she could be sure was actual human communication.

She opened the door – it was never locked – and stepped inside. There was only one window, and it was covered by heavy blackout curtains since Delmar's skin was sensitive to light. There was a dresser to the left of the door, atop which rested a lamp with an incandescent bulb. Incandescent bulbs were good for people who were sensitive to light – they provided a softer glow and emitted little blue light, the wavelength that was most bothersome to the light-sensitive. As an additional precaution, Tressa kept a gauzy red scarf draped over the lampshade to dim the light even further. The light still seemed to bother Grandpa, but he could tolerate it, and it was enough for Tressa and Kate to see by. Kate switched on the light, and the dark room was illuminated by murky crimson. Normally, Delmar drew in a soft hissing breath whenever the light came on, but this time he was in too much distress to notice, coughing and hacking, body spasming as he writhed on his mattress. Tressa kept a sheet of clear plastic beneath him at all times, and it made crackling sounds as he thrashed back and forth. He lay in a hospital bed with side rails, wheels, adjustable mattress, the whole bit. Tressa had always warned Kate to keep the mattress level, though. If anyone put the bed into a sitting position, there was an excellent chance that Delmar might try to actually sit up and drown in his own lungs. Other than the dresser and lamp, the only other piece of furniture was a chair set next to the bed. Tressa would sit there in the evenings, talking to Delmar or sometimes reading aloud to him from a book. If he dozed off, she'd stop reading and just sit and look at him. Kate wondered what thoughts went through Tressa's mind during those times Delmar slept, but she was fairly certain she was better off not knowing.

Delmar Shardlow was somewhere in his seventies, but his precise age was impossible to determine given his condition. He was naked – clothes wouldn't stay on him – with the exception of an adult diaper that had been wrapped around him so tightly that his mottled flesh bulged over much of it. The diaper was swollen full, and its contents added to the room's stink. His skin was covered with a thick pus-yellow coating that was responsible for the nasal-searing stench that filled the room like a release from Satan's rotting asshole. But as bad as the smell was – and it was fucking *awful* – the worst part of Delmar's affliction was his utter lack of bone. He was an old-man flesh-blob, and while he had all the right outer parts – facial features, hair, fingers, toes, genitals – without a skeletal structure for them to hang on, his resemblance to anything human was tangential at best. He could move, a little at least, wiggle and quiver, sometimes come close to rolling all the way over. She had no clue how he could move without any bones for his muscles to attach to, and she also didn't know how his internal organs managed to function absent a skeleton to keep them in their proper places. But somehow, impossibly, they'd continued working like this for ten years, and there was no sign that his body, such as it was, would fail anytime soon.

Too bad.

Whatever the gunk was that slicked Delmar's skin, he produced the same shit internally as well. It constantly built up inside his boneless body, and Tressa had to help him express it once or twice a day. Tressa had insisted that Kate watch her perform the procedure so she would have some idea of how to do it should the need arise – and it clearly had. Delmar's yellow crap was blasting out of every orifice – mouth, nostrils, eyes, ears, rectum – it covered him, had splattered onto the plastic beneath him, slid in large globular chunks onto the floor. As disgusting as this was, what concerned Kate was the gunk in his throat. He was choking on it, and if he couldn't get an unobstructed breath soon, he would die.

Just stand there and let it happen, Katie-Bug…. Please!

She felt a pressure behind her forehead, forceful but not painful. Before the…*accident* that had changed him, Delmar had been a highly knowledgeable and skilled practitioner of the dark arts. Kate had never 'heard' his thoughts directly before, but she wasn't surprised to learn that he could cast them and make himself understood. What *did* surprise her was how coherent his thoughts were. She'd always believed her grandfather's mind had been destroyed at the same moment his body had become so terribly distorted, and she'd never seen anything in the last ten years to disabuse her of this notion – until today. What had been different all those other times she'd been in his presence? If he'd been capable of communication all this time, why hadn't he— Then it came to her: Tressa. This was the first time since Kate had come to live with her grandparents that she had been in Delmar's room alone. Tressa had been with her every other time. Had Delmar remained silent all those times, unwilling to make contact with Kate with his wife present? Or had he tried to connect mind-to-mind to her before, maybe many times, only to have Tressa psychically block him? Tressa was not without her own skill and power, and Kate believed she could keep Delmar's thoughts from entering her mind. The question was why?

But it was a question that would have to wait. Right now, she needed to save her grandfather's life. She took a step forward, but stopped when she bumped into an invisible barrier hard and strong as a steel wall. She pressed her hands against what looked like empty air and pushed with all her strength, but she could not budge it. Another magic trick of Delmar's, and a damn good one, too. She stepped to the right, encountered another invisible wall, then stepped to the left with the same result. She tried to go backward and found she was boxed in. Meanwhile, Delmar continued choking on the thick pus in his throat; his eyes – two small orbs swimming in soft, boneless flesh – looked at her pleadingly. It was only then the full import of his earlier telepathic communication became clear to her.

Just stand there and let it happen, Katie-Bug.... Please!

Delmar *wanted* to die. He was making himself eject all that gunk so he'd choke to death, and he'd chosen to do so now because Tressa was out of the house and couldn't stop him. All he needed to accomplish his goal was for Kate to do nothing but stand there and watch him commit suicide. She understood why he wanted to die, could even empathize with his desire. If she'd been in his place, she would've wanted the same thing. Ten years living as a mostly immobile blob, never leaving his room, let alone the house, unable even to watch TV because of how much the light from the screen bothered him. And what did he do when Tressa wasn't visiting him? He'd lie in the dark, not moving, just breathing – inhale, exhale, inhale, exhale – thinking of ways he might end his cruel joke of an existence. She wanted him to die too.

But she pressed her palms on the invisible wall in front of her and pushed, putting her whole body into it. She had no magical power to draw on, only her natural strength, but she soon felt the wall of force weakening, becoming softer. It gave beneath her hands, as if it was made of marshmallow instead of steel. Delmar's energy was waning, most likely because his oxygen level had plummeted, and he was losing his ability to maintain the wall. Now it was a race to see if the wall would fail before Delmar died, or if he'd be able to keep Kate away from him until his suicide was complete.

The wall gave first.

The resistance vanished all at once, and Kate stumbled forward. A pool of pus-gunk had collected on the floor near the bed, and when Kate's foot – her *bare* foot – hit it, she slid and nearly went down. She grabbed hold of the bed's side rail and managed to keep herself from falling, but only barely. She pulled herself into a steady standing position, reached down, and without hesitation took double handfuls of Delmar's boneless body. It was like sinking her fingers into warm bread dough, and the sensation made her stomach roil. The only thing that kept her from vomiting was the idea that if she did, her puke would mix with Delmar's pus, and that was way too disgusting to be allowed to happen.

Her instinct was to help Delmar sit up, but since he had no skeleton, he couldn't sit – which meant she had to improvise. She grabbed hold of his scalp with one hand and lifted. Delmar stretched like a giant piece of well-chewed gum, his head rising and creating a neck-like length of flesh below. Kate was encouraged by this until she realized that by stretching him this way, she was actually constricting his throat, narrowing the airway to make it even more difficult for him to breathe. She lowered his head back down into the main part of his body and frantically tried to think of some way she could get him to empty himself the rest of the way without choking to death. Maybe if she took hold of him far enough below the head, she could lift enough of him to drape over her shoulder as if he was an infant, and pound his back – or at least what more or less was his back – until his airway was clear. She was afraid it wouldn't work, but she had no time to think of a better plan. But as she reached for him, she felt pressure in her head, and the next thing she knew, she was pressing her hands deep into his body on either side of his face, and when they were in far enough, she pushed sideways until her fingertips met with only a thin layer of flesh between them. Then she interlocked her fingers and squeezed – *hard*.

She was so shocked that all she could do for an instant was stare at her grandfather's slack, doughy face, watch the skin turn a deep red and then begin to edge toward purple.

"No!" she shouted. "Don't make me do this, Grandpa!"

Delmar had taken control of her body and was using her hands in place of his. Had this been his plan all along, to get her to come close enough so he could turn her – someone who didn't have the psychic defenses to protect herself – into a weapon he could use to kill himself?

Her hands were now squeezing so hard that her forearms shook with effort.

Tears rolled down her cheeks, and she found her mind going back to a time when she was a little girl, no more than five, six at the most. The entire family, Shardlows and Lintons alike, had gathered at Tressa and Delmar's home for a summer holiday. Fourth of July or maybe Memorial Day. Whichever it was, they had a cookout and pool party at what Kate (Katie-Bug back then) thought of as the Big House. She remembered sunlight glinting on sky-blue water, the sharp smell of chlorine, how cool the water was on her skin, remembered how Ethan's dad had put him on his shoulders, how Grandpa Delmar had put her on his, and how they'd played chicken fight, trying to see who could knock the other into the water first. Ethan had been a couple years older and stronger than her, but Grandpa Delmar had held tight to her legs and maneuvered her around in such a way as to give her an equal chance against her cousin. In the end, Ethan still won and Kate ended up under the water, but she rose to the surface giggling happily, and Delmar swept her up and gave her a big hug.

She felt a wave of sadness that wasn't hers, and the pressure in her head began to ease, and her arms stopped shaking. She tore her hands free of Delmar's putty-like flesh, turned, and fled the room, sobbing. As she slammed the door shut behind her, she thought she heard the words *I'm so sorry* in her mind, but it might've been her imagination.

★   ★   ★

Technically, Tressa didn't lie to Kate. She *did* go to the bank – she just didn't *stop* there.

She drove past it and continued until she'd left Ash Creek's town limits and entered the country, where she was surrounded by cornfields and farmhouses. She didn't drive much these days, and the steering wheel felt strange in her hands, a half-forgotten device that she didn't fully recall how to operate. She had to keep fighting the car's tendency to pull to the left, plus the brakes made deep grinding noises whenever she stopped. When was the last time she'd had Kate take the vehicle to be serviced? She couldn't recall. She thought fondly of the silver Lexus she and Delmar had once had. Now *that* had been a car. The ride was so smooth, it was like you were on a luxury yacht floating serenely in calm waters. But that had been back when the family had money. The best they could afford these days was a "pre-owned" Mazda, which was an ugly, garish red, and – compared to the Lexus – drove like a giant brick outfitted with square wheels.

Usually Kate ran errands for Tressa so she could stay at home with Delmar, but Kate couldn't perform this task for her. Only she could do what needed to be done.

She continued driving, making turns when appropriate, and soon she'd left the farmland behind and was traveling through thick woods, trees so tall they blocked out much of the sunlight, casting the road in shadow. The trees were taller than she remembered, but she hadn't been out this way for a decade, not since *That Night*, so of course they'd grown. The farther she traveled, the warmer she felt, as if she had the heat on in the car, but the heater had been broken for at least a year now. Her hands started trembling on the steering wheel, and at first she thought the Mazda was vibrating, that maybe its engine was on the verge of throwing a rod or something. But then she realized she was trembling, and the heat she felt was coming from inside her. Had someone hurled a curse at her? She marshalled what meager mystic resources she now possessed and cast her mind outward, searching for any sign of malign magic. But she sensed nothing.

That's because you're having a panic attack.

That wasn't possible. She was Tressa Shardlow, Seer of the Quintessence, and she feared nothing in this world or any other. But even as she told herself this, she knew she was full of shit. She was returning home – to the site of her greatest failure – for the first time in ten years, and she was not emotionally ready for it. Did she have PTSD? She supposed she might. She wondered if that was part of the reason she rarely left home, not because Delmar needed her all the time – although of course he did – but because she felt safer with walls and a roof between her and the outside world. *Safety is an illusion,* she thought, which was true, but it was also a necessary one, or else how could anyone make it through a single day on Earth, let alone an entire lifetime?

She trembled harder now, felt nauseous and light-headed. Perhaps ruminating on the nonexistence of safety wasn't the best thing for her anxiety, so she began taking deep, even breaths and tried to relax. After a few minutes, she began to feel a little better, and shortly afterward she pulled up to her old home. Stone pillars flanked the concrete driveway and a wrought-iron gate barred the entrance, not that it was any great deterrent. The property was surrounded with oak and elm trees, but it wasn't fenced in, and all anyone needed to do to bypass the gate was simply walk around it – which was exactly what she intended to do. She pulled the Mazda into the driveway and parked in front of the gate. She killed the engine, and it rattled and coughed before finally going still. She hoped the damn thing would start again when she was ready to leave.

Once, the gate had opened in response to an electronic signal, but Tressa didn't have the remote with her. She doubted the system would work after all this time anyway, plus the gate was held closed with a padlock and chain, and she didn't have the key for that, either. She got out of the Mazda, went around the vehicle's rear, and opened the trunk. Inside was a shovel and an empty plastic shopping bag. She took both, shut the trunk, and then started walking. The foliage had grown thicker since she'd last been here, and the land sloped uphill, so making her way through the trees and undergrowth was more difficult than she'd anticipated.

Halfway through the woods, the back of her neck prickled, and she sensed she was being watched. She stopped, looked around, listened, sent out psychic feelers to see who – or what – she could detect. But she saw, heard, or felt nothing. Maybe she'd only imagined she was being observed. She had plenty of reason to be nervous returning here, so it was only natural that she be overly sensitive to her surroundings. Still, it wouldn't hurt to proceed with extra caution, just in case. She continued on.

By the time she exited the woods, her knees ached and she was breathing heavily.

Out of shape, old girl.

Her fear, likely prompted by the incident in the woods, had returned full force and set up shop in her belly, where it scuttled around nervously and dug at her with cold claws. She felt feverish again, dizzy, and she knew this was her body's way of telling her to return to the car and get the fuck out of there. She was tempted to listen to it, but she forced herself to remain where she was. Events were in motion that had made Tressa's return to this place necessary, even vital, and she had to see this visit through if she didn't want the remnants of her family destroyed. Plus, Kate was going to need the items Tressa intended to retrieve from here. She had *Seen* it.

Tressa was seventy-four, slim, with short white hair. She'd dyed it black ten years ago, but she'd dropped the affectation since. Only Delmar and Kate saw her these days, and they didn't give a damn what she looked like. She wore a short-sleeved light-blue top, with dark-blue slacks, and comfortable shoes. She possessed a narrow, aristocratic face and a perpetual air of sadness hung about her, something that hadn't been present a decade ago.

The driveway – concrete cracked, with tufts of grass and weeds protruding from the fissures – was less than a dozen yards from where she'd exited the woods. She went to it now and continued walking toward the house, or rather, where the house once was. All that remained of the Shardlows' mansion, which had belonged to the family for generations, was the stone foundation and a few charred support timbers and limestone walls. The space had been overgrown with plants, primarily honeysuckle and Virginia creeper, along with some saplings. The grounds had also been reclaimed by nature, grass and weeds nearly waist high, and more young trees grew here. Tressa wondered how long it would be before the area became indistinguishable from the woods around it. Another decade? Two? She doubted she'd be alive by then. She found the thought of her death comforting, and her anxiety eased a little. When she was dead, her memories would rot with her brain, and she would be free of them at last.

She started walking toward the ruins, pushing her way through the tall grass, careful to avoid large sticker bushes. Just because she looked forward to dying didn't mean she wanted to be a pincushion for the goddamned things. Once again she had the sensation that she was being watched, and while she still couldn't detect who or what it might be, she was now certain she wasn't imagining it. She needed to be on her guard, and if she wasn't anywhere close to as strong as she once was, she'd show anyone foolish enough to attack her that this old dog still knew how to bite.

As she drew closer to the foundation, she was surprised to see that the plants in the immediate vicinity appeared to be perfectly healthy. Given the nature of the power that had caused the mansion's destruction, she'd expected the grounds to be barren and diseased. But everything seemed normal. Tressa, however, knew that normal – like safety – was an illusory concept, and often the more normal something looked, the more dangerous it was.

This is it, woman, she thought. *Shit or get off the pot.*

She stepped up to the foundation, knelt, and pressed her hand to its hard surface.

She felt it at once, a cold emptiness that pulled at her mind, a dark vortex tearing at her, desperate to pull her in and swallow her whole. And it might have, too, except its power was faint, little more than an echo of what it once was. She sensed something more, though. A presence, lurking somewhere close by, watching her intently, waiting to see what she would do next. This was the thing she'd sensed once in the woods, and again as she'd approached the mansion's ruins. She didn't know what it was, but at least she knew it was real.

She was about to remove her hand when she sensed something more. Another presence.... No, *five* presences, close by, within the area bordered by the house's foundation. She had an awful feeling she knew what these presences were, and she wasn't certain she could make herself go any farther. The thought of facing them after all this time, facing what they'd *become*, terrified her more than any dark energy that remained in the ruins or a stealth-stalker hiding and watching somewhere close by. If it hadn't been for Kate — and the destiny she'd seen in store for her poor granddaughter — she would've turned around and fled this place as fast as her aching knees would carry her. Instead she stood, stepped over the foundation, and entered what was left of Shardlow Mansion.

Once she'd done this, had truly returned *home*, she felt the tidal pull of the emptiness increase tenfold, as if she'd drawn its attention to her. The pull wasn't so strong that she couldn't resist it if she wanted to, but she allowed it to lead her to a large rectangular gap in the ground. The area showed signs of corruption — the soil around it dead and gray, the air in the immediate vicinity flat and lifeless — and there was a painful static-like buzzing in her head, which made it difficult for her to think. She gazed down into what had been the basement and saw a darkness that was more than the absence of light. It was the very embodiment of nonexistence, a nothingness so absolute that it frayed the edges of reality, blurred the boundary between what was and what wasn't. It was the most beautiful thing that she had ever seen, and she wanted to throw herself into that darkness, let it teach her the true nature of Oblivion in the last instant before she was unmade. She swayed, leaned forward, almost fell, but then a hand came down on her shoulder and steadied her.

Your work is not finished, Mother.

A man's voice, or rather his thoughts, projected into her mind. Thoughts she recognized.

"Dalton?"

She turned away from the basement and found herself facing a quintet of apparitions, human-sized distortions in the air, like the ripples of heat waves. They possessed no features, had nothing that distinguished one from another, but Tressa could tell them apart nonetheless. The apparition closest to her, the one that had kept her from hurling herself into the darkness, was her son – and Kate's father – Dalton.

She was still holding the shovel and plastic bag. She put them on the ground then reached out, tried to touch her son, but her hands passed through the space where he was, and all she felt was a slight tingling sensation. He could touch her, it seemed, but she couldn't touch him. The unfairness of it nearly made her weep. The tingling in her hands moved up her arms, into her neck, and from there to her head. It drove away the static crackling in her mind, and when the tingling subsided, she found her thoughts had cleared.

"Thank you, sweetheart," she said.

She wasn't sure, but she thought Dalton inclined his head in acknowledgment.

Another apparition came forward to stand next to Dalton, and Tressa knew this was Nila, his wife and Kate's mother. The other three were also relatives – Cordell Linton, her son-in-law and father to Ethan, Victorina Linton, the grandmother on the other side of the extended family, and Lissette, Felton's wife and Reyna's mother. These were the five who had died here a decade ago, on the night they had attempted to give birth to a god. She'd always thought they were the lucky ones, but now that she knew their shades lingered here, she wasn't so certain.

That was quite a dramatic gesture you almost made, Victorina said. *But there's no need to rush things. The Gyre will have you soon enough.*

Tressa scowled. Victorina had been a bitch when she was alive, and it appeared that death had done nothing to mellow her.

"I must confess that I am surprised to see you all," Tressa said. "How have you managed to resist the call of the void all these years?"

It will not have us, Nila said.

Not until what we started is complete, Cordell added.

Not until we've tended to the family's business, Lissette finished.

Tressa understood. Because the Incarnation had been interrupted, the five of them had been trapped in a kind of spiritual holding pattern. They had remained here for the last decade, haunting the mansion's ruins.

"I'm sorry," Tressa said.

It hasn't been all bad, Dalton said. *Teenagers come here sometimes to test their bravery at the ruins of 'The Witch House'.*

They drink, smoke, screw, Cordell said.

Laugh, tell stories, have painfully earnest conversations, Nila added.

We listen to the little shits' voices, experience what their bodies feel, Victorina said. *Through them, we get to live again, if only for a short time.*

It's nice, Lissette said.

It sounded like a very lonely existence to Tressa. "Don't you ever scare them off, just for the fun of it? I mean, you *are* ghosts."

No, Victorina said. *If we frightened them, they'd never come back, and they'd spread word that The Witch House is a place best avoided.*

"Doesn't the void try to claim them?" Tressa asked.

Yes, Nila said. *But we protect them, just as we protected you. We need them. They're the only life we have.*

Of course, we can't always protect them from everything, Dalton said.

My Felton gets hungry sometimes, Lissette added.

A low-throated growling came from somewhere close by, as if to underscore Dalton's words. Tressa had a bad feeling she knew what — or who — was responsible for the sound, and she shivered.

Afraid? Victorina said, amused. *The Tressa I knew was as tough and cold-hearted as they come.*

That version of herself had died the same time the five of them had, Tressa thought. Aloud, she said, "I've come for the eyes. Kate's going to need them."

How is she? Nila asked. Tressa could feel a yearning behind Nila's words, and as a mother herself, she understood.

"She's well. She's nineteen now, and thinks she knows everything. She works part-time at Sprinkles — it's an ice-cream shop — and takes classes at Kingsborough College, mostly online."

What does she remember of that night? Dalton asked.

"She's aware of what happened, at least in general, but I don't know how much specific detail she recalls."

It's probably better that way, Nila said. *Does she...remember us?*

Tressa smiled. "Yes, she does. Quite vividly."

Tressa felt Nila's relief. Dalton's too.

I hope the child enjoyed her time of innocence, Victorina said, *because it's over. The Incarnation will soon be fulfilled, and she will play a prime role in its completion.*

Tressa did her best to keep her thoughts shielded from the others, but she was nowhere near as strong as she once was, and she could feel the five shades probing her mind.

Don't tell me you're having doubts about the Incarnation, Victorina said. Her thought-voice sounded amused.

"As you said, the Gyre will have us all soon enough. Why rush things?"

Because it's a mercy, Cordell said. *Would you let a beloved pet suffer in pain or would you put it down out of love and end its misery?*

"An animal can't decide for itself. Humans can."

Victorina had no nose, but she still managed to make a snort of disdain somehow.

Humans are animals. They have no more sense of the true nature of existence than any other dumb beast that crawls upon the face of this pathetic mudball. It's up to those of us who are aware of what reality is to decide what's best for them. You once believed this. You were as dedicated to the goals of the Quintessence as any of us – even more. You used your Sight to identify the material needed for the Incarnation.

And you and Father gathered it, Dalton said.

All of it, Nila added.

It was true. Tressa and Delmar had eagerly done their grisly work, their actions fueled by righteous fervor. They'd believed they were doing what was necessary to free the Omniverse from the agony of continued existence. But she no longer believed in that goal. If suffering was the Omniverse's natural state, then who was she – who was *anyone* – to decide differently?

"I'm just here for the eyes," Tressa said. "It was good seeing the five of you."

She bent down to pick up the shovel and plastic bag, rose, then turned and started walking away from the shades. She felt them join forces, reach out to her mind, attempt to control her, force her to return to the basement and give herself to the void that lay within. But she was ready for them and had her psychic defenses in place. There was nothing they could do to stop her. Without turning back to face them, she said, "Look at it this way: I'm going to give the eyes to Kate, and for all I know, I could be helping the Incarnation to come into being. Why not let fate play out its hand and see what happens?"

The shades' mental assault continued for another moment, but then Tressa felt them relent and draw back into themselves.

This will not turn out the way you think, Victorina said.

"I could say the same to you."

Tressa continued walking and she didn't look back. Soon she felt the shades' presence fade, and she knew she was once more alone among the ruins of her previous life.

★   ★   ★

After the Incarnation had failed, the family had divided the parts amongst themselves. Tressa had taken the eyes, and a little more than a year later – after she'd gotten herself, Delmar, and Kate settled into their new lives – she returned to what was left of the mansion to bury the eyes. She hadn't sensed the shades then, nor had she sensed the void that had taken up residence in the basement. Perhaps none of them had been strong enough to be detected yet. Or perhaps her senses hadn't recovered from exposure to the energies unleashed by the Incarnation's failure. Most likely a combination of both, she decided. There had been a lovely old oak tree in the backyard, one she could see through the window of the master bedroom, and it was there she'd buried the eyes.

She went to the oak now. Its proximity to the mansion meant it had been touched by the energies that had destroyed the place, and it had a long scar-like rift stretching along the length of its trunk. The wound hadn't killed the tree, surprisingly enough, but it did ooze a foul-smelling greenish fluid and strange insects with iridescent shells and far too many legs made it their home. The oak was larger than the last time she'd been here, but otherwise it was unchanged. The tree still lived, still oozed green, and still housed multi-legged shiny-backed bugs. Tressa had used the spot where the tree's scar touched the ground as a marker when she'd buried the eyes. She put the plastic bag on the ground, gripped the shovel with both hands, and began digging. She felt eyes on her as she worked – eyes that didn't belong to the shades – and she did her best to ignore them. She was nervous, though, imagining that the owner of those eyes might come up behind her as she was digging, and she was relieved when she finally unearthed the cloth-wrapped object that she had hidden here nearly a decade ago. She pulled it free from the soil, brushed off the dirt, then partially unwrapped it to take a look. Inside was a sealed mason jar filled with isopropyl alcohol, and floating within was a pair of eyes, optic nerves trailing behind like grotesque tails. As she peered at them, the eyes turned toward her and the pupils narrowed. She wrapped the cloth around the jar once more, put it in the plastic bag, grabbed the shovel, and started walking in the direction of the road.

The way back was mostly downhill, something her aching knees would appreciate. But when she reached the edge of the woods, she paused, reluctant to continue. Something waited for her among the trees, a thing she'd rather not face. She had no choice, though, and besides, this had turned out to be a day for confronting the past. Why should the journey back to the Mazda be any different?

She entered the woods.

She kept all her senses alert as she walked, shovel handle on her shoulder, plastic bag swinging at her side. She imagined the eyes being sloshed around inside the jar, and she wondered what – if anything – they thought was happening. She heard only the sounds of her own feet tramping along, accompanied by birdsong and the sounds of small mammals scurrying through the undergrowth, alarmed by her presence. It all felt so normal that she was tempted to relax her guard, but she knew better, and her caution proved warranted when a few moments later, the woods fell silent. She stopped, listened, heard padded footfalls quiet as a midnight wind approaching – and then she saw him. Felton.

She remained motionless as he drew closer, nostrils flaring as he took in her scent. A soft rumble came from deep in his throat. A growl? A sign of recognition? She had no way of knowing. Not all of the family who'd survived the failed Incarnation had done so unscathed. Poor Delmar was a prime example, and so too was their son. Everything had been so chaotic that night, with the able-bodied survivors doing their best to get the others out and then swiftly returning to the basement to extricate the Lord's lifeless body before the mansion's destruction. When it was finally over, Tressa had been unable to find Felton. At first she thought he had been among the casualties, but Caprice had said she'd seen him flee into the woods.

He was changing, she'd said. *Into what, I don't know.*

Tressa had tried finding him with her mind, but her psychic abilities had been damaged by the failed rite. The resultant pain had been so intense that she'd nearly passed out. She told herself to forget about Felton for the time being. They had to get the survivors – the others who'd changed – to safety, and they needed to decide what to do with the Lord. She'd come back in a few days when she was feeling stronger and search for Felton then. But she hadn't. In those early days, she feared Delmar would die without constant attention to his needs. She had looked for Felton when she returned a year later to conceal the eyes, but she hadn't detected his presence.

He was making his presence known right now, though. He closed to within three feet from her, well within striking distance, and gazed upon her with inhuman yellow eyes. His throat-rumble grew louder, and his lips drew back from double rows of sharp teeth. His claws were down and at his sides, but the fingers flexed and unflexed, as if his hands were eager to rip into prey. He smelled like rancid blood and rotten meat. He smelled like death.

Tressa was surprised at how calm she sounded when she spoke.

"Hello, Felton. It's good to see you."

She wondered if he could tell she was lying.

His eyes narrowed in response, and he showed more of his teeth. He sniffed the air once more, frowned, then directed his gaze toward the plastic bag she held.

"They're what I came here to get," Tressa said. "They're for Kate – your niece. Do you remember her?"

Felton locked gazes with Tressa once more. He cocked his head to the side, as if he were trying to understand what she was saying but was having difficulty. She didn't know if anything of her son still existed inside this beast, but she was about to find out. She sent a slender tendril of psychic force toward him, nothing too strong – she didn't want to spook him. Tressa gently wormed her way into his mind and then she projected an image of Kate, not as she was now, but as the nine-year-old girl that Felton had known. His head jerked back, as if he'd been struck, and his throat-rumble became a full-on snarl. He bared his teeth and raised his claws, and Tressa knew she had been too clumsy in her attempt to enter his mind. She was no longer capable of the finesse she'd once had, and it had been foolish and arrogant of her to think otherwise. Now she was going to pay for her mistake with her life. She didn't care if she died – although she worried how Delmar would do in her absence – but if she couldn't get the eyes to Kate, then everything would be lost. She couldn't let that happen.

She dropped the shovel, removed the mason jar from the plastic bag, and held it up for Felton to see. His snarl died away as the eyes focused on him. His breathing eased, his body relaxed, and his hands fell to his sides. He stood frozen, as if the Lord's eyes held him in their thrall. Tressa knew that this state was a temporary one. If she removed the eyes from Felton's line of sight, he would become aggressive once more and likely attack her before she could do anything more to protect herself. There was one last thing she could try, though she had no idea if it would work. She stepped forward slowly, making sure to keep the jar up where Felton could see it. When she was close enough, she stopped walking and moved the jar toward his face. She stopped when glass touched the tip of his inhuman nose.

The eyes' optic nerves wriggled upward and affixed their ends to the inside of the jar directly in line with Felton's eyes. Then, a second later, they made mental contact.

Felton stiffened and his furry body began to shake. The pieces of the Lord still contained power, and Tressa's son was experiencing that power now. He was seeing through the Lord's eyes, and while Tressa had no idea what they were showing him, she hoped whatever it was would be enough to keep her son from killing her. After a couple moments, Felton's body calmed and his tremors ended. Tressa slowly pulled the jar away from his face and took a step back. She looked into her son's eyes, and for an instant they were human – a slate-gray that she remembered so well – but they swiftly became feral yellow again.

Felton looked at her one last moment, before turning and loping away, moving silent and swift. She watched him go until she couldn't see him any longer, then she put the mason jar back in the plastic bag, retrieved the shovel, and continued on her way, crying for her poor, lost son.

INTERLUDE

Eyes

Bradley Nunez sat alone on the couch in his small one-bedroom apartment, watching a news report, silent tears streaming down his cheeks. On the screen, a reporter stood on the side of the highway, microphone in hand. Behind her, an SUV sat in the middle of the road, surrounded by five state trooper vehicles, their lightbars flashing. A red EMS van was parked nearby, its emergency lights flashing as well. Bradley turned up the volume as the reporter began to speak.

"I'm Molly Osborne for Channel Ten Action News. I'm standing on the side of I-75, just north of Cincinnati, where only moments ago state troopers were involved in a shoot-out with a murder suspect. The male suspect died in the exchange of gunfire, but authorities will not release his name until the next of kin can be notified. One of the troopers told me they believe the deceased to be the serial killer known as the Bonebreaker."

The camera operator zoomed in on a sheet-covered body lying on the asphalt near the SUV. Blood had soaked through the cloth, creating a large crimson stain in the middle. Troopers stood near the body, and when one of them noticed the camera was focused on the dead man, he motioned to the others, and they grouped together to block the view. The camera operator lingered on the troopers for another few seconds before focusing on the reporter once more.

"The Bonebreaker is believed responsible for at least seventeen strangulation murders in the tri-state area, murders in which each victim's neck was snapped during—"

Bradley – unable to stand hearing any more – snatched the remote off the coffee table and muted the sound. He left the picture on, although he wasn't sure why. Maybe he hoped to get another look at the cloth-covered body in order to assure himself that this was actually happening. If that really was the Bonebreaker's corpse lying beneath the blood-stained sheet, that meant his brother Jerry was dead. He realized then that he was crying, reached up to touch his cheek, brought his hand away, examined the moisture on his fingers. If anyone had been present to see him cry for a man who had snapped the necks of seventeen people, they might've thought he was as insane as the killer himself. Who knows? Maybe he was.

He had been thirteen when he'd witnessed his brother kill Jasmine Beck.

It was summer, and Bradley was luxuriating in his break from school. Seventh grade had sucked donkey balls, and he didn't have any reason to think eighth grade would be much better. He was free now, though, and he intended to enjoy each glorious day. That morning he had gone down to the river with a couple friends, and they'd spent several hours wading in the shallows, looking for crawdads, skimming rocks across the water's surface, telling stupid jokes, and lying about which girls had let them squeeze their developing breasts. Bradley almost had got to cop a feel on Ginny Martin a couple weeks before behind the bowling alley, but she'd chickened out at the last moment. He hoped he'd get another shot at her before the summer ended. Maybe she'd even let him *see* her tits. He thought he'd probably spooge in his pants if she did.

He and his friends left the river around lunchtime, and Bradley entertained himself with thoughts of Ginny's boobs as he biked home. When he got there, he saw Jerry's Jeep Cherokee in the driveway, but he didn't think anything of it. Jerry was four years older than him and he came and went as he pleased. Both of their parents worked days, so the brothers were left to their own devices in the summer, which suited both of them just fine. There was nothing especially wrong with their mom and dad, but there was nothing especially *right* about them, either, and all things considered, Bradley and Jerry were happiest when they weren't around.

Jerry had a part-time job working with a local moving company. He was a big guy, tall and thick-limbed, with the largest hands that Bradley had ever seen on a human being. Because he was so big, people regularly mistook him as being quite a bit older than he was, and his time schlepping other people's shit had built up his muscles even further. Jerry Nunez was a fucking *beast*, and Bradley – all five-foot-four and ninety-eight pounds of him – hoped every day that he would hit a growth spurt and become a badass motherfucker like his brother.

Bradley left his bike lying in the front yard, despite his parents always reminding him to put it in the garage, and walked up the steps and onto the front porch. As he reached for the doorknob, he heard a *thump-thump-thump* coming from inside the house, and he knew that Jerry was blasting death metal on the family room's sound system again. Cannibal Corpse, probably, or maybe Sepultura. Bradley couldn't tell any of the bands apart. They all sounded the same to him – driving guitars, pounding beats, and growled vocals – but if Jerry liked them, they had to be cool, so he listened to them as well and tried to get into them.

He took off his muddy shoes and socks and left them on the porch before going inside. He wanted to head straight for the kitchen and get something to eat, but he figured he should let Jerry know he was home first. Besides, Jerry had already been gone when he'd gotten up this morning, and he wanted to say hi to his big brother. He walked to the back of the house, where the family room was located, and he stepped inside, prepared to yell *Hi* as loud as he could so Jerry would hear him over the music, which was turned up so loud Bradley could feel the floor vibrate beneath his feet. But when he saw Jerry straddling a girl in the middle of the floor, both of them naked, clothes strewn on the carpet, he could only stand there and stare. He knew about sex, of course, and he'd seen pictures of people fucking in magazines that his friends stole from their dads or older brothers. Jerry had some magazines like that, but they showed bound and gagged women being slapped or whipped – or worse – and Bradley didn't find that kind of thing sexy. He found it kind of sickening, actually. But Bradley had never seen a real live naked girl before, and he'd certainly never seen two people doing it, especially when one of those two people was his own goddamn brother. His dick – which had a mind of its own these days – swelled into instant hardness and strained painfully against the fabric of his jeans. He felt an instinct to reach down and touch his bulge, but he resisted it.

The whole situation embarrassed him, and he wanted to get the hell out of there before Jerry or the girl saw him. Jerry was a good brother, but he had a temper – a real bad one sometimes – and Bradley was sure his big bro would be royally pissed if he interrupted his fuck session. But just as he was about to turn and leave, he realized something wasn't right. Jerry wasn't inside the girl; he was sitting on her stomach. Those big hands of his were wrapped around her throat, and she was kicking and thrashing, pounding her fists on the hard, straining muscles of his arms. Her face was a dark red, edging toward purple, and as Bradley watched, her exertions began to lessen. And then, despite how loud the music was, Bradley felt as much as heard a loud *snap*. The girl's body stiffened then went still. Jerry, hands still tight on the girl's throat, began thrusting rapidly and Bradley saw his brother's cock – which was much smaller than he would've imagined – shoot a load of cum onto the girl's skin.

The *dead* girl's skin.

Jerry stopped thrusting, closed his eyes, leaned his head back, and breathed deeply. His own skin was coated with sweat, and for a moment Bradley thought that his brother's entire body had ejaculated, semen oozing from every pore. Then, as if alerted by some instinct, Jerry's eyes flew open, and he turned his head to see Bradley standing there, his brother's face ashen, cock wilted. An expression of cold calculation came onto Jerry's face, and something alien stirred in his gaze. For the first time in Bradley's life he was afraid of his big brother. In fact, he was fucking *terrified*.

Jerry got off the girl and hurried over to Bradley, stiff red cock bobbing ridiculously. A cum pearl oozed from the tip, and the sight of it turned Bradley's stomach. Jerry gripped Bradley's shoulders with his big hands, hands that only a few seconds ago had broken the girl's neck like a thin, brittle branch. Inside his mind, Bradley cried out in fear when his brother laid those hands on him. Outwardly, he remained silent, face expressionless. *Don't make any sudden moves,* he thought. *Don't do anything to make him angry.*

Jerry leaned his face close to Bradley's ear so he could be heard over the music.

"Jesus Christ, Brad, did you *see* that? I can't believe that happened!"

There was something off about Jerry's words, as if he were speaking lines he was reading from a script. Bradley was too scared to do anything more than listen, though. Maybe Jerry was scared too. After all, he *sounded* scared. Kind of.

Words continued rushing out of Jerry's mouth. Her name was Jasmine. He didn't know her last name, had met her last week when he'd helped move her family into a house a couple blocks away. They'd hit it off and started hanging out, kissing, doing some hand stuff, then some oral sex, and today they'd finally gone all the way.

"She told me she couldn't get off unless someone was choking her. It sounded pretty goddamn weird to me, but I figured whatever floats your boat, right? So I did it, and at first she seemed to be into it, you know? But as things went on, I got more excited, and she did too – at least, I thought she did – and then...then...."

Jerry let out a sob that was more than a little theatrical, part of Bradley's mind thought, and then embraced his younger brother. And in that moment, Bradley had a choice to make: believe Jerry had made a horrible, tragic mistake or believe he was a fucking lunatic who'd snapped a girl's neck on purpose. In the end, he went with the choice that he wanted to be true rather than the one he thought was true. He hugged his brother as hard as he could, pressed his face to his naked chest, and bawled like a baby.

★　　★　　★

Bradley helped Jerry take care of Jasmine's body. She was a petite girl, and they were able to use a couple large-size garbage bags to wrap her up. Jerry pulled his Jeep into the garage, and they loaded Jasmine into the backseat and covered her with a blanket. Bradley had gathered her clothes and put them in another garbage bag, and he stuffed this under the blanket with her. Then the two brothers drove down to the river, not far from where Bradley and his friends had been messing around that morning. They put the garbage bag with her clothes inside the ones she was wrapped in, added a bunch of rocks, and then Jerry wrapped the bags tight around her with duct tape. He lifted the bundle, rocks and all, as if it weighed nothing, and carried it partway into the river. When the water was up to his waist, the current became too strong for him, and he threw Jasmine's body toward the middle of the lake as hard as he could. She landed with a loud plastic *plap*, floated for a foot or two – during which Bradley thought his heart would stop – before finally sinking. Jerry made his way back to shore, grinning.

"Did you *see* that throw? That was something else, right?"

Bradley nodded. "Sure was."

Jasmine's body was never found, at least not officially. Bradley assumed the river's current had carried her across the bottom, and by the time she was found, she was far from their town, and since her body probably wasn't in pristine condition by that point, she'd been labeled a Jane Doe and her remains eventually disposed of. There were stories in the local paper about her disappearance, though, which is how he learned Jasmine's last name, that she played cello in the school orchestra and wanted to be a microbiologist.

He and Jerry never spoke of Jasmine again, and when Bradley graduated high school, he went to college and did his best to forget he ever had a brother. He went home for holidays, sure, but half the time Jerry didn't show, and eventually Jerry stopped visiting their folks at all, which was a great relief to Bradley. After graduating college with a degree in accounting, Bradley became a CPA and started his own business. He didn't really have any friends, and he certainly didn't date. He'd never gone out with a girl, barely even spoke with any if he didn't have to. In his mind, he associated sexual desire with violence and death, and he wanted nothing to do with it.

Then he began seeing reports on the news about a killer who broke women's necks while he was raping them, and he knew that Jerry was responsible. He thought about calling the police and telling them about his brother, but what if he was wrong? What if Jerry had made a life for himself somewhere, maybe working in a warehouse or on a construction crew? What if he'd never again harmed a woman? Bradley might not have been able to stand the thought of being in Jerry's presence, but that didn't mean he wanted to ruin him. They were still brothers, after all. But this evening, watching the report about the death of the Bonebreaker, Bradley knew deep in his heart that his brother was dead. The reporter had said he'd killed seventeen women, but those were just the ones they knew about. How many more might he have killed after Jasmine? How many of those deaths could Bradley have prevented if he'd gone to the police and told them about Jerry?

If only he hadn't gone home that day, if only he hadn't walked in on Jerry and Jasmine, if only he hadn't *seen*....

The door to his apartment exploded open then, and he jumped up from his couch, startled. A middle-aged man carrying a sledgehammer entered, followed by a middle-aged woman. Absurdly, Bradley didn't want them to see he'd been crying, so he quickly wiped the tears from his face with both hands. He might not share his brother's homicidal tendencies, but he still possessed his share of the Nunez temper, and it came out in him now.

"Who the hell are you?" he demanded, "and why the *fuck* did you break down my door?"

The pair came toward him, both of them smiling.

"I'm so sorry that you had to see what you did," she said. "But you know what the Bible says...."

"If thine eye offends thee," the man with the sledgehammer said.

"Pluck it out," the woman finished.

She raised her right hand, and Bradley saw that she held a gleaming stainless-steel scalpel. She rushed toward him then, knocked him to the floor, and straddled him, pinning his arms down with her knees. And as she leaned forward to begin her work, he thought of how Jerry had straddled Jasmine, and he began to laugh.

CHAPTER FOUR

Kate spent twenty minutes in the shower trying to get Grandpa Delmar's muck off of her. The water was almost scalding hot when she started, and by the time she finished it was ice cold. She didn't feel clean, wondered if she ever would, but she couldn't take the cold anymore, so she turned the water off and, shivering, stepped out of the stall. She grabbed a towel and wrapped it around her. It was thin and scratchy and did little to warm her. Tressa and Delmar might have been rich once, but these days they didn't have the money to buy replacement towels, and everything Kate made at Sprinkles went to help buy food and pay bills. She remembered going to her grandparents' house in the country, the place so big and beautiful it was like something out of a storybook. She was fuzzy on what had happened to change everything. She knew their house had burned down when she was nine, and supposedly she was present when it happened, although she didn't remember much about it, had only a few scattered images in her mind that she couldn't make sense out of. Whatever had happened had been bad — *really* bad — and Grandpa Delmar's current condition was a cause of it, as was her parents' deaths. She'd asked Tressa about that night many times, but her grandmother always said some variation of *You're lucky you don't remember, dear. Sometimes ignorance is a blessing.* Kate was even more unclear why the loss of the house had wiped out all of her grandparents' money. Hadn't they had insurance on the house? And it wasn't as if they'd spent a ton of money rebuilding the mansion. As far as she knew, they'd never even contemplated rebuilding. They still owned the land, though, and if they needed money so badly, why didn't they just sell it? She had a lot of questions, but whenever she tried asking them, Tressa would evade them. *That was a long time ago, honey. And your grandfather and I never put much emphasis on money anyway. Family is the only true wealth.*

Kate dried herself, and when she was done, her skin stung as if she'd rubbed sandpaper all over her body. She dressed in fresh clothes – she might have to burn the ones she was wearing when she'd gone into Delmar's room – brushed her hair, and then gave herself a once-over in the mirror over the sink. She wasn't particularly impressed with what she saw, but it would have to do. She'd left the bathroom fan running while she showered, but she could still smell Delmar's stink, and when she stepped into the hallway, it hit her full force. She knew she should go into her grandfather's room and try to clean him, that she shouldn't let him continue to lie in his own filth, but she couldn't bring herself to do it. Partially because she didn't think she could be in his room for more than a few seconds before becoming violently ill, but mostly because she was afraid he'd try to take control of her again and use her to attempt suicide. She'd known all her life that her family – Shardlows and Lintons alike – were different than ordinary people, that they had special knowledge and abilities. She'd never demonstrated any powers of her own, though, and Tressa had never taught her anything about magic or whatever it was. Delmar had power, though – *strong* power – and she didn't know if she'd be able to resist being controlled by him a second time. Best to wait until Tressa returned home. Delmar couldn't control Tressa. If he'd been able to do so, he would've used her to kill him a long time ago.

She walked down the hall to his bedroom and listened at the door for a few moments. She heard his labored breathing, so she knew he wasn't dead, and she couldn't decide if that was a relief or not. She went to the living room, sat on the couch, and lifted her phone off the coffee table. Tressa didn't have a cell phone. *I don't trust technology,* she'd once said. *It invites too many outside forces into your life.* So Kate couldn't call or text her grandmother to let her know about Delmar's...episode. She'd just have to wait for her to get home. And now that Kate thought of it, where the hell *was* Tressa? She'd said she was going to the bank, but that had been almost an hour ago. Kate might've thought Tressa had decided to run a few more errands while she was out, except her grandmother never stayed away from Delmar very long. Had something happened to her? Had she been in an accident of some kind? If only Tressa hadn't been so stubborn about carrying a phone, Kate could've—

There were three sharp knocks at the front door.

Kate was so startled she almost dropped her phone. She couldn't remember the last time someone had come to the house. Kids fundraising for school programs, religious proselytizers, and political canvassers all avoided the place, as if they sensed something wasn't right within. Whoever it was, maybe they'd go away if she ignored them. She sat, listened.

Three more knocks. Then three more after that, louder, more insistent.

Could it be Tressa? Had she forgotten her house key when she left? Kate supposed it was possible. She rose from the couch, phone still in her hand, and walked to the front door, stepping lightly to avoid alerting whoever it was outside that anyone was home. There was a peephole in the door, and Kate leaned forward, closed one eye, and peered through it with the other. She expected to see Tressa, or maybe a delivery person or mail carrier. Instead, she saw Lee.

Fuck. Fuck-fuck-fuck-fuck-fuck!

She jerked back her head as if afraid Lee could see her through the tiny glass viewer. What the hell was Lee doing here? Not only hadn't she invited them to come over, they didn't know where she lived. Kate had never told them her address, and she'd been careful to avoid saying anything that might even hint at where she lived. Her heart pounded furiously, and she felt suddenly lightheaded. She was as scared now as she had been when Delmar had tried to use her to help him commit suicide – maybe more so. Christ, and the entire house *reeked* of his filth. There was no way she could invite Lee in. But she couldn't just leave them standing there on the porch. Could she?

Three more knocks.

Goddamnit!

Kate unlocked the door, opened it, stepped outside, and quickly closed it behind her.

Lee smiled.

"Hey there, gorgeous. Before you get mad at me, I know it's rude to show up at someone's place uninvited. *And* I know that you've never told me where you live. I parked near Sprinkles one night when you were working, and I followed you home after you got off. I know that was really shitty of me and, to be honest, kind of makes me a stalker, but…." They trailed off, their smile turned sheepish, and they shrugged.

Lee Taylor was twenty-one, biracial, with thick curly black hair, and warm brown eyes. They wore a jean jacket over a white shirt, black jeans, and sneakers without socks. Lee had never worn socks the entire time Kate had known them. It was almost as if they had a physical aversion to the things.

Kate should've been furious with Lee, and she supposed on some level she was. But she was also relieved. It had been getting increasingly more difficult to keep coming up with excuses for why Lee couldn't come over and meet her grandparents. Kate was pretty sure she loved Lee, and she definitely wanted to take their relationship to the next level, but it was hard to do that when you couldn't be honest and open with your partner.

"Do you hate me?" Lee asked, only half-joking.

Kate smiled. "Not as much as I should. Look, I'm sorry that I've never invited you to come over, it's just that my grandpa is…." She searched for the right words. "Not in the best of shape. He can't talk or take care of himself, and he's stuck in bed all the time. And he…smells bad sometimes, you know? I'm not ashamed of him." She said this knowing she was lying. "But it doesn't make the house a very pleasant place to be."

She felt lighter for having spoken these words, and she hadn't realized how much of a burden keeping the truth from Lee had been. Yes, she hadn't told them the entire truth – *My grandfather is a boneless blob* – but it was close enough.

"Is it okay if we just sit here on the porch?" Kate asked.

"Yeah, but your grandpa…is he going to be okay? Is your grandmother here to take care of him?"

Kate had feared Lee would react with horror, or at least disgust, upon learning of Delmar's condition, but she'd obviously done her partner an injustice, as Lee's immediate concern for her grandfather's well-being demonstrated.

"My grandma went out for a bit, but Grandpa will be okay for a while. He's sleeping right now." She didn't know if this was true, but it satisfied Lee. They took Kate's hand, and together they sat on the porch steps. Kate rested her head on Lee's shoulder and sighed in contentment. It looked like their relationship had leveled up successfully without Lee having to learn the full truth about Delmar's condition.

Life is good, Kate thought. *Or better, at least.*

A moment later, an old red Mazda came chugging down the street. It slowed as it neared Kate's house, then turned into the driveway, steering system groaning in protest. Brakes ground as Tressa brought the vehicle to a stop and killed the engine. It rattled and coughed before finally going silent. Kate looked longingly at Lee's silver Camry parked at the curb in front of the house. She'd love to have a new car, but there was never anything left over from her paychecks to save for one. Maybe someday.

Kate felt a surge of nervousness as Tressa got out of the car, and without realizing it, she gripped Lee's hand tighter. Lee gave her a smile, stood, and pulled her to her feet. They stood like that, hand in hand, as Tressa came up the walk. A plastic shopping bag dangled from her right hand, and Kate figured she probably had stopped off somewhere beside the bank. Part of her resented Tressa taking extra time away from the house and leaving her to deal with Delmar, but she was also glad that Tressa had been able to have a break from tending to her husband. Although once she went inside the house, that break would be over.

Tressa kept her gaze downcast as she approached the porch, and Kate began to wonder if her break had done her any good at all. She seemed preoccupied and troubled, but by what, Kate couldn't guess. As she set her foot on the first step, she looked up, and when she saw Kate and Lee she broke out into a big smile.

"Is this who I think it is?"

"Grandma, I'd like you to meet Lee. They're my partner."

Tressa's smile faltered, and she looked at Kate. "Partner?"

"I'm nonbinary," Lee said. "Some people like the term *enbyfriend* instead of boyfriend or girlfriend, but I think it sounds kind of awkward. *Partner* seems to work better to me. It's *so* nice to meet you, Tressa. Kate talks about you all the time – all good stuff, don't worry."

Lee gave Tressa a warm smile, and Tressa returned it.

"Same here," she said. "Why don't the two of you come inside? I'll make some coffee and we can talk."

Kate gave her grandmother a warning look. She didn't know if Tressa could literally read minds, but the woman was so intuitive that Kate wouldn't have been surprised if she could. Tressa caught the look, her eyes widened, and she gave Kate an almost imperceptible nod.

"I should tidy up a bit first, though. It shouldn't take more than half an hour. I'll come get you when everything's ready."

Kate was grateful to Tressa. As used as she was to looking after Delmar, she should easily be able to clean him up in that time. Being able to deal with the stink that pervaded the house was another matter, but Kate didn't want to worry about that now. Maybe she could convince Lee to take her somewhere else before Tressa was finished, and they wouldn't have to go into the house at all. And if Lee insisted they stick around? She'd deal with that when the moment came.

"Thanks, Grandma."

Tressa reached up with her free hand and cupped Kate's cheek.

"Anything for you, sweetie."

She smiled at Lee a final time before stepping up onto the porch and entering the house. A slight whiff of Delmar-stench wafted out as she opened and closed the door, but if Lee noticed, they gave no sign.

"She seems like a real nice lady," Lee said.

"She is. She's been the only parent I've known for the last ten years. I—"

A spike of pain lanced into the left side of her head, as if someone had just rammed a sharp blade through her skull. She swayed, stumbled, would've fallen if Lee hadn't caught hold of her arm. The pain was so intense that she wanted to scream, but before she could, it vanished. One instant she was in agony, and the next, she felt fine, as if the pain hadn't happened at all.

"Are you okay?" Lee asked, concern in their voice.

Kate started to nod, but she feared that even a slight head movement might set off the pain again. She'd never had trouble with headaches before – certainly she'd never had any so severe – and she wanted to avoid doing anything that might make it return.

"Yeah, I'm fine. Just had a muscle spasm or something. I feel okay now."

Lee gave her a skeptical look, but they didn't press the issue.

"All right, but let's sit down again. I can give you a massage if you like. You always carry so much tension in your shoulders and neck."

"Oh, I like," Kate said, smiling. "I like very much."

*   *   *

Ethan blazed down the highway, his metallic-blue Camaro whipping past other cars like they were standing still. He had the windows up and the air-conditioning going. Southwest Ohio was a pollen-plagued nightmare in spring and summer, and even though he'd taken allergy medicine before leaving the House of Red Tears, he didn't intend to take any chances. He wouldn't exactly look intimidating with red, swollen eyes and snot constantly running from his nose.

Oakmont was well behind him, and Rockridge lay ahead. At the rate he was going, he'd be there before he knew it. He was tempted to slow down, though, maybe even get off the highway and take some back roads. It had been a long time since he'd visited his mother, and to say he was experiencing mixed feelings about going to see her now would be a massive understatement. It didn't help that he was also uncomfortable with the mission – for lack of a better word – Caprice had given him.

When the Incarnation failed ten years ago, those of us who survived had a decision to make. What to do with the Lord's body – or rather, its pieces? The mystic energies released by the rite created an unearthly fire that burned Tressa and Delmar's home to the ground within moments, but while the fire had reduced the Lord to its component parts, the parts themselves were undamaged. Some of us wanted to try for another Incarnation as soon as possible, while others of us — me, primarily — thought we needed to infuse the Lord with more power in order to bring it fully to life. We argued, fought, nearly killed each other. You don't remember of course because you weren't there. Your cousin Reyna took you and Kate into town so you wouldn't have to see how ugly things got. There's nothing so vicious as a family that turns against itself, you know. In the end, we chose to divide the pieces of the Lord amongst ourselves and safeguard them. And when the time was right, we intended to bring them together and attempt to complete the Incarnation. At least, that was the original plan.

Normally Ethan didn't like to play music while he drove. Even with soundproofed walls, the House of Red Tears could get damn noisy at times, and the only real quiet he ever got was when he was behind the wheel of his car. But his mind was buzzing with everything he'd learned today — not to mention all the things he now needed to do — and although he was excited, honored even, he was growing increasingly anxious. He turned on the radio and tuned in to a smooth jazz station. He let out a deep sigh as soft tones filled the Camaro, and he felt himself begin to relax somewhat.

Our entire family — Lintons as well as Shardlows — have belonged to the Quintessence since before Europeans came to this continent and began ravaging it. The Quintessence believes it is the destiny of all existence to eventually succumb to entropy. Reality came into being solely for the purpose of feeding the Gyre, the great Nothing that sits at the center of the Omniverse and devours all. The Quintessence, although comprised entirely of humans, does what it can to hurry entropy along — which, to be honest — isn't all that much. Murders, dark rites, curses, plagues…. They're all very well and good, not to mention fun, but their ultimate impact is less than a drop of piss in an ocean. Our family decided that what was needed was a power so great that it could deliver the entire Omniverse to the Gyre in a single stroke.

In other words, we needed a god. And since there wasn't one, we decided to make our own. The Book of Depravity had a…well, I suppose you could call it a recipe of sorts for making a dark god, and we added some of our own touches to it, and the Lord of the Feast – however imperfect it turned out to be – was the result.

But after the Incarnation failed, some of our family strayed from the faith of our people. They began to have doubts about bringing the Lord to life. They claimed that they'd come to believe that a slow progression of entropy was best, that it was what the Gyre preferred. "It gives the Gyre time to savor its food," your mother once told me. Others, like Tressa, felt the same. They continued guarding their pieces of the Lord, but they no longer intended to complete the Incarnation. Some even tried to destroy the piece of the Lord they possessed, but they didn't succeed. All of us who survived were diminished in power after the first Incarnation failed, but even at our full strength, none of us ever wielded so much as a fraction of the power it would take to destroy a single cell of the Lord's body. Fucking morons.

So I can't trust those who have betrayed the principles of the Quintessence to bring their pieces of the Lord here, so that we may complete the rite and bring the Lord fully into this world. Hell, I'm not sure I can count on any of our family to help, not after all this time. That's where you come in, Ethan. I want you to gather the components of the Lord and bring them to me. And if any of our family tries to stop you, I want you to give them the ultimate gift.

For members of the Quintessence, the ultimate gift was death. Ethan had no qualms about killing humans – he'd been doing it most of his life, after all – but he'd never killed someone he knew, let alone members of his family. He found the prospect somewhat disturbing, but at the same time, tantalizing as well. Could he do it? He'd had the same question when Caprice was speaking to him, and she answered it as if she'd read his mind.

I raised you to be a killer for this very reason, boy. Murder is second nature to you.

What if they give me their body part when I come for it? he'd asked. What should I do then?

Caprice had grinned.

Kill them anyway.

★   ★   ★

Ethan hadn't been to his mother's house – he didn't think of it as *home* – since he'd been in his early teens, and then he'd come with Caprice. Caprice was Delora's aunt, which made her Ethan's great-aunt, although he never thought of her like that. To him, she was much more: mother and father, mentor and tormentor, teacher and judge. After spending a short, awkward time with his mother during the visit, Caprice had sent him outside to play so the women could talk. He'd had no idea what they spoke of, but when Caprice came out of the house, his mother followed her outside, a blanket draped over her head, hands gloved.

Don't you ever come back here, you goddamn fucking bitch! And take that little freak with you. I don't ever want to see him again!

Caprice had given him Delora's address, and he'd entered it into his phone's navigation app. As he pulled up in front of the house, an electronic voice said, *You have arrived at your destination.*

"No shit."

Ethan parked and turned off the engine, but he didn't get out right away. Instead he looked at the house and tried to remember ever living here. Surely he should have *some* memories of doing so. It had been his home until he was eleven. But now, as he gazed upon this two-story McMansion with the small, immaculately landscaped yard located in one of the better neighborhoods in Rockridge, no memories stirred in his mind. No emotions, either. It was as if he himself had been reborn on that night ten years ago, his memory wiped clean.

He remembered something Caprice had said before sending him on his way.

All of us were diminished in power after the first Incarnation failed....

Maybe so, but Caprice had a decade to regain at least a portion of the power she'd lost that night, and who knew how strong she was now? He thought of something else she said.

I raised you to be a killer for this very reason, boy. Murder is second nature to you.

What if, in order to make him into the killer she wanted, she'd needed him to be a blank slate, one upon which she could write whatever she wanted? It was a disturbing idea. He had other memories, though, of hanging with Kate and his brother Weston when they were younger, of Reyna babysitting the three of them, all of them playing video games, watching cartoons, laughing.... Selective amnesia? he wondered. It was possible. Magic could do all kinds of weird shit.

You're stalling, he told himself. *Time to get your ass in gear and go to work.*

He got out of the car and walked across the lawn. As he approached the front door, pressure began to build in the right side of his head. It was merely annoying, but he knew it was going to get worse, and soon.

He thought of yet another thing Caprice had told him.

In the Repository, when you were close to the Lord's head, you felt a jolt of pain, didn't you? That's because you can sense the Lord's pieces, Ethan. It's an ability you gained the night the Incarnation failed. The energies released by the rite imprinted on your mind, calibrated it, and whenever you're in close proximity to a piece, you can feel it. The nearer you are to a part, the more your head will hurt.

That was an ability Ethan could have done without, thank you very much, but it would prove useful in his quest. Experiencing the pressure in his head now, slight as it was, meant that his mother had one of the Lord's pieces – the left arm, according to Caprice – hidden in the house somewhere. All he needed to do was go inside, get the arm, and hope his head didn't explode before he took it to the car.

Easy, right?

He stepped up to the front door and knocked.

He waited several moments, and he was about to knock again when he heard the *snick* of a deadbolt being turned, and then the door opened a crack.

"Who is it?"

A woman's voice. His mother's? Surely it was, but he didn't recognize it. *Selective amnesia,* he thought.

"It's Ethan."

The woman – Delora, he presumed – didn't respond for a moment, but then she stepped back and opened the door, not too wide, just enough so he could enter. He stepped inside, and she quickly closed the door behind him. She didn't lock it.

She looked the same as the last time Ethan had seen her. She'd draped a large thin blanket over the top half of her body — a beige one. Last time, it was blue. The majority of her hands were concealed, but the tips of her fingers were visible, and he saw that they were covered with white silk gloves that looked to be a size too large for her. She wore a tatty gray robe, baggy socks, and large well-worn slippers. She exuded a strong, earthy odor, and he wondered when she'd bathed last. Some time ago, he guessed.

"I know what you want," Delora said.

Ethan was taken aback by her directness, but he did his best to hide it.

"Good. That'll make things easier then."

"I didn't say I was going to give it to you."

Before Ethan could reply, his mother turned and walked away. He followed, unsure what was happening. He was fairly confident he was in no real danger. Given Delora's...disability, she couldn't harm him. At least, he didn't think so.

She led him into the kitchen and gestured toward a single-serve coffee maker on the counter. A mug with a cartoon kitten on the front with the words *Cutey Cat* underneath sat next to the coffee maker, along with several sugar packets and a small carton of creamer. Ethan could smell that the coffee had been freshly brewed.

"I didn't know how you take it," Delora said.

"You knew I was coming?"

She shrugged beneath her blanket, then winced, as if the motion caused her some discomfort. "I had a feeling you might. But I've had similar feelings before and been mistaken."

"And if you'd been wrong today?"

"I would've wasted a cup of coffee."

Ethan didn't want the coffee, but for some absurd reason he felt compelled to accept it. He went over to the counter, picked up the mug, lifted it to his face, and inhaled the coffee's rich aroma.

"I just take it black," he said, then took a small sip. The liquid was hot and delicious.

This ritual complete, Delora headed for a breakfast nook where a small round table with two padded wooden chairs rested. She gingerly sat on one of the chairs, drawing in a sharp breath as she settled. She kept the blanket draped over her and rested her gloved hands on her lap. Ethan brought his coffee over and sat across from her. They were silent for several moments, the quiet broken only when he took an occasional sip of his coffee, Delora sitting completely still, as if she didn't want to move any more than necessary. Ethan couldn't believe how awkward this was. It was the first time he'd seen his mother in nearly a decade. They should have all kinds of things to talk about, but now, sitting here, he couldn't think of a single one.

It was Delora who finally spoke. "How's Caprice? Still a gigantic bitch?"

Ethan bristled at the question, but he managed to keep his tone even as he answered.

"She's fine. The House keeps her busy."

"I imagine so, what with all the corpses that need to be properly disposed of and the rooms that need cleaning. She must spend a fortune on bleach."

Axton saw to those sorts of mundane details, but Ethan saw no point in mentioning this. Delora continued.

"Do you…. Have you…."

"Killed anyone? Yes. Many times."

"I see. Your voice is much deeper than the last time you were here. You sound like your father."

Cordell Linton had died in the aftermath of the failed Incarnation ten years ago, and Ethan's memories of him were hazy at best. He did feel a distant sadness at the thought of the man, though, as if there was an empty place inside him that could never be filled.

"Do you see your brother very much?" Delora asked.

"No," Ethan admitted. "You?"

"Weston visits me several times a month. He makes sure the house and lawn are taken care of, and he picks up groceries for me. Medicine, too. You wouldn't believe how many bottles of eye drops I go through. Weston's a good boy."

"And I'm not?"

Delora didn't respond to this. Instead, she said, "Are you still a follower of the Quintessence's teachings – are you a *true believer*?" She spoke these last two words with a venom that surprised him.

"Not to the degree Caprice is," he admitted, "but yeah, I guess I am."

"And you believe the Incarnation should be attempted a second time?"

"I wouldn't be here if I didn't."

"Of course." Then, just as she'd done before, Delora changed the subject. "Do you know why I let Caprice take you from me?"

"I...." The truth was, Ethan had always assumed Delora simply hadn't wanted him anymore. Caprice had never come out and told him this, but she'd hinted at it often enough over the years. "No, I don't."

"After your father died and I...changed, I withdrew into myself. I could barely walk or lie down without experiencing agony, and given my new condition, I didn't see how I could take care of you and Weston. When Caprice offered to take you both for a while to give me time to adjust to my new situation, I accepted. I told myself it was going to be a temporary arrangement, and that once I was better, you and Weston would return. I was a fool. I should've realized that Caprice wasn't being altruistic, that she had plans for the two of you. She hadn't established the House of Red Tears yet, you see. But once she did, she began training the two of you to be stone-cold killers. You took to the training, had an aptitude for it, a passion even. Weston did not, so he left your great-aunt and returned to me. When he told me what Caprice had been doing to you, I tried to get her to release you, but she refused. She accused me of having lost my faith, of betraying the principles of the Quintessence, and she wasn't wrong. I no longer cared about the Incarnation. I saw it for what it was – a ridiculous, dangerous folly. The one time I managed to convince Caprice to bring you for a visit, I sent Weston to stay with your Aunt Lisette. I thought it possible that Caprice might attempt to take the Lord's arm from me, and I didn't want Weston around if things got violent. She didn't say a word to me about the arm, though. Honestly, I'm not sure why she came. Maybe she wanted me to admire the job she was doing with you. Maybe she hoped to bring me back to the true faith. All I know is that when I first looked at you, I could feel the lives you had taken – *all* of them – and I was horrified. Caprice had turned my sweet little boy into a monster. I'm ashamed to say that I was revolted by what you'd become, and I told Caprice to leave and never speak to me again."

Don't you ever come back here, you goddamn fucking bitch! And take that little freak with you. I don't ever want to see him again!

The memory of those words burned like fire in Ethan's mind, and he fought to keep a tight rein on his emotions as he spoke.

"What turned you away from the path of the Quintessence? Dad's death?"

"That was part of it. But the main reason was you and your brother."

This was not what he'd expected to hear. "Don't blame us for your own choices."

He couldn't see his mother's face, but he could hear the sad smile in her tone.

"Do you ever wonder why people who claim to believe entropy is the strongest force in the universe, one so strong that it's the only thing that can truly be called *real*, have children?"

"Because the more people there are to process the Omniverse into nonexistence, the faster it will happen," Ethan said.

"That's the party line," Delora said. "But the truth is, many of us want children for the same reason anyone else does. They bring hope for the future. Caprice wants to end existence *now*, and if she succeeds, there will be no future for you, or any children you might one day have, or any of *their* children."

"Everything will surrender to Oblivion in the end."

"Yes, but there's a lot of time before that happens – maybe enough to learn how to forestall or even reverse entropy."

Ethan laughed. "You're insane, Mother! Surely you must realize that on some level."

Delora sighed. "I was afraid you'd react this way. Caprice has had ten years to make you into her creature. It was foolish of me to think I could change you during a single short visit."

Ethan was rock solid in his beliefs, but his mother's words still stung.

"I attempted to destroy the damned thing," Delora said. "I tried everything – cutting it, burning it, pouring acid on it…. Nothing worked. I'm not sure why I kept it. I hoped to prevent Caprice from ever getting her hands on it, I suppose. If even one part of the Lord is missing, the Incarnation cannot be completed."

Ethan was tired of this. All he wanted was to get the arm, get the hell out of here, and forget that he'd ever had a mother.

He stood up, put his hands on the table, leaned toward his mother.

"The arm. *Now.*"

Delora reached up, grabbed hold of the blanket with her gloved hands, and yanked it off with a single, violent motion to reveal her face. She was bald, and the skin of her face, head, and neck was covered with eyes. The eyes she'd been born with were blue, but these eyes were many different colors, and their sizes varied, from regular-sized eyes to pea-sized to several that were large as baseballs. They all had lashes and lids, and they all blinked, some faster or slower than others, but not in unison. Her regular eyes, the ones that were in the place where everyone else's were, had seemed normal at first, but now that he looked more closely, he could see that small eyes grew upon them, like some disgusting form of ocular acne.

Ethan stood frozen in shock. Caprice hadn't warned him about the nature of his mother's mutation – assuming she knew – and it hadn't occurred to him to ask. Besides, he didn't need any special preparation. After everything he'd seen and done in the House of Red Tears, he could handle whatever he encountered as he worked to gather the Lord's pieces. But *this*…. It wasn't the eyes themselves, the amount or placement of them, although all of that was deeply disturbing. The eyes gleamed with an inner light, and this is what caught his attention and held it.

Delora stood. She peeled off her gloves and dropped them onto the table. Her hands and fingers were covered with miniature eyes, and a regular human-sized orb nestled in the center of each palm. Then, moving carefully — because eye-covered hands are incredibly sensitive — Delora opened her robe and shrugged it off. She was naked now, but since her entire body was covered with eyes, she looked more like some kind of surrealist's painting of a woman than the actual thing. She stepped away from the table so Ethan could have an unobstructed view, and his head swiveled to follow her. All of the eyes — including her two natural ones — were blinking out of sync, and the longer Ethan watched them, the more he became convinced that there was a pattern to their movements, an incredibly intricate one. He thought he might be able to detect that pattern, understand what it meant, if he just watched a little longer....

Delora turned and walked to a counter, wincing. She did have eyes on the bottoms of her feet, after all. She stopped when she came to a butcher's block, drew a large knife from a wooden slot, then turned to face Ethan.

"Some of us died when the Incarnation failed. Some survived, relatively unharmed, and some of us, like poor Delmar, like *me*, changed hideously. But my change, for all its drawbacks — and don't get me wrong, there are a fuck-ton of them — came with one new advantage. When people see my eyes, they're unable to think, feel, or do anything. They become living statues, which I suppose makes me something of a modern-day Medusa, doesn't it? The effect wears off as soon as I'm no longer in their sight, but as long as it lasts, I can do whatever I want to them. Right now, I'm going to cut your throat and watch you bleed out all over my kitchen floor. I'm going to try not to cry — you can't believe the mess *that* makes when you have several hundred eyes — but I don't know if I'll manage it. But if I cry, it won't be for you, but rather for the little boy you were before that terrible night in Tressa and Delmar's basement. Don't worry. It shouldn't hurt too much. I may not have as much experience killing people as you do, but I know how to slit a throat."

She smiled, the action stretching the eyes on her lips until they began to bleed from the corners.

"Like the saying goes, I brought you into this world, and I can take you out of it."

Delora had made certain that Ethan had a clear view of her body the entire time she'd gone to fetch the knife, and so he remained immobile, hands on the tabletop, leaning forward, head turned toward her. He still felt the pressure in his head that indicated the arm was close by, but there was something else there now, a kind of whispering, almost as if a voice was speaking to him in his mind, though if it was forming words, they were in a language Ethan wasn't familiar with. And yet, he thought he understood what they were saying. *Watch the pattern. Wait for it. Then act.*

He watched. He waited.

Delora was less than a foot away. She touched the tip of the knife to the skin of his throat and started to press it in, when it happened. All the eyes that Ethan could see currently – every single goddamned last one of them – blinked closed at the same time. In that split second he could move, and he quickly closed his own eyes. Freed from paralysis, he pivoted toward his mother and lashed out with his right arm. His palm smacked the side of her head, striking a dozen of her various-sized eyeballs. She shrieked in pain, and Ethan followed that blow with another, this time driving his left fist into her side. She screamed again, louder this time, and he heard the sound of the knife hitting the floor, followed closely by the meaty smack of Delora's body doing the same. She cried out in pain once more as she fell, numerous eyes compressed between her flesh and the floor, and then she began sobbing.

Ethan risked opening his eyes.

Delora sat with her back against the wall, blood streaming from the eyes he'd damaged, tears flowing freely from the others. Her body was coated with so much liquid, it looked as if she was sweating. He felt no mesmeric effect from her eyes now. Maybe she needed to concentrate to do her Medusa thing, or maybe once the spell was broken, it couldn't capture you again. Either way, it seemed he had no more reason to avoid looking at her. That would make what he intended to do next much easier.

He knelt, retrieved the knife, then went to his mother and crouched down in front of her.

"I'll tell you where the arm is," she said between sobs.

"You can if you like. But I'll be able to find it on my own if you don't. In the meantime, let's play a game."

He selected an eye at random – one protruding from her left shoulder – and jabbed the knifepoint into it in a single swift in-and-out motion, as if he was lancing a boil. The eye popped and a mix of blood and ocular fluid leaked from the wound. Delora screamed.

"That's one," Ethan said.

He aimed for an eye on her right breast, one next to her nipple. Another quick stab, and another scream from his mother.

"That's two. I wonder how many more are left? Let's find out."

He stabbed the knife downward again, over and over, and Delora screamed, and screamed, and screamed.

CHAPTER FIVE

As Ethan pulled away from his mother's house, he looked at his throat in the rearview mirror. He expected to see a small wound, perhaps a bit of drying blood, but the skin was smooth and unmarked. Evidently, she hadn't managed to start cutting before he'd broken free of her spell.

He wasn't sure exactly when Delora died. She passed out well before he finished, and she'd stopped breathing sometime before he popped her last eye – number 982. He'd done his best to do as Caprice had taught him and not get any blood on his clothes, but 982 was a hell of a lot of eyes to pop, and there'd only been so much he could do. He wasn't drenched in gore or anything, but his shirt and pants were stippled with the red stuff. When Caprice saw him again, he'd undoubtedly get an earful from her about being sloppy in his work.

He thought he would feel guilt over killing his mother or at least regret that things hadn't turned out differently between them, but he felt great. Emotionally, that is. Physically, he had a pounding headache. Before the end, Delora had told him where the Lord's arm was – she kept it in a chest freezer down in the basement – and when she was dead, he went downstairs to get it. As he approached the freezer, his head started pounding like a motherfucker, but he ignored the pain, got the arm – which was frozen solid, despite not needing to be preserved – and wrapped it in a towel he took from his mother's linen closet. He'd put the arm in the trunk, and while his head still hurt, the pain had lessened with every step away he took from the thing. This was something Caprice hadn't warned him about either. She'd told him he'd be able to sense the parts of the Lord's body, but not that proximity to them would be so painful for him. He wondered what other things his great-aunt hadn't told him. More than a few, he suspected.

But he was in too good a mood to worry about that now. He felt light, freed from bonds he hadn't known were holding him back. He'd severed the last remaining ties to his past life, and now he could focus on fulfilling his family's destiny with a clear, sharp mind. Plus, he liked killing in pursuit of a specific goal. It was much more satisfying than killing yet another random victim at the House of Red Tears. People needed purpose, it brought their lives meaning, and for the first time since his birth, he was doing something truly important, and he liked that feeling.

He had two parts of the Lord so far – the head and the left arm. Which should he go after next? All of his relatives still lived in southwest Ohio, within an hour's drive of each other at the most, so selecting his next stop by distance wasn't necessary. He thought about the realization he'd had a moment ago, about how by killing his mom he'd put his past behind him. But that wasn't entirely true, was it? He still had good memories of Weston, Reyna, and Kate. Especially Kate. They'd been best friends when they were kids. If there was anyone he still had tender feelings for, it was her.

Which meant he needed to see her next. Hopefully, she still believed in the Quintessence's cause, and if she didn't, maybe he could persuade her to return to the fold. And if he failed...well, he'd just have to put her behind him too, wouldn't he?

INTERLUDE

Left Arm

"How's your meal, Ms. Pittman?"

Janet looked up from the iPad her niece Angela had gotten her last Christmas. She'd been reading social media posts while she ate the slop this place served instead of food, and she *hated* being interrupted when she was reading — especially since she now had twenty-twenty vision thanks to her last cataract surgery. One of the staff stood at her side, a pretty young black girl dressed in a blue polo shirt and black slacks, and she struggled to remember her name. She could've simply read the girl's name tag, but she was too stubborn. Come on.... Come *on*.... Then it came to her: Kendall. Kendall.... Something. She broke down and checked the name tag. *Kendall Ayers*. Ayers? That didn't sound right, but she supposed the girl knew her own damn name.

Janet smiled. "It's fine, dear. Thank you for asking."

It wasn't fine. Tonight's dinner was supposedly beef stroganoff but it looked, smelled, and tasted like something a dying cat would yak up. But Janet wasn't about to tell Kendall this. She never shared what she really thought and felt. Not out loud, anyway.

The dining room at Stay Awhile Assisted Living was Janet's idea of hell. Old people, most in their eighties, sitting at small round tables, some in wheelchairs, some sitting with friends, others — like her — sitting alone. Staff circulated among the diners, chatting with them, checking to make sure they were okay and asking if they needed anything. They were mostly women, half of them like Kendall, young and eager to help, half middle-aged and bitter, going through the motions so they could pick up a paycheck. Janet liked the bitter ones. At least they didn't pretend to enjoy working here. Some of the residents wore regular clothes – shirts, pants, sweaters, blouses, dresses – but most wore pajamas, robes, and slippers. They spent the majority of their time in bed, so why bother getting dressed? Janet shared this philosophy and wore a white nightgown beneath a plain brown robe. She didn't like to stand out, preferred to remain in the background, unnoticed. That way, no one paid attention to her as she watched – and she was *always* watching. As a writer, it was important to be on the lookout for new material.

The dining room smelled of cooked food, medicine, bleach, and people slowly dying. Janet didn't know how anyone could eat with this stink hanging heavy in the air, but eat they did, slowly, mouths working mindlessly like cows chewing cud, gazes as empty as those of any bovine. Christ, she hated this fucking place.

"Enjoying your new toy?" Kendall asked.

At first, Janet didn't know what the girl was talking about, but then she realized she was referring to her iPad.

"Just trying to keep up with the times. You're never too old to learn something new."

Kendall smiled broadly. "That's the spirit! You let me know if you need anything, Ms. Pittman, all right?"

"I surely will, dear."

Kendall moved on to check on other residents, and Janet sighed in relief. She found making conversation with the staff to be exhausting, plus it took time away from her real work. She put another forkful of tough beef and slimy noodles in her mouth, then picked up her iPad and resumed reading where she'd left off. She was logged on to a social media site called Chatterbox – it was where she spent most of her time online – and she'd been in the middle of reading a post from HarriedMom29 when Kendall had interrupted her.

...don't know what's wrong with me. Everyone tells me that being a new mother is supposed to be a wonderful experience, that it's a time for me to bond with my baby. But I'm so tired all the time and whenever the baby cries, I get so angry. Sometimes all I want to do is grab her and shake her until she stops crying. I haven't though! I don't go to her when I'm angry. I've tried talking to my mom

and my friends about how I feel, but they tell me it's a phase and it'll pass. I'm afraid it's NOT a phase, though, and I'm terrified that I might actually hurt my baby someday. What can I do?

Janet grinned as she began typing a reply.

Fill your bathtub with water and hold your baby under the surface until she drowns. Problem solved.

She posted the comment, which was attributed to her screen name, Truthspeaker13. Quite pleased with herself, she placed the iPad on the table, took another bite of her meal, and washed it down with a swig of acidic apple juice. Tonight's dessert was a fruit cup, and while she normally saved dessert until she was finished with the rest of her food, she thought she'd make an exception tonight. She wondered if HarriedMom29 would actually take her advice and drown her squalling brat. More likely, she'd read the comment and be shocked by it. Janet didn't care either way, big or small, as long as she caused some measure of hurt to someone, she was happy.

Janet began her career as a composer of poison pen messages when she was five. Her older brother, Ben, had pushed her down when they were playing, and to get back at him, she wrote a message to her mother and father on a piece of paper in red crayon.

Ben hurts me.

She drew an unhappy face beneath the words, and added a single teardrop falling from an eye for good measure. She put the message on her mother's pillow, and the next day Ben received the spanking of his life when their father got home. Janet had grinned the entire time as Ben cried out in pain and protested that he'd never done anything to hurt her. *That'll teach him to be mean to me,* she'd thought, and he *was* more careful when playing with her after that. The lesson she learned from this incident: words have power, and she could use that power to do whatever she wanted to whoever she wanted.

In first grade, Betty Rodgers pulled her hair on the playground, and Janet wrote a note to their teacher saying that she heard Betty call her a b-word in the restroom. Janet put the note – unsigned – on Mrs. Moore's desk at the end of the day. The next day, Betty was called to the principal's office, and when she returned to class, she was crying. It was glorious.

After Christmas break, Mrs. Moore scolded her for talking in class, so she wrote a note to the principal saying Mrs. Moore had called Daniel Hoffman a *dirty little kike*, and then it was the teacher's turn to be summoned to the principal's office.

When Janet was twelve, she discovered a box of magazines hidden in the garage. The magazines were filled with pictures of naked women, sometimes just posing, other times doing stuff with men. She assumed the magazines belonged to her father, and while he hadn't done anything to upset her, she figured her mom ought to know about the magazines, so she wrote her a note. That caused a big fight between her parents, which was a lot of fun to listen to, and a year later they were divorced. Coincidence? Maybe, but Janet liked to think her note was the spark that had ignited the flame.

In high school, she had a crush on Trevor Mitchell, captain of the football team. He was dating Amelia Wilkerson, though, and wouldn't give Janet so much as a second look – until she wrote him an anonymous letter about how Amelia was queer for other girls. Trevor broke up with Amelia and Janet swooped in. Trevor asked her to marry him the day after they graduated.

A few years into their marriage, it became apparent that children weren't in the cards for them, and since Janet didn't work outside the home, she had a lot of time on her hands. She watched her neighbors, got plugged into the local gossip network, and when she'd gathered enough ammunition, she began writing letters – a *lot* of them. No one ever knew where they came from. By this point, she was typing her missives, which was a relief. She was left-handed, and she hated always having to be careful not to smear the pencil or ink as she wrote. She never signed her letters and she never put a return address on the envelopes. The chaos that she created in her little neighborhood was delicious – arguments, broken friendships, divorces, even a couple suicides. All because she was good with words.

Once the Internet became a thing, it was like she'd been born for it. She set up multiple email addresses so she could send messages anonymously, and she created profiles on message boards, and later, on social networks when they came into being. Now that she was in her eighties, with her husband long dead and no children, her bitch of a niece had stuck her in Stay Awhile. But thanks to the miracle of technology, she was able to continue her life's work from this fucking depressing place.

God bless whoever invented computers, she thought.

Kendall was now talking with Alma Gomez and Laurie Bridges. The two women were best friends, practically joined at the (artificial) hip, and they were particular favorites of Kendall. She spent more time with them than any of the other residents, having a grand old time chatting and laughing. The three women were laughing right now, and when Kendall glanced in Janet's direction, she wondered if they were talking about her. Probably not, she decided. Still, she was irritated, so she opened up the email program on her iPad and wrote a letter to Stay Awhile's director.

I'm a resident at your facility. I don't want to use my name because I'm afraid of retribution. Kendall Ayers comes into my room when she thinks I'm asleep and plays with my private parts. I'm too scared to do anything, so I just keep my eyes shut and hope she'll leave soon. Please do something. I can't be the only one she does this to.

She read over the message, and when she was satisfied with it, she hit send.

She smiled. Life in a nursing home sucked, no doubt about it, but you could make your own fun if you tried.

★   ★   ★

Later that night, Janet was propped up in bed, watching a dumbass game show, when Kendall popped her head into the room.

"You have a couple visitors, Ms. Pittman," she said.

Janet couldn't have been more surprised if the girl had walked in, bent over, and shit out a hundred monkeys onto the floor. Who the hell would visit her? Her niece only came on holidays, and she never brought her husband with her. The fucker couldn't stand Janet, which was fine since she hated him just as much.

Kendall stepped out of the doorway, and a man and woman Janet didn't recognize entered the room. They were both in their forties, Janet guessed, and for some reason the man was carrying a suitcase.

"I'll leave the three of you to visit," Kendall said. Smiling – god, why the hell was she always so fucking cheerful? – she departed.

Janet frowned at her visitors.

"My mind may not be as sharp as it once was, but I'm pretty sure I don't know you two."

"You don't," the woman said. "But we're big fans of your work."

"The biggest," the man said.

The couple walked over to Janet's bed. A chair sat nearby in a corner. The man laid the suitcase on it, opened it, and withdrew a brown bottle and a handkerchief. He handed these to the woman, and then removed a strange-looking metal tool that resembled a cross between a knife and a saw. The device was tinged with rust, and when the man saw Janet looking at it, he said, "It's an antique. Been in the family for years. But it'll cut just fine, don't worry."

The woman unscrewed the cap from the bottle, poured liquid onto the handkerchief, and then put the bottle down on the rolling tray next to Janet's bed. She then turned to Janet and smiled.

"Did you know that you can make your own chloroform? It's quite easy. All it takes is some household bleach, acetone, and ice."

Before Janet could reply, the woman pressed the cloth to her face, covering her mouth and nose. Janet tried to push her away, but the woman was stronger, and Janet's exertions soon stopped, and her vision began to dim. The last thing she knew before she lost consciousness was the cold touch of steel on her left shoulder, and the last thing she thought was, *I'm going to write a strongly worded letter to someone about this.*

CHAPTER SIX

"Thanks, Grandma."

Kate took the warm mug of spiced tea from Tressa and set it down on the table. Lee had already gotten theirs, and they took a sip.

"This is delicious!" Lee said. "What's it called?"

Tressa smiled as she finished pouring a mug for herself.

"I'm so glad you like it. It's an old family recipe. Ancient, you could say. I'm not sure it has a name, to be honest. Not one that anybody remembers."

The three of them sat at the kitchen table, Tressa at one end, Lee to her right, and Kate next to Lee. Kate had wanted to sit between Tressa and Lee so that Lee wouldn't feel awkward, but Lee had insisted on sitting next to Tressa. *I want to get to know your grandmother,* they'd said, and Kate had accepted this, if reluctantly. At least the house didn't smell that bad. She had no idea how Tressa had managed to get rid of the worst of Delmar's stink in only thirty minutes, but she had. When Kate was younger, Tressa used to tell her that she had magic powers, and while they had been stronger before *That Night,* they hadn't deserted her completely. Given how horrible the house had smelled when Lee showed up, Tressa would've had to use supernatural means of some sort to deal with the stench. It wasn't completely gone – Kate wasn't sure there was any power in the universe strong enough to accomplish *that* miracle – but it was tolerable, and for that she was grateful. She'd have to do something special later to thank Tressa.

Tressa took a sip of her tea and nodded her approval. "So, how did the two of you meet?"

Lee glanced at Kate. "You didn't tell her?"

Kate's face reddened. "It never came up." A lie, but it was better than *I was too embarrassed by my mutant grandfather to tell Tressa much about you – I was afraid she'd insist you come over.* Although now that it was happening, she realized she'd had nothing to be afraid of. Everything was going well…so far.

Lee gave her a slight frown before facing Tressa once more.

"I came into Sprinkles one night to get a scoop of mint chocolate chip – that's my favorite – and Kate was working. I don't know what it was that got my attention first, her eyes or her smile. Maybe both at the same time. There was something…fascinating about her. We talked a little while she got my ice cream ready, and even though I'm usually shy about these kinds of things, I asked her when she got off work. She told me ten, and I asked if she'd like it if I came by around then so we could talk some more. She said yes, I left and came back, and we ended up talking in the parking lot until the sun started to rise. We've been together ever since."

"That's a lovely story," Tressa said. "Delmar – that's my husband – and I had a more traditional meeting. We belonged to the same… church, I guess you could call it. We'd known each other most of our lives, but it wasn't until we were teenagers that we started looking at each other differently, you know?" She sipped her tea and sighed. "Sometimes I think love is the only thing that matters in this… goddamned…universe."

Tressa's voice grew faint and her eyes became unfocused. Kate had the feeling her grandmother was looking at something far away from there.

Don't do this, Grandma, please! Whatever's happening, try and get control of yourself!

Tressa's face paled. She screamed, her eyes rolled back, and her body went limp. She would've fallen out of her chair and onto the floor if Lee hadn't been there to catch her.

Kate's embarrassment vanished. Something was wrong – *seriously* wrong – and Tressa needed help. She hurried over to her grandmother and together she and Lee managed to get her off the chair and into a standing position. Tressa moaned softly, and Kate knew that her grandmother wasn't completely unconscious. She hoped that was a good sign.

"Help me get her onto the couch."

Lee nodded, and together they carried Tressa to the living room, her head lolling and feet dragging the floor as they went. They laid her on the couch as gently as they could, and Tressa began shaking violently, as if she were suddenly freezing. Kate grabbed a throw blanket that had been draped over the back of an easy chair and placed it over her grandmother, but it did nothing to stop her shaking.

"What's wrong?" Lee asked. "Is she having some kind of seizure?"

"I don't know," Kate said. "I've never seen her like this before."

Tressa wasn't super old, but she wasn't young, either. Kate feared she was having a heart attack or stroke, and either meant she needed an ambulance. She pulled her phone from her back pocket and started to call 911.

"Don't..." Tressa whispered.

Her eyes were open again, and while she still shook, it was less severe than before.

"But, Grandma, you should—"

A tinny voice came from the phone's speaker. *Nine-one-one. What's your emergency?*

Tressa made a weak gesture with her hand and the call cut off.

"I wasn't ready," she said. "I'll be okay in a minute or two."

Her voice already sounded stronger and the color was coming back into her face.

Kate looked at Lee.

"I'd do as she asks," Lee said. "She already seems a lot better."

Kate debated with herself a couple seconds longer before returning her phone to her pocket.

"Thank you," Tressa said.

Kate knelt in front of the couch, reached under the blanket and took Tressa's hand. It shook only a little now.

"What happened?"

"It's Delora. She just died." Tears welled in Tressa's eyes and began running down her face.

Delora was one of Tressa's three children, Kate's aunt, and Ethan's mother. Kate hadn't seen Delora in years, but the news of her death still struck her like a gut punch. She didn't question how Tressa knew this had happened. Tressa's Sight, even diminished after the failed Incarnation, was still stronger than anyone else's in the family.

Kate glanced at Lee. They stood directly behind her, one hand on her shoulder for support. They must've been confused as hell by what was happening, but they weren't asking a bunch of inane, time-wasting questions, and Kate deeply appreciated this.

Kate turned her full attention back to her grandmother.

"How did it happen? Was it an accident?"

"I don't know. I do know she died in terrible agony. There's a plastic bag with a jar inside it sitting on the kitchen counter. Go get it for me, please."

More of Tressa's strength was returning to her by the second. She'd stopped shaking completely, and her skin tone was almost normal again. Her tears still flowed freely, though. She started to prop herself up into a sitting position, but she still wasn't strong enough to accomplish this on her own. Before Kate could step forward to help, Lee was there.

"Go get the jar," they said.

Kate smiled, nodded, and headed for the kitchen. She found the bag near the microwave, and rather than remove the jar from it, she grabbed the handles and carried the whole thing into the living room. The instant she picked up the bag, she felt a stab of pain on the left side of her head. The pain came on so suddenly that it surprised her, and she almost dropped the bag. This had happened to her before, when Tressa had gotten home and gone inside to clean up so that Kate could bring Lee in. Was it some kind of stress-related thing? Could be. She sure as fuck was stressed right now. The jolt of each step intensified the pain, and she grit her teeth and squeezed her eyes shut as she returned to the living room.

Tressa was sitting all the way up now, and while her eyes and nose were red from crying, she looked otherwise normal. Lee had grabbed a box of tissues for her, and she dabbed her eyes with one. Kate saw the grief in Tressa's eyes, and she knew her grandmother was fighting not to break down sobbing. Kate couldn't imagine having that kind of strength and control. She may only have been nine when her parents died, but she remembered what it had felt like to lose them. Still, she couldn't imagine the pain of a mother who'd just discovered she'd lost one of her children.

"Give me the jar, sweetie," Tressa said.

Without looking, Kate removed the jar from the bag. The pain in her head increased the instant her hand came in contact with the glass, and she gasped.

"Hurry now," Tressa said. "You'll feel better once you let go of it."

She handed it to her grandmother, and true to Tressa's word, as soon as the glass was no longer touching her flesh, the pain in her head began to subside. Kate looked at the jar in her grandmother's hands, saw what was suspended in the liquid inside, and her stomach gave a flip. She looked at Lee, as if to ask, *You see eyes in there too, right?* and Lee, their gaze fixed on the jar's contents, gave a quick nod.

Tressa held the jar up to her face, and the eyes inside slowly turned to look forward. Watching the things move was creepy as hell, but Kate had grown up with a grandfather who didn't have any bones, so she was more used to weird than the average person. Lee should've freaked the fuck out, but they gazed upon the eyes with fascination rather than fear or disgust.

"The Lord's eyes will show me what I need to see," Tressa said. "Past, present, or future." She was quiet for a moment, and then she drew in a sharp breath. "Oh, my poor child! What he did to you...."

"What?" Kate asked. "Did you see how Delora died?"

Tressa didn't remove the jar from her face as she answered. "Yes, but don't ask me for details. It's enough for you to know that she died hard. But it was no accident. She was murdered – by Ethan."

Lee looked at Kate. "He's your cousin, isn't he? Didn't you two used to play together when you were kids?"

"Yeah. I haven't seen him for a long time, though."

After *That Night*, Ethan had become withdrawn, nothing at all like the silly, energetic boy who'd been her best friend. His father had died, along with Kate's parents, and while they had loss in common, instead of bonding over it, they'd turned away from one another, each needing to process their grief in their own way. Kate had thought about getting back in touch with him many times over the last several years, but she'd never done it. What if he didn't want to see her again? What if she reminded him of *That Night* and brought all the sorrow and trauma flooding back to him? And now he was supposed to have killed his own mother? Kate couldn't bring herself to believe it.

"Why would he do something like that?"

"He intends to gather the pieces of the Lord, so Caprice can complete the Incarnation."

Kate hadn't seen her other grandmother for ten years, but she remembered the woman as emotionally distant and more than a little scary. Caprice had taken Ethan in after the death of his father and his mother's transformation, and while Kate had trouble imagining Ethan as a killer, she had no such difficulty picturing Caprice as one. Could a decade living with that woman as his guardian and teacher change Ethan so radically from the boy she'd known? If Tressa was right, the answer was yes.

"And he's coming here," Tressa added. "To get the eyes. I should've—" She broke off. As she'd spoken, she'd shifted her head slightly, and now the eyes in the jar were looking at Lee. Tressa didn't say anything for a moment, then she lowered the jar. She looked at Lee appraisingly, and Kate thought she was going to say something about them, but she picked up where she'd left off. "I should've left them where they were. He still might've gotten them in the end, but at least he would've had a harder time doing it. I wish I could stop him, but I'm not strong enough to go up against him and Caprice. She's worked hard to rebuild her power all these years, while I used what I had left to keep your grandfather alive. I shouldn't have, I know that, but I just couldn't let him go."

Tressa had kept Delmar alive and trapped in his own personal hell all these years — *and* she'd supposedly done it out of love? Kate couldn't wrap her mind around the thought.

"Lee, take this."

Tressa held the jar out to Lee. Lee hesitated, but then they took the jar. The eyes inside moved to look at them, but other than shuddering at being the object of the eyes' scrutiny, Lee showed no reaction.

"It hurts Kate to hold it," Tressa said. "Any part of the Lord's body will cause her pain if she's too close to it."

Lee must've thought Kate's entire family was insane by now, but they nodded to Tressa, as if they accepted what she said. Tressa rose from the couch and stood. Her legs were shaky, but they held her. She put her hands on Kate's shoulders and looked intently at her, as if she was trying to memorize the way she looked at this exact moment. *No,* Kate thought. *As if this is the last time she's going to see me.*

"You need to leave right away. Ethan will be here soon, and we can't afford to let him get all of the Lord's pieces. They can't be destroyed, but they *can* be hidden. Keep the eyes from him, and try to get any other of the parts that you can. Other members of the family have them. If you want to save them from Ethan, you'll need to get to them and take the pieces they're guarding before Ethan can reach them. Start with Reyna and Weston. They'll be the most inclined to help you. I'm so sorry, sweetheart. I'd hoped you'd never have to deal with any of this, but there's nothing I can do to protect you now. Go, and take my blessing with you, for whatever it's worth."

She pulled Kate to her and hugged her tight. Kate only half understood what was happening, but she knew Tressa was saying goodbye to her, and that there was a chance they would never see each other again. She hugged her grandmother back as hard as she could. She would've stayed like that for the rest of her life if she could, but then Tressa gently pushed her away. She turned to Lee.

"Help her however you can."

"I will," Lee said.

Kate had the sense that there was more being communicated here than was apparent by their words, but she had no idea what it might be.

"Take Lee's car," Tressa said. "Ours is a piece of shit and would probably die on you before you got out of town. And Ethan doesn't know Lee exists, which means he won't recognize—" she paused before continuing, "—*their* Camry."

"Look at you," Kate said, smiling although there were tears in her eyes, "using someone's preferred pronouns."

Tressa smiled. "Who said you can't teach an old dog new tricks?"

★   ★   ★

Lee put the eyeball jar back in the plastic bag, and when they got into their Camry, they wrapped it in a windbreaker and secured it in the trunk. Kate, sitting in the passenger seat, still felt pressure in her head, but the pain had receded to the point where she barely noticed it. Lee climbed behind the wheel, started the car, and pulled the vehicle away from the curb. Kate looked through the window at the house that had been her home for ten years, over half her life. She had the terrible feeling that she would never be back here again. Tressa stood in the open doorway, struggling to smile, tears running down her cheeks. She blew Kate a kiss, and Kate waved back. Then Lee reached the end of the street, turned left, and Kate couldn't see her grandmother anymore. She faced forward then, and although she wanted to cry – really bad – she forced herself not to. If everything Tressa had told her was true, Kate had work ahead of her, and she needed to keep a clear head, needed to be able to think straight, if she wanted to get it done.

"So…" Lee said. "What the fuck was *that* all about?"

Kate tried to think of a way to explain everything to Lee, but she had no idea where to start.

"Maybe it's better if I show you."

★   ★   ★

Tressa remained standing at the doorway until the Camry was lost to sight. She'd always known the day would come when Kate would leave the nest. It had happened with all three of her children, and she knew it would happen with her granddaughter too. It was the natural progression of things, of course, but she hadn't expected it to happen quite so soon. It might've been a cliché, but it was true – they grew up too fast. And while one grandchild had left, another was approaching. She hadn't seen Ethan in a long time, and she wasn't looking forward to his visit now, especially after what he'd done to dear, sweet Delora.

She was also concerned about what the Lord's eyes had shown her regarding Lee. She wondered if she'd been mistaken to trust Lee to guard Kate; she'd done so more on her own instinct than anything the eyes had revealed to her. She might be iffy on whether she could trust Lee, but she *did* trust her intuition – it rarely led her astray throughout her life – although *rarely* wasn't the same as *never*.

Enough. She needed to prepare to receive Ethan properly. She shut the door and headed to the kitchen to get started. She might've said a prayer for Kate's safety, but she had no deity to ask such a boon of, and the one time she'd attempted to help custom-make a god for her family, it hadn't gone so well.

CHAPTER SEVEN

Ethan couldn't remember the last time he'd been in Ash Creek. His parents had moved to Rockridge shortly before he was born, and while they had taken him to Grandma and Grandpa Shardlow's house many times when he'd been a child, they'd lived in the country outside town. It was possible this was his first time in Ash Creek proper, and from the look of things, he hadn't missed much. The town consisted primarily of middle-class to lower middle-class suburban neighborhoods, the sort of place where people had a vehicle up on blocks in their driveway, an American flag hanging by the front door, and a large barking dog – usually a pit bull – chained up in back.

Welcome to Shitsville, he thought.

Tressa lived in one of Ash Creek's dumpier neighborhoods – which was saying something – and Ethan felt like the resale value of his Camaro was dropping every second he stayed here. He checked his phone's display, and the directions app said he was close. As he drove deeper into Tressa's neighborhood, making right and left turns whenever the app prompted him, he passed a silver Camry going in the opposite direction. He felt a pull from the vehicle, as if there was something about it, or its driver, that he recognized. He didn't know the person at the wheel, he was certain of that, but the pull remained until both vehicles had put some distance between them. Then it stopped, so completely it was as if he'd never felt it at all. Weird.

The first thing he noticed as he approached Tressa's house was the piece of shit Mazda sitting in the driveway. It was hard to believe that Delmar and Tressa Shardlow, who'd once owned a fucking mansion, and – at least to his child's way of looking at things – had possessed more money than God, had come so far down in the world. *Entropy in action,* he thought. He pulled his Camaro into the driveway next to the Mazda, reluctantly, as if afraid his vehicle might catch some kind of machine disease from the old beater, got out, and headed for the porch. As he mounted the steps, he saw that the front door was open. It seemed he'd been expected.

Be cautious when approaching Tressa, Caprice had warned him. *I don't know how much of her Sight she still has, but even without it, she's a tricky bitch. Remember, she's the one who identified the donors for the Lord's body, and she and Delmar harvested the parts. They were extremely dangerous in their day, and regardless of their current situation, you should still treat them as such.*

Ethan hadn't thought to arm himself before coming here. He was young, strong, and an experienced killer, skilled in using a variety of instruments – including his bare hands – to end lives. He'd given no real thought to how he would confront Tressa, other than that he would improvise with whatever objects were at hand. A gun would be pretty damn useful right now, though. He could walk in, point the barrel at her, and demand she hand over the Lord's eyes, easy-peasy. But nowhere near as much fun.

Grinning, he stepped into the house.

"Grandmother," he called out in a singsong voice. "It's your darling grandson, Ethan. Won't you come out to greet me? It's been *so* long since I've seen you. I'm dying to give you a great big hug."

He listened but heard only silence.

Had her Sight warned her he was coming? If so, had she left before he got here? The Mazda was in the driveway, but that wasn't necessarily the only vehicle she owned. And she could've gotten a ride from someone else, someone like....

"Kate! We had such good times when we were kids, didn't we? Let's sit down, have some coffee, and reminisce about the old days."

More silence.

Irritated, and beginning to worry that he'd arrived too late, Ethan moved further into the house. The place had a rank odor, one that reminded him of a plaything he'd had at the House of Red Tears once, an older woman whose body had been riddled with cancer. When he'd opened her up, a similar smell had wafted forth, a stink of corruption and death.

He passed through the living room, found nothing, then moved on to the kitchen. He saw a teapot and three mugs on the kitchen table, and he went over to check on them. He placed his hand on the teapot and found it still warm. He dipped his finger into one of the mugs and held it up to his nose and sniffed. The tea was strongly spiced, and he recognized the odor. Caprice made tea like this – well, she had Axton make it from a family recipe – and the familiar smell made him feel a pang of guilt. Tressa, Delmar, and Kate were family. He couldn't kill them, or at least he shouldn't. Then again, he *had* killed his own mother....

He rummaged around in the kitchen drawers in search of a suitable weapon. He found plenty of knives, but he ignored them. He'd used a knife on his mother, and he disliked repeating himself if it wasn't necessary. It was a lot easier in the House of Red Tears, when you had tools laid out for you and you could take your pick. But searching for a weapon was fun, like a macabre scavenger hunt. Killing out in the real world might be more difficult than at the House of Red Tears, but it was way more fun. He eventually found a metal meat tenderizing hammer with pyramid-shaped points on each of its two sides. It had a nice heft to it, and he gave it a couple experimental swings to try it out. It felt good.

We've got a winner, he thought, and continued exploring the house.

None of the rooms he came to were locked, but no one was inside. He found what he assumed was Kate's room, although it didn't have much personality – no art on the walls, no objects on top of her dresser, bed neatly made. It could've been a hotel room for all the individuality it possessed. The sight of it depressed him. He remembered his cousin as being full of life, a nonstop dynamo of energy, but he saw no sign of that girl here. He closed the door and moved on. He found a bathroom (empty), and then another bedroom (also empty). At first, he assumed the latter belonged to Tressa and Delmar, but then he saw that the bed wasn't large enough for two people. Had they divorced or had Delmar died? Caprice had told him that Delmar had changed after the failed Incarnation, but she hadn't told him how and he hadn't asked. Maybe his change had something to do with why there was only a single bed in the room. He closed the door. Only one more room to go.

He'd become aware of two things as he'd proceeded deeper into the house. One was that the bad smell grew stronger the further he went, and the other was that he felt no pressure in his head which would indicate the presence of the Lord's eyes. He hadn't seen a basement door yet, and he assumed the house didn't have one, so where the hell could the eyes be? Had Tressa and Delmar hidden them somewhere else, maybe well away from the house where he'd never be able to find them on his own? If so, he'd just have to do his best to make them tell him where the eyes were, wouldn't he? He gripped the handle of the meat tenderizer tighter and opened the last door with his free hand.

A wave of stink so strong it felt like a solid wall slammed into him. The room was so dark that he couldn't make out anything. He took a step inside, reached out with his free hand, and felt the wall for a light switch.

"Grandma Tressa, are you here? Delmar? Kate?"

He heard a rustle of cloth, the scuff of a foot on the wooden floor, and he sensed movement in the dark. He swung the meat tenderizer in front of him, more as a precaution than because he'd identified a specific target, and he was rewarded with a solid *thunk* and a loud expulsion of air.

Gotcha!

But it turned out he was got, too. He felt hands grab his shirt, pull him forward, spin him. He stumbled further into the room, his feet struck a soft, yielding object lying on the floor, and then he lost his balance and fell. He landed on something warm and mushy, like a bean bag chair filled with hot water, and then he felt another presence in his mind, a pressure, but not like when he was near one of the Lord's parts. This was as strong as that, but it wasn't painful.

I'm sorry, Ethan, but the Incarnation must never be completed.

The voice was in his mind, but it wasn't his. It felt like Delmar's. Had he fallen on his grandfather? Was Delmar this disgusting fleshy blob beneath him?

That's Grandpa *Disgusting Fleshy Blob to you, boy.*

Ethan's eyes were starting to adjust to the room's dimness, and he saw Delmar's boneless hands slithering toward his mouth like a pair of smooth, scaleless snakes. Now he knew where the awful smell that permeated the house originated. Delmar's flesh was coated with some kind of foul muck the human body had never been designed to produce. He tried to push himself off his grandfather, but his body refused to obey him. Delmar might be malformed, but it seemed he still possessed some measure of mental abilities, and he'd used them to place a psychic block in Ethan's mind to paralyze him. He could do nothing but lie there as the rubbery tips of Delmar's fingers reached his lips, and pressed against them, wriggling like worms as they began to squeeze their way into his mouth.

He wants to asphyxiate me, Ethan thought. Not the most pleasant way to die, but he could think of worse. Hell, he'd *done* worse. But he was wrong. Delmar wasn't meant to be his executioner – he was meant to be a distraction. Tressa emerged from the shadows in a corner of the room and came rushing toward Ethan, a huge butcher knife in her hand. Her expression was a mix of determination and sorrow, as if she was conflicted by what she was about to do, but Ethan knew she wouldn't hesitate. He wouldn't, if he'd been in her place. He couldn't help but admire the efficiency and ruthlessness of his grandparents' plan, though. Caprice had been right about how dangerous they were, and although it seemed strange to feel proud to be related to people trying to kill you, Ethan did. Unfortunately for Tressa and Delmar, there was one possibility they had failed to plan for. While Caprice had made sure the bulk of Ethan's education had been in the homicidal arts, she'd also tutored him in magic. He was by no means an expert, but he knew how · to break free from another's mental control.

Tressa took a two-handed grip on the knife and raised it above her head as she flung herself toward Ethan. When the tip of the blade was within two feet of penetrating him, he threw off his paralysis, spit out Delmar's fingers, and rolled to the right. If Tressa realized what was happening, it was too late for her to do anything about it. She fell onto her husband and the butcher knife *chukked* into his chest. Both of them cried out, and it was impossible to tell which of them felt more agony based solely on the pain in their voices. Ethan was willing to bet the winner would be Delmar. After all, he was the one with a knife sticking out of him.

Ethan pushed himself into a sitting position. "Sucks not to have a rib cage, huh?"

Tressa let go of the knife, leaving it lodged in Delmar's chest. That told Ethan she'd stabbed a human being before, not that he was surprised by this. Only someone with experience knew that a stab wound bled more if you removed the object that had caused the injury. Her head whipped toward Ethan, her face no longer that of a woman in her seventies. She'd become fury personified, and anger blazed from her eyes with almost physical force. *This* was Tressa Shardlow, matriarch of one of the Quintessence's most powerful and respected families, a woman who had once come close to creating a god – and she was *pissed*.

"You killed my husband *and* my daughter, you little shit!"

Ethan felt her gathering her mental resources in preparation for a psychic strike on him, and while he thought it would be interesting to see if his power could measure up to the old woman's, he had work to do. He still held the meat tenderizer, and he swung it at Tressa's left temple as hard as he could. The impact caused a jolt of pain to shoot through his forearm, and he felt part of her skull cave in from the impact. Her head snapped to the side, and she collapsed, the bottom half of her body across her husband's putty legs, pinning them down. Her eyes were closed, and there was a concavity now where her left temple had been. The skin there had been shredded by the tenderizer's pyramid points, and the wound bled freely. Ethan didn't know if she was dead, but he could no longer sense her mental presence. If she still lived, she wasn't going to be capable of mounting another psychic attack anytime soon, if ever.

He looked at Delmar and saw the man wasn't dead yet. His breath came out as a gurgling wheeze, but his chest rose and fell visibly, meaning he was still getting a good amount of air. Given that Delmar had no skeleton to contain his internal organs, they could shift around inside him to a certain degree, and it was possible the knife hadn't hit anything vital. If it had pierced his heart, he'd have died almost instantly. This was good. Ethan had a few questions he needed answered.

"This probably wasn't the kind of reunion you'd imagined when you thought about seeing me again," Ethan said. "If you ever thought about me at all, that is. I'm sorry to see what happened to you. Clarice never filled me in on the details, assuming she knows them. I'd imagine that life as a blob hasn't been a laugh riot for you these last ten years."

Without a skull to anchor his muscles, it was impossible for Delmar to display a facial expression, but his eyes – which looked like large doll eyes floating in a flabby mass of flesh pudding – burned with an anger as intense as Tressa's had a moment ago.

"If I were you, I'd pray for death every fucking moment of every fucking day. I'd just want it *over* with, you know?"

Some of the anger drained out of Delmar's eyes, replaced by sadness and – maybe – a little hope.

Ethan continued. "The knife's already in you. All I'd have to do is stir it around in there real good a few times, and that should do it. I suppose you could try to do it on your own, but I'm guessing your hands don't have much gripping strength the way they are."

The last of the anger left Delmar's gaze. His eyes now pleaded with Ethan to finish what the butcher knife had started.

"I'm happy to do it, Grandpa. What's family for, after all? But there's one question I need you to answer first. Two, actually, and I'm beginning to suspect they may be connected. Where is Kate and where are the Lord's eyes?"

Delmar's lips opened and closed silently, reminding Ethan of some kind of fish. A flounder, maybe. Weren't they supposed to be flat?

"You can think your answer to me. I'll hear it."

Kate left…before you got here. Took the eyes…with her.

Delmar's thought-voice wasn't as strong as before, but Ethan could still make out his words.

"And *where* is she taking the eyes?"

Instead of words, this time images flashed through Ethan's mind. He saw Kate — all grown up — sitting at the kitchen table with Tressa and someone he didn't recognize. A friend of Kate's? That felt right. This was followed by an image of a silver Camry pulling away from the curb in front of his grandparents' house. Kate was sitting in the passenger seat, her friend behind the wheel.

"You couldn't have seen these things. You can barely move. Did Grandmother tell you about them?"

Yes.

Ethan remembered feeling an odd sensation as he was driving through Ash Creek to get here, a similar sensation to when he first got close to the leg his mother had kept stored in the basement freezer. Had he passed a silver Camry when he'd felt that? He couldn't recall for certain, but it seemed likely.

One final image came to him, a small white building with a sign above a wooden door that read *High Strangeness*. He smiled. He knew precisely where Kate was going. In fact, it was already on his list of stops for the day.

"Thank you, Grandfather. I hope you enjoy Oblivion."

He grabbed hold of the knife handle, shoved the blade in deeper, and stirred it around inside Delmar with swift, violent motions. Delmar gasped, his eyes widened, and his pores exploded with jets of yellowish gunk. Then a final soft breath escaped his lips and he fell still.

"You...disgusting...piece of...."

He turned, saw Tressa, conscious now, struggling to rise.

Ethan yanked the knife from Delmar's dead body, and laid open Tressa's throat with a swift backward slash. As she coughed and choked on her own blood, Ethan rose to his feet.

"Thanks for a lovely visit, Grandmother."

Ethan was covered with Delmar's yellow gunk, both from having fallen on him and from when the man had shot the last of it out as he was dying. Ethan knew he couldn't keep wearing these clothes. The stink would tell everyone he was coming from a mile away. He needed to ditch the clothes, take a quick shower, and see if he could find some replacements. Delmar wouldn't have any clothes – you couldn't get a shirt and pants onto a blob – but maybe Kate had something that would serve. He'd have to look. But first, the shower.

He dropped the knife and headed for the bathroom.

★   ★   ★

"So this was your grandma and grandpa's original home."

The plastic bag containing the jar with the eyes dangled from Kate's left hand. She hadn't felt comfortable leaving it in the car, but she didn't feel comfortable having it with her, either.

She nodded. "Doesn't look like much now, does it?"

She tried to keep her tone light to cover how much seeing the ruins of her grandparents' house was affecting her. This was the first time she'd been back here since *That Night*, and while she'd imagined what the place must look like a thousand times, the reality was both more dramatic than anything she'd envisioned while at the same time being depressingly mundane. A stone foundation, a couple limestone walls, some charred support timbers, a gaping pit that had once been the basement, grass and weeds growing all around. Nature hadn't fully reclaimed the area yet, but it was only a matter of time.

"Entropy is All," she whispered.

"What?"

"Sorry. Just something my family used to say."

Lee took her right hand and held it firmly, and Kate gave them a grateful smile.

Kate wasn't completely sure why she'd brought Lee here. After what had happened at Tressa's place, she felt she owed them an explanation, but now that they were here, she wasn't sure how to start. How did you tell your partner that you were raised in a family that belonged to an entropy-worshipping cult that had tried – and failed – to create a god whose purpose was to bring about the early death of all reality? She remembered something Tressa had once told her. *It was supposed to be a mercy killing. What arrogant fucking morons we were.*

She wondered what was happening at Tressa's now. Had Ethan arrived yet? If so, how had he reacted to learning that Tressa no longer had the Lord's eyes in her possession? Tressa had said that Ethan had killed Delora, his mother and Tressa's daughter. If she was right — and Kate had no reason to think she wasn't — what would Ethan do to her and Delmar?

"We should've stayed with Tressa," she said. "We should've helped her."

"You did what your grandmother wanted you to do. If all of this weird shit is true, then the worst thing you could've done is stay back there and give Ethan a chance to get hold of the eyes."

"And if it's not true?"

Lee shrugged.

"Then there's no harm in doing what your grandmother asked, is there?"

They were silent for several moments after that, then Kate began speaking again.

"I guess I wanted to bring you here to show you some kind of physical proof that what's happening is real. But some old ruins don't prove much, do they?"

"The eyes are pretty convincing," Lee said. "They move like they're real. And there's something about this place…. It feels like we're being watched. And do you see how dark it is inside the basement? The day's overcast, but there's still plenty of light. The shadows shouldn't be so thick in there, but it's pitch-black, like the inside of a deep underground cavern. And it feels *wrong*. I don't like it."

Kate had been so worried about Tressa that she hadn't paid the ruins much attention. But now that Lee pointed it out, she could see what they meant. She could sense the wrongness too, experienced it as pressure in her head. Her instincts told her not to get any closer to that darkness — because it was *hungry* — and she intended to heed them.

"Tell me what it was like," Lee said. "That night, I mean. You've told me a little, about how there was a fire, and several of your relatives lost their lives in it, including your parents. But that's really all I know."

That was all Kate had told them because that was mostly all she'd been able to remember. But now, standing here among the ruins of where it had happened, she found her memories returning – and they were far more horrific than she could've imagined.

"I...I'm not sure I can talk about it."

"Just try." Lee squeezed her hand. "It'll be okay. I'm right here."

Kate nodded, took a deep breath, and began.

★   ★   ★

Kate, nine years old, sat on a large sectional couch with her cousin Ethan, twelve, and her 'big' cousins Weston and Reyna. Weston was a teenager and was taking driver's ed classes, and Reyna was an actual adult. She was old enough to drink alcohol, and she even *worked* in a bar. Kate had never been inside a bar before, had only seen them on TV and in movies. Grandma and Grandpa Shardlow had a full bar down here on the other side of the basement – which they called the *rec room* – but Kate didn't count that as a *real* bar. It was more like a pretend one, a barroom playset instead of the actual thing. Normally a thought like that would've made her giggle, but not now. There was nothing funny about what was going on here tonight.

The adults were gathered around the pool table – Kate's mother and father, both sets of grandparents, Ethan and Weston's parents, as well as Reyna's, and Great-Aunt Caprice, who Kate thought of as the boss of the whole family, Shardlows and Lintons both. Reyna should've been standing with them, Kate thought, but she'd gotten stuck babysitting her, Ethan, and Weston. *It's too dangerous for you kids to participate*, Kate's mother had told her. *If it's too dangerous for us, then it's too dangerous for you*, Kate had shot back. Her mother hadn't responded to that, but she hadn't changed her mind. Ethan and Weston's parents evidently felt the same way, because they were exiled to the couch with her. Reyna didn't seem to mind babysitting duty, though. In fact, Kate thought she seemed kind of relieved that she didn't have to *participate* with the older adults.

The only light in the base— In the *rec room* came from the glass-covered fireplace in front of the couch. The fire's flickering glow made everything seem soft-edged and slightly unreal, as if she was dreaming. Dark ambient music – if you could call it music – played at low volume over the sound system: guttural chanting voices accompanied by discordant instruments that she couldn't identify. The adults were dressed formally, as if for a wedding…or a funeral. Freshly pressed suits and expensive dresses, all purchased especially for this occasion. Mom had taken Kate shopping with her when she picked out her dress – which made Kate feel very grown up – but she wouldn't tell Kate what the outfit was for. When Kate asked, all she'd said was, *You'll see.* She'd seemed excited, and maybe a little scared, too. Kate, Ethan, Weston, and Reyna all had new clothes too. Kate thought the boys looked funny in their suits, although she'd never say so. Certainly they looked uncomfortable, Weston especially. He kept tugging at his collar as if it was too tight, and his face was redder than normal. Kate liked her dress, even if it wasn't as fancy as Mom's, but Reyna usually wore jeans, and she kept crossing and uncrossing her legs, as if she didn't know what to do with them, and smoothing out her skirt with her free hand.

She's scared, Kate thought, but she dismissed the notion as soon as it occurred to her. Reyna was smart and tough. Kate couldn't imagine her being afraid of anything or anyone. She admired the hell out of Reyna and wanted to be like her when she grew up.

Kate sat between Ethan and Reyna, and she held her big cousin's hand. She wasn't certain, but she thought Reyna was just as grateful for the contact as she was. She leaned her head close to Reyna's ear and whispered, "What's happening?"

Reyna didn't answer right away. She didn't look at Kate either, instead kept her gaze fixed on the adults.

"They're trying to make something. Something special."

"Something *dangerous*," Weston said.

Reyna shot him a warning look, and he didn't say anything more. Kate looked at Ethan to see if he had any reaction to his brother's words, but he was watching the adults with fascination and appeared not to have noticed what Weston said. Kate remembered her mom and dad arguing about whether or not to bring her tonight. Dad thought it was important that every member of the family be present during the Incarnation – Kate wasn't sure what that word meant, but it sounded important – even if they weren't directly participating in the rite. Mom was less certain.

What if something goes wrong? she'd said.

The only thing that can go wrong is the rite fails, Dad had said. *That'll be a disappointment but hardly a disaster.*

And if it goes right?

Then Kate will sit with us at the right hand of our god.

Kate trusted her parents, and if they thought it was safe to bring her, then everything should turn out okay, shouldn't it? But despite Reyna's confident front, Kate could feel her nervousness, and it was making her start to have doubts. If her grown-up cousin was scared, then shouldn't she be scared too? At that moment, for the first time in her short life, she realized that maybe her parents weren't always right about everything, and that thought was absolutely terrifying. If she couldn't trust Mom and Dad, who or what *could* she trust?

Grandpa Delmar stood at one end of the pool table, holding a book open in front of him. Kate had heard the adults talking about this book before, usually when they thought she wasn't listening, but she didn't know much about it, other than that it was really old – even older than her grandparents – and that it could help people do amazing things. Before the rite started, Kate had asked Grandma Tressa why the book was so special. *Because it has power, child,* she'd said. Kate didn't really understand Tressa's answer, but she'd nodded as if she had. The other adults were gathered around the pool table, Grandma Tressa on Delmar's left, and continuing clockwise, Mom and Dad, Felton and Lissette (Reyna's parents), Delora and Cordell (Ethan and Weston's parents), Elisha and Victorina (Kate's other set of grandparents), and then finally, standing on Delmar's right, Great-Aunt Caprice. They were turned inward, facing objects lying on the pool table that looked to Kate like life-sized doll parts: head, torso, arms, legs.... A pair of eyes lay to the right of the head, a brain to the left. The head had no top and its eye sockets were hollow. Kate didn't think the parts were real. For one thing, they didn't match up. Some were larger, some smaller, some looked like they came from men, some from women, and the skin was different shades. Another reason the parts seemed artificial was that there was no blood on them. They were all clean, the edges where they ended neatly trimmed.

Maybe the pieces were prepared, Kate thought. When Mom cooked meat for dinner, there usually wasn't much blood, and what there was disappeared when the meat was cooked, except for the rare steaks Dad liked. Maybe the adults had done something to the parts to get them ready for tonight. But the idea that the pieces were real, that they had come from actual human beings, made her feel sick to her stomach, so she decided to go on thinking of them as doll parts. It was easier.

Delmar began reading aloud from the book, which had a funny name: *Liber Pravitas Itineribus.* He spoke one sentence at a time, pausing so that the other adults could repeat the words after him. Kate didn't understand much of what they said, although she caught words like *Gyre*, *Oblivion*, and *The Great Nothing*, and they beseeched something or someone called *The Multitude* to help them. Kate wasn't sure what was supposed to happen, but she felt the atmosphere in the basement grow heavy, like the air right before the eruption of a violent thunderstorm. The temperature dropped as well, becoming winter-cold in an instant, and she hugged her arms and shivered. Something appeared in the air above the pool table.... No, it was more like the ceiling was gone now, and above them was...was.... Kate didn't want to look at it, felt she might die or go mad if she did, so she kept her gaze focused on the pool table. The doll parts began to shake, and then in less time than it took Kate to blink, they were joined. The eyes had wormed their way into the sockets, and the brain had nestled inside the head and made itself at home. There were visible seams where the neck, arms, and legs had joined the torso, but the pieces seemed to be firmly affixed. This was confirmed an instant later when the creature's eyes flew open and it sat up.

Kate had never seen anything more beautiful or more terrible.

The adults fell to their knees, raised their arms high, and gazed upon their homemade god with a combination of adulation and shocked disbelief.

"I'll be damned," Reyna said softly. "They actually did it."

Weston's eyes were wide, and Ethan grinned from ear to ear.

The Lord of the Feast looked around, taking in its surroundings, and then it rose to its feet, moving stiffly, as if not used to its conglomerate body yet. Its mismatched legs weren't the same length, causing it to stand lopsided, and one arm hung lower than another. The top half of its head was missing, and the upper part of the brain was visible, reddish-pink and pulsating. Waves of power rolled off the creature with physical force, and Kate felt her body being pressed back into the couch, as if a large hand had shoved her. A sound issued from the Lord's mouth, so high-pitched that it was almost beyond the range of human hearing, and it cut into Kate's head like a red-hot knife. She cried out in pain, and then grabbed Reyna's arm and began shaking her.

"We have to go," Kate said. "Now!"

"Are you crazy?" Ethan spoke without taking his eyes off the Lord. "It's just getting good."

Reyna was also looking at the creature, but her face was pale and she was trembling.

"I think you're right," she said to Kate. She grabbed Kate's hand and stood, pulling Kate up with her. "Come on, you two," she said to Weston and Ethan. Weston stood, but when Ethan didn't budge, Weston took hold of his brother's wrist and yanked him off the couch. Ethan protested, but Weston was bigger and stronger, and he tugged Ethan behind him as the four of them hurried toward the basement stairs.

When they were halfway up, Kate couldn't keep herself from looking at the Lord of the Feast once more. It crouched low now, and it faced Kate's mom. Kate couldn't see her mother's expression – she was facing the other way – but she did see the Lord grab hold of Mom's head, give it a quick, savage twist and then yank. She heard the *crack* of snapping bone, the moist tearing of flesh, and then her mother's head came free from her body in a spray of blood. Everyone screamed as her headless body slumped to the floor, and the Lord lifted her head to its mouth and began drinking from the ragged opening, blood streaming down its face and onto its naked body.

The adults screamed, and so did Kate, and then Reyna pulled her through the open basement door, and the four of them ran like hell.

★　　★　　★

"Jesus," Lee said.

"The next thing I remember is standing outside in the night air with Reyna, Ethan, and Weston, watching the house burn. The fire was a strange reddish color, and it blazed hotter and faster than a normal fire would. I don't know what started it. Maybe the Lord did it, or maybe one of my family members created the fire to try and stop the creature they'd brought to life. A few minutes later, Tressa, Caprice, Delora, and Elisha joined us. Delmar leaned on Elisha. Delmar was changing, his bones beginning to lose their solidity. They'd be completely gone in a few days. Ethan's mom had bumps all over her body. The next day, they opened and revealed they were eyes. No one else made it out. We huddled together and watched the house burn down – it didn't take long – and then we left. Tressa told me later that she and the other surviving adults came back to the ruins a week later. They found the remains of the Lord. The fire had caused the creature to separate, but its pieces were undamaged. When the adults realized the parts couldn't be destroyed, they decided to divide them up between them and keep them safe until the day came to attempt the Incarnation again."

"What happened to the book?" Lee asked.

"They never found it. Most of my family thought it had been destroyed in the fire, but Tressa once told me that a book like that is too stubborn to die so easy. I don't know when the basement got the way it is now, though. Maybe the rite left a residue of negative energy that expanded over the years. All I know is I wouldn't climb down in there for anything."

"Me neither," Lee said. "So what did your family want to make a god for anyway?"

Kate told them about the Gyre and how the Quintessence wanted to bring out the premature death of the Omniverse. The feeling that they were being watched increased while Kate was talking, and she turned her head this way and that, expecting to see someone standing nearby. She didn't, but then again, she did – sort of. To their left, about twelve feet away, was a patch of air that didn't look quite right. She could almost make out shapes, five of them, featureless outlines of human forms.

"Do you see those?" Kate pointed toward the shapes.

Lee looked in that direction, squinted, then shook their head. "I don't see anything. Wait. I do see something, but it's farther to the right, over there, by that tree."

Now it was Lee's turn to point, and Kate turned her attention to a large oak tree that Lee had indicated. It grew a dozen yards from where they were standing, and had a deep split running vertically down the length of its trunk. Kate remembered that tree. She, Ethan, Weston, and Reyna had used it as home base whenever they played hide and seek. The crack hadn't been there then, though, and she assumed it had happened in the years since, probably as a result of the energies released during the failed Incarnation. The rift oozed some kind of weird green gunk, and strange insects crawled over it. There was something behind the tree, a dark shape that was leaning out just far enough to peek at them, revealing only a single yellow eye and a small portion of its head. The sight of the thing – even if it was only a partial view – gave Kate a sick, queasy feeling. She and Lee were in danger, she was sure of it, but just how much danger, she didn't know.

"I'm going to use the eyes," she said, "see if I can get a better look at these things."

She reached into the plastic bag and pulled out the jar. The instant her hand touched the glass, she felt a sharp stab of pain in her head, and almost dropped the eyes.

Lee took the jar from her hands.

"I'll hold it while you look. Just tell me where to point it."

The pain was already receding, and Kate gave Lee a grateful smile. She pointed to where the almost-shapes were, and Lee held the jar in front of her face. At first nothing happened, but then Kate's vision blurred, and when it sharpened once again, she saw five people standing shoulder to shoulder – three women, two men. Even with the eyes' help, their features didn't come all the way into focus, but she felt that she knew them. It was her parents, Ethan's dad, her other grandmother, and her aunt: Nila and Dalton, Cordell and Victorina, and Lissette. She should've felt joy at seeing them, at knowing that their spirits had survived death, but instead she felt afraid. An inhuman coldness emanated from them, and while she detected no animosity to it, she knew that these weren't her family members, not exactly.

"Turn the jar toward the tree."

Lee did as she asked, and suddenly it was as if the tree vanished. Kate saw a lean, black-furred beast standing on two legs. Its hands terminated in wickedly curved claws, and its head was like a wolf's or bear's, with high pointed ears and a pair of yellow eyes that seemed to glow in its black face. Another relative she sensed, this one…yes, Uncle Felton, her dad's brother. He'd changed, like Delmar had, although his transformation had been far different. There was nothing insubstantial about him – he was definitely no ghost – but Kate felt only a rudimentary intelligence in him. There was almost nothing human left. Felton remained hidden behind the tree and showed no sign that he intended to attack, but Kate feared that might change any moment.

"Look through the jar," she told Lee. "See if you can see them."

Lee did so. "Nope. I don't see anything that I didn't before. What are they?"

Kate told Lee who she thought the five ghosts and the beast were.

"This is wild," Lee said. "Beyond wild."

Kate handed Lee the plastic bag and they put the jar inside. They kept the bag instead of handing it back to Kate.

"What should we do now?" Lee asked.

"I think we should leave. Slowly. And maybe not turn our backs on him until we reach the woods."

"Sounds like a plan."

Lee sounded scared but determined, and Kate loved them for it. They did as Kate suggested, moving backward, one slow step after another. Without the aid of the Lord's eyes, Kate couldn't clearly see the ghosts, but she could still make out the suggestion of their forms, and she saw they remained where they were. Felton did too, although he leaned a little farther out from the tree to better track their progress. Kate had to fight the urge to turn and run. She might've grown up around some weird shit, but that didn't mean she was comfortable with being in the presence of ghosts and monsters. And just because these particular ghosts and this particular monster had once been her relatives didn't mean that she trusted them not to hurt her and Lee.

But the two of them reached the woods safely, and only then did they turn around. They began making their way back to Lee's car, moving as fast as they could through the underbrush. Kate listened for sounds of pursuit the entire way, but heard none. Still, she didn't relax until they were back at the front gate and inside Lee's Camry, windows up and doors locked.

"I shouldn't have brought you here," Kate said. "I didn't realize it might be dangerous."

"It was my choice to come with you. Besides, it turned out okay."

"I wanted to show you the place where the Incarnation happened – or almost happened – so you'd believe my story. But that was selfish of me. I wasn't thinking about your safety."

"I'm okay, Kate. *Really*. A little freaked out – okay, maybe more than a little – but nothing bad happened."

"This time. My family created this mess, so it's my responsibility to try and fix it. But you don't have to, and I can't stand the idea of putting you in any more danger. I *do* need a car, though, so I'd appreciate it if you could lend me yours. We can drive back to your apartment and drop you off, and then I can—"

"I'm going with you. You said your family created the Lord so it could destroy the entire universe, right? Well, I live in the same damn universe you do, so I'd say I have a vested interest in helping you."

Kate laughed. "Does this mean you believe what I told you?"

"I believe enough of it." They paused, then added, "More importantly, I believe in *you*."

Lee reached over and took Kate's hands in theirs.

"I know we've been dating less than a year, but I really love you, and I don't want you to go through this alone. Besides, tough and smart as you are, you could probably use some help."

Kate feared she was being selfish again, but she was relieved by Lee's offer to accompany her on her bizarre mission. Truth was, she was scared to death at the thought of doing this at all, let alone doing it by herself.

"Okay. Thanks."

She leaned over and kissed Lee.

When they pulled apart, Lee started the car and backed out of the driveway. Once they were on the road and moving, they asked, "Where to next?"

"Tressa said we need to go see my cousin Reyna. She has a bar in Oakmont, and she's probably working there right now."

"Oakmont it is."

They drove in silence for several moments, then Lee said, "Try not to worry about me, Kate. I've got a pretty good idea what I'm getting into."

Kate sighed. "That makes one of us."

★   ★   ★

The five shades watched Kate and her friend depart. When they were gone, Felton padded out from behind the split oak and crept closer to them, but not *too* close. The beast he'd become a decade ago was reluctant to trust anyone, including the ghosts of family members.

Was that Kate? She's so much older, Victorina said.

Time doesn't mean the same thing for us as it does for them, Cordell said. *I'm sure my Ethan is older too.*

Reyna too, Lissette said.

It was so good to see her, Nila said. *But so sad as well.*

Our girl has a difficult job ahead of her, Dalton said.

A virtually impossible one, Victorina said.

Felton snorted, as if in agreement with her, but there was no way to know how much, if any, of the conversation between the shades he understood.

Perhaps Tressa was right, Lissette said. *Perhaps it's the Omniverse's destiny to suffer. Suffering purifies and clarifies. It shows one who they really are, deep down at their core. Suffering is growth, it's life. It's the Gyre's way of showing it loves us. It wants to make us the best we can be.*

The tastiest we can be, you mean, Victorina said. *Suffering is how the Gyre seasons its food.*

Flavor to the feast, Lissette agreed.

The shades thought on this for a time.

It was Cordell who eventually broke their silence.

Tressa is gone.

Yes, we can all feel it, Nila said.

She cannot help Kate any longer, Dalton said.

We could help her, Victorina said. *We know where this will end. If we can get there in time....*

The farther we travel from the basement's void, the weaker we will become, Cordell said. *We might not be able to maintain our presence on this plane long enough to reach our destination, and even if we do, we might not be strong enough to make any difference.*

But we can try, Lissette said.

We have to, Nila said. *Kate has her friend, but there's no telling what a friend will ultimately do. They're not family.*

Felton let out a chuffing bark, as if he agreed with Nila. The five shades waited to see if any of them had anything to add. When no one spoke again, they began moving toward the edge of the woods, floating soundlessly above the grass. After a moment, Felton followed, making no more noise than they did.

CHAPTER EIGHT

Ethan drove down the highway, heading back toward Oakmont. After his visit with Tressa and Delmar, he felt *good* — calm and relaxed. He was looking forward to arriving at High Strangeness and seeing Kate and Reyna. Last he heard, his brother was working there too, and he was hoping to see him as well. It had been a while since they'd been together. Neither Weston nor Reyna liked Caprice much, and they thought she had an unhealthy hold over Ethan. They had no moral qualms about what took place in the House of Red Tears, although Reyna had once told him she found Caprice's business tawdry. But they felt Caprice was using Ethan for her own ends, especially Weston, who had tried on several occasions to convince Ethan to leave their great-aunt's home. When Ethan told Caprice about how his brother and cousin felt, she'd said, *They've fallen from the true faith. They preoccupy themselves with small degradations that do little, if anything, to speed entropy. They resent me because I remind them of what they've turned their backs on: their beliefs, their history, their family....*

Ethan figured that Caprice was right, but Weston and Reyna *were* still family, regardless of what they thought of their great-aunt and him, and he hoped that when they came to understand that the Lord's Incarnation was going to occur at last, they'd return to the fold. And if they didn't? He'd brought along the butcher knife Tressa had tried to stab him with. It lay on the passenger seat, the blade and handle clean. Plus, a bar had dozens of glass bottles that, once broken, made excellent weapons, and chair and table legs made good clubs. One way or another, he'd manage.

He was in such a good mood that he didn't even mind the way he was dressed. It had been slim pickings in Kate's room, but he'd eventually a found a T-shirt that was larger than the others in her dresser, gray, with the words *I Wanna Rock and Roll* on the front. A past boyfriend's? Maybe Kate had worn it to sleep in, or maybe she just liked listening to rock music and being comfortable. All that mattered was that the shirt fit him well enough. He was a skinny dude, but even so, he hadn't been able to find pants that would fit him. The best he'd been able to do was a pair of jeans that were too tight and which he couldn't zip up all the way or button. Luckily, the front of the T-shirt hung down far enough to hide this fact. Shoes had been a near-complete bust. His feet were simply too big for any that Kate owned. In the end, he'd been forced to make due with a pair of bright yellow flip-flops that had plastic daisies on top of the straps.

He might look ridiculous, but he still liked these clothes better than the white monkey suit Caprice was always trying to get him to wear. He had no interest in looking like Axton's mini-me.

His phone lay on the passenger seat next to the knife, and it began vibrating. At the same time, music started playing, Black Oyster Cult's 'Don't Fear the Reaper'. Too much on the nose for a ring tone, he supposed, but he liked the kitschy absurdity of it. He picked up the phone and steered with one hand as he answered it.

Caprice started speaking before he could say hello.

"Did you give my regards to your mother?"

Ethan grinned. "Not in so many words, but I think it's safe to say she got the point – multiple times, actually."

Caprice sighed. "What did I tell you about making after-murder puns?"

"That it mocks the holy solemnity of entropy. You know, you can be a real buzzkill sometimes, Caprice."

She ignored the dig. "So you got the left arm?"

"I did."

He hoped to hear her praise him, but of course she didn't. She continued as if he hadn't spoken.

"Have you gotten any other pieces?"

His first impulse was to lie, but she almost always knew when he wasn't telling the truth.

"I visited Tressa and Delmar."

"So you've got the eyes as well."

"Not exactly."

He told Caprice about what happened with Tressa and Delmar, leaving nothing out.

"I made Delmar tell me where Kate was going before he died. She's heading to High Strangeness, and I'm on my way there now. Not only will I get the eyes, Reyna has the right arm, and I'll get that, too."

Caprice was silent for so long that Ethan thought the call had been dropped. But he wasn't that lucky.

"If Kate gets there before you, she can warn your cousin, and Reyna might make a run for it and take the arm with her. It's more likely Kate would take it, though."

Ethan frowned. "If Kate's no longer a believer, I can see why she wouldn't want to help us, but why would she take the arm from Reyna?"

Caprice ignored his question.

"I'm disappointed that you let the eyes slip away from you, Ethan. And if Kate intends to work against us – which I'm sure she does, given that her mind has been poisoned by Tressa all these years – I think we need to step up our timetable. The sooner we collect all the Lord's pieces, the better. I'm going to have to call in some backup."

"I can do this – I don't *need* any help!"

"Clearly you do. Make sure you get the eyes and that arm."

She disconnected.

"Fuck!"

Ethan threw his phone in anger. The device struck the passenger door, bounced off, and hit the floor. He didn't care if he'd broken it. If he had, at least he wouldn't have to listen to Caprice's bullshit if she tried to call him back.

He couldn't believe this. For ten goddamned years he'd done everything Caprice had told him to do, had made himself into the thing she wanted him to be, all for one purpose: to be ready to gather the pieces of the Lord when she'd collected enough energy in the Repository to complete the Incarnation. And now that the time had finally come and he was fulfilling his destiny, Caprice had decided he wasn't performing to her satisfaction and intended to call someone in to help. For fuck's sake, he'd just started! The least she could do was give him a little time to prove himself. But not Caprice. Now wasn't soon enough for her. She wanted everything yesterday, or better yet, last week. His face burned with anger and shame, and he wondered who she was going to get. Not Axton. If she thought he had the stones for this work, she'd have used him in the first place.

He decided it didn't matter who she called. He'd show Caprice that he could do this job on his own. He was Ethan Fucking Linton, a member of the Quintessence and a stone-cold killer. He'd gather the pieces of the Lord and perform the Incarnation all by himself if he had to. And when the god manifested in the flesh, he'd ask a single boon of it.

Kill Caprice first.

★   ★   ★

Caprice made a call when she was finished with Ethan and had a brief but satisfying conversation with an old friend. She then placed her phone on the table next to a sledgehammer whose face was covered with blood, brain matter, and chunks of hair. The other implements spread out on the table were equally as gore-slick. She shook her head.

"I swear, that boy…."

She picked up a cat-o'-nine-tails, turned away from the table, and walked toward the center of the room. She was naked, but her skin was covered with so much blood she looked like she was wearing a crimson wet suit. Normally, she liked to do her killing neat, but sometimes she needed to let go and have a little fun – especially when she was stressed. Five corpses lay on the floor, all mutilated and broken to various degrees, surrounding a black leather-padded pillar to which a naked Axton was chained, arms stretched tight above his head. Like Caprice, Axton's body was slick with blood. Unlike her, some of it was his own.

"I couldn't help overhearing," he said as Caprice approached. "You asked the Mister and Missus to fetch the torso?"

Caprice took up a position in front of Axton, and slashed the whip across his lower abdomen, just above his penis. He grunted and his body jerked, but he didn't cry out. They were playing one of Caprice's favorite games – Make Axton Scream. So far, the most she'd gotten out of him were a few brief cries of pain and a couple pathetic mewling sounds. She was going to have to work harder. Maybe she should turn him around, work on his back and ass for a while.

"I did."

The two of them had entered the room so Caprice could work out some nervous energy while she waited for Ethan to finish his errands. She'd had five playthings brought up from the holding pens in the basement for her and Axton to enjoy, a mix of ages, genders, and races. She insisted on being brought a random selection whenever she played. She was a huge proponent of nondiscriminatory killing. After all, the Gyre accepted everyone. And while she had more than enough spirits saved in the Repository to restore the Lord, adding a few more to their number wouldn't hurt.

She swiped the whip across Axton's nipples, and a soft "Ah" escaped his lips. As it did, his penis twitched.

Now we're getting somewhere, Caprice thought.

"And you're sending to them get which piece? The torso?"

"Yes."

She struck his left inner thigh this time, and his cock become half erect. He didn't make any sound, though, so she struck the other thigh harder. This time he let out a louder "Ah", and his dick hardened fully.

"I've never understood why you let Haksaw keep it."

Caprice had been aware of Haksaw for some time. Someone in her business needed to keep track of any independent killers in the area, in case they drew the attention of law enforcement and, in turn, the media. Her clients paid for anonymity and safety, and she'd do what she had to in order to ensure both. Caprice had considered having Haksaw killed, but he possessed a fierce dedication to his art, and she admired that, so she decided to keep an eye on him, and if he became too troublesome, then she'd have him eliminated. One day the torso disappeared from the House, and a review of security tapes showed that Haksaw had been the culprit. She didn't know how he'd learned about the torso. Perhaps it had called to him somehow. Her first impulse was to track down Haksaw, kill the bastard, and bring the torso home. But upon further thought, she'd changed her mind.

"He's remained close by all these years, and he protects the torso more obsessively than anyone else on the planet would, including me. It's been safer with him than anywhere else. And I suppose the perversity of the situation amuses me, to be honest. But it's time that I got the torso back, and that's where Yes and No come in."

She swatted his penis with the whip three times in rapid succession: *thwap, thwap, THWAP!*

Axton screamed at last, and Caprice smiled. She dropped the whip to the floor, turned around, and backed up to him until his throbbing, bleeding cock was inside her.

Axton gasped and said, "I hope they succeed."

Caprice started moving back and forth.

"They will. Haksaw's dangerous, but he's nothing compared to those two."

Then the time for words was over, and when Caprice was finally finished with Axton, he released a very different kind of scream.

★   ★   ★

Mr. Yes ended the call and slipped his phone into the inner pocket of his suit jacket. He'd stepped out of the bathroom to take the call, and now that he was finished, he reentered.

"I'm afraid we're going to have to cut this short, darling."

Mrs. No didn't look at her husband as he spoke. She stood bent over a rectangular marble tub that matched the marble floor and walls, making it seem as if the bathroom hadn't been built but had rather grown naturally. The tub was filled with scalding hot water, and an overweight, balding man in his sixties wearing only a red bathrobe knelt next to it. Mrs. Yes held the man's head beneath the water, and while he struggled and flailed mightily, he couldn't escape her grip. If she felt any pain from having her hand submerged in the hot water, she gave no indication.

Mr. Yes was in his early forties, tall, with an athletic build. His hair was midnight-black and freshly cut. He was clean-shaven, not so much as a hint of stubble on his always-smiling face. He was dressed in a dark blue suit, a blue shirt and tie, and brown shoes. Mrs. No was the same age and height as her husband and also possessed an athletic build. She wore her black hair pulled into a ponytail so it wouldn't get in the way when she was working. She wore all black – suit jacket, blouse, slacks, shoes. Both carried Glocks in shoulder holsters and had various knives concealed about their persons, as well as extra ammo. They possessed similar facial features, so similar that they were often mistaken for brother and sister instead of husband and wife. Whenever anyone commented on their resemblance, Mrs. No said that she and her husband were clones. She never smiled when she said this, and although most people thought it was a joke, they didn't laugh.

She raised the man's head out of the water, let him take a gasping breath, then shoved him back under. His hands smacked the sides of the tub, his feet drummed against the floor, but he could not escape Mrs. No.

"Who called?" she asked.

"Caprice. She has a—"

"Job for us. Did you tell her that—"

"We're busy at the moment? Yes. She said it was of vital importance and so she'd—"

"Double her usual fee?"

"Triple."

That got Mrs. No's attention. She yanked the man's head out of the water and let him catch his breath. She looked at her husband.

"Interesting. Did she sound desperate?"

Mr. Yes considered. "I wouldn't go that far, but I *would* say she sounded as if there was a certain degree of urgency to the matter."

Mrs. No turned to the gasping man. His dripping face was red, as if he'd gotten a bad sunburn, and his flesh was swollen so badly his eyes were barely visible.

Dwayne French was a plastic surgeon, and by all accounts a very good one. His house in the richest, most exclusive neighborhood in Columbus was testament to his success. He also, unfortunately, was overly fond of alcohol. Last month, he was performing a breast augmentation procedure on the wife of a city councilwoman, and he'd had a three-martini lunch beforehand. It was a simple boob job, and it wasn't as if he needed to be at the top of his game or anything. But during the operation, his hand slipped and his scalpel nicked an artery that was located in a place he hadn't expected it to be. French and his nurse had tried to stop the bleeding, but he failed and his patient died. This was the third patient of his to die on the table, which Mr. Yes supposed wasn't all that bad a track record for someone who'd been in medical practice for thirty years. Still, French's medical license had been suspended pending a review of the incident, and the good doctor – who did feel a certain amount of regret over the woman's death – was giving serious consideration to retiring, although he had no intention of giving up drinking. The councilwoman was inconsolable over the loss of her wife and burned for revenge. And so she'd hired the best assassins in the Midwest – Mr. Yes and Mrs. No. Her instructions were as simple as they were direct: Make French suffer as much as possible for as long as possible before he died.

"I don't know..." Mrs. No said. "We've barely begun, and if we kill this fucker too quickly and easily, we'll be violating the terms of our contract. That's not very professional, is it?"

"True," Mr. Yes acknowledged. "But triple our fee, dear heart."

"You have a good point." She turned to French. "It's your lucky day, Doctor."

He blinked and squinted, attempting to see past the swelling around his eyes.

"You're letting me go?"

Mr. Yes and Mrs. No laughed. Then Mrs. No slammed French's head against the sharp edge of the tub, one, twice, three times. When she was finished, little of his face remained and he was quite dead. She let go of him and stood. His corpse slid to the marble floor, his ruined face leaving a smear of blood on the side of the tub, and he flopped over on his side. Mr. Yes and Mrs. No regarded French's body for a moment.

"Not our best work," Mrs. No said.

"True," Mr. Yes acknowledged. "But this is what comes from—"

"Being the best. I know. Always in demand. Victims—"

"Of our own success," Mr. Yes finished.

Mrs. No bent down and dried her hands on French's robe. When she was finished, she straightened and followed Mr. Yes out of the bathroom.

"Where are we headed?" she asked.

"Oakmont. We can be there in an hour, maybe a bit less if I drive with a heavy foot on the accelerator."

"Sounds like the situation calls for it. After all—"

Mr. Yes grinned. "Triple our fee."

*   *   *

Mr. Yes and Mrs. No met when they were preteens. Not only did they live in the same town, they lived on the same block. They'd seen each other around in the neighborhood before, but they'd never interacted until that day Mr. Yes – who, like Mrs. No, had a different name back then – visited a small park near his house. He carried a pocketknife with him, which he'd stolen from his father's dresser, and he'd come in search of a ginger tabby cat that he'd seen prowling around the park. He found the cat, but it was lying dead behind a bush, its abdomen flayed open, the girl who would one day be Mrs. No kneeling next to it, holding an X-Acto knife, the razor-sharp blade dripping with blood. Mr. Yes had wanted to yell at the girl for cutting up *his* cat, but she looked so pretty kneeling next to the mutilated animal, knife in hand, that his anger instantly dissipated.

The girl looked at him for a moment. She gripped the X-Acto knife tighter, and he had the sense that she was making a decision. Then she relaxed her grip on the knife and smiled.

"Would you like to—"

"Share? Yes, I would. Very much."

He took out his pocketknife, unfolded the blade, and knelt beside her.

They were inseparable after that, and no animal in the neighborhood – domestic or wild – was safe from them.

They killed their first human on Mrs. No's sixteenth birthday, a toddler that had strayed out of his parents' yard. Mr. Yes found the boy, who was lost and crying, and took him to Mrs. No's house. Her parents were gone, and she had no siblings, so they took the boy down into the basement and enjoyed him together. When they were finished, they made love for the first time.

After they graduated high school, they decided to go into business as partners, and – after murdering both sets of parents – they set out to make a living doing what they did best. They were successful right from the beginning, and the money kept rolling in. They married when they were both twenty-two, and for their honeymoon, they visited a place they'd learned about from others like them, people who killed for fun and profit: the House of Red Tears. They enjoyed their stay so much that they returned every anniversary and also spent their birthdays there. The owner and proprietor – Caprice Linton – got to know them and started throwing work their way. Sometimes they captured new playthings for her, other times they eliminated deadbeat clients who refused to pay, or would-be entrepreneurs who made the mistake of trying to compete with her. Caprice paid well, but she wasn't one to squander money, so when she offered to pay them triple their fee to go to Oakmont and retrieve a human torso from some low-level killer who went by the name of Haksaw – an embarrassing *nom du mort*, complete with intentional misspelling – they knew how important this job was to her. And once they'd killed Haksaw and delivered the torso, maybe they could use what they'd done for her as reason why they should be allowed free visits to the House from now on.

Or at least discounted ones.

⋆　　⋆　　⋆

Haksaw woke so abruptly that he was sitting up and looking around before he was even aware he was conscious.

Something's wrong.

After a lifetime of performing acts that most of society deemed monstrous – and having to avoid the law because of them – he'd developed a heightened instinct for danger that was almost as keen as an animal's. Something bad was coming. Whatever it was, it wasn't here yet, but it was on its way and approaching fast.

"Don't worry, my love, I'll protect you. Don't I always?"

He pulled back the sheet and gazed upon his sweet love. It had no head, arms, or legs, and while it possessed male genitalia – which unfortunately were incapable of erection and ejaculation – Haksaw never thought of his love as a *he*, always an *it*. It just felt right. The torso lay chest down, its buttocks smeared with petroleum jelly. Haksaw did his best to keep the torso clean, but he usually fell asleep directly after they had sex, often before he had a chance to wipe his lover clean. He used a corner of the sheet to remedy this now, then rolled his love onto its back.

He reached down, pressed his hand against the muscled abdomen, and a shiver of joy rippled down his back. With the torso, every touch felt like the first, new and exciting. His love couldn't think without a brain, obviously, but it could still *feel,* and Haksaw had gotten very good at understanding and interpreting his love's emotions over the years, and while it wasn't scared right now, it *was* deeply concerned – which meant that whatever was coming was even worse than Haksaw had first thought.

He ran his fingers up across its chest. He never ceased to be amazed at how supple the flesh of his love remained after all these years. They'd been together for nearly a decade now, and in all that time, it hadn't shown a single speck of decay. It hadn't aged, either. He hoped his love's perpetual youth would rub off on him, but so far it hadn't. Maybe it never would, in which case he'd enjoy however much time they had together. That would be enough. More than enough.

Haksaw was fifty-two, short, bald, with several days' growth of beard. His teeth were yellowed with plaque and his breath reeked like an open sewer. Every day he wore the same outfit, whether he was in his room sleeping or out on the street working: a black hoodie, no shirt underneath, jeans, and sneakers. His clothes were old, stained, and smelled like dried blood and piss. His real name, which he barely remembered, was Evan Horton, but he liked Haksaw better, like the way he spelled it without the C. It was cooler like that. Despite his rough-looking exterior, he had a disarming aura of perpetual kindness and gentleness about him, a trait that lulled his victims into a false sense of security. It was the most important weapon in his arsenal.

The torso was a perfect lover for him. It had no eyes with which to gaze upon his ugly visage, no nose to be offended by his malodorous body, and no ears to grow tired of listening to his grating voice. He had first become aware of the torso on a bitterly cold winter night nine years ago. He was lurking in the vicinity of the House of Red Tears at the time. He'd heard rumors on the street about it, a place where killers paid to have victims brought to them in a room where they could do whatever they wanted to them without fear of being caught by the police. It seemed too good to be true, and while he didn't have the cash to get in, he was intensely curious, and so he watched, standing in the mouth of shadowed alleys, crouching alongside foul-smelling trash bins, hiding behind parked cars and streetside mailboxes. He didn't look like a homeless person on purpose, but because of his appearance, people rarely paid attention to him. It was the perfect camouflage for his line of work, and it served him in good stead during his surveillance of the House of Red Tears.

After several days, he came to the following conclusions:

The House of Red Tears was open twenty-four-seven.

The proprietor must have paid off Oakmont's police, because no cruisers ever came through the neighborhood.

The House catered to a varied clientele. Some customers looked like ordinary, unremarkable men and women, while others wore leather and were heavily pierced and tattooed. Some wore expensive suits and dresses and arrived in chauffeur-driven vehicles, while others looked like villains who'd escaped a cheap slasher movie, garbed in coveralls and wearing creepy masks. And some...well, they didn't look quite human. Haksaw knew about Shadow, the dark realm that lies alongside everyday reality and which few people can detect and even fewer enter. Shadow was particularly strong in Oakmont, and Haksaw figured that's where the House's more *unique* customers came from.

There was always someone guarding the door. He never once saw it unattended.

A steady stream of smoke rose from the House's chimney produced by, he assumed, an on-site crematorium.

Vehicles periodically stopped behind the House to unload manacled people who were taken inside by employees. An establishment like this had a constant need for fresh supplies. He briefly entertained the idea of applying to be a delivery driver for the House, but he could never give up his independent status.

He heard some of the employees mention the name *Caprice*, and he assumed this was their boss, and perhaps the House's owner as well.

There was something inside that wanted him to come find it.

It took several days of observing the House before he came to this last conclusion. It began when he realized his fascination with the place had taken such a hold on him that he couldn't remember the last time he'd eaten or drunk anything. And when he tried to leave so he could take care of those needs, he found he couldn't. He could move from one vantage point to another, but he could not walk away from the House. Then he began feeling a pull toward it, a compulsion to find some way to get inside. If he'd had the money, he would've simply paid for admission like anyone else, but he wasn't exactly rolling in cash. The compulsion deepened, until entering the House was all he could think about. He began hearing a voice inside his head, too. It didn't speak words, and it didn't communicate in images. It spoke in feelings, and it was weary of being imprisoned in the House and longed for its freedom – freedom only Haksaw could give.

That night, when a black van pulled up to the rear entrance in the alley behind the House, Haksaw snuck up and joined the crowd of captives and the guards who unloaded them. The guards all wore white polo shirts and white slacks, and one of them – a broad-shouldered woman with a tattoo of a black widow covering her face – eyed him suspiciously as the van drove off.

"Why aren't you in manacles?"

"They said I smelled too bad to come near."

She sniffed the air and made a face. "Damn, they weren't kidding. Come on."

The woman might've questioned him further, but it was freezing outside, and she was likely in a hurry to get back inside and get warm. There were two other guards, and all three of them ushered the 'fresh supplies' into the House. Because he stank so bad, they let Haksaw stay at the end of the line, and Haksaw kept hanging farther and farther back until they'd left him behind. He thought there was a good chance they'd never noticed he was missing. Assuming people ever noticed him at all, they often quickly forgot about him. He'd spent most of his life living in Oakmont's Cannery District, and the presence of Shadow was strong here. Maybe a little had rubbed off on him, which was why people seemed to have trouble perceiving him at times. And maybe that was why he heard the not-voice so clearly.

He followed the not-voice then, and it led him to an elevator. Once inside, he felt the need to go down – all the way down – but there was a keyhole next to the button for the subbasement. He didn't have a key, of course, and he had no idea where he could obtain one. He was pondering his situation when the elevator doors closed and the car began to descend on its own. He felt a sense of almost smug satisfaction from the not-voice, and he knew who was responsible for the elevator moving. When the car reached the subbasement, it stopped, and the doors slid open. Ceiling lights came on as Haksaw exited the car, and he found himself facing a large stone wall with an iron door set into it. The surface of the door was covered with symbols he didn't recognize, but which were pleasant to look at. They made him feel warm and welcome here. He stepped forward and tried to pull the handle, but the door was locked and wouldn't budge.

Haksaw lowered his hand and waited. After a moment, the lock *snicked* and the door opened of its own accord. Trembling with excitement that might've been his, might've been the not-voice's, but most likely was a combination of both, he walked through the doorway. It was dark inside – the light in the outer chamber was unable to enter this one for some strange reason – but he slept during the day and walked the world at night, so his eyes were accustomed to making do with little-to-no light. Inside it was like a cave, although whether it was natural or artificial, he couldn't say. There was a large, black half-dome on the ceiling, and he wondered what it was for. He could sense power in it – immense power – but he'd never experienced its like before. He felt presences in the chamber with him that weren't the not-voice. These weren't anywhere close to that strong, but they were definitely present. They had not-voices too, but very weak ones, and he couldn't understand what they were trying to say. It didn't matter, though. He hadn't come here for them. He'd come here for....

He sensed it before he saw it, resting in the wall close by, within a recess carved into the stone. He started toward it, guided by the not-voice, and behind him faint white light came into being. He glanced over his shoulder and saw human-shaped masses of what looked like glowing fog, maybe a few dozen of them, gathered together. They made no move to come at him, merely watched. He sensed their interest in him, in what he was about to do, but that was all. He turned back toward the wall and continued to the two recessed areas. The top one contained a human head, which was missing its eyes as well as the top half of its skull. He was impressed by how fresh the thing looked, and he could feel the power it contained, but it wasn't the source of the not-voice. Besides, he'd never really been into heads. The lower recessed area contained a second body part, this one larger, and from the difference in skin tone, Haksaw guessed it had come from a different owner than the head.

It was a torso.

It was also the most beautiful thing that he'd ever seen.

Like the head, it showed no signs of decay, and when he reached out a trembling hand to touch it, he found the skin was warm, as if it had been harvested only moments before. He had the sense the torso had been here longer than that, though.

Like any other human, serial killers have different preferences when it comes to what they enjoy about their work. Some are fixated on a certain type of victim – say, a petite redhead with freckles – or they hunt primarily with a beloved weapon, such as a knife, a machete, or a gun, treating it as if it was an extension of themselves. Haksaw, true to his name, preferred to capture a victim, render them unconscious, then take them back to the abandoned apartment house where he lived and use saws to dismember them in a bathtub. They were bound and gagged so they would offer a minimum of fuss, but fuss they did, especially when he made the first cut. He removed the head, the arms, and the legs. He had no use for them. But the torso…now *that* was perfection. Male or female, young or old, one race or another, it made no difference to him. All torsos were beautiful. The torso was like the trunk from which a mighty tree grew, the head, arms, and legs like branches extending outward from it. It was where the heart and lungs were located, the stomach and intestines, the liver and kidneys, the genitals – all the organs that made life possible. The torso was the true seat of the soul. The brain was a mere calculating machine, entirely dependent on the torso for its survival. Haksaw disposed of the rest of the body immediately and kept the torsos of his victims as long as he could, which was only a few days. The internal organs tended to spoil rather quickly, but when he tried removing them, the hollow thing left behind didn't satisfy. A true torso had all its inner bits and pieces intact. So he'd learned to live with the fact that all his loves would be temporary ones.

But this torso was different. It wouldn't rot, he could *feel* it. It would remain with him and be the everlasting love he'd always dreamed of. He felt the not-voice then, its emotions so strong and clear this time that he had no difficulty translating them into words.

I may not be able to give love. But I can receive it.

Haksaw considered this. What he really wanted was a love that would stay with him, one that could accept all that he had to give. This beautiful, magical thing before him could be exactly that.

Haksaw pulled the torso out of the recessed area where it had been stored and ran like hell for the doorway. He kept running even after he was back in the frigid alley, and he didn't stop until he reached the abandoned building where his apartment was located, and collapsed onto the soiled mattress lying on the floor, which served as his bed. He lay there next to his new love, gulping air, sweat pouring off of him. He felt the torso's gratitude wash over him, and while the torso had claimed it could not love him, this sensation was a perfectly acceptable substitute. Haksaw spent the rest of the night fucking the torso, and by the time the sun rose, his dick was chafed and sore, but he had never been happier.

Haksaw still killed people after that night – he and the torso had an understanding – but not as many and not as often as before. He still removed the heads and limbs from his victims, but he no longer kept the torsos. Why would he? None of them could come close to measuring up to his love. Haksaw had lived contentedly like this for years, and now something was threatening his happiness. He didn't know what it was, but he'd find out, and then he'd fucking destroy it. But first, he had to make sure his love was safe. He wrapped the torso in the yellow, stained sheet, and carried it out of the bedroom.

"It's going to be okay, my love. I'll take care of you. I always will."

He felt the torso's reply.

I know you will.

CHAPTER NINE

Haksaw didn't have much in the way of living quarters. He'd selected one of the apartments in the building to be his, but the only furniture he possessed was the mattress in his bedroom and a broken office chair that he'd rescued from a trash bin and which he kept in the living room. There had been blinds on the windows when he'd moved in, so he hadn't had to bother covering them with newspaper. The kitchen cupboards and drawers were bare, except for his collection of saws, along with the oven cleaner and stainless-steel brush he used to cleanse them. The place had no electricity or running water, but that was okay. He liked the simple life. It provided clarity, helped a man think. He shared his quarters with rats and roaches, but they never went near the torso – something about it repelled them – so he didn't mind his verminous roommates. Live and let live was his philosophy. Well, except for the people he killed, of course.

The apartment door had both a deadbolt and a chain lock, and Haksaw also used a security bar wedged between the knob and the floor for added protection. While the other units in the building didn't have permanent residents, people sometimes crashed here for days, even weeks at a time. Drug addicts, alcoholics, and the mentally ill, mostly. He needed to prevent anyone from entering to see if he had anything worth stealing, because he most certainly did.

He didn't have a key to the deadbolt, so he had no way to lock the door behind him when he went out. No way in hell would he leave the torso unguarded, so he always brought it with him when he left. It was lighter than it looked, so he had no problem carrying it. He would take it down the stairs, go out the building's back entrance, and into the alley. He kept a shopping cart there, one he'd stolen from the parking lot of a FoodSaver several blocks away. He'd lined the bottom of the cart with newspaper, and he kept several flattened cardboard boxes in it. He'd place the torso on the newspapers then arrange the cardboard so it concealed his love. Then he'd push the cart ahead of him as he walked, just another homeless person wandering around the Cannery District scavenging. It was a very effective disguise, one that had worked for him for years. No one ever bothered him or tried to look in his cart. Who the hell was interested in a bunch of cardboard?

This was his intention now – to get the torso out of the building, into the shopping cart, and wheel it away before whatever danger was coming arrived. He removed the lock bar and laid it on the floor, then unlocked the deadbolt and chain. But as he opened the door and stepped into the hallway, he realized he was too late.

A man and a woman were walking down the hallway toward him, both smiling, eyes cold and dead. Neither had any weapons on them – at least none that were obvious – but Haksaw was a predator, and he recognized others of his kind when he saw them. He knew at once that these two were as bad as they came.

"How nice of you to wrap it up for us," the man said.

"Extremely thoughtful," the woman agreed.

Haksaw didn't hesitate. He rushed back into his apartment, slammed the door, grabbed the lock bar and jammed it back in place. An instant later there was a loud *thud* and the door shook. One of them, most likely the man, Haksaw thought, had kicked the door. He quickly threw the deadbolt and hooked the chain, for whatever small good they might do. A second thud came, then a third.

"Not a very hospitable welcome," the woman said.

"Downright rude, if you ask me," the man said.

Another thud.

Haksaw thought furiously. The only potential weapons he had were his saws, and with two opponents, he'd need to use both hands, which would mean putting the torso down. If he did that, it would be easy for one of the couple to attack and keep him busy, while the other snatched up the torso and ran. Too risky, he decided. He would not let his love out of his hands for any reason. He'd die first.

The man kicked the door again, and Haksaw saw that the hinges were starting to pull away from the wall. Another kick or two, and the door would give and the couple would enter. He didn't know who these people were, and he didn't care. All that mattered was they wanted the torso, and he didn't think he could successfully defend himself against the two of them. Whatever he was going to do, he had to do it fast.

He ran back to the bedroom.

He'd feared this day would come eventually. Perhaps the couple had sensed the torso just as he'd once had, and they'd felt compelled to obtain it for their own. Or perhaps the owner of the House of Red Tears had finally tracked him down and decided to reclaim what she viewed as her property – as if anything as magnificent of the torso could ever be owned by a mere human, especially one who could never appreciate and love it as much as he could. But as he'd known someone would come to take the torso from him eventually, he'd made preparations. He rushed to the bedroom closet and slid the door back, revealing a square board propped against the closet's wall. Haksaw had painted the board white – the same color as the closet's inside – to make it look as if it belonged here. He slid it aside to reveal a large hole that he'd created, one that led into the bedroom closet of the apartment next door. He shoved the torso through, crawled after it, and then turned around, reached through the hole, and pulled the board back into place. He knew the crude concealment wouldn't fool anyone for very long, but he didn't need it to. He only needed it to fool his pursuers long enough for him to reach the ground floor.

He picked up the torso and ran through the apartment to its front door. Like the one in his place, it was locked and additionally secured with a lock bar. He removed the latter and placed it on the floor quietly, then he slowly undid the chain and turned the deadbolt. He listened, and when he heard the crash of his door giving way, he waited for a two count, then opened the door to this apartment and stepped into the hallway. He half expected one of the two to have remained in the hallway to keep watch, but neither had. Relieved, he started down the hall, jogging as quietly as he could. Halfway down was the door to the stairwell that served as the building's fire exit, and when he reached it, he opened it, stepped inside, and pulled the door closed behind him, careful not to make any sound.

The building only had two stories, so it took him almost no time to reach the ground floor. He exited the stairwell and turned left, not toward the building's front entrance, nor toward the rear one. Instead, he headed for apartment 13-A. He kept the door to this apartment unlocked, and once he was inside, he slid the chain in place, threw the deadbolt, and picked up the lock bar he had left here long ago and jammed it between the knob and the floor. He then ran for the bedroom. He put the torso on the floor, unlocked the window, then opened it wide. The window was on the east side of the building, and it faced the skeevy laundromat next door. Haksaw picked up the torso, climbed through the window, and jumped down into the alley.

Only then did he start running.

*　　*　　*

Mr. Yes and Mrs. No found the escape hole in the bedroom closet within moments after gaining entrance into the apartment. Mr. Yes climbed through while Mrs. No hurried back to the hallway in case their quarry was only now exiting the adjoining apartment. The door opened as she approached, but it was Mr. Yes who stepped through.

"I assume you—"

"Saw no sign of him? Correct."

Mr. Yes sighed. "We're going to have to search the whole damn building, aren't we?"

Mrs. No nodded. "Even though it'll be a waste of time. He's surely out on the street by now. But we must be thorough and methodical, dear."

"I know. But it's a real pain in the ass sometimes."

"Agreed."

They began searching. They could've done the job in half the time if they split up, but Mr. Yes and Mrs. No rarely left the other's side, even when it was in their best interest to do so. The thought never even occurred to them.

They found nothing on the second floor, except for some trash and used hypodermics left behind by recreational drug enthusiasts. They moved on to the first floor, and before long they discovered an apartment in which the bedroom window was wide open.

"This is how he got out," Mrs. No said.

"Undoubtedly."

Still, there were a few apartments left to check, and they did so, just on the off chance that the man had opened the window in the one apartment to throw them off the track and was still hiding in the building. The remaining apartments were empty, with the exception of the last one they came to. Unlike most of the other doors in the building, this one was locked, and when Mr. Yes kicked it open, he and his wife stepped inside to find a young boy and girl, both middle-school aged and dressed in dirty clothes, standing in the middle of the living room, holding on to each other and looking at these unexpected arrivals with wide, fearful eyes.

"Looks like we found a couple runaways," Mrs. No said. She looked at the kids. "I don't suppose either of you saw a man carrying a human torso leave the building." The kids – a brother and sister, Mrs. No guessed – looked at each other then back to her. They both shook their heads.

"Too bad," she said. "For you, that is." She turned to her husband. "Want to blow off some steam and kill them before we leave?"

His mouth curved into a slow, bloodless smile. "Oh *yes*. Do you think we should be merciful and do it swiftly?"

"Oh *no*."

Grinning, Mrs. No closed the apartment door, and she and her husband approached the boy and girl, both of whom began sobbing. It was the least interesting sound they'd produce over the next half hour before they died.

INTERLUDE

Torso

On a chilly October night close to one a.m., Carl Wheeler, seventeen, drove his used Elantra through a fast-food drive-thru. He ordered a double cheeseburger, large fries, and a large Coke, and once he'd paid for and received his food, he pulled into a space next to the restaurant's entrance. He left the engine running so the heater would keep the vehicle warm, and he tuned the radio to an oldies station that tended to play sad, depressing music. It suited his mood. He planned to sit, listen to music, and eat his food, but the smell of it turned his stomach. He let his burger and fries remain in the grease-stained bag and thought about the first time he realized his father was raping his sister.

He'd been sixteen, and Kristi fourteen. Their bedrooms were on opposite sides of the hallway, and Kristi's was next to their dad's. Louis Wheeler worked as a welder for a construction company, and he often worked late and on weekends, so the kids didn't see him much. He was a tired, sullen presence that they caught glimpses of now and again, and Carl and Kristi had to fend for themselves most of the time. They did the household chores as well. Maybe not as regularly as they should have, but the work got done – eventually. Their mother had died from breast cancer the previous year. The doctors had caught it late, and although they treated it aggressively, they couldn't stop the poisonous cells' rampage through their mother's body.

Louis had never been an emotionally demonstrative man, and he became even worse after the death of his wife. He hardly ever spoke, and when he did it was in toneless monosyllables. He started drinking whiskey instead of beer at night and too much of it. Sometimes the kids would hear him sobbing in his bedroom — the one he'd shared with their mother — in the hours before dawn. Hearing his father cry like that scared Carl. If a strong man like his dad could become so broken, what chance did he have of making it through life unscathed?

Carl and Kristi grieved their mother's loss too, of course, but since their father couldn't see past his own emotional wounds to comfort them, the kids comforted each other, singing silly songs from cartoons and playing game after game of Uno. After six months, the cloud of depression that had hung over their house ever since their mother's death began to lift, at least a little. Carl and Kristi started smiling more and playing Uno less. Boys were starting to ask Kristi out, and she'd usually say yes. Carl started getting jealous — but not in a creepy way. He didn't think of his little sister like *that*. That was gross! He just missed spending time with her the way they once had. In many ways, she was the only real friend he had. But he told himself that if she was happy, he should be happy for her too.

Their father, it seemed, was not so accepting of Kristi dating. He scowled whenever she asked for permission to go out, and insisted that whichever boy she was dating come inside and *meet your goddamn father*. The way he always stressed these words made them sound like a threat rather than a request. When the boy arrived to pick her up, Kristi would bring him inside, and Louis would look him up and down, and then say, *You touch my daughter, I'll pull your cock off with my bare hands,* or *You'd better keep it in your pants tonight, junior, or I'll jam my hand down your throat, grab a fistful of your guts, and turn you inside out.*

Kristi never got asked out on any second dates.

Around this time, their dad started looking at Kristi funny and making comments like, *You look more like your mother every day,* and *You've got her eyes. I used to stare into those eyes when we…well, you know.* Kristi may not have been sure what their father was alluding to, but Carl did. And one night, he decided he'd better do something about it. He waited until Kristi was in the bathroom, then he went into the living room where his dad sat on the couch, half-empty whiskey bottle in his hand, watching a singing competition show. He sat down next to his father, and – before his courage could desert him – began talking.

"I've seen the way you stare at Kristi sometimes, Dad. And sometimes you make…inappropriate comments about the way she looks. It makes her feel—"

He didn't get any farther. His dad raised his whiskey bottle and brought it down hard on Carl's head. Glass shattered and white light exploded behind Carl's eyes. The next thing he remembered clearly was sitting in the front passenger seat of his dad's pickup, holding a bunched-up towel to his head, as they drove down the road.

"Don't you dare tell anyone what really happened," Dad said. "I'll make up some story, and they'll believe me. Teenagers are always doing stupid things that end up with them getting hurt."

He'd gazed straight ahead the entire time he said this, but he now turned toward Carl.

"You hear me, boy? Otherwise, I'll give you worse than a little love tap to the head – a *lot* worse."

"Yes, sir," Carl whispered. "I'll go along with whatever you tell them."

Louis looked at him for a moment more before finally saying, "Good," and turning his attention back to the road.

Carl stayed out of his father's way the rest of the week, and nothing more happened between them. Kristi asked about his injury, and he mumbled something about stumbling on a curb, falling, and hitting his head. He couldn't look Kristi in the eye as he spoke, and when she asked him if anything else was wrong, he told her no. He doubted she believed him, but she didn't press the issue.

It happened that Saturday night.

He was asleep, and he heard music. At first he thought he was dreaming, but the music continued playing, and the longer it went on, the more it pulled him out of sleep until finally he woke. He opened his eyes and gazed up at the ceiling as he struggled to orient himself. He was in his bedroom, but he couldn't figure out where the hell that music was coming from. He recognized the tune, one from Katy Perry called—

He bolted upright, suddenly wide awake.

It was called 'Teenage Dream', and it was coming from his sister's room. He checked the time on his phone: 12:38 a.m. He threw off the covers, climbed out of his bed, and walked to his door on the balls of his feet so he wouldn't make any noise. His door always squeaked a little when he opened it, but he hoped the music would cover the noise. He eased it open, crossed the hallway, and slowly pressed his ear to his sister's door.

The song came to an end and faded out. He listened, hoping he wouldn't hear anything, knowing he would.

The rhythmic squeaking of a mattress. Harsh, labored breathing. A soft voice saying *no* over and over. *No no no no no no no no no no....*

The song started again, and Carl felt sick to his stomach. Dad was in there. He'd had Kristi put on music to cover the noise they were making, and had he chosen this particular song because he thought it suited the occasion, helped set the proper mood? The song choice might've been a coincidence, but Carl didn't think so.

Rage flared bright and hot within him, an anger stronger than anything he'd ever known before. He had to get in there and help his sister. The door was probably locked, but he'd break the goddamned thing down if he had to, rush inside, yank his father off Kristi, and beat the shit out of the bastard, make the fucker bleed and break some bones while he was at it. And when Carl finished, he'd call the police and tell them to come pick up the piece of shit who'd been raping his own daughter.

That's what Carl wanted to do. But he stood there, ear to the door, frozen, pulse thrumming wildly in his ears. *Go on,* he told himself. *Start pounding on the door, you fucking coward!*

Still, he couldn't move.

He remembered what it had felt like when the whiskey bottle had shattered against his skull, remembered the threat his father had made on the way to the emergency room.

I'll give you worse than a little love tap to the head – a lot worse.

Once he was in Kristi's room, could he take the bastard? Louis was strong, and despite his drinking, still goddamned tough. Carl was thin and he'd never been in a real fight before. The closest he'd ever come was watching people fight in movies. If he broke into the room and interrupted what was happening, Louis would be so angry that he might not stop at beating up his son. He might keep going until Carl was dead.

Fuck that noise! He was Kristi's big brother. It was his job to protect her! His right hand curled into a fist, and he raised it, intending to slam it into the door.

But he couldn't make himself do it.

The mattress squeak grew louder, and its tempo increased. His father's breathing became faster too, and Kristi's litany of *no*s picked up speed as well.

Carl turned away from the door, went back to his room, slowly closed the door, then lay down in bed and folded the pillow up over the sides of his head to muffle the sounds coming from across the hall. It helped – a little.

He cried the rest of the night.

Life went on this way for three and a half months. Louis raped Kristi once a week, sometimes twice, always to the same song, and Carl lay in bed afraid and hating himself. Then one night when Louis went to Kristi's room, he shouted something Carl couldn't make out, then Carl heard him running down the hallway. Carl got out of bed, opened the door to his room, and hurried across the hall.

He stopped in Kristi's open doorway and whispered, "Sis?"

She didn't reply.

It was dark in her room, so he reached inside, found the wall switch, and turned on the overhead light. He saw his sister, lying on her bed, skin pale, eyes open wide. She was wearing a long T-shirt as pajamas, and there was a knife on the floor next to her bed. She'd sliced open her wrists and so much blood had soaked her mattress, spreading out on both sides of her, that it almost looked as if she had crimson wings.

His knees gave out and he slumped to the floor. All he could do was stare at his poor sister while he heard Louis calling 911 in the kitchen.

Thankfully, Kristi wasn't dead – just very close to it – and the EMTs who arrived were able to stabilize her and get her to the hospital in time. Louis rode in the EMT van with Kristi, and Carl followed in his Elantra. After a couple days, when Kristi was strong enough, she was sent for psychiatric evaluation, a standard procedure for people who attempted suicide. The psychiatrist who examined Kristi decided she was at immediate risk of making another attempt to kill herself and ordered her to remain in the hospital for another seven days so she could be treated with a combination of therapy and drugs. Carl felt so sorry for Kristi, but he was encouraged as well. She was in a place where she could tell the truth about what their father had been doing to her and she would be believed. Louis was in shit-deep trouble now, and Carl couldn't wait for his father to be revealed as the sick fuck he was.

But Kristi didn't tell the doctors the truth. She made up a story about a boyfriend cheating on her with another girl, and how emotionally devastated she had been, so much so that she'd tried to kill herself. During her week's stay, she was a model patient, and when she was released, her psychiatrist assured Louis that she thought this was a one-time event and unlikely to be repeated. She wrote Kristi a prescription for antidepressants and anxiety meds, and she gave him the card of a therapist she wanted Kristi to start seeing. After that, Kristi was free to go.

Carl wanted to drive her home, but Louis insisted she ride with him.

"I *am* her father, after all," he said.

During Kristi's time in the hospital, he and Louis hadn't spoken about her near-suicide, and Carl hadn't confessed that he knew what his father was doing to her every night. He couldn't come up with a good excuse why Kristi should ride with him, and in the end she'd gone with Louis. She gave Carl a sad smile as she got in the pickup, and he had a very bad feeling, although he didn't know why. He figured Louis wanted to be alone with Kristi so he could interrogate her about what she'd said – and not said – to the doctors about him and her, but he didn't think their father would do anything to hurt her. Still, Carl was uneasy and he followed them home in his car.

For part of the drive home, they needed to travel on the highway, and when Louis's pickup approached an overpass, the vehicle suddenly began to swerve all over the road. Carl feared the pickup had blown a tire or maybe something had gone wrong with the steering. Then the pickup angled toward one of the concrete support columns beneath the overpass and smashed into it. Carl slammed on his brakes when it happened, and he nearly got rear-ended by a semi that was behind him. He pulled his Elantra onto the shoulder, got out, and started running toward the mangled, twisted hunk of metal that had been the pickup. He needn't have bothered. There was nothing anyone could do for his sister or father now.

The police declared the cause of the accident as undetermined, but Carl knew what had happened. Kristi had decided to take her life again, only this time she'd decided to take their father with her. She'd grabbed the steering wheel, Louis had tried to wrestle it away from her, but he'd failed, and Kristi had driven them into the support column. *Bang! Crash! Crunch!* He hoped it was fast for her, and that it had hurt like hell for Louis.

Both sets of grandparents were still alive, and they helped Carl take care of burying Kristi and Louis. They decided on a double funeral, which made Carl want to puke. His bastard father didn't deserve to be anywhere near Kristi in life *or* in death, but there was nothing he could do unless he was willing to tell everyone exactly what kind of man Louis Wheeler had been.

The funeral had been two months ago, and the house had been sold and Carl had moved in with his mom's parents (no fucking way was he going to stay with his father's). His junior year of high school started in late August, but he'd been sleepwalking through his classes, barely aware of what was happening around him. His grandparents and his teachers were sympathetic. *Give him some time. He'll be okay eventually. This isn't the kind of thing you recover from easily.* Yes, Carl was grieving his sister's death, but he also hated himself for being too afraid to stand up to Louis and stop him from abusing Kristi. His fear had led to Kristi slitting her wrists and then crashing Louis's pickup. She would still be alive if he'd had the guts to stand up and be a man. Instead, he'd betrayed his sister, and now she was dead and he couldn't stand living with the guilt and shame.

Which was why he was now sitting in this parking lot. He'd come here for a last meal, and then he planned to get on the highway and once he drew near the overpass where his sister and father died, he would jam the accelerator to the floor, aim for the same support column they hit, and end his miserable excuse for a life. But now that he'd actually bought the food, he not only wasn't hungry, the smell of it made him want to vomit. He didn't want that smell to accompany him on his last ride, so he grabbed the bag and the plastic cup of soda, got out of the car, and walked to the nearest waste receptacle. He tossed the so-called food in the trash, and then turned to head back to his car, but he stopped. A man and a woman around his grandparents' age stood between him and the Elantra. Both of them were smiling, and the man was holding an ax.

The woman spoke first. "Hello, Carl. I'm Tressa Shardlow, and this is my husband, Delmar."

The man inclined his head in greeting, and the woman continued speaking.

"This may be hard to believe, but I See things. I Saw you would be here tonight, and I Saw *why*. I also Saw that you have something we need."

"We need your torso," Delmar said. "And since you're going to kill yourself anyway, it would be a shame to let it go to waste."

"We're building a god, you see," Tressa said.

"I can make it fast," Delmar said. "You'll barely feel a thing."

Carl stared at the ax head. He liked the way the metal gleamed in the parking lot's fluorescent light.

"Can you make it hurt?" he asked. "Like, a lot?"

Tressa and Delmar exchanged a look.

"I think I can manage that," Delmar said.

Carl smiled. "Good. Then go ahead and take what you need."

Delmar nodded, raised the ax, and stepped forward.

CHAPTER TEN

"That's it."

Kate pointed to a long, narrow building with white siding and a flat roof. There were no windows, only a door in front with a wooden sign above it – *High Strangeness*, painted in bright green letters on a black background. The words were surrounded by small white stars, a yellow crescent moon, and an ugly orange blob that might have been meant to represent Saturn. It was late afternoon, but the parking lot was nearly full. Most of the vehicles were popular sedans, SUVs, and pickups, some newer, some older, and a few that looked like they'd recently been in a demolition derby – and lost. But several parking spaces had been taken by less recognizable vehicles. One was the length of two cars, low to the ground, and had a dozen small wheels on each side. Its body was a black so deep that it looked like it swallowed light instead of reflecting it. There didn't appear to be any windows for a driver to see through or, for that matter, any doors to allow ingress and egress. Another vehicle looked like a hansom cab from England's Victorian era, but instead of being harnessed to horses, it was strapped to a glowing blue orb roughly twice the size of a basketball, which made a slight humming sound as it floated above the ground. And the third odd vehicle was a motorcycle that appeared to have been constructed entirely from gleaming silver scales, including the tires.

Lee pulled into the lot, took one of the few empty spaces, and turned off the engine. They both got out of the car, and Lee looked around.

"So this is the famous Cannery District."

"You know about it?"

"I've heard rumors. People say that if you want to have a really wild time, head to Oakmont and check out the Cannery. I got to say, it looks like any other rundown post-industrial area. Ohio's full of them." Lee pointed to the orb-and-hansom-cab vehicle. "That thing's pretty cool. What is it, a prop or something? I mean, the place *is* called High Strangeness after all."

"I don't think it's a prop," Kate said. "It's real, and so are those other weird vehicles. The stories about the Cannery District are true. It's a place that's...." Her voice trailed off. Her eyes grew watery, and she rubbed them to stop herself from crying.

Lee went to her and put their arms around her.

"Hey, now. What's wrong?"

Kate leaned her head against Lee's chest.

"I should've called 911, told the cops that someone was trying to break into Tressa's house. Maybe they would've gotten there in time and stopped Ethan. But everything was happening so fast, and I was so confused, it didn't occur to me until now."

"Don't beat yourself up. I didn't think of it either. I mean, this isn't exactly a normal situation we're dealing with."

Lee hugged her tight and Kate closed her eyes, felt the warmth of Lee's body against her, and for a moment she felt that she was safe, loved, and everything would be all right. When they separated, Lee said, "Maybe your grandmother's okay. If she didn't have what Ethan wanted, he might've just left. Why don't you give her a call, see if she's all right?"

"Okay."

Kate took her phone from her back pocket, called Tressa's number, and listened. It rang and rang and then went to voicemail.

"Hello, this is Tressa. Please leave a message."

Kate almost started crying when she heard her grandmother's voice.

"Grandma, it's me. I hope you're all right. Call me when you get this. I love you."

She disconnected, put the phone back in her pocket, wiped her eyes. She didn't feel any better for having called, but she didn't feel any worse, either. At least she'd tried.

"Sorry you didn't reach her," Lee said. "That doesn't necessarily mean something bad happened, though." But they didn't sound fully convinced of their own words. To change the subject, they said, "What should we do about the eyes? Do you think they'll be safe if we leave them in the car, or should we take them inside with us?"

Kate hadn't considered this, and she honestly wasn't sure which was best.

"Leave them, I guess. That way we won't have to explain them if anyone sees them – and if we don't have them on us, no one can try to take them."

The Cannery District lay on the edge of Shadow, which was what gave it its reputation as a place where you could go for a 'wild time'. But it could be dangerous, too – at least that's what Tressa had told her when they'd visited. She didn't know if any of the bar's customers would be able to sense what the eyes were if she took them inside, but she didn't want to risk it. The eyes had power, and power was a temptation. Best not to tempt anyone if they didn't need to.

She opened the passenger side door, shoved the plastic bag with the eyes beneath the seat, then closed the door again. Lee locked it with their key remote and turned to Kate.

"Let's go talk to your cousins."

Kate nodded and together they headed for the bar's entrance.

At nineteen, Kate was below Ohio's legal drinking age, but Lee wasn't, and the two of them had gone to bars together before. No one had ever bothered carding Kate, and she'd always been careful not to drink too much. She didn't want to get drunk, cause a scene, and give bartenders an excuse to toss her out on her ass. That would've been a less than optimal end to a date night. Tressa had brought her to High Strangeness when she was younger to visit Reyna and Weston, although it had been a long time since she'd last been here. Her cousins had several rooms in the back that served as a living space for them, and Kate remembered thinking as a child that it was weird they lived in the same place they worked. Even though she'd seen the parking lot was full, she wasn't prepared for the amount of noise and activity in the bar, and stepping inside was an assault on her senses. The place was packed, and everyone was talking, laughing, and yelling. Strange music played on the sound system, a mix of bizarre atonal noises like a symphony composed on some distant alien world. The décor was a kitschy blend of paranormal paraphernalia – framed posters of UFOs and various cryptids. Ouija boards and tarot cards hung on the walls, along with mystic and occult symbols that Kate didn't recognize.

The bar's patrons, like the decorations, were an eclectic mix, and there appeared to be no class distinctions here. People wearing filth-encrusted clothes sat alongside people in expensive tailored suits. Customers so tatted and pierced they seemed like a different species sat with plain-dressed men and women who looked like they'd dropped by after a church service. Some had eyes too large, mouths too big, skin rough and pebbly like a toad's or so thin you could clearly see the bluish network of their circulatory systems.

"Wow," Lee said.

"Wow is right."

There were a couple open seats at the bar, and Kate took Lee's hand and led them over. They sat, and a bald man next to Kate smiled at her, revealing teeth that undulated like tiny serpents. Kate quickly looked away. Two people were working behind the bar, a woman in her early thirties and a man in his mid-twenties, both wearing T-shirts with *High Strangeness* printed on them in bright green. The woman came over to them, smiling.

Reyna's light brown hair hung past her shoulders. She had a sharp nose and a small mouth, but her most striking feature was her bright green eyes. Whenever she focused them on you, you felt you had her full and undivided attention.

"So what can I get you two—" She stopped, looked at Kate, frowned, and then her smile became a huge grin. "Katie-Bug?"

Kate grinned back. "Yep."

Reyna came out from behind the bar, ran over to Kate, threw her arms around her, and hugged her fiercely. Kate hugged her just as strongly. They remained that way for several moments, and when they finally released each other, Kate saw that Weston had joined them.

Weston was a beefy guy, with thick black hair and a full mustache and beard. His grin was just as wide as Reyna's had been.

"It's good to see you, cuz."

His hug wasn't as bone-crushing as Reyna's, but it felt just as good to Kate. When they pulled apart, Kate introduced Lee, and they shook hands with them both. Lee then looked at Kate with a mischievous smile.

"Katie-Bug?"

Kate felt her face redden.

"It's what the family used to call me when I was young."

"She was the last of the grandkids born, so she's always been the baby in the family," Reyna said. "Like a tiny little bug, you know?" She turned to Kate. "But now that you're a grown-ass woman, I don't suppose Katie-Bug is all that appropriate, huh?"

Kate kind of liked hearing Reyna use her old nickname, but she didn't want to admit it – *especially* in front of Lee. They'd tease her about it every chance they got.

"It's been years," Weston said. "What brings you slumming around the Cannery?"

Weston was older than Ethan by several years, but the brothers resembled each other so much that Kate wondered if she was basically seeing what Ethan looked like now. Ethan was probably more slender – he'd always been the thinner of the two – and she had no idea if he had facial hair or not, but otherwise she felt she was looking at Ethan himself. Her once-beloved cousin who, in all probability, had killed Tressa and Delmar, and who would be coming after the Lord's eyes.

Try not to think about that, she told herself. *There's nothing you can do for them right now. If you want to honor your grandmother, do as she asked: gather as many pieces of the Lord as you can and keep them from Ethan and Caprice.*

It was a logical, rational approach to her situation, and once she decided on it, she felt better. A little, anyway.

"It's a long story," Kate said. "And not a very nice one."

Reyna and Weston stopped smiling.

"Let's go in the back," Reyna said. "We can talk there." She raised her voice. "Hey, Lonnie!"

One of the customers – a man with a grayish cast to his skin – rose from a table and came over to Reyna. His movements were stiff, and when he stopped, he stood so motionless it appeared he wasn't even breathing. His clothes were dotted with what looked like clumps of mold.

"You mind watching the bar for a few minutes?" Reyna asked.

Lonnie's eyes were coated with a milky layer, and he smelled like meat on the verge of spoiling. He didn't speak, merely inclined his head a few inches.

"Great. And don't let anyone bullshit you about how they always get free drinks from me. No one *ever* gets free drinks around here. Got it?"

Lonnie gave another minimal nod.

"Good." Reyna turned to Kate. "C'mon."

She started walking and the others followed. Lee looked back over their shoulder at Lonnie.

"Is he...."

"Dead?" Weston asked. "Yes and no. In Shadow, life and death aren't binary. They're more like different points on a spectrum, you know? Today Lonnie's closer to the death side of things, but tomorrow, who knows? He could be the healthiest-looking person in here. It all depends on his mood."

"He's...existence-fluid?" Lee asked.

Weston grinned. "That's a good way to put it."

Lee turned to Kate. "When I woke up this morning, if you told me that I was going to meet a guy who was kinda-sorta-dead but kinda-sorta-not, I'd have said you were insane."

Kate smiled. "And now?"

"I'm beginning to think *I'm* the crazy one."

Kate gave Lee's hand a reassuring squeeze. She'd been a part of this world – or at least on the fringes of it – her entire life. She'd had plenty of time to adjust, but this was all new to Lee. All in all, Lee was doing great, a lot better than most people would've in their position. She was so grateful that her love was willing to stand by her instead of fleeing this madness, but she was scared that Lee might end up paying a terrible price for their loyalty. Maybe they'd *both* end up paying a terrible price in the end, but if so, at least they would be together.

Reyna led them into the back room that served as her office, a space so small there was barely enough room for a desk and two chairs. Reyna sat behind the desk, and gestured for Kate to take the chair in front of it, leaving Lee and Weston to stand. Kate sat, a little guiltily, and looked around. Had she ever been in Reyna's office before? She couldn't remember. There wasn't much to it. A laptop computer was the only item on the desk, and an out-of-date calendar featuring cute puppy pictures was the only object hanging on the wall. There were no filing cabinets, no shelves, not even a small plastic trash receptacle. One woman, one laptop, one desk, two chairs, one expired calendar – that was it.

"So," Reyna said, "what's up?"

Kate wasn't sure where to start, so she began with Tressa atypically going off on errands this morning and ended with her and Lee's visit to the ruins of the Shardlow mansion.

When she was finished, Reyna said, "Busy day."

"And it's not over yet," Weston said. "Not as long as Caprice wants the Lord's body parts."

Kate sighed. "I was afraid you were going to say something like that."

"You know that Ethan and I lived with her for a while," Weston said. He looked at Lee. "Our mom came close to having a mental breakdown after our dad died, and Caprice offered to take Ethan and me so she could work through her grief. She didn't do it out of love, though. She wanted disciples that she could groom. I got out of there after a couple of years, but Ethan stayed."

The bitterness in Weston's voice surprised Kate. She remembered him as a happy, easygoing kid, and maybe part of that Weston still remained, but his time with Caprice had hardened him. It sounded like there was little love lost between him and Ethan too. That saddened her. The brothers had always been so close.

Reyna picked up the thread then.

"After the Incarnation failed, the family became disillusioned and drifted away from the Quintessence. Maybe they still believed in the group's basic principles, but they'd lost too much during their attempt to create the Lord of the Feast, and they were done being fanatical followers. This did not sit well with Caprice. She saw the rest of the family as traitors and became determined to complete the Incarnation on her own. She decided that the reason the rite failed originally was because they didn't have enough power to infuse the Lord with. If you're going to make a god, stands to reason you'd need a hell of a lot of energy to do it, right? So Caprice figured out a way to get that energy – she created the House of Red Tears."

Kate frowned. "Tressa never mentioned that to me."

"It's possible she didn't know about it," Reyna said, "but it's more likely she simply wanted to spare you the knowledge that Ethan and Weston were part of it."

Reyna looked to Weston, as if signaling him to continue the story. He gazed at a wall as he spoke, as if he couldn't bring himself to look any of them in the face.

"To create life, Caprice *needed* life – and a lot of it."

He went on to describe how Caprice used the House of Red Tears to collect and store life energy from the people who were killed there.

"My god, that's horrible," Kate said.

Lee was pale. "So Caprice believes that if she gathers all the parts of the Lord together and somehow infuses them with all this ghost energy, the god will finally come to life? What does she think she is, some kind of occult Frankenstein?"

"Caprice may be crazy," Reyna began. "No, strike that. She *is* crazy. But she's also the one with the most mystical ability in the family." She glanced at Kate. "Except for maybe Tressa. But if Caprice thinks she can do it, she probably can."

Kate looked at Weston.

"Reyna said that Caprice involved you and Ethan in her plans...."

Weston didn't meet her gaze as he responded. "She trained us to be killers so we could help harvest the life energy that she needed. I hated what she made me do, what she made me *become*, but Ethan took to it like he was born with a blade in his hand. The Ethan we knew died in the House of Red Tears and was reborn as a cold, cruel, methodical murderer."

Kate couldn't believe that Weston had ever taken a human life, but by his own admission, he had. How many people had he killed? Did he remember their names and faces? Looking at him now, hearing the regret and self-loathing in his voice, she thought he did. But if Ethan was the stone-hearted killer Weston claimed, she was certain that Tressa and Delmar were dead. Why would Ethan leave them alive to possibly interfere with Caprice's plan to resurrect the Lord of the Feast? It would be illogical to do so.

But Tressa had managed to interfere one last time. She'd retrieved the Lord's eyes, warned Kate about Caprice's plans, and charged her with trying to stop the crazy-ass bitch. Then she'd remained behind with her husband to await Ethan's arrival and do what she could to slow him down. Kate knew that Tressa hadn't exactly been a saint, that she'd done terrible things to help make the first attempt at the Incarnation possible. But Kate loved the woman and admired how tough she'd been. In the end, Tressa had tried to do the right thing, and that had to count for something, didn't it?

"Do you have one of the parts?" Kate asked. "Tressa said you did."

Reyna and Weston exchanged a glance.

"We each got one: the right leg and the right arm," Reyna said. "We keep them together in a storage unit we rented."

"Nothing personal," Kate said, "but a storage unit doesn't sound like the most secure place to keep two pieces of a god."

"Did you see the mystic symbols on the walls when you came in? Those aren't for decoration. They're wardspells designed to prevent anyone from entering the bar, and I activate them every night after we close." She smiled. "I may not be as skilled or strong in magic as Tressa and Caprice, but I know a few tricks, and I used them to protect the storage unit as well. No one can get in unless they have the key."

Reyna reached into her shirt and lifted out a key attached to a black string around her neck. She held it up, and Kate felt a small twinge of pain in her head, a response, she assumed, to the magic the key possessed. Had she inherited some of Tressa's mystical ability, enough to allow her to sense the presence of magical power? Maybe.

Reyna tucked the key into her shirt once more, and when it was out of sight, the pain in Kate's head went away.

"So what do we do now?" Lee said. "Go get the arm and leg?" They shook their head. "I can't believe I just said that."

"Tressa told me to gather the body parts," Kate said.

"I understand that," Reyna said, "and I have the deepest respect for Tressa's abilities. But I don't see how the parts would be safer with you than where they are now. No offense."

Kate didn't blame her cousin for feeling this way. She had no special mystic training, and it had been years since the two of them had seen each other. Why would Reyna agree to give her the arm and leg? How could she hope to protect them from Ethan? In truth, she had no idea how she could do that, let alone know what she was ultimately supposed to do with the parts she managed to collect. Tressa said they couldn't be destroyed, and that meant the best Kate could do was hide them. Maybe Reyna's storage unit would be the best place for them. Reyna had said it was magically warded, and it already had two body parts inside. If they put the eyes in there as well, Ethan wouldn't be able to get at any of them. Kate didn't need to collect all the Lord's body parts. She just needed to ensure that Caprice couldn't obtain the complete set. Even if one part was missing – let alone three – she couldn't resurrect the Lord.

She was about to tell Reyna her thoughts when she was interrupted by the *crack* of a gunshot followed by screams – some of fear, some of fury – coming from the bar.

★   ★   ★

Haksaw was having trouble catching his breath, and his legs felt like they were full of pins and needles. He'd been running – or at least jogging – since fleeing the apartment building, and he hadn't paused to rest once. He'd had no destination in mind when he'd started, had only wanted to get his love to safety. But as he pushed the shopping cart into the parking lot of High Strangeness, he knew that the torso had guided him here. He wasn't sure *why*, but that wasn't important. He trusted his love completely, and that was all that mattered. He stopped by one of the lot's light poles, put a hand on it to steady himself, leaned over, and gulped air. He was covered with sweat and his throat was dry as sandpaper. His pulse seemed erratic too, and he wondered if he was on the verge of a heart attack. He wasn't a young man anymore, and he didn't get regular exercise, unless you counted killing victims once or twice a month, and while dismembering a body could be physically challenging, it hardly took the place of cardio.

When he could breathe more or less normally again, he straightened, put his hand inside the shopping cart, and slipped it beneath the flat cardboard boxes to touch his beloved.

"What should I do now?"

He received a sensation of quiet stillness which he interpreted as meaning *Wait*.

So he'd wait. He could do with a rest anyway.

He sat down on the ground, back against the light pole, knees to his chest, and took hold of one of the cart's legs to keep it from rolling away. He closed his eyes and smiled contentedly. He wasn't concerned about what might happen next. The torso would provide.

It always did.

★　　★　　★

"This is embarrassing. Not to mention painful," Mrs. No said.

Mr. Yes drove their gun-metal gray Mercedes Benz while Mrs. No looked out the open passenger window, her hair blowing in the breeze. Yes thought she never looked so beautiful than when she was angry. No's left hand rested on the seat next to her, a towel wrapped around it, the white fabric slowly turning crimson.

Not only hadn't they obtained the torso, they hadn't even gotten a good look at Haksaw. Caprice had told them where the man lived – if you could call it living – and what he generally looked like, but her description hadn't been much help. *He looks like a bum because that's what he is. He's middle-aged, dirty, and smelly. What else do you need to know?* More than that, as it turned out. The Cannery District had no shortage of people who fit the description Caprice had given them. They stopped and asked a few if they knew who Haksaw was and if they'd seen him go by. One woman just stared at them, and then her eyes melted and slowly ran down her cheeks like thick, viscous tears. A man they asked said he had, but rather than provide any details, his body collapsed into a mass of black flies that flew off in different directions. *The Cannery District is a pain in the ass,* Mrs. No had said, and Mr. Yes agreed with her.

The third person they stopped to ask had been sitting on a sidewalk next to a metal trash receptacle, slumped over, looking more like a pile of rags than a human being.

Do you mind if we ask you a quick question? No had said.

The being – it was impossible to determine a gender – rose to its feet and walked toward their car. It moved with lopsided, lurching motions, and Yes saw that where its face and hands should be were only folds of dirty cloth. In fact, its entire body was made of stained and blackened pieces of cloth.

It's a Rag Man, Yes thought. He'd heard of them, but he'd never seen one before. Supposedly they lurked in plain sight, camouflaged, feeding off the negative emotions of the humans that passed by them unaware of their presence or who'd simply mistaken them for homeless people.

"Mind?" the Rag Man said. "To mind I'd have to have a brain, wouldn't I?"

Its voice sounded incongruously beautiful given its appearance, like two bolts of the finest silk sliding slowly across each other. The Rag Man laughed then, a soft *tssh-tssh-tssh* sound. No ignored his joke. Yes knew she wasn't intimidated by the creature. There was nothing in existence that could frighten her. What could possibly scare a nightmare made flesh like his wife?

"We're looking for a man called Haksaw," No said. "Have you seen him?"

"Yes. He passed this way only a few minutes ago. I don't think he saw me. Most people don't unless they look directly at me. I know where he was heading, too. He kept muttering the name of his destination under his breath as he walked, as if he feared he might otherwise forget it."

"Tell us," No had said. "We'll pay you well for the information."

The Rag Man let out another laugh. *Tssh-tssh-tssh.* "I have no use for money. But you are very beautiful, and I've enjoyed talking with you. I would like a small souvenir so that I might better remember our meeting."

Yes started to object, but before he could get a word out, No looked at him and said, "Triple our usual fee."

Yes kept silent.

"What do you want?" No asked.

"Hold one of your hands out the window. Either will do."

No didn't hesitate. She stuck her left hand through the open window. The Rag Man sprang forward, wrapped its cloth fingers around her wrist, and lunged its head toward her fingers. Yes caught a flash of sharp white teeth buried somewhere in the creature's cloth face, and then No screamed.

The Rag Man released her wrist and stepped back. Blood now smeared the cloth where its mouth should be.

"Your pain is delicious. Haksaw is going to High Strangeness. It's a bar, about a mile farther down the street."

The Rag Man shuffled back to where it had been sitting and flopped down. This time it looked more like a pile of old, discarded cloth than anything remotely human. No continued holding her hand out the window, and Yes saw that the tip of her pinky was gone, and the wound was bleeding freely.

"Don't just sit there!" she'd snapped. "Get me a towel!"

They kept a number of work supplies in their trunk, and Yes put the car in park, got out, and fetched a towel from the trunk for her. She'd wrapped it around her hand, and they continued on.

"It could've been worse," Yes said now. "The Rag Man could've taken your entire hand."

No gave him a withering look. "Next time we need to pay for information with flesh, it'll be your turn to pony up."

It wasn't that great a loss. After all, No was right-handed and losing the tip of a pinky wouldn't prevent her from doing her job. Her ego likely hurt more than the wound did, he suspected. No was likely furious that she'd been bested by the creature. Once they finished this job for Caprice, he wouldn't be surprised if she insisted on hunting down the Rag Man, pouring gasoline all over it, and dropping a lit match on its head. *Flame on*, he thought, and smiled.

They arrived at High Strangeness soon after their encounter with the Rag Man, and Yes pulled the Benz into the parking lot. He and No weren't strangers to the Cannery District, although they didn't spend a great deal of time there. The Shadowers – those who moved back and forth between Shadow and the regular world – had their own methods of solving problems, many of them far worse than simple murder, and they rarely needed the services of professional assassins. Yes and No's visits to the House of Red Tears were pretty much the extent of their connection to the Cannery District. So as the couple got out of their car and headed for the bar's entrance, their attention was on the stranger vehicles in the lot – the orb-drawn hansom cab, the scaled motorcycle, the long, low car with multiple tiny wheels – and not on a shabbily dressed man sitting against a light pole, dozing while holding on to a shopping cart containing flattened cardboard boxes concealing a very special passenger. For that moment at least, Haksaw was as invisible as a Rag Man.

★ ★ ★

I can't believe this, Ethan thought, *but I'm actually nervous*.

He was back in Oakmont, headed for High Strangeness. Although he lived in the same town as Weston and Reyna, he rarely left the House of Red Tears and so never saw them. But that was only part of the reason, wasn't it? The truth was they disapproved of Caprice's plan to complete the Lord's Incarnation, and they disapproved of his being part of it. They thought Caprice had turned him into her pet killer and that she held such complete control over him that he could no longer think for himself. Weston and Reyna had told him so several years ago, which – not coincidentally – had been the last time he'd seen them. He hated to admit it, but he wanted their approval. No, he *needed* it. And if he couldn't have that, then he wanted them to fear him. Best case scenario: he would be able to convince them to willingly give Caprice the body parts they were custodians of – the right leg and the right arm – and they would join him in helping their great-aunt finish her holy work. Worst case scenario: he'd have to kill them both and take the arm and leg.

And what about Kate, assuming she was still at the bar when he arrived? Reyna and Weston would surely have filled her head with lies about him. Would she even listen to anything he had to say? Or would she look at him as if he were a mindless servant of Caprice's, a machine-like killer who dispatched humans with no more artistry than a slaughterhouse worker? Move 'em in, move 'em out, kill, kill, kill, kill, kill…. He imagined seeing the look of disgust in her eyes when she saw him, and he didn't know if he could take it. He wasn't in love with her or anything. He wasn't interested in romance or sex, never had been. Besides, they were *cousins*. But for a time she had been his best friend, as close to him as Weston was, and in some ways maybe closer. Of all the family members that he wanted to join him in his quest to bring the Lord to life, Kate – Katie-Bug – was the one that mattered to him the most.

Looking at it another way, though, his feelings about Kate were a weakness, weren't they? Maybe his greatest weakness. Caprice had long ago taught him what to do when he detected a weakness in himself. Large or small, it didn't matter – you destroyed it. Maybe that's what he needed to do in this case: kill Kate the moment he saw her, along with Weston and Reyna. If he severed his familial bonds to them, it would only make him stronger. And honestly, how hard could it be? He'd already killed his mother and one set of grandparents. They'd been good practice, but now the main event was coming up. He needed to prove to himself that he could do this, that he had become the death-dealing monster that Caprice had trained him to be.

Now that he'd made this decision, he felt much better. And if there was some small part of him that remained unsure, he pretended it didn't exist.

As he approached High Strangeness, he saw it was busy for a late afternoon. Shadowers could sometimes sense when and where something bad was going to happen, and they would flock to that place to witness it go down – and join in if they could. If that was the reason for the crowd, so be it. He'd have preferred to have as few people in his way as possible. Not only did it make the work more efficient, a minimalistic approach had an elegance that appealed to him. But he could work with whatever circumstances he encountered. He was a professional, after all.

He pulled his Camaro into the lot and parked next to a nearly new Mercedes Benz. Nice car. Maybe he'd get himself one after all this was over. If he did, he hoped he'd have enough time to enjoy it, at least a little, before the Lord of the Feast delivered the Omniverse into the vast maw of the Gyre. He believed in the inevitability of entropy, but there was no harm in having a bit of fun before everything ended.

He picked up his phone and the knife he'd taken from Tressa's house then got out of the car. He slipped his phone into his pocket, but he decided to carry the knife. He might need it soon. He locked the car, but before he started walking toward the bar, he considered the wisdom of leaving the Lord's left leg – the part he'd gotten from his mother – in the trunk. The leg was in no danger of spoiling, and there was no reason for anyone to suspect there was anything special in the trunk to steal. What the hell would anyone want with a leg, anyway? Then again, this *was* the Cannery District. Any number of Shadowers could find a use for a severed limb, whether it belonged to a god or not. He couldn't take the leg into the bar with him, though. Not only did he have no way to conceal the damn thing, his head hurt like a motherfucker whenever he got too close to it. He decided it would be okay where it was. If all went well, he wouldn't be away from it for long.

As he crossed the lot, he noticed a homeless-looking guy sitting on the ground in front of a light pole, head lowered, one hand holding on to a grocery cart containing…flattened cardboard boxes? That was weird. What kind of value did boxes like that have? None, unless you were planning to move, and since the man looked as if he didn't have a home to move into or out of…. He winced as a sudden sharp pain cut through the left side of his head. Was he still too close to the car? The leg hadn't bothered his head while he'd been driving, and he was farther from it now than he had been then. Whatever. This shit was magic, not science. It wasn't always consistent, at least not in ways humans could fully understand. He continued walking toward the bar's entrance, knife held at his side, and his pain lessened with every step until it vanished.

He forgot all about the homeless guy.

*   *   *

As soon as Ethan entered the bar, Haksaw woke, or rather, was woken. Emotional impressions flooded into his mind from the torso, and they resolved themselves into four words: *Go to the Camry.*

His back complained as he stood. He stretched to try and loosen the muscles, but it did no good. *Getting too old for this shit,* he thought.

He pushed the cart toward the Camry – he didn't have to ask which one; his love had shown him – and when he reached it, he felt a sense of recognition from the torso, as if it was familiar with the vehicle. No, with something *inside* the vehicle. He sensed another emotion from the torso then, one he'd never known it to feel before: joy. Whatever was inside the car made his love happy…happier than he ever had, maybe than he ever could. The realization cut through Haksaw like one of his own tools, and he felt deep, dark despair well up inside him. Close on the heels of this emotion came jealousy, which quickly turned into rage.

He didn't have to listen to the torso. He was in charge! Hadn't he been the one who heard his love's call and liberated it from the chamber below the House of Red Tears? Hadn't he kept it safe all this time, protected it, *loved* it? If nothing else, he still possessed a whole, intact body, and the torso needed him to get around. Without him, the torso couldn't do anything but lie around like a hunk of mindless meat. If he didn't want to share the torso with whatever was in the car that had it so enthralled, he didn't have to. He could leave right now and find a new place to live, somewhere hidden where the two of them could be alone for the rest of Haksaw's mortal life. And after he died, if he was fortunate, his spirit would join with the torso, and they would be together for eternity.

Haksaw gripped the shopping cart's handle and started to back away from the Camry, but then he stopped. If he truly loved the torso, he shouldn't stand in the way of its happiness. If there was something inside this car that called to the torso the same way it had once called to him, then it would be the height of selfishness to take his love away from it.

He sighed. Relationships were hard.

"All right, we'll wait here for the owner of the car to return. Hopefully, we'll find out what's inside that's got you so worked up."

Haksaw felt a wave of warmth come from the torso, the psychic equivalent of a hug, and he couldn't help smiling.

"I love you too," he said.

★   ★   ★

"For Oblivion's sake, Lonnie, can't you pour any faster?"

You try mixing drinks with dead hands, Lonnie thought. Aloud, he only moaned. When he was in a non-living phase, he wasn't the most talkative person.

He'd worked in bars himself before he'd become a Shadower, and he didn't mind helping out when Reyna asked, regardless of where he was at on the life-death spectrum that day. But when he was on the deader side — and not exactly at his most dexterous — some customers would think it hilarious to challenge him to make complicated drinks and watch him struggle to make his stiff, numb hands work. Jimmy

Sandoval — who was an asshole at the best of times — had asked him to make a Long Island iced tea. A bartender standard, to be sure, but it required a cocktail shaker filled with ice, over which was poured vodka, gin, rum, tequila, Triple Sec, and lemon juice. You covered the shaker, shook it vigorously, and poured. Easy enough to make when your hands worked normally — a bitch when they didn't.

Fucker, Lonnie thought. It came out as another moan, but the meaning was clear.

"Yeah?" Jimmy said. "Well, fuck you too."

Lonnie was in the process of pouring the gin when a man and woman in suits walked into the bar. His thought processes might be slower when he was in this stage, but they were hardly nonexistent, and he could tell right away that these two were going to be trouble. They moved with the strong, confident ease of predators, and they swept their gazes around the room as they entered, sizing up any potential threats. They both smiled, but there was no emotion in their expressions. They might as well have been robots who'd been programmed to mimic smiling without having any notion of what the action was for. Lonnie saw that the tip of the woman's left pinky finger was missing, and from the fresh look of the wound, she'd lost it recently. Blood dripped from the mutilated digit onto the wooden floor where it was absorbed. Reyna *hated* it when people bled in the bar. *A few drops of blood, and the goddamned place wants to be fed all the time. It can take weeks to wean it off the stuff again.*

When you lived on the edge of Shadow, as people in the Cannery District did, you quickly gained a sense of who was a danger and who wasn't. Reyna's friends who had entered earlier: not dangerous. These two: *extremely* dangerous. Everyone in the bar sensed it too, and all heads turned toward the couple. Their smiles remained firmly in place, but their eyes went cold as arctic ice.

"Anyone here Ethan Linton?" the woman asked.

No one in the bar spoke, and the dark ambient music playing on the sound system only added to the tension in the air. Lonnie had continued pouring gin all this time, and now it overflowed the shaker and spilled onto the countertop. He barely noticed. People began whispering to one another, and he caught the words *Mr. Yes* and *Mrs. No*. By rights, Lonnie shouldn't have been able to feel anything in his current state, but a chill shivered down his back upon hearing those names. If they really *were* those two, then the patrons of High Strangeness were in even more trouble than he'd thought.

He needed to get Reyna. *Now.*

As he started to put down the gin bottle, he concentrated on becoming all the way living again. He couldn't always force the transition – it usually happened naturally, in its own time – but sometimes, if he tried hard enough....

Warmth flooded through his body, his limbs became loose and limber, and his vision cleared. The gin bottle *thunked* down on the counter – making a small splash in the spilled alcohol – and Lonnie let go of it. He turned, intending to head for the back room, but before he could take more than a single step, he heard the man speak.

"Did I tell anyone it was okay to move?"

Then he heard a gun go off, felt something hard punch his head, and he collapsed to the floor. He lay on his side, watching a pool of blood widening on the tile around him, his eyes clouding over once more, this time for good.

Well, shit, he thought, and died.

*   *   *

Jimmy didn't like Lonnie, and he knew the feeling was mutual. But that didn't mean he wanted some motherfucker to walk into his favorite bar and blow the jackass's head off. Hell, he'd hoped *he'd* get to be the one to kill Lonnie for real someday. Furious, he grabbed the mostly empty bottle of gin and smashed it on the edge of the counter to break off the bottom half. Now that he had himself a weapon, he turned toward the couple—

And immediately caught a knife in the throat.

"Excellent throw, sweetheart!" the man with the gun said.

The woman grinned. "And I made it with my wounded left hand too. Fuck you, Rag Man!"

Jimmy tried to look down to see how much he was bleeding, but the knife blade stuck in his neck made the movement impossible. He tried to speak, but all that came out was a thick gargling. That was okay, though. He had no idea what to say anyway. Then he began to fall, and darkness claimed him before he hit the floor. His last thought before he was gone: he really wished he'd had a chance to drink that Long Island iced tea before he died.

Fucking Lonnie.

CHAPTER ELEVEN

The bar became chaos after that. Half the patrons wanted to flee or hide, and the other half wanted to get at Mr. Yes and Mrs. No and tear out their goddamned hearts for killing two of their friends. No drew her gun, and she and Yes started blasting away. Blood sprayed the air and bodies fell one after the other.

Yes couldn't think of a more pleasant way to spend an afternoon.

★　★　★

Ethan heard the first gunshot before he reached the door, and he ran the last few feet to get there. Not because he feared his brother and cousins were under attack – at least, that's what he told himself – but because if they died, they couldn't tell him where the parts of the Lord they possessed were being kept.

He yanked the door open and rushed inside.

The moment he set foot inside the bar, a man in a blue suit armed with a Glock spun toward him and fired. Without any conscious thought on Ethan's part, his knife hand swept upward and he heard a metallic *ping* as the bullet was knocked aside.

Everyone in the bar stopped what they were doing and gaped at him.

"That was impressive," said the woman standing next to the man who'd fired on Ethan. She wore a black suit and held a Glock. "Can you do it twice in a row?"

She raised her gun and fired. Once again, Ethan's hand swept out and batted aside the bullet with his knife blade.

"I guess he can," the man said.

The woman frowned. "By any chance are you Ethan Linton?"

Ethan was so stunned by what he had just done – when the hell had he become a super ninja? – that he almost didn't understand the woman's question.

"Uh, yeah. I am."

"Caprice sent us to help you," the man said. He lowered his weapon, and the woman did likewise. He nodded toward Ethan's borrowed T-shirt. "Ready to rock and roll, huh? Cute."

"Not as cute as those sandals, though," the woman said.

Ethan ignored the two and allowed his knife hand to drop to his side. Seeing the man and woman reminded him that Caprice didn't believe he was up to the job she'd given him. If he hadn't still been trying to process the fact that he'd just deflected two bullets, he would've been extremely pissed off. As it was, he was only minorly irritated. But he was now more determined than ever to prove himself to Caprice, even if he died in the attempt.

He remembered then why he'd come here, and he looked around the bar, trying to see if he could spot Kate, Reyna, and Weston. But they weren't among the people – living, dead, or wounded – present, and he was surprised by how relieved this made him.

"Do you know why I've come here?" he asked his 'helpers'.

"Yes," the woman said. "Your cousin owns this place, and she has something you want."

"Something I *need*," Ethan corrected. "And these people are all in my way. We need to get them out of here."

The man looked at the woman and smiled.

"Do we want to let them leave alive?" he asked.

"*No*, we do not. Do we want to kill the shit out of them?" she replied.

"Oh *yes*."

Ethan sighed. "Fine, but let's be quick about it."

He raised his knife, the couple raised their guns, and the three of them went to work.

★　　★　　★

It grew quiet in the bar for several moments, then a gun went off again. Once, twice. A few more moments of silence, and then the gunfire resumed and people began shouting and screaming once more.

"Fuck!"

Reyna opened one of her desk drawers and pulled out a pair of handguns. Kate didn't know what kind they were, but they looked big enough to do some damage. Reyna handed one to Weston, and he gave the weapon a once-over, making sure it was loaded and in working order, and Reyna did the same with hers.

Reyna looked at Kate. "Sorry I don't have any more guns."

"I wouldn't know what to do with one," Kate said.

Lee didn't speak. They looked scared, and Kate didn't blame them. What was happening was terrifying – or at least it should be. Kate was scared too, but nowhere near as much as she should've been. She'd never experienced violence before – unless *That Night* counted – and she had no idea how to defend herself in a fight, let alone one where people were shooting at each other. But her thoughts were clear and well ordered. Maybe she was one of those people who didn't fall apart until after a crisis was over. If so, that was good. It might just keep Lee and her alive.

Reyna and Weston looked angry instead of scared.

"I'm sorry I brought this down on you," Kate said. "I didn't know something like this would happen."

"It's not your fault," Weston said. "It's the rest of the family's. They were the ones obsessed with creating a fucking god."

He started toward the office door, and Reyna followed. But before Weston could open it, Reyna grabbed hold of his shirt and stopped him. She looked back at Kate.

"It's too dangerous for you two to stay here." She hesitated, then pulled the key from beneath her shirt, removed it from around her neck, and tossed it to Kate. "Go out the back, sneak around to your car, and get the hell out of here as fast as you can. Stronghold Self-Storage in Collier. You'll need to enter a PIN to open the gate and get in. Ours is 3722. Now go!"

Reyna turned away and she and Weston ran out the door.

Lee looked at Kate, eyes wide, and Kate saw they were trembling.

"So I guess we leave now?" they asked.

Kate looked at the key Reyna had thrown to her. It had a number engraved on the side: 342. She put the string around her neck, tucked the key into her shirt, then stood.

Additional gunfire echoed from the front of the bar, and Kate knew Reyna and Weston had joined the fight.

"Definitely," Kate said.

She grabbed Lee's hand and pulled them toward the door.

★   ★   ★

While his two helpers blazed away with their Glocks, Ethan carved bloody swaths through the crowd with his blade. Two blades, actually, as he'd taken one from a woman who'd attacked him and then used it to slice open her throat. He had fallen into a zen-like state of calm as he slashed and stabbed, spun and whirled, moving like he was a dancer in an intricately choreographed and nightmarishly gruesome ballet. And the patterns the blood made as it sprayed the air were nothing short of breathtaking. He didn't bother trying to keep from getting any on him. Not only was it impossible given how much of it was flying around, he *wanted* it on him, wanted to be a living canvas for the crimson work of art that he was creating with sharp steel. There was a poetic elegance to death when it was visited upon someone prematurely, but when it happened like this, killing one person after another, it was, in a small way, like being the Gyre itself. An endless darkness devouring all light and life, forever hungry, never sated.

"Ethan!"

He spun around to see Weston and Reyna, both armed with 9mm pistols, standing shoulder to shoulder, dead and dying customers around their feet, floor slick with blood. Weston had been the one who'd called out to Ethan, and both he and Reyna had their weapons trained on him. He felt a pang of betrayal upon seeing them like this, guns aimed and ready to fire, but he supposed he couldn't blame them. He hadn't exactly made the most subdued of entrances, and his new helpers had only made a bad situation worse. Ethan wished he had more than a pair of knives with which to defend himself. He really should get in the habit of carrying a gun himself.

He'd deflected bullets with these blades — although he had no idea how he'd managed that miracle — but that had been when only one round at a time was fired at him. Could he deflect two or more bullets coming at him at once? He'd rather not find out.

He lowered the knives.

"It's good to see you, Wes. You too, Rey. Sorry about your customers. Things got a little out of hand."

He was trying to sound calm and reasonable, but the fact that he was drenched in blood likely created a very different impression, he thought. He had no choice but to press on.

"Where's Kate? I'm so looking forward to seeing her again."

They ignored his question.

"We know why you're here," Reyna said, "and we know what you want. We won't ever—"

A pair of shots rang out and Reyna and Weston's heads snapped back in a double spray of blood. They fell backward, Reyna striking a table before hitting the floor, and Weston — who'd been hit a split second after Reyna — falling on top of her. Ethan stared at their bodies for several moments, unable to bring himself to believe what he'd witnessed. Then he spun around to face his two helpers.

"Why the fuck did you do that?" he demanded.

The man grinned. "Why the fuck not?"

"They *were* pointing guns at you," the woman added.

"You goddamned morons! They knew the location of two of the Lord's body parts. How the hell am I supposed to get that information from them now? And besides that, they were *family*."

He gripped his knives tighter and took a step forward. The man and woman trained their weapons on him.

"Careful," the woman said. "Your aunt's paying us to help you, but we won't hesitate to take you out if you threaten us."

"We're big believers in proactive murder," the man said. "Shoot first—"

"And don't bother asking any questions," the woman said.

"Keeps things simple."

"Tidy."

Even with a pair of guns pointed at him, Ethan considered attacking the couple. Maybe he would be able to deflect their bullets, and when he reached them, he'd carve them up into so many pieces that you wouldn't be able to tell which parts came from which person. Then again, maybe he wouldn't be able to stop their bullets.

He lowered his knives, and a moment later, they lowered their guns.

He resisted an urge to look back at Weston and Reyna's bodies. He sensed it would be a mistake to display any sign of weakness in front of these two. Working with Caprice had taught him that souls were real, and while he had no idea if Weston and Reyna's spirits still lingered here, and if so, whether they could detect his thoughts, he sent them a message anyway.

I'm sorry. I didn't mean for it to work out like this.

He felt no reply, and really, he hadn't expected to.

"We came here looking for a man who your aunt claims has the Lord's torso," the woman said. She gave a quick glance around the room. "I don't see him, though."

Ethan knew who they were talking about – the serial killer who called himself Haksaw. He'd planned to go to the man's home last, since he knew exactly where he lived and, according to Caprice, the man rarely left the place. But now it sounded as if these two idiots had caused Haksaw to leave his hidey-hole and take the torso with him. The fucker could be anywhere in the Cannery District now. There were tons of places he could hide here, especially among the Shadowers. This was all due to Caprice's control-freak nature and her inability to trust him to do the job she'd assigned him. If she'd just stayed the hell out of his way and let him do his work, everything would've been fine. But no, she had to send the Fuck-Up Twins to babysit him, and now things were more screwed up than they'd been before.

Had he arrived before Kate got here? She wasn't among the dead. Had she decided not to come here for some reason? Just because Delmar had thought she was coming to High Strangeness didn't mean she'd followed through. Or the old bastard could've lied to him. The family was tough, and he had no problem imagining that Delmar could resist torture and interrogation. So not only was Haksaw loose in the wind somewhere, so was Kate.

This day kept getting better and better.

"We should work together from now on," the man said. "That way we can be the most help to you."

Ethan almost burst out laughing. Some fucking help they'd been so far! But he supposed it was necessary, even if it might not be a good idea. He could use the extra firepower, and if they were with him, he could keep an eye on them and make sure they'd didn't mess up anymore.

"All right," Ethan said.

"I say we search the place," the woman said. "See if we can find the Lord's parts on the premises."

Ethan shook his head. "It would be a waste of time. Reyna wouldn't have stored them here. Too many people coming and going throughout the course of a day. She and Wes would've stored the pieces off-site somewhere. Of course, since both of them are dead, we can't—"

A needle of pain jabbed his brain then, and with it came not a vision precisely, but a feeling, so primal and strong it was almost like instinct.

"The parking lot."

Without waiting for the man and woman to respond, he ran past them, careful not to trip over any bodies or lose his footing on spilled blood. He sensed he only had moments, and he had to make them count.

He threw open the door and ran outside.

★　　★　　★

Kate and Lee came around from behind High Strangeness to see a mass exodus occurring in the parking lot. A number of drivers were jockeying to get to the exit and onto the street – resulting in more than a few minor collisions – while others said to hell with it and drove over the curb, and some people didn't bother getting into cars at all and simply ran for it. Kate thought these people had made the most rational choice, and if the Lord's eyes weren't still in Lee's car, she would've done the same. As they ran past the hansom cab, its orb glowed bright blue and then the vehicle vanished with a *whump* of inrushing air. Whatever the thing was, Kate wished she had one. Right now, she would've loved to be able to push a button or pull a lever and *poof!* be somewhere else instantly.

There was so much commotion in the parking lot that Kate didn't notice the man standing next to Lee's Camry until they were almost on top of him. He was filthy, smelled like a clogged sewer, and had his hand on the handle of a shopping cart filled with cardboard. Lee unlocked the car using the key remote, and Kate hoped the man would get out of their way so they could get inside, but he didn't budge.

"Can you step back, please?" she asked. "We need to leave."

She could hear more gunfire in the bar, and she hoped Reyna and Weston would be okay. She'd hate to lose them so soon after their brief reunion.

"I'm supposed to go with you," the man said. "That's what my love says, anyway."

He removed the cardboard from the cart and tossed it to the ground, revealing a human torso, its arm, leg, and neck stumps bloodless.

Pain flared in Kate's head, and she drew in a sharp breath. She had no idea who this man was, but she instantly recognized the object in his cart as one of the Lord's pieces, the largest, as a matter of fact.

She quickly calculated the odds of their being able to take the torso from this man, get it into the car, and haul ass out of there before whoever was shooting up the bar – Ethan was the most likely culprit – came out looking for them. Assuming, of course, that Reyna and Weston didn't manage to stop him. The odds, she decided, were not in their favor.

"All right, you can come with us."

Lee looked at her as if she was insane, and maybe she was.

"We'll toss it in the trunk and—"

"No!" the man shouted. "My love stays with me."

There wasn't time to argue. "Fine. The two of you can get in the backseat then."

She opened the rear door on the driver's side and stepped back to make room. The man lifted the torso out of the cart, carried it to the Camry, and climbed in. Kate closed the door after him, and he hugged the torso close.

Lee gripped Kate by the shoulders.

"Are you crazy? We don't know who he is. And given the way he looks – not to mention smells – I don't know if it's a good idea—"

"Look, we can argue about it later. Right now we need to get out of here."

"But—"

"It's the right thing to do. I can *feel* it."

Lee sighed. "Okay, but if he ends up killing us, I swear I'm going to haunt your ass for eternity."

Kate smiled. "Deal."

They got in, Lee fired up the engine, and aimed the Camry for the curb. A couple hard bumps, and they were on the street and heading south. They drove for several moments before Kate realized her head didn't hurt anymore.

★　　★　　★

Ethan made it outside in time to see the last of the fleeing vehicles – a silver Camry – drive off. He had no reason to think the car had anything to do with Kate, but an almost-voice whispered in his mind that it did. *She's in that car,* he thought, *and she has at least one body part with her, maybe more.* He had no idea how he knew this, but he did. Maybe he possessed more of his family's mystic ability than he'd thought. He also sensed that the more parts that were together, the easier it would be for him to feel their presence, maybe even track them. It was like the more there were, the stronger signal they put out.

But he could already feel that signal fading as the Camry drove farther away, and he knew that if he didn't hurry, he'd lose the trail. He started running toward his Camaro, not caring if his helpers followed. If they kept up with him, they could ride in his car if they didn't have their own, and if they didn't keep up with him, fuck 'em. There was no way in hell he was going to let that Camry get away.

He heard a gunshot behind him, felt something punch the back of his left shoulder. He stumbled forward, fell, put out his hands to catch himself. But when his left hand came down on the asphalt, his shoulder screamed, his arm buckled beneath him, and he rolled onto his left side – which caused his shoulder to scream even louder. It was only then that he realized he'd been shot.

He looked back toward the bar's entrance, saw Reyna – half of her face covered with blood. Her right arm was outstretched, and even though she looked as if she could barely stay on her feet, her gun hand was steady as a goddamn rock.

Ms. Blue Suit turned to Reyna, raised her own gun, and put a bullet into Reyna's right eye. Reyna's head jerked to the side, blood sprayed, and she collapsed.

"This time stay down." The woman looked at Mr. Blue Suit. "I hate it when they don't die the first time."

"Most inconsiderate," the man said.

Using his right arm, Ethan pushed himself up into a sitting position and looked to the street.

The Camry was no longer in sight.

★   ★   ★

Kate kept checking the side-view mirror to see if anyone was coming after them, but since she didn't know what kind of vehicle any pursuers would be driving, she wasn't sure how much good it did. No one was tearing up the road to catch up to them, so that was good. She doubted they were completely in the clear – the odds didn't favor that – but she thought it a good bet that they'd at least managed to buy a little breathing room.

Speaking of breathing room, Kate had rolled down the Camry's four windows to try to cut their new companion's stench, but it only helped so much. The man's rank body odor reminded Kate of the monkey house in a zoo she'd visited as a child, only his stink was much stronger.

The Lord's eyes were still beneath her seat, and although she was close to them, she wasn't experiencing more than a mild headache – and that was with the torso now in the car as well. Whatever had been causing her pain when she was close to any of the Lord's body parts, she seemed to be adjusting to it.

She turned around in her seat to look at the man who'd joined them. He held the torso close and stroked its ribs with his fingers, mouth leaned close to the neck hole, whispering as if he was talking to the thing. She couldn't make out what he was saying, but the tone was gentle, even loving. At first, she didn't realize what was going on, then her stomach lurched when she understood. This man was talking to the torso as if it could understand him, and he was speaking in a voice reserved only for a lover's ears, soft and intimate. When the man noticed Kate was staring at him, he looked up and smiled, displaying teeth that looked as if they hadn't been cleaned since the day they'd come in.

"You have another in here, don't you?" the man said. "My love can feel it."

"Another...? Oh, yes. Yes, we do."

"Can I see it?"

Lee gave Kate a warning glance, and she could guess what they were thinking. They had no idea who this man was or what he was doing with the torso. Could he be connected to Caprice somehow, maybe someone else she'd sent out to gather the Lord's parts for her? If so, he might try to take the eyes when Kate showed them to him. She hesitated, unsure what to do, and then she felt warmth radiating outward from the torso, and with the sensation came, not a word so much, but a concept that in her mind was translated as *Trust*, as in, it was okay to trust this strange man.

She decided to take a risk. She reached down, pulled the bag with the eyes from beneath the seat, removed the jar, and held it up for the man to see.

His own eyes widened when he saw the Lord's, and he leaned forward to get a better look. The eyes focused on him at first, but then they lowered to gaze upon the torso.

"They're beautiful," the man said. He didn't ask her to hand him the eyes, and he didn't reach out to try and take them. Kate let him look at them a few more moments before putting them back beneath her seat.

"I'm Kate," she said. "This is Lee. What's your name?"

"Haksaw. Like the tool, but without a C."

Weird name, but okay. "Do you live in the Cannery District, Haksaw?"

The man nodded. "Have most of my life. I've always had the Eye." When Kate didn't respond, he said, "You know – the ability to see into Shadow. Not everyone can. And if you can't see it, you can't enter it. It can always see *you*, though, and it can reach out and pull you in whenever it wants. It's better if you can see it coming. Gives you a fighting chance to avoid it, you know?"

Kate did. Her parents, and then later Tressa, had taught her about Shadow, the basics, at least.

"Do you have a job?" Kate didn't think it likely, given the man's appearance – and odor – but she thought it was only polite to ask.

"Sure. I kill people. One or two a month. I don't like to be too greedy, you know? Better to spread them out. Of course, I don't really want the whole person, so I cut off the parts I don't like and get rid of them. It's easy to dispose of meat in the Cannery. All I have to do is toss the unwanted parts into an alley, and usually a couple Dog-Eaters will show up and take care of them. They prefer dogs, of course. I mean, that's in their name, right? But they'll eat any kind of meat, as long as they don't have to put up too much of a fight for it. I use a hacksaw to cut off the bits I don't want to keep. That's how I came up with my killer name. Do you like it?"

Kate was too shocked to respond. She'd allowed a serial killer to get into the car with them, and they didn't have any kind of weapons to protect themselves. Maybe the guy wasn't a killer; maybe he just liked to pretend he was to fuck with people. But when she looked into his eyes, she saw deep madness there, and she knew he was telling them the truth.

"Can you guess what my favorite part is?" he asked. "I'll give you a hint."

He lifted the torso in front of his face and waggled it back and forth.

"Fuck this!" Lee said.

They yanked the Camry's steering wheel to the right and whipped the car into a pharmacy's parking lot. There were only a few other vehicles present, and Lee parked well away from them. They turned off the engine, got out of the car, and slammed the door shut behind them.

Kate glanced back at Haksaw. "I need to go talk to them."

"Sure," Haksaw said. "Lovers' quarrel. I get it. You'll work it out."

A serial killer is reassuring me about my relationship, Kate thought. *Nothing weird about that.*

She got out of the car. Lee was pacing back and forth behind the Camry, scowling and muttering to themself.

"Let's give a ride to a fucking lunatic, sure, no problem, what could possibly go wrong with that?"

Kate stopped when she reached Lee. Lee kept pacing, and she wanted to reach out and grab them, make them stop and look at her, but she didn't. Lee was upset, and when they got like this, they needed to bleed off energy.

"What's wrong?" she asked.

Lee continued pacing as they answered. "What's wrong? *Everything's* wrong! I find out my girlfriend comes from a family of witches, that they tried to create a god who would bring about the end of the universe, and that we needed to go on a road trip to collect all the god's parts before it could be brought to life again. Then we end up barely escaping a massacre at a bar, and now we've got a fucking serial killer riding in our backseat with his pet torso. And all of this happened in just a few hours! Pardon me if I'm having a bit of trouble adjusting to this insanity."

Kate bristled. Lee hadn't come out and said so, but from their tone, Kate thought they blamed her for everything that had happened, at least partially.

"It hasn't exactly been a barrel of fucking laughs for me either. My grandparents and my cousins are dead, and my other cousin wants to kill me too."

Events had been happening so fast that she hadn't had time to fully feel the loss of her family members. She knew it would hit her sooner rather than later, and when it did, she would probably become so overwhelmed with grief that she'd be unable to function – which was why she had to keep her emotions at bay. This was a time for rational thinking. She could grieve later, assuming she survived.

Lee stopped pacing and faced Kate. "I'm sorry for your losses, I truly am. But they're proof that this is too goddamn dangerous for you to continue. If you keep going the way you are, you're going to end up dead, too. Maybe your cousin will kill you or maybe Haksaw will decide he wants to add another torso to his collection. Either way, you'll be just as dead."

"I have to do this. There isn't anybody else."

"No, you don't have to. Even if your great-aunt gets hold of all the body parts, who's to say she'll be able to bring the god to life? Your whole family tried to do it the first time, and they failed. How can Caprice succeed on her own? She could attempt the rite only for her house to end up burning to the ground around her."

"But what if she succeeds?"

"Whatever the god is, it can't possibly be powerful enough to destroy the entire universe. All Caprice would do is succeed at creating a monster that'll more than likely turn against her. Isn't that what these kinds of monsters do, betray their creators in the end? I don't want you to be there when that happens. Please don't throw your life away."

Kate was touched that Lee wanted to protect her, but at the same time, she was also offended. She wasn't some little kid who needed looking out for. She was a fucking Shardlow, born to death and darkness. Her family was Evil with a capital E, and it was her responsibility to stop them from bringing the Lord of the Feast into the world. Why couldn't she make Lee see this?

"I have to do this. I *have* to."

Lee looked as if they might cry. "Fine." They pulled the Camry's key remote from their pocket and tossed it to Kate. "Then go ahead without me. I can't be a part of this any longer. I can't watch you basically commit suicide."

Kate wanted to protest, to tell Lee that she needed their support if she was to have any chance of succeeding. But she also didn't want Lee to end up getting killed like Tressa, Delmar, Delora, Weston, and Reyna. It was better this way. Whatever happened, at least she would know that Lee was safe. Unless of course she failed to stop Caprice and the entire universe went down the fucking drain, but best not to think about that now.

Kate and Lee looked at one another for a moment, then Lee turned and headed toward the sidewalk. Kate watched them go, and when they were lost to sight, she got back in the Camry, this time in the driver's seat, and started the car.

"I take it Lee isn't going with us?" Haksaw asked.

"No."

Haksaw grinned. "Then I call shotgun!"

He got out of the car and took the front passenger seat. He brought the torso with him, of course, and while Kate's head gave a twinge at its proximity, the pain was mild and easily endured.

"Where are we headed?" Haksaw asked.

"Collier. There's a storage facility there I need to visit."

"More parts?"

"More parts."

Haksaw smiled. "This is fun!"

Kate backed the Camry out of the parking space and pulled onto the street.

At least one of us thinks so.

★   ★   ★

Good god, that girl was stubborn! Normally, it was one of the qualities Lee found most attractive in her. They liked how Kate knew her own mind and went after what she wanted, consequences be damned. But today's events had shown Lee that this trait was one Kate had inherited from her family, and they feared it would lead to her ruin, just as it had for the other Shardlows and the Lintons. Lee loved Kate, they truly did, but there was no way they could continue to support her self-destructive behavior – even if it was their duty to do so.

Lee didn't have a destination in mind. They'd probably end up calling an Uber and getting a ride back to their apartment eventually, but right now they just wanted to keep walking until they calmed down. They passed a bus stop where a lone man stood waiting. He was a big guy, middle-aged, with snow-white hair and beard. He wore glasses, a loud Hawaiian shirt, a pair of black slacks, and black shoes. As Lee walked by, the man turned and followed.

"Lee," he said.

Lee stopped and turned to face him. The man caught up to them and gave a friendly smile. They didn't recognize him, had never seen him before, and yet they knew who he was, or rather, who he represented.

"Been a big day for you, hasn't it?" the man said.

Lee didn't respond.

"I have to say, we're a little disappointed that you gave up so easily. We thought you were made of tougher stuff."

"Yeah, well, I guess I'm not."

"You've been on this assignment for almost an entire year, and just as things finally start to heat up, you decide that's it, you're out?"

Lee lowered their gaze to the sidewalk. "I couldn't stand watching Kate put herself in danger."

"That's the job. Watching and reporting. You didn't allow yourself to develop feelings for her, did you?"

Lee met the man's gaze once more. "You know I did. You – or someone like you – are always watching."

The man smiled. "All right, yes, we knew. But as long as your emotions didn't interfere with your work, we could look the other way. But they're interfering now, and we can't have that. Not when Caprice Linton is getting closer to resurrecting the Lord of the Feast."

"Why don't you send someone else to help Kate then? Why don't *you* do it?"

"That's not how we do things, and you know it. The Unbroken Court must retain its neutrality."

"But not so neutral that you don't send operatives to deal with situations when it suits you."

"When the need is great enough, yes. And no one forced you to become an agent of the Court. It was your choice."

"A choice I'm beginning to regret."

"The Court asks much of us, and we all come to regret serving it sooner or later. But that doesn't mean we stop doing so." The man sighed. "I sympathize with your situation, Lee, I truly do. Forget the whole end-of-existence stuff and ask yourself this: If you really love Kate, how can you refuse to help her, no matter the cost?"

Without another word, the man turned away and started walking in the direction Lee had come from. They didn't bother chasing after him. He would speak no more on this matter. Officers of the Court were like that. They showed up, made their pronouncements, then left. It was up to you whether or not you acted on them. But in this case, Lee didn't really have a choice.

They removed their phone from their pocket, tapped a few buttons, and summoned an Uber. They returned their phone to their pocket and waited. Lee could've called Kate and apologized, but they didn't want her wasting time by driving back to get them. They knew where Kate was going – Stronghold Self-Storage in Collier – and they'd have the Uber take them there. With any luck, they'd arrive before Kate opened the storage unit containing the Lord's arm and leg, *and* before Ethan showed up to try and take them *and* before Haksaw decided to kill her.

Lee waited for their ride, their anxiety increasing with each passing moment.

Stay safe until I can get back to you, my love, they thought.

★   ★   ★

Ethan sat in the backseat of his helpers' Mercedes. Mr. Yes was driving and Mrs. No sat in the passenger seat, window down, eyes closed, enjoying the feel of the sun and air on her face. It was a lovely image, Ethan thought, one that would make a great painting. Evidently Yes and No — stupid names — were regular clients of his aunt's. Ethan was familiar with most of the regulars, even if he knew none of them very well, but he'd never so much as heard of Mr. Yes and Mrs. No. There were some clients who demanded anonymity, though, and Caprice made sure they got it while they were in her house. He assumed Yes and No were among the latter. They weren't exactly maintaining a low profile today, though. Then again, after he'd been shot, Mrs. No had gone back into High Strangeness to finish off anyone who hadn't been dead while Mr. Yes saw to his wound. The couple obviously wanted to leave no witnesses behind. Smart.

The bullet Reyna had fired at him had gone all the way through his shoulder, so there had been no bullet to dig out. Yes, with quick, efficient motions, cleaned and bandaged it. Then he'd given Ethan a handful of pills and told him to swallow them. When Ethan asked what they were, Yes had simply said, *Medicine*. Ethan took the pills, and they'd kicked in almost immediately. His shoulder still hurt like it was on fire, but he felt distant from the pain now, and it was tolerable. The Mercedes' trunk was like a killers' convenience store, containing weapons, ammo, rope, and restraints, but also a fully stocked med kit, snacks and bottled water, towels and wet wipes, and fresh clothes. His skin and hair were more or less cleaned of blood, but the clothes he'd taken from Kate's room were unsalvageable. No had put them in a plastic garbage bag and stuffed them in the trunk. *We'll toss them in a dumpster once we're far enough away from the bar,* she'd said. Ethan wasn't worried about the police finding the bloodied clothes. Caprice paid them quite handsomely to ignore what went on in the House of Red Tears, and if necessary, she could toss a bonus their way to cover up what had happened at High Strangeness. The cops were usually only too happy to overlook whatever weirdness took place in the Cannery

District anyway. So No's precaution likely wasn't necessary, but Ethan appreciated the woman's thoroughness and professionalism.

There hadn't been a lot to choose from among Yes and No's spare clothing, and he'd ended up selecting a pair of black running shorts with red stripes on the sides, a plain white T-shirt, and a pair of well-worn sneakers that were a half size too large for him. The outfit was way less embarrassing than the *I Wanna Rock* T-shirt, too-small jeans, and flip-flops with plastic daisies he'd stolen from Kate, so he wasn't about to complain.

Since Ethan was in no shape to drive due to his injury and the 'medicine' he was on, they'd taken the Mercedes. He'd switched the Lord's left arm – the part he'd gotten from his dearly departed mother – from the trunk of his Camaro to the Mercedes, and Yes had driven them out of the bar's parking lot. Now they were traveling aimlessly through the Cannery.

"So what's our next destination, Ethan?" Yes asked. "Your aunt sent us to get the torso from Haksaw—"

A task you failed at, Ethan thought.

"But she didn't tell us the location of any other parts," No said. "Your cousin has the eyes, correct?"

"I think she may have the torso as well," Ethan said. "I'm not sure why. Just a feeling."

"Your family is good when it comes to witchy shit like that," Yes said. "So I bet it's more than a feeling."

"I don't think Kate has anything else, though," Ethan said. "Not yet, anyway."

"Another feeling?" No asked.

"Not really. I know how my brother and cousin think – *thought* – and I can't see them storing the body parts they were given custody of at the bar. They wouldn't have been secure there. Too many people in the Cannery would've sniffed out the power the parts contained and attempted to steal them. I'm sure Reyna and Weston stored the parts off-site somewhere."

"But you don't know where," Yes said.

"No. But I know how to find out." *I hope.*

He took his phone from his pocket, wincing as the action jostled his wounded shoulder, and called Caprice.

CHAPTER TWELVE

"I'm sorry, but these things do happen."

Caprice sat behind the desk in her office, Axton standing at her side, his hands clasped behind his back. Sitting in front of them was a killer who went by the sobriquet the Silent Man – although he wasn't being particularly silent now. He wore a black bodysuit, black gloves, and a black hood with eye holes. The effect would've been more sinister if the man would lose a few pounds, Caprice thought, but then who was she to judge?

"I paid good money for my session today, and I expected to get a victim that could go the distance. Instead, mine has a heart attack and dies before I even touch them!"

"I'm sure it's because you're so terrifying," Axton said drily.

Caprice suppressed a smile. "All of our playthings are given medical exams to ensure they're in acceptable health before we offer them to clients. Unfortunately, given the stressful situations playthings experience, unforeseen medical events do occur from time to time. Please accept my apologies. I'll have a fresh plaything brought to you, and I'll make certain the medical staff double-check it first to ensure it's in prime condition."

She hoped this would placate the Silent Man. If all went according to plan, the Lord of the Feast would be Incarnated soon, but while she knew the god would bring about the end of all existence, she wasn't sure exactly how soon it would happen. *The Book of Depravity* gave no indication how quickly the Lord would work, just that it would greatly accelerate the Omniverse's collapse into total entropy. But what did *rapidly* mean on a cosmic scale? A century? A millennium? An epoch? An eon? The Lord would most likely start with Earth, but there was still a possibility that

Caprice would live out the rest of her natural life before the planet was destroyed, in which case she'd continue to keep the House of Red Tears open. Strictly speaking, she wouldn't need to, for there would no longer be a need to harvest life energy to complete the Incarnation. But she liked running her own business. After the first attempt at the Incarnation failed, she'd needed money to establish the House, and a lot of it. So, with the help of professional thieves, she'd stolen all the wealth the Shardlows and Lintons had acquired over the years and used it to fund her project. She'd worked damn hard over the last decade, and she'd succeeded beyond her expectations. No way would she give it up as long as she lived. Besides, she could always find fun ways to use the additional life force she'd acquire. All of this was the reason why she didn't tell the Not-So-Silent Man to fuck off. As long as she was still running the House of Red Tears, she'd act as a businessperson, and that meant maintaining good relationships with customers.

"Screw you!" the Silent Man snapped.

Caprice blinked. "Excuse me?"

The Silent Man stood, placed his gloved palms on Caprice's desk, and leaned forward.

"I can't just pick up where I left off. The mood is completely spoiled now. I spend *days* mentally preparing myself before a kill. I'm not some impulsive butcher who kills on a whim. Those animals are the premature ejaculators of the serial killer world. I am a serious devotee of the homicidal arts, goddamnit!" He punctuated *goddamnit* by slamming a fist on the desktop.

Out of the corner of her eye, Caprice saw Axton start toward the man, but she raised her index finger, and Axton restrained himself. The Silent Man continued his rant.

"You may think you have a monopoly on providing killers with victims and a place to ply their trade, but you're wrong. I know of at least three others in this country, along with one in Canada and two in South America. After today's cock-up, I'm going to be taking my business to one of them, and I intend to tell every killer I meet that the House of Red Tears isn't worth the money. And speaking of money, I expect a full refund, and I expect it—"

Caprice nodded and Axton sprung forward. He pulled an ice pick from his white suit jacket's inner pocket and plunged it into the Silent Man's eye sockets with two quick jabs, wiggling it back and forth each time. When he was finished, he stepped back. Thin lines of blood ran from the man's eyes. Red tears, indeed.

"—now," the man finished. He remained in that position, hands on Caprice's desk, staring at her quietly, silent at last.

"Nicely done, Axton."

Axton wiped the ice pick clean on the Silent Man's arm.

"I've been practicing. You never know when you're going to need to perform a quick lobotomy."

Caprice would've been content to allow the Silent Man to leave – until he said he was going to bad-mouth her business to others. Word of mouth was the only type of advertising a place like hers had, and she wasn't going to allow some self-important prick to poison the House's reputation.

"Take him down to Processing," Caprice said. "Tell them to ask around and see if any of the clients currently on the premises would like an extra plaything – on the house."

Axton grinned. "Yes, Caprice." He gently took hold of the Silent Man's arm and helped him into an upright position. He then removed the man's hood to reveal a perfectly ordinary face. The man looked at Axton quizzically, as if he thought he knew who he was but couldn't quite place him.

"If you'll come with me, sir," Axton said.

Keeping a hand on the man's arm, Axton led him to the office door. He opened it, and as they stepped into the hall, the Silent Man gave Caprice a silent look. Then Axton closed the door.

Caprice sighed. That was one problem dealt with. She hoped there wouldn't be any more today. She—

Her phone rang. She checked the display and saw Ethan was calling. Could he have procured all the Lord's parts already? She hoped so. She could use some good news right now.

She answered. "Ethan, my boy! How are things going?"

She listened.

When Ethan was finished, she was in even a worse mood than she had been when the Silent Man was barking at her. She briefly considered having Axton lobotomize Ethan, but things hadn't gotten that bad. Not yet.

"I think I can help. I'll call you back."

She disconnected.

She put her hand to her face, stroked her lower jaw as she thought. Despite what she'd told Ethan, she wasn't certain that what she had in mind would work. But she could see no other way to get the information he needed, and the little bastard sure as hell needed assistance. He still only had the left arm that he'd gotten from Delora. Kate had the eyes and, if his hunch was correct, the torso, and he believed she was on the way to get the parts Weston and Reyna had been charged with guarding. Caprice couldn't believe how fucked up this had gotten. She'd hired Mr. Yes and Mrs. No to retrieve the torso, and they'd obviously failed. She wondered what had happened to Haksaw. Had Kate found him and taken the torso from him? Had she killed him? No, killing wasn't in her nature. She was very much the white sheep in the family in that regard. She should never have let Haksaw keep the torso all these years. At the time, she believed she made the right choice, had sensed that was where the torso needed to be, but she'd clearly made a mistake. Haksaw had taken the torso not long after the first Incarnation failed. Caprice thought she had escaped any bad aftereffects from that night, but what if her judgment had been impaired and she hadn't realized it?

It was too late to worry about such things now. She needed to focus on the present, and that meant finding out where Reyna and Weston had stored the Lord's right arm and right leg. And she could think of only one place where she might come by that knowledge.

She needed to make another visit to the Repository.

*　　*　　*

The spirits of Nila, Dalton, Cordell, Victorina, and Lissette moved alongside the road, unseen by passing motorists, although more than a few felt a cold chill as they drove by the revenants. They would have a difficult time falling asleep that night, and when they finally did slumber, their dreams would be uneasy ones. Felton kept to the woods that bordered the road, and when there were no trees to provide cover, he moved fast and low to the ground. He wasn't concerned about being seen – what could mortals do to harm a creature like him? – but animal instinct told him to be cautious, and he obeyed without question.

The spirits traveled faster than a human could walk, but not as fast as a car could move, and they found this frustrating. They did not have physical bodies, were beings composed primarily of thought, emotion, and memory, but they were forced to behave as if they were corporeal. This meant they could not simply vanish from one place and reappear in another, which would've been much more convenient. They needed an anchor to remain in this world, and the void in the basement of the Shardlow mansion had fulfilled that function for them. Felton served as their anchor now, which meant they could not stray far from him. To make matters worse, they could feel themselves growing weaker with each moment that passed. The dark energy that emanated from the void had not only anchored them in this world, it had sustained them as well. Without it, they would eventually weaken to the point where they faded into nonexistence, and while this prospect did not frighten them, they needed to reach the House of Red Tears while they still possessed enough strength to stand against Caprice.

They did what they could to slow their weakening. They absorbed the life energy from grass and weeds they drifted over, the plants turning black and withering. They drained the vitality from insects and small animals – snakes, lizards, toads, mice – leaving them desiccated husks that Felton would snap up for whatever nutrition remained in their tiny empty bodies. What they took wasn't enough to halt their weakening, but it helped slow it.

As they traveled, two additional spirits joined them. They immediately recognized Tressa and Delmar's essences, and the family members enjoyed a reunion, albeit a melancholy one. Felton approached the newcomers, sniffed them, sensed the patterns of their energy, and if he had a tail, he would've wagged it.

They continued on together, a beast and seven spirits now, and as they drew closer to Oakmont and the House of Red Tears, more would join their ranks – Delora, Reyna, Weston…. All of them with a single shared goal: to stop the second Incarnation from succeeding—

—and to make Caprice and Ethan suffer as much as possible in the process.

★   ★   ★

Caprice went to the Repository by herself this time. If Axton had known what she planned to do, he would've tried to stop her, and she might've let him. There was an excellent chance that this would fail spectacularly and result in her death, or worse, but she could see no other recourse. If the Lord of the Feast was ever to be born, she had to take the risk. She was afraid – something she would never admit to anyone in this world, including Axton – but she hadn't done everything she had over the last decade to turn aside from the path now. She was Caprice Fucking Linton, and she had a god to create.

When the elevator opened on the subbasement, she stepped out and the antechamber's fluorescent lights activated. The air here felt colder than usual, and the runes and sigils etched into the Repository's iron door seemed to be glowing faintly. Before she could lose her nerve, she stepped forward, spoke the words that would allow her to pass through the Repository's wardspells unharmed, then unlocked the door. She drew in a deep breath, pulled the door open, and stepped inside.

As usual, the light from the antechamber failed to penetrate the Repository, and she found herself surrounded by darkness. She waited and within moments soft white pinpoints of light began to glow all around her as the Gathered manifested. The specks grew larger, joined, formed featureless humanoid shapes. The wraiths flowed through the air like ethereal swimmers moving through invisible water, slowly at first, then with increasing speed. They whirled around Caprice, and she felt like a small fish surrounded by a school of hungry sharks. The protective spells that prevented the Gathered from immediately attacking anyone who entered the Repository would only keep them at bay for so long, so she needed to work fast.

She wished she had *The Book of Depravity* to guide her, but it had been lost in the destruction of the Shardlow mansion. She had acquired other occult tomes over the years, but none as powerful, and none contained spells designed to accomplish what she hoped to do here now. She would have to wing it, and when it came to conducting magic, improvising was dangerous as hell.

Enough stalling, she thought.

She raised her arms, hands up, palms outward, and began.

"You who have been freed from the shackles of mortality, heed me! You can see many things which are hidden from the living, and I command you to use that sight to aid me now. My niece and nephew hid two of the Lord's parts from me, and I desire to learn their location. You are in the presence of the Lord—" she gestured to the recessed area in the wall that contained the eyeless, brainless head, "—and thus you are connected to the great one. Use that connection to trace the parts I seek and tell me where I might find them! Tell me what I need to know to succeed!"

The Gathered didn't respond at first, and Caprice thought she'd failed to reach them. But then the wraiths coalesced, merged into a single glowing form, its light so intense that Caprice was forced to shield her eyes. A thin tendril extruded from the mass and stretched toward the Lord's head. The tip of the tendril curved down into the skull cavity, and the eye sockets blazed with light. The tendril emerged from the Lord's mouth, streaked toward Caprice, and stabbed her forehead. She felt as if a metal spike had been driven into her mind, and she let out a cry of pain. An image appeared in her brain, row after row of storage units. She saw a sign that said *Stronghold Self-Storage,* and then she saw a number: *342.* She heard a word whispered in her ears. *Collier....* Other images flashed through her mind, ones she sensed were unconnected to the storage unit. A small nondescript building with a plain white door and three people walking toward it. There were two words on the door, painted in black letters. The words were blurry at first, but after a moment they came into focus.

Caprice grinned in triumph. She'd gotten more than she'd bargained for! She'd bade the spirits tell her what she needed to know to be successful, and they'd not only given her the information she'd come for, they'd given her more. She needed to leave and call Ethan back so he—

She felt the icy tendril drill deeper into her brain, into her very soul, and she screamed in agony. She heard a chorus of voices echo within the stone chamber then, speaking as one.

You Gathered us, now we Gather you. We will tear the spirit from your body and use you as our plaything. Pain is different for beings such as us. So much more intense than the merely physical, and there are so many new levels to experience…. We're going to enjoy introducing you to them all.

Caprice felt energy draining from her body, and she knew the wraiths were killing her. If she couldn't find a way to break free from them in the next few moments, she knew she was a dead woman, and she had no doubt the spirits would make good on their promise to hurt her in ways that she couldn't yet conceive of. The pain spread throughout her body, and she found it almost impossible to think. She tried to concentrate past the agony and search her mind for a spell that would allow her to repel the Gathered's attack, but she couldn't focus. She continued to weaken, and she knew she was going to die. The Incarnation would not be fulfilled, and the Lord of the Feast would never come into being. She had failed, and the Omniverse was doomed to suffer slowly as the Gyre devoured it one subatomic particle at a time over the course of a trillion-trillion years.

"I'm so sorry," she whispered, voice faint and thin. "I tried…."

The Gathered laughed with malignant glee, but as Caprice's awareness dwindled, she caught a flash of movement in her peripheral vision, and she heard Axton shout her name.

★   ★   ★

She returned to consciousness in the elevator, Axton's arm around her waist, holding her up. She felt so small, so frail.

"What..." she began, but was unable to complete the thought.

"I tried to use the elevator, but when it took too long to come up, I realized it had been stopped at the subbasement. Only you and I have reason to go there, so I went down to the Repository to see if there had been a security breach of some kind. I found you lying on the floor, the Gathered all around you. I picked you and carried you out of there. The Gathered tried to stop me, but I made it out. What the fuck were you *thinking*, Caprice? You almost died!"

The elevator reached the basement level where the living quarters were, and when the door opened, Axton helped her out of the car. She wanted to walk on her own, but she wasn't strong enough yet. She allowed Axton to take her to her room, and once there, she motioned for him to put her in the chair next to her bed.

Axton stood close by, clearly concerned.

"You should really lie down, Caprice. You need to rest, regain your...your strength."

There was something about the way Axton was looking at her that she didn't like, but she couldn't figure out what it was. It didn't matter right then. She needed to get the information she'd learned to Ethan. She reached inside her suit jacket and pulled out her phone. Her hands felt too stiff and achy to operate the device, so she handed it to Axton.

"Text Ethan. Tell him Stronghold Self-Storage in Collier, unit 342. He'll know what it means."

Axton started to do so, and as he worked her phone, she looked down at her hands to see why they hurt so. At first, she didn't understand what she saw. The hands weren't hers – they couldn't be! The finger joints were swollen, skin liver-spotted and paper-thin, and they shook with small, constant tremors. They were the hands of an old woman, one in her eighties or even nineties. She reached up with one of those trembling hands and touched her cheek, found the skin soft, saggy, wrinkled. She understood then what had happened. The Gathered had drained her life energy, just as theirs had been absorbed after their deaths and transferred down to the Repository. Axton had pulled her out of there before the wraiths had been able to drain her completely, but not before they'd turned her into a crone.

She started laughing then, the sound a strained cackle. Fuck those ghosts! She was still alive, and she'd gotten the information Ethan needed. Soon the Lord would walk the face of this world, and even the dead would tremble in its presence.

"Also, tell him not to hurt Kate, that we need to have representatives from both sides of the family during the Incarnation and she should be present during the rite."

Axton frowned. "That's not precisely true."

"No." She tried to stifle a yawn but it came out anyway. "But I can't very well tell him the complete truth, can I?"

"Point taken." Axton tapped on the phone screen for a few moments, then said, "Text sent." Instead of returning Caprice's phone to her, he put it on the nightstand next to her bed.

She looked at the phone. Her eyelids were drooping, and it was all she could do to keep them open. Wasn't there one more thing she was supposed to tell Ethan, an additional bit of information that she'd acquired from the Gathered? Something about a small building with a white door? She was so very tired, though, and she couldn't remember the details. Maybe they would come to her later.

"Thank you. Now, if you wouldn't mind, could you help me to the bed?" She yawned again. "I could use a nap."

★   ★   ★

"That's it."

Kate pulled the Camry up to unit 342, parked, and cut the engine. Stronghold Self-Storage was an outdoor facility, and all the units looked alike – ugly rectangular orange doors set in long, flat-roofed buildings without much space between them. The car fit in the aisle with room to open the doors on each side of the vehicle, but just barely. Haksaw sat in the passenger seat next to her, hugging the torso tight to his body, as if he feared it might somehow try to escape him.

If anyone had told Kate this morning that by late afternoon she'd be riding around with a necrophiliac serial killer sitting next to her, she'd have told them to lay off the drugs for a while. She wasn't sure why she'd come to accept Haksaw's presence so easily. Maybe it was because the whole day had been crazy since Tressa had given her the Lord's eyes and charged her with collecting the rest of the god's parts before Ethan did. Maybe she was in shock from having lost four family members in the course of only a few hours, and she wasn't thinking straight. Maybe it was because she came from an extended family of cultists who worked with magic tomes that had titles like *The Book of Depravity*. Or maybe it was a combination of all these things. Whatever the reason, Haksaw was, for the moment, a necessary evil – even if she wasn't yet sure *why* he was necessary. That didn't mean she trusted him, though.

Her stomach gurgled loudly. She hadn't eaten anything since breakfast this morning and it was close to dinnertime now. She might've picked up something at a drive-thru along the way but breathing in Haksaw's horrific body odor during the drive to Collier had made it impossible for her to seriously consider eating. She doubted she'd be able to keep anything down. Hell, the way she felt right now she never wanted to even think about food again.

Lee will never get this stench out, she thought.

Tears threatened then. She'd done her best not to think about her argument with Lee while she'd been driving, but she'd kept her phone on the seat beside her in case they called or texted. But they hadn't. She wondered if she'd ever hear from them again.

Of course, you will. They'll need to get the car back eventually.

Maybe they'd be able to talk things out then. She hoped so. But right now she didn't have time to worry about her relationship. She had work to do.

"Are you okay?" Haksaw asked.

"Hmm? Oh, yeah, I'm all right. Just thinking."

"About your friend. Don't worry. The torso says you'll be together at the end."

At the end. Kate didn't like the sound of that.

"It also tells me that there *are* other parts inside this unit. It's very excited to be close to them again." Haksaw patted the torso's back. "Be patient, love. They'll be here soon."

Kate didn't sense the parts that Reyna and Weston had stored here. Even this close to the torso, she only felt a faint echo of the pain she'd once experienced when in the presence of one of the Lord's parts. She supposed she was getting used to it or maybe being in the proximity of the parts was changing her somehow. She didn't want to think about that, so she opened the car door and got out. A moment later, so did Haksaw. He arranged the torso on the passenger seat and buckled the safety belt around it to keep it in place.

"I'll be close by," he said, then closed the door and walked over to join Kate. "So now what? We just unlock the door, roll it open, take the arm and leg, and leave?"

"Seems too easy, doesn't it?"

Kate removed the key from around her neck. It looked ordinary enough. She'd had to use it in order to get the facility's security gate to open, and presumably all she needed to do now was insert it into the lock on the door, turn it, and voila! Access would be granted. But there had to be more to it than that. Reyna had said that she and Weston had placed wardspells on the unit to protect the arm and leg. What if she needed something more than the key to deactivate them? Thinking of her cousins almost started her crying, but she told herself that she couldn't give in to sorrow right now. She needed to stay strong and ensure their sacrifice wasn't wasted.

You also need to be careful, she thought. Once the door was open — assuming they managed to open it — Haksaw would be able to get at the arm and leg. He hadn't tried to take the Lord's eyes from her when she'd shown them to him earlier, but that didn't mean he hadn't wanted them. He might've been biding his time, waiting for the perfect opportunity to take them. And once he added the arm and leg to his collection, he would be well on his way to having a complete set. He claimed the torso spoke to him, at least in some fashion. What if it *wanted* to join with the other parts and become the Lord of the Feast again? It could be manipulating Haksaw into acquiring the rest of its pieces, and since the man was a killer, Kate doubted he'd hesitate to murder her if she stood in his way. Now she really wished Lee was here. She would've felt safer knowing they had her back.

Reyna hadn't given her any special instructions on how to use the key, maybe because there hadn't been time, but maybe because none were required. She hoped it was the latter.

"You might want to stay back," she told Haksaw. "Just in case."

The man smiled, displaying his rotten teeth. "Don't have to. Nothing connected with my love would ever hurt me."

"I hope you're right."

She stepped up to the door, inserted the key into the lock, and then – after hesitating only a second – turned it. There was a soft *click*, but that was all. No shrieking alarms sounded, no mystic defense systems activated. Evidently Reyna had enchanted the key so that when it was used, the defenses were deactivated. Kate removed the key from the lock, put it around her neck again, then bent down to grip the door handle. The door had been closed a long time, and she expected it to be hard to open, but it rolled upward smoothly and with minimal effort on her part. The unit was empty except for a pair of towel-wrapped objects lying in the middle of the concrete floor. She felt a twinge of pain in her head, not severe, but enough to let her know that she'd found what she'd come here for: the Lord's right arm and right leg.

She started forward but then she felt a hand come down on her shoulder.

This is it, she thought. *He's attacking me.*

She spun around, ready to defend herself – although she had no idea how she might do so – but Haksaw made no threatening move toward her. He wasn't even looking at her. Instead, he was looking into the storage unit.

"The corners," he said.

She turned back to the unit. At first she didn't know what he was talking about, but then she saw it: thick shadows clustered in the corners, and the longer she looked at them, the more she realized there was something wrong. The shadows were moving.

"What *is* that?" she said.

"Something bad," Haksaw said.

No shit.

The shadows flowed out of the corners like thick black liquid and moved toward the storage unit's entrance, taking on shape, separating, becoming....

"Rats," Kate said.

Not ordinary ones, though. These were the size of small dogs, with prominent, almost tusk-like teeth, and their eyes blazed with burning crimson light. They glided toward the wrapped bundles – the arm and leg, Kate assumed – and surrounded them. The creatures fixed their baleful gazes on the humans that dared to invade their territory and hissed. The creatures didn't move to attack, though, and for this Kate was grateful.

"They don't like the light," Haksaw said. "That's why they're not coming at us."

It made sense. This was likely the first time in almost a decade that unit 342 had been opened. These things weren't used to light. Good thing, too. Kate didn't know whether she and Haksaw could've made it back to the Camry before the rats could swarm over them.

"Have you ever seen rats like these before?" Kate asked.

"Yeah, in the Cannery. When things live too close to Shadow for too long, they change, you know?"

Evidently that was also true for things that lived near the Lord's body parts. She glanced at Haksaw. He'd had the Lord's torso in his possession for years, and from what she'd seen, he handled it constantly. What changes had it caused in him?

As long as she and Haksaw remained out here in the sunlight, they'd be safe, and it would be several hours before the sun started to go down. The shadow rats would be confined to the storage unit until then, which was good, but Kate didn't see how she and Haksaw could get at the Lord's arm and leg while the creatures guarded them, which was bad.

"How do people in the Cannery deal with creatures like these?"

"We stay the hell away from the fucking things," Haksaw said. "But when we can't, we bring the light to them."

He walked to the Camry's passenger side, opened the door, reached past the torso, took hold of the rearview mirror, and yanked. The mirror snapped off easily, and he withdrew his arm, shut the door, and returned to Kate. She smiled as he handed the mirror to her.

"Smart."

She looked up to check the sun's position, then she experimented with the mirror, turning it one way then another to see which position was best to catch and reflect its rays. The rats hissed in anger and fear when the reflected beam came close, and when it finally struck some of them, they squealed in pain and fled toward the back of the unit, smoke curling from their ebon hides. She moved the mirror around, directing the beam at the other rats with similar results. The problem was that once the beam moved away from where the rats had been, they swiftly returned. She moved the mirror faster, trying to drive away all the rats and make them stay away, but it was no good. Smoking hides or not, they always returned to the arm and leg in the middle of the floor and clustered around them, hissing louder.

"Looks like I've managed to piss them off, but that's about it."

"One of us will have to stay out here and work the mirror while the other goes in and gets the parts. We won't be able to make the shadow rats leave the unit – they're too addicted to being near the arm and leg's power – but if we're fast enough, we can keep them at bay so we can liberate the parts."

"*If* we're fast enough."

"You're young and can run faster than I can," Haksaw said, "so you should go in."

He held out his hand for the mirror, but Kate didn't hand it to him right away.

"How do I know I can trust you to keep the light shining on the rats? This would be an excellent opportunity to get rid of me. Then you'd have the right arm and leg, the eyes, *and* the torso."

Haksaw gave her an exaggerated hurt look that would've been comical if the circumstances had been different.

"I can't believe you would say such a thing!"

"Right. *I'll* stay out here and *you* go inside."

"How do I know *I* can trust *you*? You want the torso. Don't deny it; I can feel it. You could just as easily kill me, then *you'd* have all the parts."

Kate wanted to tell him that he was wrong, that she'd never hurt anyone before, and she didn't intend to start now. But her cold practical side wasn't so sure. Haksaw was a killer, not some innocent who'd gotten swept up in all this. Who knew how many more people he might kill before he finally died? By killing him here and now, she'd be saving the lives of his future victims. While the rats were devouring his body, she'd be able to get the arm and leg, and exit the storage unit before the creatures could attack her. Then she'd close the door and drive off with her two prizes – three, if you counted the torso – and let the rats finish their meal in peace.

Her thoughts must've shown on her face, or perhaps it was a case of takes one to know one, because Haksaw smiled and his eyes glimmered with darkness.

"I like the way you think, Kate."

Horrified and ashamed, she thrust away all thoughts of killing Haksaw. She may have been born a Shardlow, but that didn't mean she had to behave like one.

"Looks like we have a stalemate here," Kate said.

"Looks like," Haksaw agreed. He didn't sound upset about it, though. If anything, he sounded amused.

"I guess it's a good thing I showed up then."

Kate and Haksaw turned to see Lee walking toward them. Kate wanted to play it cool, but she was so happy to see them that she ran to them, threw her arms around them, and gave them a big kiss. When she pulled away, Lee laughed.

"You weren't supposed to do that until *after* I said I'm sorry."

"How'd you get here?"

"Took an Uber then climbed over the outside fence." Lee glanced into the open storage unit and frowned. "What the hell are *those* things?"

"Shadow rats," Kate said. "And they'd rather we didn't take their friends away. They don't like light, so we were going to reflect a beam into the unit and scare them away from the parts."

"Is that my rearview mirror?" Lee asked.

"We needed it," Haksaw said.

Lee shot the killer a dirty look but didn't reply.

"We were just about ready to try it," Kate said.

"Now that there's three of us, it'll be a lot easier," Haksaw said. "I can shine the beam inside, and each of you can run in and grab a body part."

"I don't think so," Kate said. "Lee can work the mirror while you and I go in."

Haksaw looked at Lee doubtfully. "I don't know...."

"Lee won't let the rats get at you. There's too great a risk that they'd end up getting me, too."

Haksaw thought for a moment, then smiled.

"Makes sense. But I'm only doing this because the torso wants to be with the rest of its family. Don't get me wrong, I like you. You have a lovely torso of your own." Haksaw looked at Kate like he was imagining sawing off her limbs, and she shivered. "But all I care about is getting those parts out of there. Understand?"

"It's every woman or serial killer for themselves. Got it."

"You know," Lee said, "this would be safer if we used fishing poles. We could shoot a sunbeam in there to drive off the rats, cast our lines, hook the towels, and pull the arm and the leg out."

"It's a good idea," Kate said, "but I don't think we have time to run to a sporting goods store and buy some. Ethan is going to show up here probably sooner rather than later, so we need to get those parts out now. Unless you happen to have a couple fishing poles in your trunk...."

"I'm afraid not. Okay, so it's the mirror by itself then. Let me practice with it a few times."

Lee stepped closer to the entrance, and as Kate had done before them, they tilted the mirror at different angles to learn the best method of reflecting sunlight onto the shadow rats. After much angry hissing and scratching of rodent claws on concrete as the creatures fled and returned, fled and returned, Lee announced that they were ready.

"Stay close to the sides of the unit until you're ready to grab the parts," they said. "That way you won't block the beam any more than you have to."

Kate nodded, then she looked at Haksaw.

"Ready?"

Haksaw grinned. "On your mark...."

Kate couldn't help grinning back. "Get set...."

Lee got into position and raised the mirror.

But before any of them could act, the roar of a car engine came from the direction of the gate, followed by the sound of crashing metal. Someone had broken into the facility, and Kate didn't have to guess who.

Ethan had arrived.

CHAPTER THIRTEEN

"Remember, we can't hurt Kate," Ethan said.

"Why is that again?" Mrs. No asked.

"Because both sides of the family have to be present during the Incarnation."

Ethan was merely repeating what his aunt had texted him. He didn't understand why this should be so, and he hoped No wouldn't question him further.

"I don't really get magic," Mr. Yes said.

That makes two of us, Ethan thought.

As they approached Stronghold Self-Storage, Yes pressed the accelerator to the floor.

"Think we can break through the gate?" he asked, grinning.

No grinned back. "It'll be fun to find out."

Ethan grabbed hold of the back of No's seat to brace himself. He really hated working with these two.

Yes swung the Mercedes into Stronghold's driveway, then gripped the steering wheel tight as the car raced toward the metal gate. Ethan was certain that the gate would hold and the Mercedes' front end would crumple like tissue paper, but one teeth-grinding impact later, the gate burst open and they were in.

"I'll be damned," Yes said. "I didn't think that would work."

"Live and learn, love," No said.

"Remember, we're looking for unit 342," Ethan said.

"Row three, unit forty-two," Yes said. "Got it."

The numbers were prominently displayed on the end of each row, and Yes quickly found Number Three. He turned the Mercedes into the aisle, and Ethan saw the silver Camry – the one he'd watched drive away from High Strangeness – parked near an open storage unit. He grinned.

Gotcha! he thought.

As Yes raced toward the Camry, Ethan saw three people standing near the open unit. Was that Kate? She looked so different, but…yes, he saw the little girl he used to know in the shape of her face and the color of her hair. He felt an unexpected pang of sadness upon seeing her. They'd been close once, best friends, really. And now they were on different sides of a small-scale war whose outcome would determine the fate of all who lived. Life sure was weird sometimes.

Ethan didn't recognize the other two people.

"Hey, that's probably Haksaw!" Yes said. "What the hell is he doing here?"

"Who cares?" No said. "The Gods of Blood and Death have smiled upon us this day, sweetie. If Haksaw is here, so's the torso."

Ethan was elated. Once they were finished here, he would have the Lord's left and right arms, the right leg, the eyes, and the torso – and of course, Caprice had the head in the Repository. That meant he'd only have the left leg and the brain to retrieve. Easy-peasy.

Earlier, he'd slipped his two knives into the storage pocket on the back of No's seat. He drew them now and gripped their handles tight.

"Pull up behind the Camry," he said, "and let's get this over with."

*   *   *

With a sinking feeling, Kate watched as the Mercedes – its front end badly dented – parked by Lee's car. She was acutely aware that they were armed only with a broken rearview mirror, and although she'd never held a gun in her life, let alone fired one, she wished she had one now.

"What are we going to do?" she asked.

"Stay quiet and don't move," Lee said. Before Kate could ask what they intended to do, Lee began walking toward the Mercedes.

"Don't!" She started after Lee, but Haksaw grabbed hold of her arm and stopped her.

"There's a scent on Lee," he said. "Like Shadow but not Shadow. I don't know what it is, but there's more to that one than meets the eye."

"Let me go!" She struggled to pull free of Haksaw's grip, but the man was too strong. All she could do was watch Lee approach the Mercedes and hope her partner wasn't throwing away their life for nothing.

Three people emerged from the vehicle – a man and a woman wearing suits and holding handguns, and a younger man in a white T-shirt armed with a pair of knives. Ethan was ten years older than when she'd last seen him, but she recognized him right away. The thing that had changed about him the most was his expression. She remembered him as a normal kid, smiling, laughing, joking. This Ethan's face was expressionless, eyes cold as the grave. God, what had Caprice done to make him like this? She had no idea who the other two people were, but she didn't need to know their identities to recognize they were dangerous. It was in their hard, calculating gazes and the relaxed way they held their weapons, as if the guns were part of their bodies. She noticed the tip of the woman's left pinky finger was missing, the wound uncovered. What was up with that?

Lee stopped when they were within five feet of Ethan and the suits. The latter trained their guns on Lee, but they didn't fire.

"Who are you?" Ethan asked. "I like to know the name of the person I'm about to kill."

"I'm Lee Taylor."

Kate was impressed by how calm Lee sounded. They were obviously tense, but not pants-wetting terrified, like she was right now.

Lee went on. "I'm an Observer for the Unbroken Court, and I invoke my right to Aequus."

Ethan frowned. He looked to the two suits and they shrugged. Then he turned back to Lee.

"What the hell does that mean?"

"It's Latin. It means fair, balanced, equitable. Although I suppose in this instance, the best translation would be *level playing field*."

From above came the sound of movement, and everyone looked up to see what was causing it. Everyone but Lee. They kept their gaze focused on Ethan and his two companions.

Figures leaned over the edge of the rooftops on either side. There were a dozen in all, men and women, different ages and races, all dressed normally in everyday casual clothes. They said nothing, but their expressions were grim. Then one of them – a big guy in a loud Hawaiian shirt – waved a hand, and the blue-suits' guns and Ethan's knives jerked out of their hands and flew upward. Several other knives jumped out of the suits' clothes and streaked upward to join the other weapons. People on the roof caught the deadly objects as they ascended and then withdrew. The man in the Hawaiian shirt gave Lee a stern look before he went.

"Who the fuck were *they*?" Ethan said.

Lee turned back to look at Kate. "That's all the help they're going to give us. We're on our own now."

Kate had no idea what had just happened, but she understood that Lee had somehow given them a fighting chance, and they couldn't afford to waste it.

"Come on, Haksaw! It's time to do what you do best."

"Take care of my love?"

Kate didn't bother explaining. Either the man would figure it out or he wouldn't. She started running toward Ethan and the suits, and as she passed Lee, she said, "After this is over, you and I are going to have a talk!"

Lee started running alongside her. "Agreed!"

Ethan remained standing and watched them come. The suits, however, weren't so patient. They ran forward to meet Kate and Lee, savage grins on their faces, as if they weren't upset about the loss of their weaponry, but were actually grateful for it. *They're born killers,* Kate realized, and they didn't need guns or knives to do their work. It suddenly looked like a frontal assault wasn't the best idea she'd ever had. A thought came to her then.

The woman's wounded finger is the most logical first point of attack.

When the black-suited woman reached her, she tried to drive a knifehand strike into the side of Kate's neck with her right hand. But

Kate, moving faster than she ever had before, ducked, grabbed hold of the woman's left wrist, pulled it to her mouth, and bit down on her wounded finger close to where it joined the hand. The woman screamed and reflexively tried to jerk her hand away, but Kate bit down harder, her teeth cutting through flesh and hitting bone. The hot metallic taste of blood filled her mouth, and for a moment she feared she might vomit, but then she thought, *It's just blood. It can't hurt you, but the woman whose body it's flowing from can.* She blocked the blood-taste from her mind, and thrust the heel of her hand upward toward the woman's face. It collided solidly with her nose and made an extremely satisfying crunching sound. Blood sprayed from the woman's nose, and she made a thick, liquidy *gah* sound. She pulled backward, and the rest of her pinky finger came off with a tiny *pop-crack*, the severed digit remaining in Kate's mouth like a cigarette made of flesh and bone. Kate turned her head and spit the finger onto the ground.

While the black-suited woman was distracted, Kate risked a quick glance to see how Lee was doing. The answer: surprisingly well. As far as Kate knew, Lee had never taken any martial arts classes – they'd never mentioned doing so, anyway – but now they were blocking the blue-suited man's attack strike for strike. Lee had an expression of fierce concentration on their face, but there was absolutely no sign of fear in their eyes. This was a side of Lee Kate had not only never seen but never suspected existed. She had two simultaneous and very different reactions to this. She had never really known Lee at all, and she couldn't believe how hot they looked kicking ass.

Bright light flashed behind Kate's eyes as something hard collided with her left jaw. It took her a split second to realize that the black-suited woman had punched her. She took a couple stagger-steps to the side and stood there, unable to believe what had happened. She'd never been hit before, and she was as shocked by the experience as she was by the actual pain of the blow. The woman – blood streaming from her nose and wild fury burning in her eyes – brought her bleeding hand around for a second knifestrike, going for the neck once again. Kate began to bring her arm up, hoping to bat the woman's hand away, but as soon as she started, she knew she wouldn't be fast enough. Could the woman kill her with a single blow? Given how galactically pissed off she was, Kate thought she probably could. She was surprised by how little the prospect bothered her. If she died, at least she wouldn't have to deal with her family's fucked-up legacy anymore.

Then Haksaw stepped forward and slashed his hand down toward the black-suited woman's. She cried out in pain, blood sprayed, and Kate saw the woman no longer had any fingers on her left hand, just her thumb. The woman stared at the four bleeding stumps with shocked disbelief. Haksaw held up his hands, and Kate saw that lines of serrated bone now thrust outward from the pinkies to the wrist. They were moving rapidly back and forth, making *chkk-chkk-chkk-chkk-chkk* sounds.

Haksaw grinned. "Look what my love gave me."

Kate had wondered if long-term exposure to the torso had mutated Haksaw. Now she had her answer.

Kate realized then that she didn't know what Ethan was doing. Was he readying an attack? No, he was standing by the Mercedes, not doing anything, just watching.

He's waiting for his moment, a voice inside her that both was and wasn't hers said.

Lee and Mr. Blue-Suit were still fighting, neither able to gain an advantage over the other. As they'd fought, they'd moved in front of the open storage space, and they now stood only a few feet from its edge. The shadow rats had gathered close by, coming as near to the sunlight as they dared, crimson eyes shining with anticipation. Kate decided to do the little monsters a favor. She ran toward Mr. Blue-Suit and shoved him as hard as she could. He stumbled away from Lee and across the boundary between outside the storage space and inside. That was all it took. The shadow rats swarmed, engulfing him in a surging, clawing, biting mass of darkness, and he screamed. The black-suited woman, her wounded hand pressed against her side to staunch the bleeding, cried out as if she were being eaten alive as well.

Kate stood next to Lee, watching in fascinated disgust as the rats did their grisly work. She caught a flash of movement in her peripheral vision then, and her first thought was that Ethan had decided to attack while they were distracted. She was half right. He *had* chosen to act, but instead of coming at them, he ran past and into the storage unit.

He's going for the arm and leg, the voice said.

Kate didn't hesitate. She ran after him.

By the time she caught up to him, he had already picked up one of the cloth-wrapped bundles and was reaching for the other. Kate kicked his hand away before he could grab it, and he glared at her. He shifted his grip on the limb – the leg, she thought – and for a moment she thought he was going to use it like a club and hit her with it. But then a shadow rat came racing toward them. Ethan stomped on the vermin before it could attack either of them, and it popped like a balloon filled with foul-smelling black pus. Kate looked and saw that Mr. Blue-Suit – who no longer screamed – had fallen to the floor. Rats still covered him, but evidently there wasn't enough left for all of them, and some were beginning to leave his body and look around for new prey, and Kate and Ethan were prime candidates.

Kate lunged for the arm and snatched it up before Ethan could get it. They glared at each other for a moment, and then both turned and ran like hell for the storage unit's entrance. Kate heard the frantic scratching of claws on concrete, and she knew the rest of the shadow rats were coming for them. Despite everything Ethan had done, she hoped he would make it. He was a killer, but despite that, he was her cousin, and in memory of the boy he had been – if nothing else – she wanted him to survive.

They ran into the sunlight, several of the shadow rats close on their heels. The instant the little bastards were outside the storage unit, they squealed, writhed in pain, and then evaporated. The rest of the rats stopped short of the entrance, red eyes glittering with inhuman malice. Kate looked for Mr. Blue-Suit, but there was no sign of him, not a drop of blood, nor a scrap of cloth. The rats had devoured every bit of him.

"You fucking bitch!"

The black-suited woman came running at Kate, wounded hand still pressed to her side. Her face was a mask of hate – eyes wild, teeth bared

— and although she held no weapons, Kate knew the woman would kill her if she got hold of her, claw out her eyes with her good hand, rip out her jugular with her teeth. But Lee and Haksaw stepped in front of Kate. Lee fell into a defensive posture while Haksaw held up his saw hands, the blades ratcheting back and forth. Black-Suit showed no sign of slowing, but when she came in range of Ethan, he swung the leg and struck her on the side of the head. Her eyes rolled white, her legs folded beneath her, and she dropped to the ground. She was still breathing, but Kate didn't think she'd be getting up anytime soon.

Ethan looked at Kate. "It's good to see you, Katie-Bug."

"Wish I could say the same."

Ethan ignored the jab. "Come with me. Caprice would love to see you."

"She'd love to take the parts of the Lord I have," Kate said.

"True. But don't you want to see the Lord be born? Don't you want it to relieve the interminable suffering of the Omniverse? Sometimes at night, I lie awake, and I think I can hear the fabric of existence screaming as it's ripped apart, its tattered pieces slowly devoured by the Gyre. Reality is in *pain*, Kate. You must sense it."

Kate wanted to tell him that she didn't sense shit, but somewhere in the back of her mind, she thought she might — faint echoes of despairing voices, trillions of them, hurting and crying for release.

"I'm not a killer," Kate said.

Ethan grinned. "Mr. Yes would beg to differ, I think. Except he's in the bellies of a couple dozen shadow rats and isn't in a position to speak right now."

Everything had happened so fast that it hadn't had time to hit her yet, but Kate realized Ethan was right. She *was* a killer now. She might not have planned what she'd done to the man — to Mr. Yes — but she'd known what would happen to him when she'd knocked him into the storage unit. He would've killed her if he'd gotten the chance, she was sure of it, but that didn't make her feel any better about what she'd done.

You did what you had to do, a voice inside her said. *It was the only logical move.*

"We wouldn't be killing the Omniverse for the fun of it, Kate – although I imagine it will be magnificently beautiful. We'd be killing out of mercy, out of love." Ethan looked at Haksaw. "Surely you understand. You kill one person at a time. Can you imagine what it would be like to kill everyone everywhere?"

"If everyone was gone, there'd be no new torsos born," Haksaw said. "That would be a tragedy."

Ethan rolled his eyes then looked at Lee. "There's no point trying to convince you, is there? The Unbroken Court has a reputation for being inflexible. Hence its name, right? Never once, in all its long existence, has it wavered from its duty. Admirable, if unimaginative."

Lee said nothing.

Ethan turned to Kate. "I don't suppose I can convince you to give me the parts you have."

"No. And you can't take them from me. The odds are not in your favor."

Ethan smiled. "Not at the moment, perhaps. But odds have a way of changing. See you soon, cousin."

Ethan turned and started walking to the Mercedes.

"What about your friend?" Kate asked.

"Mrs. No is no longer of any use to me. You can have her if you want."

He got in the car and started the engine. Given the damage done to the front when they'd rammed through the gate, Kate didn't know if it would start. The engine strained and whined, but it turned over, and he began backing the Mercedes away from the storage unit. When he reached the end of the aisle, he turned, put the car in drive, and pulled away.

"So that's Ethan," Lee said drily. "Nice guy."

Kate ignored them. She wanted to know what the hell the Unbroken Court was and how Lee was connected to it, but now was not the time for that conversation.

"What should we do about her?" She nodded toward Mrs. No. *What the hell kind of name is that?*

"We could toss her into the storage unit and let the shadow rats have her," Haksaw said.

Now that Ethan was gone and there was no longer a threat, his bone-saw blades had retracted into his hands.

Kate and Lee looked at Haksaw.

The man shrugged. "It's just an idea."

It's a good one too, the voice inside Kate said. *Once she's eliminated, she'll no longer be a threat.*

Kate wasn't sure.

You killed her boyfriend or husband or whatever. You saw how she reacted. She was devastated. You can bet that once she comes to, she's going to come after you — and she won't kill you easy. She'll want you to suffer. A lot.

Kate looked at the woman. She lay less than two feet from the storage unit's entrance. The shadow rats were clustered nearby, their beady red eyes fastened on her unmoving body, almost as if they were attempting to will her to wake up and crawl toward them.

"Don't do it," Lee said. "Don't go down that road."

Don't listen to them. You took your first step down that road when you killed Mr. Yes. The first step is always the hardest. The second will be easier, and it will prepare you to take the third and the fourth. Or do you really believe that you're going to be able to prevent the Incarnation happening without killing anyone else? You need to be ready, and killing Mrs. No will help get you there.

The reasoning was cold, but it seemed sound. She was almost convinced, but then the voice inside her said, *Besides, you're a Shardlow. Killing is in your blood.*

Kate stepped forward, pulled the storage door closed, and locked it. She had no idea what would happen to the shadow rats now that the Lord's arm and leg were gone. Would they find a way out of the unit and go off in search of prey or, without access to the residual power in the Lord's limbs, would they eventually fade away? She hoped for the latter.

"Let's go," Kate said. She didn't know how badly Mrs. No was hurt, but they couldn't afford to take the time to transport her to a hospital. After they left the facility, she'd call 911 and report a wounded woman at Stronghold Self-Storage, and then Mrs. No would be someone else's problem.

Lee put their hand on Kate's arm.

"Kate, I—"

"You're driving," Kate said, and started toward the Camry. A moment later Lee and Haksaw followed.

INTERLUDE

Right Leg

Elena Burton was four years old when the family German shepherd tried to kill her.

She was playing alone in the backyard, plucking dandelions and putting them into a small blue plastic bucket, while humming a tune she'd heard on *Sesame Street*. She enjoyed the warm feeling of sun on her skin, along with the green smell of grass and the rise and fall of cicada chittering. Mommy had told her that cicadas were big bugs that liked to sing, but while Elena liked the strange sounds they made, they didn't seem much like music to her. She was picking dandelions because she'd watched a cartoon yesterday where a bunny, who wore a cute blue dress and lived in an underground home with tiny furniture, went outside to pick pretty flowers that she later put in a vase on her dining table. *Doesn't this brighten up the place?* she'd said when she finished. Elena wasn't sure what *brighten up* meant, but the bunny had seemed so happy that Elena thought if she picked some flowers to put on her family's dining table, maybe her mom would be happy too. Mommy wasn't happy very often. She spent most of her time sitting in her chair in front of the TV, smoking menthol cigarettes and drinking Tab. She didn't say much, and when you tried to talk to her, she'd answer with one or two words, never taking her eyes off the TV screen. Elena's daddy drove a truck for his job, and sometimes she wondered if Mommy was so sad because Daddy was gone a lot, or if Daddy was gone a lot *because* Mommy was so sad. Maybe a little of both.

But if she could gather a lot of *really* pretty flowers, maybe Mommy would feel better, and then she might talk with Elena, maybe even *play* with her. Elena couldn't remember a time that Mommy hadn't sat in front of the TV, and sometimes she imagined Mommy starting out as a baby in that chair, growing into a kid, then a teenager, then a grown-up, all the while drinking soda and smoking one cigarette after another. But the flowers would change all that, Elena *knew* it. She just had to get a lot of them.

Their family had one pet – two, if you counted the mangy stray cat that prowled around their front door every morning, hoping for a handout. Tonya was a German shepherd who lived in the backyard, chained to a metal spike driven into the ground in front of a dilapidated doghouse. Tonya's house was positioned toward the back of the property, close to the chain-link fence that enclosed the backyard. She had two plastic bowls – one for water, one for food – and both of them were empty. Elena couldn't remember the last time she'd seen either of them full. She liked Tonya, but she was a little scared of her too. The dog wagged her tail whenever she saw Elena, but she was a big dog, and Elena was a little girl. Still, she couldn't leave Tonya without anything to eat or drink, could she?

She put her bucket down and started walking toward Tonya.

"Good girl," she said. "*Good* girl."

Elena had heard her mommy say these words when she approached Tonya, so she said them now too. She didn't know if Mommy was saying Tonya *was* good or reminding her to *be* good. Either way, speaking the words comforted her, made it easier for her to keep putting one foot in front of the other.

Tonya lay on the ground, watching Elena as she came. When Elena was within several feet of the doghouse, Tonya rose to her feet and continued watching, her tail wagging slowly, uncertainly.

"Good girl."

Elena reached the doghouse and bent down to pick up Tonya's bowls, and that's when the dog attacked.

In the future, whenever anyone would ask Elena about the incident, she'd claim that she didn't remember. But in truth, she remembered every second of it: Tonya knocking her down, getting tangled in the dog's chain, hot breath on her skin, growling loud in her ears, sharp teeth penetrating her flesh, tearing and ripping…. One thing she truly couldn't remember was how she got away from Tonya. One moment she was on the ground in front of the doghouse, screaming and bleeding, and the next she was in her mommy's arms, Mommy's tears falling onto her face.

Elena's daddy had Tonya *put down*, which she eventually figured out meant *killed*, and this made Elena very happy. The thought that Tonya was gone forever and would never come back sustained her through her time in the hospital as well as the dozen surgeries she suffered through to make her look normal again, although she never really did. When she was old enough to go to school, the kids called her Patches because her skin grafts were a slightly different color and texture than the rest of her face.

She kicked her first dog – a stray mutt that came up to her on the sidewalk when she was walking home from school – when she was six. She didn't kick it hard, just enough to send it running, but the feeling of power she experienced afterward was euphoric. She kicked the next dog harder, and the one after that even harder. If they didn't come close enough to kick, she'd throw things at them. Rocks, usually. Big ones.

In her twenties, she began treating the neighborhood dogs to chunks of raw meat laced with rat poison. It was an efficient – and painful – method of removing them, but nowhere near as satisfying as kicking them. She liked the solid feel of their bodies when her foot struck them, liked the way they yelped and gave her confused, betrayed looks as they fled. It was the closest to pure bliss she'd ever come.

One day when she was in her thirties, Elena – who worked as a loan officer at a local bank – went out for a walk during her lunch hour to get some fresh air. She had to be careful, though, as her skin grafts were sensitive to sunlight and burned easily. She was standing at a crosswalk, waiting for the light to change, when an elderly woman walked up, holding on to a leash with an ugly chihuahua on the other end. Elena sneered at the dog, but as much as she wanted to kick the little fucker, she couldn't do so in broad daylight with the owner standing right here.

Too bad. She faced forward once more and continued waiting for the light to tell her it was okay to cross. She felt something warm and wet on her ankle, and when she looked down, she saw the goddamned little rat-dog was pissing on her. She was so shocked that for a moment she could do nothing but watch as the chihuahua, one leg lifted, squirted a thin stream of urine onto her.

"Oh my god, I'm so sorry!"

The dog's owner sounded mortified, but she did nothing to stop her dog from peeing on Elena. Fury overwhelmed Elena – who sometimes in her own mind still thought of herself as Patches – and she bent down, yanked the leash from the older woman's hand, picked up the startled chihuahua, and hurled it out into the street. There was a *thump* as a van struck the dog in midair, and then another when the animal hit the asphalt. The older woman screamed, "My baby!" as the van screeched to a halt. The woman ran into the intersection toward the mangled and bloodied lump of meat that had been her dog, and Elena – still fuming – turned and began walking back toward the bank. Her walk was spoiled now, so she might as well get some work done, *after* she stopped in the restroom to wash the dog's pee off her foot.

"Excuse me."

The voice came from behind her, and Elena turned to see who had spoken. At first she thought it was going to be someone who'd witnessed her throw the chihuahua into traffic and wanted to make a federal case out of it. She intended to tell them to fuck the hell off if they didn't want to end up smacked by a van too. It was a man and a woman, both older than her, although not so old as the chihuahua's owner.

"I'm sorry," Elena said, "but I don't have time to—"

The man stepped forward and jammed a small black object against her neck. Electricity coursed through her body, and she spasmed uncontrollably. The woman caught her before she could fall, and together, she and the man carried Elena into an alley and behind a building. They then let go of her and she collapsed to the ground.

"I like dogs," the woman said.

"Me too," said the man.

Then they started kicking Elena, and they didn't stop until she was dead.

After that, they removed her right leg.

Her dog-kicking leg.

INTERLUDE

Right Arm

3:37 a.m.

Latoya Holmes sat on the couch, tears streaming down her face, pistol held in her right hand, the safety off. She didn't know if she could do it, but she knew she had to. It was only a matter of working up the courage. She wiped her eyes with her left hand, took several deep cleansing breaths, and then stood.

It's okay, it's going to be okay.

The house was quiet, the only sounds the ticking of the grandfather clock in the hall and the *whirr* of the refrigerator in the kitchen. Latoya mounted the stairs to the house's second level, and climbed them slowly, feeling each step give beneath her weight, listening to the wood's soft creaking. Her back gave a twinge of pain, and she winced, remembering how David had thrown her down these stairs yesterday evening, while Kathy and Johnnie stood at the top, sobbing and begging their daddy to stop hurting Mommy. He did as they asked, and left her lying at the bottom of the steps, half conscious and in pain, as he turned his attention on them.

She hadn't been able to get up for almost an hour, and she'd had to listen to the sounds of her husband striking their children the entire time. It had been hell for her, but she knew it had been far worse for the kids.

She and David started dating in high school. They'd both been fifteen, and back then he had been kind, gentle, and considerate. He listened to what she had to say – really listened – and just as importantly, he *heard* her. He valued her opinions and insights, and he never made her feel small or unimportant. He could get angry sometimes, sure, but only when someone treated her badly, and then he'd come down on them like the wrath of God. They had sex, of course, but David respected her. He never pressured her to do anything she didn't want to, and he always used a condom. Like a lot of high school kids, they'd drunk and used drugs, usually just at parties, but they were careful not to overindulge. David asked her to marry him the day after they graduated from high school, and she'd felt like the luckiest woman in the world. Of course she said yes.

That had been ten years ago.

Latoya didn't know when things had started to go wrong in their marriage. It occurred so slowly, bit by bit, that she hadn't been aware it was happening. No, that wasn't true. She'd known. She hadn't wanted to believe it, that's all. David leaving all the household chores to her. *I work* outside *the home, honey.* She did too, but that didn't seem to count. David coming home late from work a few nights a month. *I'm on salary. When the boss needs me to put in some extra hours, I gotta do it.* David sitting in front of the TV watching sports and ignoring the kids. *A guy needs to relax sometimes, okay? Stop fucking nagging me.* Money disappearing from their joint checking account until it was overdrawn. *I make money and that means I get to decide how to spend it.* Needle marks on his arms. *Those are just bug bites, baby. Maybe we should have an exterminator come over and check out the place.* The violence began with him grabbing her arm when he was angry, progressed to him wrapping his fingers around her hands and squeezing tight, from there to a tentative slap on the cheek, to a full-fledged flesh-stinging slap, and then ultimately to him hitting her with his fists, usually in places where the bruises wouldn't be visible when she was dressed. Once, she tried to talk him into counseling for his anger issues, but he'd beaten the hell out of her, and that was the last time she said anything about that. When he started beating the children, she intervened and took the punishment meant for them. Sometimes his rage would be satisfied then, and he'd leave the kids alone. Sometimes he wouldn't.

Try as she might, she couldn't determine the cause of his anger. They both had good jobs and a nice house in an upscale neighborhood. They had friends and supportive relatives, and they had two beautiful children. They had it all, so what the hell did David have to be so angry about? He'd once told her that his father had possessed a hair-trigger temper, although he'd never said anything about the man beating him, his siblings, or his mother. But she thought David's father must've been an abusive bastard and, whether through genetics or having witnessed his father's violent behavior up close and personal, David had become infected with it, and now his own family was paying the price.

But they wouldn't be paying it much longer.

She'd hoped to divorce David, had actually gone as far as to consult a lawyer. But when David had found out, he told her that if she continued pursuing divorce, he'd kill her, but not until after he'd killed Kathy and Johnnie first – and making her watch while he did it. Maybe it had been an empty threat, but she hadn't thought so, and she never spoke with the lawyer again.

When she reached the top of the stairs, she had a decision to make. Go to the kids' rooms first, or go to the bedroom she shared with David? If she started with one of the kids, the noise would wake David and alert him. He'd come rushing out of their bedroom to see what was happening, and she didn't know if she'd be able to fire on him when he came at her. He'd most likely yank the gun out of her hand, press the barrel to her forehead, and shoot.

She started toward the master bedroom.

She used a pillow as a silencer when she shot David so as to not wake the kids, and she did the same with each of them. Within the space of nine minutes, her family was gone, freed from the tyranny of David's anger. She hoped they could rest now, and if there was an afterlife, she hoped that one day they'd be able to forgive her for what she'd done.

She trudged back down the stairs, barely conscious of her actions. Her heart still beat and her lungs still breathed, but for all intents and purposes, she was already dead. She returned to the couch, flopped down on it, and sat there, staring at nothing. Her face, clothes, and hands were stippled with blood splatter, but she barely noticed.

People had funny attitudes toward suicide. She hadn't asked to be born, but once she had been, her life belonged to her. It was her choice how to use it, including ending it early if she wished. People called it the coward's way out, and maybe it was, but it wasn't easy, that was for damn sure. Her hand shook slightly as the brought the gun to her head and pressed the muzzle against her temple. She sat that way for a long time, finger on the trigger, staring off into space, unable to bring herself to fire. She was considering putting the gun down, calling the police, and telling them she'd killed her family. Let her spend the rest of her life rotting in a prison cell. But then, as if of its own volition, her finger tightened on the trigger. There was a split-second blast of thunder, and then she was gone.

★　　★　　★

"She really made a mess of this couch, didn't she?" Delmar said.

"I'd say. Shame. It was such a *nice* couch," Tressa said.

"Look at it this way, she's already done half our work for us."

"Considerate of her."

Delmar placed the edge of the bone saw against Latoya's upper right arm and began cutting.

CHAPTER FIFTEEN

Kate, Lee, and Haksaw were on the highway headed back to Oakmont, Kate driving the Camry. The right arm, still wrapped in cloth, sat on the backseat next to the jar with the eyes. The torso sat next to the passenger-side window, as if it wanted to look out at the passing scenery, and Haksaw sat in the middle of the seat, arm around the torso, smiling serenely.

"Let's see if I got this right," Kate said. "There are three basic powers in existence: Corrupters, Prolongers, and Balancers. The Unbroken Court prosecutes crimes committed by both Corrupters and Prolongers, which puts them in the Balancer camp."

Lee didn't take their eyes off the road as they answered. "Yes."

"The Court has agents all over the world, and they monitor Shadower activity. They're officially neutral, but if they feel they absolutely must intervene to protect the Balance between Life and Entropy, they will."

"Yes."

"And you're one of the Court's Monitors, and your assignment was to watch me."

"Yes. Because your family are Corrupters who nearly succeeded in Incarnating the Lord of the Feast. We were aware of what your family was doing, but when the rite failed, there was no need to take them into custody. Some had died, others had changed horribly, and the rest found themselves plagued by failure and regret, their lives in tatters. The Court deemed this punishment enough. Still, the decision was made to monitor your family, in case they ever tried to Incarnate the Lord of the Feast again, which is what Caprice is now doing."

"So our relationship wasn't real. I'm just a job to you."

"No! At first, monitoring you *was* only an assignment, but I fell in love with you."

"And when you realized you loved me, you told me the truth about who you really are and what you were assigned by the Court to do." Kate couldn't keep the bitterness she felt out of her voice.

"Monitors are strictly forbidden to reveal the truth about ourselves. Plus, I was afraid that once you found out the truth you wouldn't want to have anything to do with me. Your family had already been through enough weirdness. I didn't think you'd want to get mixed up in more."

Kate couldn't dispute that. She could've happily gone through the rest of her life without ever having to deal with Caprice and the Incarnation.

"You should have told me the truth," Kate insisted.

"You didn't tell me about your family. You didn't know that I already knew what they were and what they'd tried to do. You didn't tell me because you didn't want to scare *me* off."

Kate wanted to argue, to tell Lee that their situations were completely different. Except, were they? They'd both kept secrets from each other, held back on divulging details about their backgrounds.

"You said the Unbroken Court tries to remain neutral. So why did those other Monitors – I assume that's what they were – help us?"

"Yes, those were Monitors, except for the guy in the Hawaiian shirt. He's an Officer of the Court. And they helped us because I invoked the right to Aequus. If Monitors find themselves in a situation that's unbalanced—"

"Like going up against three armed killers when you have no weapons."

Lee nodded. "Exactly. When an Officer of the Court is presented with a request for Aequus, they have no choice but to grant it. But that is *all* the help they'll give, and you can only ask for Aequus a few times in your career. And you have to wait a long time between requests."

"So we can't count on the Court's help from here on out," Kate said.

"Correct." Lee smiled. "Hey, you said *we*."

"As of right now, you're on partner probation. If we manage to save the world – and survive – we can work out the details of our relationship then."

"Agreed."

"It's wonderful when lovers make up," Haksaw said.

Kate and Lee looked at each other and made *eeeww* faces.

They drove in silence for a time after that.

"So what's our next move, guys?" Haksaw said. "By my count, there's only one of the Lord's parts left to collect. Caprice has the head, I have the torso, you have the eyes and the right arm, and Ethan has the left arm and right leg. That leaves only the left leg. Unless the Lord was cut into more pieces than that."

"There's the brain," Kate said. "But I assume that's with the head." She looked at Lee. "Do you know of any more parts?"

Lee thought for a moment. "Seems like a complete list to me."

Kate frowned. That wasn't exactly a yes. She was about to ask Lee to elaborate, but then Haksaw said, "Ethan is probably going for the left leg now, assuming he knows where it is."

"Caprice has been working toward this for a decade," Lee said. "You can bet she knows exactly who in the family had which body part, which means Ethan is well on his way there now."

"I could use the eyes to try and find out where he's going," Kate said. "Maybe we can catch up to him and take the parts he has. I saw you fight back at the storage place, Lee. You've got some moves. And Haksaw has his mutant saw hands. We can take Ethan."

"There's a good chance he'll get hold of more weapons," Lee said. "Especially after he witnessed what Haksaw and I can do. Martial arts and handsaws are fine, but they aren't a match for a trained killer who's fully armed."

"*I'm* a trained killer," Haksaw said. He sounded as if he was pouting.

"Yes, you are," Lee said, "but you're a specialist. Ethan is a generalist. That gives him more options when it comes to fighting us."

"So what are you saying?" Kate asked. "That it's hopeless, that no matter what we do, Caprice and Ethan are going to win?"

"No. But our goal isn't to beat them, is it? It's to prevent the second Incarnation from happening. Caprice needs *all* the Lord's parts in order for the rite to succeed."

"What are you suggesting? That we take the parts we have and hide them somewhere?"

Lee shook their head. "If Caprice has gathered enough power to conduct the rite, she'd be strong enough to locate the parts, no matter how well we hid them."

"So we just keep driving for the rest of our lives, moving from one place to another, never stopping long enough for Caprice to get a fix on us?" Kate didn't like the idea of becoming a lifelong nomad, but if that's what it took to prevent the Incarnation from happening...

"That could work," Haksaw said. "Caprice will eventually die of old age, Ethan too, and then there will be no one left who knows about the Lord. The body parts would be useless then." Haksaw looked to the torso. "Oh, my love, I'm so sorry! I didn't mean that you're *completely* useless, just that no one would know how to use you to recreate the Lord of the Feast." Haksaw sighed. "Now I've hurt its feelings."

"As long as the parts exist, there will always be a chance someone who knows what they're doing will find them and finish the work Caprice started," Lee said.

"Could we take the parts we have to the Unbroken Court?" Kate asked. "Would they guard them?"

"Maybe...." Lee thought for a moment. "But the power the parts possess would be very tempting. Someone in the Court might try to tap into that power and use it for what they'd tell themselves was a good reason. But the power in the Lord's body parts is pure Corruption, and nothing good can come from it."

"What about the Prolongers you mentioned? Could some of them handle the parts without being tempted by them?"

"It's possible," Lee allowed, "but I wouldn't want to risk it. Anyone can be corrupted by power, no matter how pure their initial motives."

"So we're back to the place where there's nothing we can do and we're fucked," Kate said.

"There is one thing we could try," Lee said. "It won't be easy, and it'll be dangerous, but it might have a chance of working."

"Might." Kate sighed. "I guess that's better than no chance at all. What is it?"

"We could destroy the Lord's body parts."

"No!" Haksaw pulled the torso close to his chest and hugged it protectively.

"But they *can't* be destroyed," Kate said. "That's part of their magic."

"They can't be destroyed by *ordinary* means," Lee said. "But if you want to fight magic, you need bigger magic. In this case, the magic that created the Lord of the Feast in the first place."

"The book," Kate said. "The adults used a book to help them perform the rite of Incarnation."

"*The Book of Depravity*," Lee said. "Your family believed it was lost when the Shardlow mansion was destroyed, but I know where we might be able to find a copy."

"There's that *might* again," Kate said. "So you think that if the book has a rite for creating a god, it'll have one for destroying it too?"

"Possibly. If such a rite exists, we can use it to destroy the parts we have—" Lee glanced over their shoulder at Haksaw, "—or most of them, anyway. And as long as even one part of the Lord is missing...."

"The god can never come into being," Kate finished.

She thought about Lee's suggestion for several moments. There were a lot of uncertainties to the plan. What if they couldn't find the book? What if they found it, but it didn't contain a rite for destroying the Lord's parts? What if it *did* have such a rite but they couldn't understand how to perform it? Hell, what if it wasn't even written in English? But it beat the hell out of all the other plans they didn't have.

"Let's give it a try," Kate said.

"I was hoping you'd say that. It's why I started heading toward Oakmont. That's where the bookstore is."

"You mean Tainted Pages?" Haksaw said. He shuddered. "That place scares me."

Great, Kate thought. *We're headed to a place that an insane killer thinks is scary.*

"The fun never stops, does it?" she said.

Lee took one hand off the steering wheel, reached down, and clasped one of hers. She still didn't know how she felt about Lee lying to her – or at least withholding the truth – but she was grateful for their touch right then. She leaned closer, laid her head on Lee's shoulder, and they continued on toward Oakmont.

★   ★   ★

Wake up, sweetheart. You still have work to do.

Mrs. No liked the cool, soothing darkness that surrounded her, but she didn't like this voice disturbing her peace.

"Go away."

Open your eyes.

"Fuck off."

Open your eyes, the voice repeated, this time with a touch of impatience.

"Five more minutes," she pleaded.

The one who killed me is getting away.

No's eyes snapped open, and she tried to push herself into a sitting position. Unfortunately, she attempted to use her left hand – the one which now only possessed a thumb – and the agony that resulted woke her the rest of the way. Her head pounded like a motherfucker, and while she had no memory of being hit, when she reached up to touch her scalp, she found a massive bump and her hand came away sticky with blood. It had to have been Ethan, the little prick. She'd had the other three in her sight when she lost consciousness. She supposed one of the agents from the Unbroken Court could've struck her, but violence wasn't their style.

It was Ethan. He clonked you on the head with the leg before taking off in our car.

The voice was faint, but it sounded like her husband's. That was impossible, though. Yes was dead, devoured by the shadow rats. In her mind, she saw the girl with the short red hair run toward Yes and shove him into the storage unit. She saw the shadow rats swarm over him, once more heard his agonized screams.

I'm going to kill that bitch, she thought. *But I'll make her suffer a thousand ways first.*

She rose to her feet, head swimming, stomach roiling with nausea. She knew both sensations were a result of her head injury, and she ignored them. They'd get better or they wouldn't, and right now she didn't give a shit either way.

She raised her wounded hand, examined it, wiggled the thumb. At least she'd still be able to grip things with it, more or less. The wounds were open and raw, but the blood had clotted somewhat. The storage unit was closed, and the Camry – which she presumed the two young people and Haksaw had arrived in – was gone. She looked upward to see if any of the Unbroken Court agents were watching her, but she didn't spot any. She wasn't surprised. Those fuckers could be standing right next to you, and you still wouldn't see them unless they wanted you to. Even Caprice, with all her magic, would have a difficult time detecting the presence of one.

Her thoughts were muddled, which only made sense, given that her brains had been scrambled by the blow to her head. But she could've sworn she'd heard Yes's voice a moment ago. Had he somehow survived the shadow rats? She didn't see how. He was good, but nobody was *that* good.

It all depends on how you define survive.

The air in front of her rippled like heat waves, and she thought the distortion almost formed a shape – a *human* shape.

"Yes?"

That's me. Or what's left of me, anyway.

He sounded amused.

"I'm talking with your ghost."

You think I'd let a little thing like death stand between us?

She wanted so badly to believe it was really him, but she was too practical minded.

"You're not real. You're a hallucination brought on by my head injury."

Maybe. But do you really care if I'm real or not?

"No," she said after a moment's thought. "I don't."

I know where Ethan and Kate are going. Kate's the girl who killed me. I guess technically the shadow rats killed me, but you know what I mean.

"Kate," she said. The name made her think of the word *cut*. She would cut off Kate's limbs, slice meat from bone, then feed the flesh to her one gobbet at a time.

And I know something else. I know where both Kate and Ethan are going to end up. Two birds—

"One stone," she finished. "Where?"

The House of Red Tears. All you need is a ride.

Stronghold Self-Storage was an automated facility, so there were no employees on-site, but she was certain they'd set off any number of alarms when they'd rammed the Mercedes through the front gate. The police were undoubtedly on their way, and might be here already.

Mrs. No smiled. Good.

⋆　　⋆　　⋆

Craig Goodwin was having a bad day, and unknown to him, it was about to get a hell of a lot worse.

He'd been a patrol officer with the Collier PD for four years now, and while the work was okay, what he really wanted to do was become a detective. He knew it was a cliché, but he'd loved watching mystery TV shows and reading whodunnits ever since he'd been a kid, and there was nothing he wanted more in life than to solve murders. He liked the puzzle-solving aspect of the work – the challenge of it – and he also liked that he would be getting killers off the street, bringing justice to the deceased, and providing some measure of closure for victims' families and friends. To this end, he'd taken the promotion exam a couple days ago, and while he'd done well, this morning his chief told him that another candidate, one who'd been with the department longer, was getting the promotion instead.

That disappointment had set the tone for the rest of Craig's day. A shoplifting teenager had called him a fascist killer and spit in his face, a lawyer who'd had way too much to drink during a business lunch – and who'd gotten violent when the bartender cut her off – had vomited on his shoes when he'd tried to calm her down, and he'd had to tell a homeless couple they couldn't stay in a small stretch of woods behind a grocery after the store's manager called the police and complained. Now here he was, responding to a call at Stronghold Self-Storage. Someone had rammed a car into their front gate – probably thought the gate would open automatically for them – and fled the scene, likely due to extreme embarrassment. A security camera had hopefully caught an image of the vehicle's license plate, and the driver would be found. All he had to do was check out the scene, look around to make sure everything was okay, and write up a description of what he found while he waited for the owner to arrive. Hardly the sort of case Sherlock Holmes would get, but then he was no Holmes, was he? The chief had made sure of that.

So he was in a sour mood as he approached Stronghold, but that mood vanished the instant he saw the woman standing in front of the mangled gate. She had blood on her clothes, blood running down the side of her face, and – Jesus! – it looked like she'd lost four of the fingers on her left hand. What the ever-loving fuck?

He pulled into the facility's driveway and parked. He got out of his vehicle and approached the woman.

"Ma'am, are you all right? What happened?"

He was walking into an unknown situation and should've had his hand on his gun as a precaution. But the woman didn't look dangerous. She looked like she'd been through hell.

The woman smiled shakily when she saw him, took a step forward, and then her eyes rolled white and she collapsed to the ground.

Craig ran the rest of the way to the woman. He knelt and placed two fingers to her neck to check her pulse.

"Can you hear me? Ma'am, can you—"

The woman sat up abruptly, grabbed hold of his shoulders, fastened her mouth on the side of his neck and bit down hard, severing his carotid artery in the process. Blood gushed onto her face as she turned and spit a mouthful of his flesh onto the ground. She then shoved him backward and stood. He lay on his back, legs folded beneath him, consciousness already deserting him. It didn't take long to bleed out when you had a wound this bad, and he thought, *At least it'll be fast.* He wondered who the hell this woman was and why she'd felt the need to tear out his throat as if she was some kind of wild animal. These were the two biggest mysteries he'd ever encountered in his career, but unfortunately, he'd never get to solve either of them.

Then he was gone.

★　　★　　★

No licked blood from her lips as she looked down at the dead cop. Humans were ridiculously easy to kill if you weren't squeamish.

She removed the man's Glock from its holster and took his baton as well. He'd left his vehicle running, and she got in, put her new toys on the driver's seat, and closed the door. She looked to her right and saw the heat-distortion shape of her husband sitting in the passenger seat.

Messy, but nicely done.

"I thought you liked it messy."

Flirt.

Smiling, she put the vehicle in reverse and, using her good hand, backed out of the facility's driveway. Next stop, the House of Red Tears.

★　　★　　★

The spirits of the Shardlows and Lintons, along with the beast-man that had once been Felton, approached Oakmont. Delora's ghost had joined them along the way, and Reyna and Weston waited for them next to the cheery *Welcome to Oakmont* sign. No words were exchanged as the spirits came together, but none were needed. There were eleven of them in total now, a majority of the family, and they continued on into town, traveling slowly but purposefully, Felton darting from one place of concealment to the next. Soon they would reach the Cannery District and the House of Red Tears, and when they did, they would reveal themselves to Caprice. They couldn't wait to see the look on her face.

Just before they tore it from her skull.

★   ★   ★

Ethan was surprised the damaged Mercedes managed to make it back to Oakmont. The engine had sounded like a dying wildebeest the entire way, and the front end shimmied, as if the tires were on the verge of falling off. It was a damn sin how Mr. Yes and Mrs. No had treated such a fine machine. Couldn't they have found a different way into the storage facility other than ramming the gate? He was glad to be rid of those two lunatics and working on his own once more. Fewer complications this way. His shoulder wound still hurt like a bitch, but Mr. Yes's bandage was holding up nicely. He could really use some decent painkillers, though. Too bad he didn't have time to stop and rob a pharmacy.

It had been weird seeing Kate after all this time, especially considering the circumstances, but it had been good too. He was glad he hadn't been forced to kill her. He remembered her as a happy child, one who loved being part of an extended family. She'd looked up to him back in those days, and he hadn't realized until now how much that had meant to him. It was too bad that she had fallen away from the pure faith of the Quintessence. Maybe once the Lord of the Feast was fully born and began its sacred work, she would gaze upon its glory and realize that she had been wrong to ever oppose its Incarnation. Then the two of them could witness the end of existence together. He'd like that.

He'd been surprised to see that Kate had joined forces with Haksaw, but he'd been even more surprised by the revelation that her other companion was a member of the Unbroken Court. Given her reaction, it seemed she'd been unaware of her friend's allegiance as well. He didn't know a great deal about the Court, only that it prosecuted crimes committed in Shadow. While he'd never heard of the Court acting to prevent crimes, they *were* Balancers, which meant that they worked to preserve the orderly dismantling of reality. They opposed the Quintessence's goal of bringing the Omniverse to an early, merciful end, so in this case they might choose to intervene in order to prevent the Lord's Incarnation. He would have to remain on guard as he proceeded.

He had to admit that he hadn't done a very good job so far. He'd only managed to acquire the Lord's left arm and right leg, and Kate had the rest – not counting the head, which Caprice kept in the Repository, and the final piece, the left leg. His current plan was to get the leg before Kate could and then, somehow, to take the pieces she'd gathered from her. He wasn't sure how he was going to accomplish this, but he'd find a way. He had to.

In the meantime, he would pay a visit to Grandfather Elisha. He was Caprice's brother and Victorina's husband, and he had been entrusted with the guardianship of the Lord's left leg. Caprice had told Ethan about Elisha before she'd sent him out on his grotesque scavenger hunt.

Of all of us, Elisha had the most doubts about creating the Lord. He'd always been a weak-minded sort, ever since we were kids. Sometimes I think it was his lack of faith that caused the Incarnation to fail. I was against letting him take the left leg, but the other surviving members of the family outvoted me. Idiots. He did well enough for the first couple years, but he couldn't stop thinking about the family members who died or were transformed during the Incarnation. He saw himself as at least partially responsible for what happened to them, and the guilt gnawed at him until he couldn't take it any longer.

Caprice had urged Ethan to save Elisha for last since he'd remained in the same place for the last eight years and hadn't once left. Gehenna was located on the edge of the Cannery, in a four-story building that had once been a hotel. On the outside it looked long abandoned – windows boarded up, brick walls darkened from years of car exhaust, façade cracked and crumbling. The asphalt of the empty parking lot was shot through with fissures from which grew ugly, spiny weeds. The lot was empty, and Ethan had his pick of spaces. He parked near the building's rear entrance and turned off the Mercedes' engine. The motor rattled and made a loud *ker-chunk* sound, and the silence that followed – along with the smoke that curled from beneath the vehicle's hood – told Ethan that the Mercedes had made its final voyage. He patted the dashboard.

"Rest well, faithful steed."

The leg and arm he had were stored in the trunk, and he figured they would be safe enough there while he visited Elisha. He got out of the car, locked it, and started walking across the parking lot, careful to give the spiny weeds a wide berth. He didn't like the way the plants turned to follow his progress, and he preferred not to find out what those spines might do if they pierced his flesh. Shadow was filled with all sorts of nasty surprises.

He walked around to the front of the building. The original name of the hotel was carved into the stone above the entrance, letters faint, eroded by time and the elements: *The Golden Star.* Someone had painted *Gehenna* over the letters in thick red. The entrance was a pair of cracked glass doors with rusted metal handles, and Ethan took hold of one of those handles and pulled. Despite its appearance, the door opened easily and silently, and he stepped inside. The lobby was in equally as bad a state as the outside of the building, if not worse – walls covered with mold and creeping vines, floor sunken in, as if it might collapse any moment, tile yellowed and curling at the edges. The air smelled of must and mildew, sweat and desperation. The lobby had a few chairs and a pair of couches, upholstery faded and torn, and several people sat reading ancient magazines with ripped covers and crinkled pages. Ethan caught some titles: *Transgression Today, Veniality Monthly, Deviant Living, Apostate Review....* The men and women looked ordinary enough, but they shared a haunted look in their eyes, along with a communal aura of sorrow. The front desk was staffed by a lone employee, a thirtyish woman in a violet blazer and white blouse who wore her hair in a bun. She smiled at Ethan as he approached.

"Welcome to Gehenna. How may I help you?"

The woman's cheerful demeanor was at odds with her surroundings, and her too-perfect teeth looked as if they'd been painted on. Her eyes were an artificial blue, and she didn't seem to blink. It was like she was a mannequin who'd been brought to life, and considering this was the Cannery, maybe she was.

"I'm here to visit Elisha Linton. I'm his grandson."

The woman's smile didn't waver as she turned to a desktop computer so old it looked as if it had been built in the stone age. Her fingers tapped the keyboard for a moment, then she peered at the screen. She turned back to Ethan, still smiling.

"He's in room 437. You can go on up."

"Thank you." He was about to turn away, but he stopped. "Those people over there." He nodded toward the magazine-readers. "What are they waiting for?"

"For rooms to become available," the woman said. "Gehenna is very popular."

"No offense, but I'm surprised people are so eager to get in."

"We perform a vital function," the woman said. She pointed across the lobby. "The elevators are over there. Despite the look of the place, they're in good condition, so please don't hesitate to use them."

Ethan thanked her and started toward the elevators. He looked back once and saw that she was watching him, smile still firmly in place, doll eyes unblinking. He suppressed a shudder as he faced forward once more. There were a pair of elevators, paint on the doors flaking, surfaces scored by crisscrossing marks as if someone had taken a knife to them – or scratched them with their fingers. Ethan chose the elevator on the left and pushed the button to summon it. The tip of his finger came away greasy, and he wiped it on the wall. Despite the doll-eyed woman's assurance that the elevators were in working order, machinery whirred and clanked laboriously as the car descended, and it stopped at the first floor with an audible *thud*, as if it had fallen the last six inches. The door only opened halfway, but there was enough room for Ethan to slip into the car, and he did so. He pushed the button for the fourth floor, and the door made a scraping sound as it slowly closed. Once it had, the elevator began to rise. The machinery made loud noises again, and the car vibrated as it ascended. It stopped for several moments between the second and third floors before moving again. When it finally reached the fourth floor, the door opened all the way this time, and Ethan jumped out, half afraid the damn thing was going to plummet downward. But it didn't, and a moment later the door scraped shut. He let out a sigh of relief. After everything he'd been through today, it would be more than a little embarrassing if he was killed by a rickety elevator. Although he supposed there would be a certain ironic poetry to it.

He turned away from the elevator and started walking down the hall.

The floor, walls, and ceiling were in the same poor condition as the lobby, and the smell up here was worse. As he passed rooms, he heard noises coming from behind the closed doors. Sometimes it was people talking in relaxed tones, as if they were having a civil conversation. Other times people shouted and cursed, as if in the midst of intense arguments. Still other times, there were wails of sorrow and despair, or screams of pain and terror. Ethan didn't want to think about what might be going on in those rooms.

Gehenna is named after a place in Hebrew lore, Caprice had told him. *It was a valley where the wicked were condemned to suffer until they atoned for their sins.*

Ethan didn't know how this version of Gehenna worked, but it sure sounded as if the residents were suffering. He tried to block out the noises as he searched for Elisha's room. When he at last came to room 437, he wasn't sure what to do. He leaned his head close to the door, attempting to hear what was happening inside, but there was only silence. He knew from his experiences in the House of Red Tears that suffering wasn't always loud. In fact, the worst suffering was often the quietest. He raised a hand, knocked, stood back, waited. When he received no reply, he tried the doorknob and found it unlocked. He opened the door, stepped inside—

—and found himself in the past. Specifically, in Tressa and Delmar's basement, on the night they'd attempted to Incarnate the Lord.

He felt a dizzying sense of déjà vu. On the sectional couch, in front of the glass fireplace, sat his eleven-year-old self, dressed in what he recalled as an extremely uncomfortable suit. Nine-year-old Kate, wearing a dress, sat next to him. Reyna, also in a dress, was on the other side of Kate, and lastly was Weston, also in a suit. Reyna was in her twenties, Weston in his teens. They all looked so young. The adults were dressed in their finest clothes and stood around the pool table, Delmar at its head, *The Book of Depravity* open in his hands. Everyone was there – both sets of grandparents, Caprice, Kate and Reyna's parents, and his and Weston's. Seeing them all like this, younger, alive, unchanged, was a shock. Seeing Tressa, Delmar, and his mother was an even greater shock, as he'd killed all three of them today. And his father…. He hadn't seen Cordell in a decade, not since, well, not since the night he currently found himself in. He felt an almost overpowering urge to go over and speak to his father, but he had no idea what to say.

Hi, Dad. It's me, Ethan. I've become a highly experienced killer who's trying to complete the task that you and the rest of the family fucked up.

The basement was dark except for the flickering light coming from the fireplace, and dark ambient music played at low volume over the sound system. Delmar was reading from *The Book of Depravity*, one sentence at a time, the adults repeating his words. Lying on the pool table's surface was…. Ethan frowned. What should've been there were the pieces of the Lord's body, but instead a figure made entirely of shadow lay there. No, not entirely. It had a real left leg. Elisha stood on the Lord's right-hand side, Victorina next to him. He had been chanting along with the rest of the adults, but now he stopped and turned to look at Ethan. His eyes widened, and Ethan knew his grandfather – or at least this version of the man – had seen him. Elisha blurred out of focus for a second, and when he became clear again, he looked very different. He was ten years older, for one thing, in his late seventies now. He was thinner, too, with long greasy gray hair, and a thick bushy beard to match. His eyes were sunken in, watery and haunted. He wore a brown flannel shirt, faded jeans, and a tattered red ballcap that said High-Stakes Casino on the front.

"Ethan? Is that you?"

"Hello, Grandfather."

No one else in the basement seemed to notice Ethan. The adults continued conducting the rite of Incarnation, while young Ethan, Kate, Reyna, and Weston looked on apprehensively.

Elisha broke into a huge grin, dry, cracked lips pulling away from yellowed teeth. He hurried over to Ethan and gave him a hug. The man's arms were light and thin as sticks, and Ethan thought he could break Elisha's bones simply by breathing too hard on them. He smelled as if he hadn't bathed during his entire stay at Gehenna.

He was grateful when Elisha released him and took a step back. The man regarded him for a moment then shook his head in disbelief.

"I knew I'd been in here awhile, but I hadn't realized how long it had been. You've grown into a man."

Ethan saw no reason to prolong their reunion.

"I've come for the leg, Grandfather."

Before Elisha could reply, Ethan felt the atmosphere in the basement change. The air became charged with electricity, and his skin began to tingle. In response, Delmar and the other adults raised their voices and chanted faster, clearly excited. Pressure built in the basement, as if they were underwater and sinking rapidly, liquid pressing into them from all sides. The temperature plunged, and Ethan began shivering. Elisha didn't seem to notice.

"This is my favorite part," Elisha said.

The shadow being that lay in place of the Lord stood up on the pool table. The adults fell to their knees and raised their arms in supplication. Power rolled off the Lord in waves, and a sound issued from it, a high-pitched shriek that cut through Ethan's ears like a red-hot razor. He remembered this moment, and reliving it now, he began to tremble uncontrollably. Even this poor version of the Lord, one which had only the original's left leg, was absolutely terrifying. He saw Reyna get up from the couch, grab Kate's hand, and begin to lead her to the basement stairs. Young Ethan didn't move at first, and Weston had to take hold of his hand and pull him along after them. They rushed up the stairs, and

Ethan knew that Reyna would lead them outside in time to escape the mansion's destruction.

The Shadow-Lord bent toward Nila, grabbed her head, ripped it off, and raised it to its mouth and drank the blood pouring from the ragged opening. Nila's body slumped over, blood jetting from her neck stump, and the adults screamed. It was one thing to believe in the Lord of the Feast when it had been an abstract concept, but the reality of the god was a different thing entirely. The entire Omniverse dying? No problem. *Your* dying? That was another story. The adults jumped to their feet and fled toward the stairs, even Caprice, who Ethan thought hadn't possessed the capacity for fear. The first crimson flames began to flicker around the Lord's body, and then with a loud *woosh* they burst outward, filling the basement. Ethan had come to regard the basement and everything in it as some kind of illusion, and perhaps it was, but the flames *felt* real, and when they engulfed Ethan a scream of purest agony tore from his throat. The pain seemed to last an eternity, but it passed, and Ethan found himself on his hands and knees, gasping for breath, the ground beneath him charred black.

"The fire's a real kick in the balls, isn't it?" Elisha said. "You get used to it after a while, though."

He held out a hand for Ethan. Ethan, almost too weak to move, reached up and took it. Elisha helped him to his feet, and Ethan looked at his hands and was relieved to find them unburnt. The rest of the basement was a smoking ruin, though, and the ceiling was gone. Above them was open sky, stars scattered across the blackness. There were five mounds of ash lying on the floor in various places – those family members who'd perished during the failed Incarnation. The only other item was the Lord's left leg. It lay among the ash piles, its skin clean and undamaged. The door to the room, however, showed no sign of the fire having touched it.

Elisha began talking.

"We'd severely underestimated the amount of raw power required to fulfill the Incarnation. *The Book of Depravity* held enough power to create the Lord, but not enough to sustain it. The Lord was only able

236 • TIM WAGGONER

to exist a few moments in our reality before it fell apart. But in that short time, it managed to unleash the fire that destroyed the mansion and killed so many of our family, your father included. And the mystic energy the fire gave off mutated your mother, Delmar, and Felton. The rest of us escaped unharmed." He gave Ethan a sad smile. "Physically, at least."

Ethan tried to speak, but his throat felt sandpaper dry. He swallowed a couple times and tried again. His words emerged as a painful rasp, but at least they came out.

"We have the power now, Grandfather. Caprice has worked to gather it for the last ten years. All we need are the Lord's parts, and then we can complete the Incarnation. That's why I've come for the leg."

Ethan's own legs barely felt capable of supporting him, but he managed to take a step forward. Elisha stopped him before he could take a second.

"You can't have it."

Ethan looked at his grandfather in disbelief.

"I originally came to Gehenna to expunge the guilt I felt for my role in the failed Incarnation. Here, I could relive that night over and over, watch everyone die, feel the Lord's fire purify me. I hoped the fire would eventually burn the guilt out of me, but that didn't happen. What *did* happen was much better. I came to understand."

If Ethan hadn't felt so weak, he would've shoved his grandfather to the ground, taken the leg, and departed. As it was, he could barely stand. He needed time to recover his strength, so he decided to let Elisha keep talking.

"Understand what?"

"The true meaning of life, of course."

"The only purpose existence has is to feed the Gyre," Ethan said.

"That's what the Quintessence believes, and our family came to adopt that view. But we were wrong. The purpose of existence isn't to end – it's to *suffer*. Only through suffering do we come to learn who we really are. It refines us, purifies us, reduces us to our core. Pain is enlightenment. Pain is love. This is the Gyre's great gift. By devouring the Omniverse slowly, the Gyre maximizes its suffering. Only by accepting our pain and experiencing it fully can we truly live."

"You're insane," Ethan said.

Elisha smiled. "Oh yes."

Before Ethan could react, Elisha headbutted him. Pain exploded behind Ethan's eyes, and he dropped to the floor and rolled onto his side. His shoulder wound screamed.

"You may be younger than me, but you'll never be meaner than me."

As if to illustrate his words, Elisha raised a foot and brought it down hard on Ethan's left knee. The pain was nothing compared to what he'd felt when the Lord's fire had embraced him, but it still hurt like a bitch and he cried out. Elisha stomped his knee again, for good measure.

Elisha smiled lovingly. "You've just taken your first step to enlightenment. You're going to stay here with me, boy, and learn what true suffering is all about."

The basement wavered around them, and when it solidified once more, it was restored to its previous state. Young Ethan, Kate, Reyna, and Weston sat on the couch while the adults – minus Elisha – stood around the pool table chanting. The scenario of the failed Incarnation was repeating itself.

Ethan knew what his grandfather intended. He planned to cripple him so he couldn't leave. He would be forced to remain here in Room 437 with Elisha and be engulfed by the Lord's flame again and again, suffering unimaginable torment until he was as batshit crazy as his grandfather.

He heard a voice in his mind then.

Just because he's insane doesn't mean he's wrong. Caprice wanted you to become a cold-hearted murderer so that you would be able to kill your family members to obtain the Lord's body parts if necessary. But what did you really learn in the House of Red Tears? If you truly believed in hastening entropy, you would've killed your playmates seconds after you walked into the room, and you would've done so as efficiently as possible. But you learned to prolong their agony, to draw out the suffering. You made killing into art. You already believe as Elisha does, you just express that belief differently.

Ethan didn't have time for bullshit philosophy. If his grandfather fucked up his other knee, he was never going to get out of there. He rolled to his side as Elisha's foot came down where his right knee had been. He pushed himself up onto his good leg, then gently put weight on his bad one. The broken knee shouted in protest, but the leg held, and that was all he needed for now. He turned to face Elisha, thinking of a dozen ways he could disable the man. But before he could try any of them, Elisha swept out his foot and knocked Ethan's left leg out from under him. Ethan crashed to the ground once more, his injured knee hurting twice as much as before, his shoulder wound burning like fire.

"Looks like I'm going to have to hamstring you, boy."

Elisha walked past the pool table and the chanting adults to the bar on the other side. He reached behind it, grabbed a bottle of scotch off the shelf, and broke it on the bar's edge. Liquor splashed onto the bar's surface, along with fragments of glass. Elisha held the neck of the bottle, beneath which was a jagged portion of glass, more than sharp enough to perform the procedure he wanted. He started back toward Ethan, broken bottle held at his side, eyes gleaming with the bright light of madness. Ethan knew he was looking at the result of eight years of being repeatedly burned by the Lord's fire, and he understood then that suffering wasn't merely life. It was power, too.

The Shadow-Lord stood on the pool table. Its shriek filled the air, the adults fell to their knees, and Reyna and Weston fled the basement with the children. The Lord tore Nila's head from her body and drank from it, and the adults screamed in terror. Elisha ignored it all. When he reached Ethan, he looked down and smiled.

"This is going to hurt a great deal. I hope you enjoy it."

Elisha began to kneel, and that's when crimson flame exploded from the Shadow-Lord and roared through the basement. Even though Ethan knew what to expect this time, the pain was still more than he could manage. He could only let it toss him about like a leaf in a hurricane until it ran its course. When it was over and the basement had once more become a charred ruin, he sat up. Elisha had a beatific expression on his face, as if he were a devout worshipper who'd just had a personal visit from his god. He was so caught up in this feeling that he didn't react when Ethan grabbed the back of his head with both hands and plunged his thumbs into his eyes. Elisha screamed as blood flowed down his face. He grabbed hold of Ethan's wrists and tried to pull his hands away, but his strength was no match for his young grandson's.

"I'm sorry to tell you this, Grandfather, but your suffering is over."

He gave a last hard push with his thumbs. Elisha's body juddered as if he were in the throes of a seizure, and then went limp. Ethan pulled his thumbs free with a pair of sucking sounds, and Elisha's body fell to the floor. The basement blurred out of existence and was replaced with a small empty room with no windows and only a single lightbulb hanging from the ceiling for illumination. The Lord's left leg lay in the center of the room, waiting for Ethan. He wiped his thumbs off on his grandfather's shirt, stood, limped over to the leg, picked it up, and left the room. He made his way back downstairs, and as he walked across the lobby, he looked at the doll-eyed woman at the front desk.

"Room 437 just became open," he said.

INTERLUDE

Left Leg

Sophia Wen wished she hadn't had a second coffee this morning. She felt hot, almost feverish, and her pulse pounded hummingbird-fast in her ears. Today was the day. She patted the ring box in the front pocket of her jeans.

You can do this, you can do this, you can do this....

Her therapist thought this was a terrible idea. *Spectacularly awful* was how he'd put it, but what the fuck did he know? Had he ever been in love? She doubted it, otherwise he'd understand what she was doing, what she *had* to do.

As she'd done so often before, at least a dozen times a day, she thought about when she'd met Tracy. They both went to the same gym, Feel the Burn Fitness, a twenty-four-hour-a-day members-only facility. Sophia was a hospital ICU nurse who worked third shift, and she exercised during what, for her, would be the end of the day, but which for most people was early morning. She was leaving after a particularly intense workout – it was early December and she wanted to lose the extra weight she'd put on at Thanksgiving – when she stepped off the curb in front of the building and somehow twisted her left ankle. She went down on her knees and fell forward, catching herself with both hands. Ankle throbbing and palms stinging, she maneuvered herself into a sitting position and reached down to assess her injury.

Oh my god, are you all right?

She looked up and there, framed in early morning sunlight, was the most beautiful woman she'd ever seen. Strawberry-blond hair, lean aristocratic features, and Caribbean-ocean blue eyes. The goddess smiled, and Sophia felt as if she were a mug that had just been filled with warm cocoa.

She could barely bring herself to speak.

I'm okay. Just twisted my ankle a little. I think I can—

She tried standing, but a bolt of pain shot through her ankle, and her leg buckled. The goddess wrapped an arm around her waist to catch her, and Sophia thought she might die of happiness right then and there.

C'mon, let's get you inside.

The goddess – who Sophia would learn was called by the earthly name of Tracy Ellis – helped her hobble back into the facility. They chatted while Sophia iced her ankle and wrapped it, then they left together. Tracy was late for work and had to go. By the time Sophia pulled out of the parking lot, she knew she was in love.

After that, she made it a point to talk to Tracy every morning at the gym, but while Tracy had seemed to enjoy getting to know her at first, eventually she began showing up later and later, skipping some days altogether. Then she stopped coming entirely. Sophia told herself not to take this personally, that Tracy had probably found a gym that she liked better. That was okay. She knew where Tracy worked – Complete Protection Insurance – and all she'd have to do was give her a call and find out where she was exercising now. Sophia would then quit Feel the Burn and join the new gym. She didn't want to be a pest, so she waited until nine fifteen to call, figuring that would give Tracy enough time to get in and get settled at her desk. Tracy answered on the second ring, but the call did not go as Sophia hoped.

To be honest, I switched gyms because you were starting to creep me out, Tracy said. *Don't get me wrong, you're a nice person. But you can be kind of… intense at times, you know? Too intense for me. Sorry.*

Then she ended the call.

Sophia had been devastated. When she told her therapist about it at their next appointment, he said that Tracy had only been setting healthy boundaries for herself. Dumbass. She and Tracy were good for each other. If her therapist could see them together for just a few minutes, he'd understand that. She and Tracy had something special, something with the potential to be so much more than it already was. She couldn't allow that to die without a fight, and she knew that deep down, Tracy wouldn't want her to.

She sent emails to Tracy's work address. She left voice mails on both her home and work phones. She sent presents – flowers, candy, a mug that said *Trust Me, I'm an Insurance Agent,* and more. Tracy's only response was an email asking Sophia to please leave her alone. Sophia knew she didn't really mean it, though. When she wasn't working at the hospital, she began to follow Tracy. She'd wait in the parking lot of Tracy's building, then follow her car when she left work. She learned where Tracy preferred to buy groceries, which bars she liked, and most importantly, where she lived. One night, when Sophia didn't have to work, she showed up on Tracy's doorstep. Tracy was not happy to see her and demanded she leave.

Sophia's therapist told her that her *obsession* (his word) with Tracy had gotten way out of hand. She'd told him he was full of shit and that Tracy was just confused and didn't know what she wanted. But Sophia knew. Tracy needed to be shown how deeply Sophia cared for her and how much she wanted them to be together. And she knew exactly how to do it.

The elevator dinged and the door slid open. She got out, consulted the directory next to the elevator, then headed down the hall toward Complete Protection Insurance. There was a large blue CPI logo on a glass door, and – trembling a little – Sophia pushed it open and stepped inside. She'd never been in Tracy's office before, but it looked more or less like she'd imagined it: blandly professional, with people sitting at desks in the outer office, more people sitting at desks in smaller, individual offices, all working at computers beneath fluorescent light. The receptionist's desk was the one closest to the door, and she walked over. The woman sitting there favored her with a decent facsimile of a friendly smile.

"Can I help you?"

Sophia reached down and gripped the ring box through her jeans.

"I'm here to see Tracy Ellis."

The woman's smile didn't falter as she raised a hand and pointed. "That's her office over there."

Sophia looked, saw Tracy sitting at her desk and talking on the phone. It had been almost seventeen days since she'd seen her goddess, and she was so beautiful Sophia wanted to cry.

"Thank you."

Sophia approached Tracy's office at an angle so she wouldn't see her coming. Sophia wanted to surprise her. When she got close enough, she could hear what Tracy was saying.

"—totally covered. That's right, one hundred percent. Yes. Yes. I'm looking at the numbers on my screen right now, Charlie, and they—" She broke off as Sophia stepped into the doorway, smiling. Tracy did not smile. "I'll have to call you back."

She hung up and stared at Sophia. Sophia tried to read her expression, but she couldn't. She swallowed. *Here goes.* She removed the ring box from her pocket, got down on one knee, and it opened it to display the diamond ring inside. She thought she'd picked out the right size for Tracy, but if it didn't fit right, they'd get it adjusted.

"Will you marry me?"

Tracy's eyes widened as they focused on the ring. This was it! Tracy would realize just how much Sophia loved her. She'd break down crying, throw her arms around Sophia, say *Yes, yes, yes!* and then they'd cry together.

Instead, Tracy screamed. This wasn't a cry of fear, though. It was one of absolute frustration. She jumped up from her desk, hurried past Sophia – nearly knocking her down in the process – and rushed into the outer office.

"Call the police!"

Sophia didn't know who she was addressing. The receptionist? Anyone in the office who would listen? It didn't matter, not now. She stood, gently placed the ring on Sophia's desk, and then left her love's office. The outer office was in turmoil. Everyone was talking at once, unsure of what was happening or what they should do about it. Some of them looked at Sophia with puzzlement, some with wariness, and others with derision. There was no sign of Tracy. One of the individual offices was closed now, and Sophia guessed that Tracy had sought sanctuary inside with a friend. The door was no doubt locked and they were on the phone to the police already.

She left the office and didn't look back.

She took the stairs this time, but instead of going down, she climbed them until she reached the door to the roof. It was unlocked and opened easily. She stepped outside without bothering to close it behind her and walked to the building's edge. The building wasn't huge, only six stories, but it was tall enough. It would do. Without her goddess, there was no point in going on. Sophia knew she wouldn't be able to take the pain of living without Tracy. The only thing she regretted was that when her therapist found out she'd killed herself, he'd say something like, *I knew that bitch was crazy*, and then forget all about her. Asshole.

She hoped the impact would kill her immediately. She didn't want to survive long enough for paramedics to arrive and save her. She might even end up in her own hospital, and the doctor and nurses would all shake their heads and cluck their tongues over a colleague who'd been too emotionally fragile to make it in this oh-so-cruel world.

She raised her left leg. She decided to step off with this one first, as a poetic gesture, since it had been her twisted left ankle that had brought her and Tracy together in the first place. But before she could lean forward and fall off the roof, a voice behind her said, "Excuse us."

She was so startled, she started to pitch forward, but someone caught the back of her shirt and steadied her. She turned to see an older man and woman, both of them smiling.

"We don't mean to interrupt your suicide," the man said.

"But we can't have you damaging your left leg," the woman said. "We need it."

The woman raised a bone saw and the man forced Sophia to lie on the roof. He held her down while the woman quickly and efficiently took off her left leg. When they were finished, the man raised her to her feet — well, to her *foot* — and set her at the edge of the roof. She was in shock and dizzy from blood loss. Blood ran down from her wound and pattered on the roof like red rain.

"As you were," the man said, then planted a foot between her shoulder blades and pushed.

As Sophia plummeted toward the ground, she hoped that she'd fall past the window of the office where Tracy was hiding. She wanted one last glimpse of her goddess, however blurry and fleeting, and she wanted Tracy to see what she'd done by spurning her love. She would never know she was on the opposite side of the building from where Complete Protection Insurance had its offices. She did, however, get one of her wishes granted. She hit the parking lot pavement head first, and there was no way a paramedic – however dedicated and gifted – could possibly save her.

CHAPTER SIXTEEN

Axton was worried about Caprice. Since helping her into bed, he hadn't left her side. He sat in a chair, holding her hand, marveling at how light it felt, almost as if it weren't really there at all. Being so old was one step away from being a ghost, he thought. You were still in the land of the living, but only barely. He wished she'd told him of her plan to seek information from the Gathered. He could've helped her, could've donated a portion of his own life energy so she wouldn't have had to sacrifice so much of hers to obtain the knowledge she needed. But she was stubborn and self-reliant, and when she wanted something, she'd move heaven and hell to get it. And if she'd told him of her plan, he would've tried to talk her out of it. He would've failed, of course, which was likely another reason she hadn't said anything. She hadn't wanted him to feel guilty for being unable to stop her. She could be surprisingly kind, in her own way. In fact, it was one of these small kindnesses that had brought them together.

Construction had been finished on the House of Red Tears, but it wasn't open for business yet. Caprice had invited a few friends to come try out the rooms, and she'd acquired her first set of playmates for them. She was looking to get as much feedback as possible so she could work out any remaining kinks before officially opening. Axton had been among the first group of victims brought to the House – captured one evening when he'd been out walking the family dog – and he had been terrified when he'd been taken into a room, strapped naked to a chair, and then left there. He had no idea how long he waited, but eventually *she* walked into the room – Caprice. He had gotten her by the luck of the draw. If anyone else had walked into the room, he knew he never would've left it alive. Axton felt drawn to her the instant he saw her.

She moved with the ease and strength of a predator, and he couldn't take his eyes off her. She examined all the instruments laid out on the table, and once she was satisfied with their number and arrangement, she turned around to look at him. He had a full erection, and when her gaze dropped to his cock, she noted it, but she gave no other reaction. She walked to the chair and took her time checking his leather restraints. Having her so close was intoxicating, despite knowing that she'd come to torture and most likely kill him. Or maybe partly because of that. One of the straps wrapped around his neck, and when she tugged on it, he gasped.

"Too tight?" she asked.

"A little," he said.

He was surprised when she loosened it.

"Better?"

"Yes, thank you."

After that, she went to work. It hurt, of course – a *lot* – but there was a tenderness there as well. The way she slipped blade edges beneath his flesh, slid sharp objects into his orifices.... No ham-fisted hacking or bludgeoning for her. She took *pride* in her work, and he felt honored to be part of it, the canvas upon which she would paint her art. He supposed he loved his wife and children, but they were too nice, too simple, too boring.... This woman was the exact opposite of those things, and it wasn't until that moment, when he was bleeding from a dozen different wounds, that he knew she was what he had needed his entire life.

He came then, harder than he ever had before, and when he was finished, Caprice looked at him for a long time, as if appraising him. Finally, she went back to the table, put down the scalpel she'd been holding, and walked out of the room without saying a word. Sometime later, two of her employees came to get him. They unstrapped him from the chair and took him to a small infirmary where they treated his injuries. He remained there for two weeks, and when he had recovered enough, he was taken to Caprice's office. They'd made love there for the first time, and Axton had remained at the House of Red

Tears ever since, helping Caprice in every way he could. He became a devout believer in her cause – the Incarnation of the Lord of the Feast – and he'd pursued its consummation with the wild-eyed zealotry of the convert.

But if Caprice was too weak to perform the rite, or Oblivion forbid, she died before she could attempt it, the Incarnation would never occur. He knew the ritual inside and out, had studied it obsessively over the years, but he didn't have the gift for performing magic, at least, not at Caprice's level. She'd trained Ethan how to do it, but Axton knew the boy could never hope to substitute for her. Only Caprice had the strength and knowledge needed to Incarnate the Lord, and only she would be able to harness the combined power of the Gathered and channel it. No, it had to be her, and she needed to be at full health in order to fulfill her destiny. And Axton could think of only one way to make this possible.

"Caprice?" He shook her hand gently. "Caprice, wake up."

She didn't respond right away, and he feared the worst, but then her paper-thin eyelids opened.

"A-Axton?"

He clasped her hand tighter, and she moaned in pain. He quickly loosened his grip, just like she had once loosened a leather strap around his neck.

"Consulting the Gathered took too much from you," he said. "You have to replenish your energy. You must take mine."

"No...." It came out as a whisper, and her head moved almost imperceptibly back and forth.

"If the Lord is to be reborn, you have no choice. Can't you hear the Omniverse screaming all around us? Its pain must be ended, and you are the only person in all existence who can do it."

"Don't...want to...hurt you."

"You won't let it hurt, my love. I know you won't."

He leaned over the bed, lowered his face to hers, pressed his lips gently to her mouth. At first, nothing happened, but then he felt his lips begin to gently tingle. The sensation grew stronger, and with it came a draining feeling. His life was leaving him and entering her, and it was far more intimate than mere sex could ever be.

Yes, he thought, *take it all....*

He felt himself grower weaker, and Caprice — stronger now — gripped the back of his head and pressed him harder against her mouth. Using her magic, she drew every iota of life energy from his body, and when she was finished, she had been restored to her more youthful self. Younger even than she had been before she'd entered the Repository that last time. Axton, however, had not fared so well. His skin was a dull gray and drawn tight to his skeleton. His internal organs had all shrunken, and his shriveled eyes had receded into their sockets. His lips had drawn back from his teeth, making him look as if he were grinning in death. Who knows? Maybe he was.

"I was wondering how long it would take you to offer yourself to me. Idiot."

She shoved his desiccated corpse onto the floor and got out of bed. Her phone was on the nightstand, and she picked it up and called Ethan. The Gathered had given her one additional bit of information that she hadn't been able to recall before, but she was young and strong again, and she remembered it now.

The building. The door. The words painted on it in black: Tainted Pages. And walking toward it, Kate, Lee, and Haksaw.

It wouldn't be much longer. Soon, everything and everyone would be in place, and the Incarnation could begin.

She couldn't wait.

★   ★   ★

"This is it?" Kate said.

"You sound disappointed," Lee said.

She kind of was. She'd thought Tainted Pages would be some kind of spooky gothic-looking place, like a Halloween haunted house. But it was a simple one-story building, so small it looked more like a shack than a house. There were no windows, and no indication that there ever had been any. There was no sign. Instead, the name of the place was painted on the front door in neat black letters.

"This reminds me of that old meme," Kate said, "the one with a sketchy-looking van with the words *Free Candy* spray-painted on the side."

Haksaw chuckled. "I used a van like that once, a long time ago. I painted *Free Pussy* on the side, though."

Kate and Lee exchanged glances.

"Did it work?" Kate asked.

"You bet! I got more torsos than I knew what to do with. If the damn thing hadn't broken an axle, I'd still be using it."

"And on *that* lovely note...."

Lee parked the Camry in front of the store, and the three of them disembarked. Lee got a blanket out of the trunk and placed it over the body parts in the backseat to conceal them, locked the car, and then they all headed for the building. Kate would've been more comfortable if Haksaw remained behind, but she knew they couldn't trust him with the body parts. What if he got it into his mind that he wanted his precious torso's 'siblings' for himself? Better he stay with them for now.

It was dusk, the sunlight dim and the shadows long. The place was old and weathered, but the door didn't creak when they opened it. Inside, the air was thick with the musty smell of ancient paper, and Kate's eyes immediately began to water.

"This is why I prefer e-readers," she said.

The place was filled with shelves, all of them crammed to bursting with books, some that looked so new they could've been printed yesterday, some that appeared hundreds of years old. There were scrolls too, rolled up and bound with ribbon or bits of twine. The shelves were placed so close together that there was barely room for one person at a time to walk between them. There were no discernable sections – no signs, no labels, and the uncovered lightbulbs on the ceiling were so dim, Kate couldn't make out any words on book spines. She had the sense that a lot of them weren't in English, though.

"How are we supposed to find anything in this mess?" she asked.

"We ask the Bookman," Lee said, as if the answer was obvious.

They led the way through a maze of shelves, far longer than should've been possible given how small the building had appeared from the outside. They seemed to walk for a long time, and Kate began to feel claustrophobic. What if they got lost in here? How would they ever find their way out?

Relax, a calm voice said inside her mind. *Lee knows the way in, and that means they know the way out.*

Of course. Kate's nervousness eased, but it didn't leave her entirely.

Eventually they came to an open area where curved bookshelves surrounded a circular counter. Instead of a computer, there was an old-fashioned cash register on the counter's surface. The man standing behind the counter – the Bookman, Kate assumed – looked pretty old-fashioned himself. He was middle-aged, wore glasses, had a light blue shirt with a blue-striped tie, and sported a neatly trimmed black mustache and goatee. His eyes were a soft brown, at least at first. But as Kate watched, they began to change, shifting from human eyes to a cat's, then lizard, goat, fish, bird, and insect before repeating the sequence. The effect was creepy as hell, but also kind of cool in a strange way.

"Welcome to Tainted Pages," the Bookman said. "How may I help you?"

Kate turned to Lee, but Lee nodded toward the Bookman. The message was clear: Kate was to take the lead now.

"Hi, we're, uh, looking for a book."

The Bookman smiled, and Kate felt like a dumbass.

"A specific book," she hurried to add. "It's called *The Book of Depravity.*"

The air was filled with a strange rustling sound, and she felt the floor vibrate beneath her feet.

"Please don't say that title again," the Bookman said. "The store doesn't like it."

She realized that the rustling she'd heard was the sound of paper moving.

"I guess not," she said. She plowed on. "Do you have a copy?"

"There are no copies of such books. They exist outside of normal spacetime, however, so it's possible to find what *looks* like two copies sitting side by side. It doesn't happen often, though."

"Uh-huh. So...do you have it?"

"Of course. My shop contains every occult tome produced on this world or any other."

He reached below the counter, brought up a thick book, and laid it down gently, almost reverently. The cover appeared to be made from old, yellowed bone. There was no title visible, but it looked like the book Kate remembered her relatives using *That Night*. The edges of its cover and pages were darkened, and the whole thing smelled of smoke and ashes.

"Don't worry," the Bookman said. "It took several years for the book to heal from the fire that resulted when the last person attempted to use it, and while it's still a touch crispy here and there, every word is legible."

"Can I look inside?" Kate asked.

"At your own risk." The Bookman smiled. He might have been making a joke, but Kate couldn't read anything in his constantly shifting eyes, so she wasn't sure.

She touched the hard, cold cover and she felt a sick squirming sensation in her stomach. She forced herself not to jerk her hand away, and she opened the book and began turning pages. They were thin and made of dry, mottled leather that she hoped to God wasn't human flesh, the words dark red, as if written in blood. What they *weren't*, however, were English letters. Just looking at them made Kate's eyes hurt, and she struggled to keep them in focus. Sometimes she thought she could almost make out a word here and there, but the meaning always eluded her.

"Can either of you two read this?" she asked.

Lee and Haksaw leaned over to look at the book.

"Not me," Haksaw said. "I almost hear it whispering to me, though." He looked at the Bookman. "Does it talk?"

"To some," the Bookman said.

"I can't read it, either," Lee said. "It's above my pay grade."

"What good is it to us if none of us can read it?" Kate asked.

"You need a special mind to read a book like this," the Bookman said. "That you have. But you also need special eyes." He pointed to his own constantly morphing orbs. "Your grandfather had the training to read it, and the power to enhance his vision, but he didn't possess the right mind."

"You know who I am?" Kate asked. "How?"

"Like this gentleman said—" the Bookman nodded to Haksaw, "—the book talks. When it finally made its way back to my shop, it told me what had happened to it. It recognized you the instant you touched it, and it told me all about you."

"I suppose you have special ears too," Lee said.

The Bookman grinned. "I have special everything."

That was a line Kate refused to touch. "Did the book tell you why we need it?"

"It did. It also said that if you take it, you'll end up delivering it into the hands of your great-aunt. Is that what you want?"

"What we want is to find a way to destroy the Lord of the Feast's body parts so that it can never be brought to life," Kate said. "Can this book show us how to do that?"

Before the Bookman could reply, the pages of *The Book of Depravity* rippled, as if an unseen finger trailed down them.

"It says it can," the Bookman translated.

Kate felt hope for the first time since she and Lee had left Tressa's house.

"Will you let us borrow it?" she asked. "I promise we'll bring it back."

"Never make promises you may not be able to keep," the Bookman said. "But that aside, you do not need my permission to take a book from my store. Tainted Pages belongs to me, but the books do not. They belong to themselves. I merely give them a home until they decide to leave. Sometimes they return, sometimes they don't. If the book wishes to go with you, it will. If it doesn't, no force in existence can move it."

"So it wanted to go with Delmar?" Kate asked.

"Yes."

"Does that mean it *wanted* to help Incarnate the Lord?" Lee asked.

"Not necessarily," the Bookman said. "Books have their own reasons for doing things, many of which may remain forever unknown to their readers. But a book like this—" he nodded toward *The Book of Depravity,* "—exists for only one reason: to cause trouble. It doesn't care who it causes trouble for or why. As long as chaos results from its use, it's content."

"So it could just as easily turn on us as help us," Lee said.

The Bookman smiled. "Yes. And it might do both. Who knows?"

Lee turned to Kate. "Maybe we shouldn't take it."

"It was your idea to come here."

"I knew about this place, but I didn't know much about this kind of book. From what the Bookman says, it's too dangerous to trust. Remember, it said that if we take it with us, it'll eventually end up in Caprice's hands. By taking it from the shop, we could help Caprice bring the Lord of the Feast to life."

Kate closed the book.

"Or maybe it would backfire on her. There's no way to know ahead of time."

"Why don't you see what the book wants to do?" Haksaw said. "If it doesn't want to go with us, it won't."

"Good point."

Kate took a breath, then she put both hands on *The Book of Depravity* and lifted. The book came off the counter easily.

"There's your answer," the Bookman said. "I wish you luck preventing the premature end of the Omniverse. There's a chance my store and I would survive if you fail, but since there would be no one left to read, what would it matter?"

Kate wondered if the Bookman was just joking or if he was serious. If he was, how powerful would he have to be to escape the end of everything?

The Book of Depravity was surprisingly light for something so large, and Kate was able to carry it easily.

"I hope we see you again," Kate said. "Actually, I hope we get to see *anything* after tonight."

Kate turned to go, and Lee and Haksaw followed.

"Happy reading!" the Bookman called out after them.

★   ★   ★

The return trip through the bookstore seemed much shorter, and they were outside more quickly than they expected. It had been dusk when they'd entered, but it was almost night now. Only a faint blue lined the western horizon, and soon it would be full dark.

"So what now?" Lee asked.

"We go somewhere and try to figure out how to read this damned book," Kate said. "With any luck, it will have an index with an entry for *Lord of the Feast, body parts, destruction of.*"

"Wouldn't that be nice," Lee said.

"You know what would be nicer? If you three were in our bellies right now."

The voice came from somewhere in the shadows near the Camry. A male's voice, one Kate didn't recognize. It was followed by a female's.

"Betcha taste good," she said.

"Betcha taste *great,*" the man amended.

There was a shuffling of feet and a pair of shadows detached themselves from the surrounding darkness and approached. Kate couldn't make out their features clearly, but she could see they both had shaved heads and carried large knives. *Hunting knives,* she thought. She couldn't tell their ages in this light. They could be anywhere from their twenties to forties.

"Look, it's been a long day," she said. "Who the fuck are you two and what the hell do you want?"

"They're *Dog-Eaters,*" Haksaw said, voice dripping with disgust.

Lee groaned. "I *hate* Dog-Eaters."

"What *are* Dog-Eaters?" Kate asked.

"The lowest of the low," Haksaw said. "Which is something, coming from me."

"No we ain't," the male said.

The pair had come close enough now that Kate could see their sharp teeth. They seemed to be the same shape and size, and she wondered if they were natural or had been filed to look this way.

"We ain't Cat-Eaters or Rat-Eaters," the female said. "They's worse'n us."

"*Lots* worse," the male agreed.

"They literally eat dogs?" Kate asked.

Lee and Haksaw answered in unison. "Yes."

"Then why are they bothering us?"

"Because we don't *only* eat dogs," the female said. "We just prefers 'em."

"No dogs around right now, and we're hungry," the male said. "So you'll do."

The two ran toward them, knives held high. Kate raised the book, as if she intended to use it as a weapon, and she heard a ratcheting sound that told her Haksaw's handsaws had emerged.

"Watch out!" the male said. "The older one's got blades on 'im."

"We got blades too," the female said. "And ours are bigger'n sharper."

The Dog-Eaters laughed and attacked. They swiped their hunting knives through the air, forcing Kate and Haksaw back toward the store. Kate swung *The Book of Depravity* in front of her, and at one point a knife tip scratched the cover. She felt the book writhe in her hands, and she heard a soft squeal of pain.

"Fuck!" the male shouted, and Kate was pretty sure Haksaw had managed to tag him with one of his handsaws.

The parking lot lights' automatic timers kicked in and they came to glowing blue-white life. Kate saw blood dripping from a small cut on the book's cover, as well as from the back of the male Dog-Eater's hand. The two Dog-Eaters looked around, then they tucked their knives into belt sheaves.

"That's it for us," the female said. "We're outta here."

"Have a good rest of yer night," the male said.

Kate gaped as the two turned and began walking away.

"That's it? You attack us and then all of a sudden you just…leave?"

"We did what we were paid t'do," the female Dog-Eater said. "Job's over, so we're out."

"We don't hang around meat-thieves for fun," the male said.

"They weren't trying to hurt us," Haksaw said. "They wanted to distract us."

The Dog-Eaters stopped and turned around.

"You're smarter than y'look," the male said.

"Which ain't sayin' much," the female said.

The two laughed, the sound like the high-pitched yapping of small dogs.

"Distract us from what?" Kate said.

"Where's Lee?" Haksaw asked.

"Lee's right—" Kate looked around, but there was no sign of Lee. She shouted their name, once, twice, but received no reply. She ran to the Camry in case Lee had for some reason decided to get inside, but the vehicle was empty.

"No," she said. "Oh god, please, no."

Without thinking, she put *The Book of Depravity* on the Camry's hood then ran over to the Dog-Eaters. They dropped their hands to their knives as she drew near, but they didn't draw the blades.

"Where's my friend?"

The male shrugged. "Don't know. We was paid to keep you two busy, and that's it."

"Who paid you?"

The female bared her sharp teeth. "Why should we tell you?"

"Because we have meat."

Haksaw stood at Kate's side. She hadn't been aware of him joining her, but he was a predator and could move silently when he wanted.

The male cocked his head. "What kinda meat?"

"Special meat," Haksaw said. "It's been infused with magic so that it always stays fresh and warm."

The two Dog-Eaters exchanged glances then the male looked at Haksaw once more.

"We don't eat meat that's got magic in it," he said.

"Spoils the flavor," the female said.

"I've been handling it all day. Take a smell, see what you think."

Haksaw stepped forward and held out his hands, but the Dog-Eaters hesitated.

"I'll keep my bone blades inside, okay?" The lengths of serrated bones subsided into the flesh of his hands. "And if it'll make you feel better, I'll close my eyes and you can draw your knives. That way you'll be able to gut me before I can even take a swing at you."

The male and female consulted once more, and finally the female nodded.

"Close yer eyes," she said.

Haksaw did so.

The Dog-Eaters drew their knives and warily approached Haksaw. When they were close enough, they began sniffing his hands, tentatively at first, then with increasing enthusiasm. They became so excited that they started licking his hands.

"I've never tasted anythin' like it!" the male said.

"It's sweeter than pure-bred Tibetan Mastiff!" the female said.

Haksaw lowered his hands and opened his eyes.

"We've got almost a full human body's worth of the stuff in our car," he said. "We'll give you each a piece if you tell the girl what she wants to know."

The male's eyes narrowed. "No tricks?"

"From one predator to another, I promise," Haksaw said.

The Dog-Eaters turned to Kate.

"We don't know his name," the female said. "He's related to you, though. We could tell by the scent."

"Cousin probably," the male said. He looked to the female for confirmation.

"Yeah. First cousin, I'd say."

"Ethan," Kate said.

"We held up our end of the bargain," the male said. "Now how about you hold up yours?"

"Of course," Haksaw said. "You won't need your knives, though. This meat is so tender it practically falls off the bone."

The Dog-Eaters looked doubtful, so Haksaw held out his hands for them to sniff once more. Drooling, they quickly sheathed the blades. Smiling, Haksaw stepped between them and put his hands on their shoulders.

"Come with me," he said. "You won't believe what you're about to experience."

The Dog-Eaters allowed Haksaw to begin leading them to the car, but they were only halfway there when Haksaw turned his hands palms up and his bone saws emerged. He jammed them against the Dog-Eaters' necks and they shrieked in pain as the ratcheting blades chewed into their flesh. Blood sprayed from their wounds, their bodies jerked and spasmed, and then fell to the ground. Kate barely noticed. She was too busy trying to figure out what Ethan's game was.

If he'd wanted to kill Lee, he could've done so when the Dog-Eaters were distracting them. Hell, he probably could've killed all three of them, especially if he'd told the Dog-Eaters to help him. So if he hadn't wanted Lee dead, that meant he'd wanted to abduct them. But where would he take them, and why? The answer came easily. The House of Red Tears. He'd abducted Lee in order to lure Kate there. Caprice would hold Lee hostage in exchange for the parts of the Lord she had as well as *The Book of Depravity*. The book had said she would deliver it to Caprice's hands, and it looked like it had been right.

You don't have to do what Caprice wants, the voice inside her head said. *You can take the book and the body parts and leave town. You can keep running and hiding until Caprice finally gives up or dies, whichever comes first.*

"She'll kill Lee."

Yes. But Lee is only one person. What does their life matter when stacked against the lives of every being in the Omniverse? Those currently living and those yet to be born?

The voice was right. Given the circumstances, this option was the only logical course of action.

"Fuck logic," she said.

260 • TIM WAGGONER

She started toward the Camry, barely glancing at the dead Dog-Eaters on the way. Haksaw stood next to the car, waiting for her.

"You don't want to collect their torsos?" she asked.

"Hell, no! Dog-Eaters are nasty. Hey, you don't happen to have a key for this thing, do you?" He jerked a thumb over his shoulder toward the Camry.

"Uh.... No. No, I do not."

★   ★   ★

Felton smelled the House of Red Tears long before they reached it, the blood-reek permeating the air like the scent of salt near an ocean. There was fear in this scent, as well as pain and despair, and thick ropey strands of saliva dripped from his muzzle. Lissette's ghost cuffed him, her touch cold as winter, as if telling her husband to stay focused. Felton growled in irritation, but he did his best to ignore the sweet stench of the slaughterhouse ahead of them.

Night had fallen, and in the Cannery – where shadows held sway even during daylight hours – it was darker, in every sense of the word. There were eleven of them, the Shardlows and the Lintons, and when they were within a block of the House, Elisha's ghost joined them, making them a dozen. Almost all the family were present now. Only Caprice, Ethan, and Kate still lived...well, and Felton, if you considered his condition as *living*. In many ways, he was like a ghost trapped in a beast's body. They were in the part of the Cannery that overlapped Shadow, and most of the people on the street could sense the ghosts' presence if not actually see them. More, they could feel the fury burning within these shades, and they suddenly found better places to be. In short order, the area around the House of Red Tears was deserted, and word had begun to spread through the Cannery that the place was best avoided this night.

While Felton smelled the miasma of nearly a decade of murder, the ghosts sensed others like them, hundreds upon hundreds, held captive in the lowest level of the House. The Shardlows and Lintons still desired vengeance against Caprice – and Ethan – but they also intended to free their fellow spirits who, no doubt, would want their own revenge on Caprice.

This was going to be *fun*.

They continued on.

★   ★   ★

Ethan marveled at the wraiths' beauty as the glowing spirits swirled around them like exotic undersea life-forms, their bioluminescence holding the darkness at bay. Too bad they weren't going to be around much longer.

Caprice stood next to him, smiling as she too watched the Gathered do their dance. The Lord's eyeless head was on the floor in front of her, face up, as if waiting patiently for the rest of its body to arrive. The left arm and right leg were in their proper places, and Ethan thought the arrangement looked like a macabre puzzle that was only half-completed. Caprice looked younger than when Ethan last saw her, but he figured that was due to her excitement. She was nearing the culmination of a decade's worth of work. More than that, the realization of everything the cult of the Quintessence had strived to accomplish for millennia. Who wouldn't feel good about that?

Actually, he didn't. At best, he was ambivalent, and with each passing moment, that ambivalence grew.

Lee sat on the floor nearby, wrists and ankles bound by leather restraints, ball gag in their mouth. Despite how angry they must be, they gazed upon the wraiths with wonder, and not for the first time, Ethan thought of how much beauty there was in death.

You can't have death without life, a voice inside him said. *Once the Gyre has feasted on everything, even death will be no more.*

It was a disturbing thought.

Capturing Lee had been even easier than he'd thought. Caprice had called him after he left Gehenna and told him where he could find Kate and the others. She sent a car for him – driven by one of her employees and *not* Axton, praise Oblivion – and the driver gave him the vehicle, along with a semi-automatic pistol, and departed. Ethan took the Lord's left arm and right leg from the trunk of the dead Mercedes, transferred them to the new car, then drove to within a block of Tainted Pages and parked. He found a pair of Dog-Eaters who he paid to distract Kate and Haksaw, and while the Dog-Eaters did their work, Ethan stole up to Lee in the near-darkness and placed the gun's muzzle against their right temple.

"Don't make a sound or I'll blow your head off," he whispered into Lee's ear. He forced Lee to accompany him, and when they reached the car, Ethan clunked them on the head with the butt of the gun and rendered them unconscious. and then drove to the House of Red Tears. Lee didn't come to until Ethan had them in one of the House's playrooms, bound and gagged. He would've loved to spend a few hours testing Lee's pain tolerance. Were members of the Unbroken Court tougher than the average human? Had they been trained to withstand pain that would break an ordinary person? Unfortunately, there wasn't time, and Ethan had brought Lee to the Repository, as Caprice wanted. He wasn't certain about her plan, though.

"Do you really think Kate will come here with the body parts and the book?" he asked her.

"Yes, to save her friend. But even if we didn't have this one—" she nudged Lee with her foot, "—Kate would still come. She doesn't have a choice."

Ethan didn't know what Caprice meant. He hated it when she spoke cryptically.

"Where's Axton?" he asked.

"He's no longer with us," Caprice said.

Ethan smiled. He knew what the euphemism meant, and it was the first truly good news he'd had all day. He wouldn't miss the officious prick.

He glanced toward the Repository's open door. While the antechamber's lights were on outside, their illumination could not pass the room's threshold. Sound was cut off too, which meant that when

Kate – and presumably Haksaw – came down to the subbasement, he and Caprice would have no warning of their approach. The gun was tucked into the waistband of his pants, pressed cold and hard against the small of his back, and he was glad to have it. Magic was all well and good, but few things beat solid ammunition. The open door made him uncomfortable, though.

"Is it wise to keep the Repository door open?" he asked. "Won't the Gathered be able to escape if it remains that way too long?"

"In ordinary circumstances, yes. But now that the Incarnation is about to start, I'm using some of my power to keep the Gathered restrained." She smiled. "I have a little extra in the tank right now. Besides, it would be rude to close the door. We want our guests to feel welcome, don't we? Try to relax, Ethan. It won't be long now."

Ethan had become skilled at many things since his great-aunt had taken him in, but being patient wasn't one of them. He watched the wraiths swimming through the darkness around them and wondered how the events of this night would play out.

CHAPTER SEVENTEEN

Kate and Haksaw walked down the sidewalk, the serial killer pushing a rusted shopping cart containing the Lord's parts and atop them, *The Book of Depravity*. Haksaw had broken one of the Camry's rear passenger windows, and they'd been able to extricate the Lord's body parts. Kate had thought at first that they would be able to carry them to the House of Red Tears, but the torso, the jar of eyes, and the right arm – along with the book – proved to be more awkward than she'd anticipated. Plus, even though this was the Cannery, seeing a man and a woman carrying body parts out in the open would raise more than a few eyebrows. Luckily, High Strangeness was on the way to the House, and Haksaw's shopping cart was still in the parking lot. Returning to the bar filled Kate with sorrow. She'd only gotten to spend a short time with Reyna and Weston before they'd died, and while she knew Ethan would've killed them anyway, she couldn't help feeling as if she was responsible for their deaths.

"I'll stop her," she'd said softly as Haksaw retrieved his cart. "I don't know how, but I will."

The book's pages riffled as if in agreement.

It occurred to her then that she might be able to read the language the book was written in if she looked at it through the Lord's eyes. As Haksaw loaded the other parts into the cart, she sat cross-legged beneath one of the lot's fluorescent lights, laid the book in front of her, turned to a random page, then lifted the jar containing the Lord's eyes up to her face and looked down. The words made no more sense to her than they had before, and she was about to give up when the strange scrawl started to become clear to her. The letters shifted, reformed, became the alphabet she was familiar with. Or maybe she merely saw them that way.

However it worked, she was able to read *The Book of Depravity*. She quickly learned, though, that reading is not the same as understanding. She understood individual words, although many were unknown to her, but the meaning of the sentences eluded her. As she flipped through the book, she saw references to things she recognized, such as the Gyre and the Quintessence. But there were far more she'd never encountered before: The Alabaster Order, Purgatum, the Beside, the Lightbringers, the Hierarchy.... She could find no definitions for these words, though. It was as if the reader was expected to already know them.

It was no use. She'd need time to study the book to make even the slightest bit of sense out of it. Days, weeks, months, years.... And time was one thing she didn't have, not if she wanted to save Lee.

"Having trouble?" Haksaw asked. He'd finished loading the other body parts into the cart and had wheeled them closer to Kate.

She slammed the book closed. "I can't find what I'm looking for."

"Ask the book to help you."

She stared up at Haksaw. "What?"

"It's kind of alive, right? Who else would better know its contents?"

Feeling silly, but also quite aware she had nothing to lose, she said, "Book, do you have any information on how to destroy the Lord of the Feast?"

The cover flipped open and pages began turning themselves rapidly. They came to a stop about two-thirds of the way through the volume. Kate raised the Lord's eyes to her face once more and read. She expected to encounter a long, involved rite, but what she found was a passage only two sentences long.

The Lord of the Feast cannot be killed until it is born, for nothing may die until it has lived. Once born, the Lord can only be destroyed by giving it what it most desires.

She read the sentences several times before lowering the jar. The letters returned to their previous indecipherable state and the book slammed shut of its own accord.

"Did you find what you needed?" Haksaw asked.

"I'm... not sure. I'm going to have to think about it for a while."

She picked up the book and stood. She placed it and the jar in the shopping cart with the body parts, and concealed them beneath the cardboard.

"Let's go," she said.

They started walking once more, Haksaw pushing the cart, Kate lost in thought.

★   ★   ★

Kate had never seen the House of Red Tears, and when she and Haksaw reached it, she was surprised by its appearance. The buildings in the Cannery generally were crumbling remnants of the area's industrial past, but the House resembled a large country mansion. *Like Tressa's mansion,* she thought. *Only bigger.* Caprice had not only wanted to recreate the family's glory days, she'd wanted to outdo them. Lee was in there somewhere, and she hoped they still lived.

It's in Caprice's best interests to keep Lee alive, the voice inside her said. *At least until you've given her what she wants.*

Alive was not the same as unharmed, though. What would prevent Caprice and Ethan from torturing Lee if they wished?

The voice had no response to this.

Kate and Haksaw stood across the street from the House, and she was struck by the foul, greasy air. Haksaw pointed to a smokestack atop the House.

"They burn the bodies when they're finished with them," he said. He inhaled deeply. "Invigorating, isn't it?"

Christ, if she didn't need this lunatic....

"Do you know how to get in? I mean, we can't exactly go through the front door."

The book and body parts were covered with cardboard, and Haksaw reached under it to pat the torso.

"I know a way. I used it when I answered my love's call and carried it to freedom."

Whatever happened tonight, Kate was glad she wouldn't have to listen to Haksaw talk about his beloved torso anymore. She was grateful that being in the presence of the Lord's parts no longer gave her a headache. She needed to be pain-free to focus her thoughts.

"Show me."

Haksaw led her across the street and into an alley alongside the House. It was empty – no vehicles, not even any trash – and halfway down was a side door.

"Through here," Haksaw said. He sounded worried.

"Something wrong?"

"I'm afraid to take my love inside. Caprice might separate us, and we'll never be together again. But it's what the torso wants, and so I have to do it. That's what love is, right? Wanting what your partner wants, even if you fear it might hurt you."

Kate's definition of love had nothing to do with hurt of any kind, but this wasn't the time to get into a discussion about relationships, especially with an insane serial killer. She put her hand on the doorknob, but before she could turn it, she felt a prickle on the back of her neck, as if someone was watching them. She looked the way they'd come, saw nothing, looked the other way, and saw.... She frowned. The air wavered as if distorted by heat, and a dark form crouched close to the wall, mostly concealed by the shadows. The longer she looked, the more she had the impression that instead of one large distortion, there were a number of smaller ones, all of them human-sized.

"Do you see that?" she asked, pointing.

Haksaw looked where she indicated. "I don't...." He leaned forward. "Maybe? What is it?"

"I don't know. Whatever it is – whatever *they* are – I don't get a bad feeling from them. Let's go."

She opened the door and held it so Haksaw could push the shopping cart inside. Then, after one last look at the things at the other end of the alley, things that for some reason seemed very familiar to her, she followed and closed the door behind her.

★   ★   ★

It was quiet inside the House, which surprised Kate. Given the activities that went on here, she'd expected the corridors to be filled with the sounds of cracking whips and revving chainsaws, accompanied by screams of agony and moans of despair.

Caprice has gathered all the power she requires, said the voice in her head. *There's no need for any more killing.*

You're not me, are you? she thought back. The voice didn't answer, which, she supposed, was answer enough.

They saw no one as they made their way through the House. Either Caprice had given her staff the night off or they'd been instructed to stay out of Kate and Haksaw's way. Whatever the reason, Kate was grateful they weren't going to have to fight to reach the elevator. She wanted to conserve as much of her strength as possible for what was to come. She did have the feeling they were being followed at times, but whenever she looked back, she saw nothing. Maybe a slight distortion in the air, or a furry hand or foot withdrawing around a corner, but she told herself these glimpses were only products of her imagination. She didn't believe it, though.

"Here it is," Haksaw said.

They'd come to an elevator in the middle of a hallway. Kate pressed the button to summon it, and they waited. She couldn't believe how ordinary the House felt. A place like this, where hundreds of people had lost their lives in the most awful ways imaginable, was a virtual hell on Earth, and should possess an appropriately oppressive psychic atmosphere.

It's because no ghosts walk these halls. They're all downstairs in the Repository.

The elevator arrived with a ding. The door slid open, Haksaw wheeled the cart into the car, and Kate stepped in after him. She looked at the panel to the side of the door and saw a key inserted next to the button for the subbasement.

"Looks like we're expected," she said. "Big surprise."

She pressed the button, the door slid shut, and they began to descend. She was afraid, no doubt, and part of her wished she could be anywhere else on Earth at this moment. But although she could feel her fear pushing inside her chest, struggling to get out, it was more or less under control. Maybe growing up in her family had given her more tolerance for the bizarre and dangerous than most people. Or maybe she'd been through so much weirdness already this day that she'd run out of fucks to give. Or maybe, somehow, she was getting help managing her fear.

"What do we do when we get there?" Haksaw asked.

"Whatever it takes to get Lee out."

She wished the Unbroken Court would show up for a last-minute rescue, but Lee had already gotten their help once today by invoking Aequus, and Kate doubted they'd be inclined to help a second time. She had no doubt Monitors were somehow watching them right now, but whatever happened, they would not act.

The elevator continued its descent.

*   *   *

Mrs. No walked in through the House of Red Tears' front entrance, Mr. Yes's ghost drifting along beside her.

"You'd think Caprice would have locked the doors tonight," she said.

She left them unlocked so her grand-niece would have no trouble getting in.

"How do you know that?"

I'm dead. I know a lot of stuff now.

"Must be nice."

Not really. I'd rather be able to drink a cold beer, you know?

"Or fuck."

That too.

No carried the Glock she'd taken from the dead cop in her right hand, and she'd stuck the nightstick in her back waistband. Her head throbbed with each step, and she strongly suspected she had a concussion – not that she gave a shit – and her left hand still hurt like a motherfucker. She figured she should probably clean the finger stumps soon or else they'd get infected, but she didn't really give a shit about that either. All she cared about was finding Kate Shardlow and making the bitch pay for killing her husband.

There was no one staffing the reception desk, which was odd, and she saw no one in the waiting area. Usually there were a half dozen or so clients sitting on chairs, watching snuff films on a big screen TV while waiting for their turn to have fun in one of the playrooms. The fucking TV wasn't even on.

"This place is empty as a goddamn graveyard," she muttered.

Caprice canceled all client appointments and sent the staff away for the evening. Only the playthings are left, and they're locked in their cages.

"Guess Caprice doesn't want any interruptions tonight," No said. "Too bad we can't accommodate her."

She turned toward Yes — or rather the rippling distortion in the air that was the only visible indication of his presence.

"You know where we're going, right?"

Yes. We need to go down to the subbasement. That's where all the fun is going to be.

"Then the sooner we get there, the better."

No started jogging, ignoring how much more this made her head hurt. Yes floated next to her, keeping up easily. She knew where the elevator was, she and Yes had come here often enough, and it was right around this corner....

She stopped. Standing in front of the elevator were a group of figures that looked like her husband — semi-visible ripples in the air. There was also some kind of big black dog that was standing on its hind legs. The dog, or whatever it was, whipped its head toward her and growled. She started to raise the Glock.

Don't, Yes said. *Let me talk to them.*

He drifted down the hall toward the other ghosts — at least, that's what she assumed they were — but the bipedal dog-thing started padding toward her, nails scratching the tile floor as it came. As it drew closer, she saw that its features were a bestial amalgamation of canine, feline, and ursine. It also had long, wicked-looking claws, and yellow eyes that gleamed with feral malice. Yes had told her not to shoot, but it took every ounce of control she had not to fire on this monster. The creature closed the remaining distance between them and looked into her eyes for a long moment. Yes thought she was going to die in the next few seconds, which meant she could start a new ghost life with her husband, but she was disappointed that she wasn't going to get to make Kate pay for what she'd done.

But then the monster lowered its muzzle to her wounded hand, sniffed the bloody finger stumps, and began licking them. At first she thought the beast was tasting her, but then she realized it was, in fact, attempting to clean her wounds.

"Uh… thanks?"

One of the ghosts came drifting over. She thought it might be Yes, but she wasn't certain until she heard his voice. The monster continued licking her.

You're not going to believe who those guys are!

And as he told her, the furry creature continued cleaning her wounds, and in return she gave it a good scratch behind the ears.

Oh, and would you mind pressing the button for the elevator? None of us has fingers.

★   ★   ★

The elevator arrived at the subbasement, dinged, and the door slid open to reveal a small antechamber carved from rock and lit by fluorescent lights set into the ceiling. Directly across from the elevator was a large steel door. It was open wide, but all that was visible was a wall of solid darkness.

"I take it that's the Repository," Kate said.

"Yes. You can't see what's inside from here," Haksaw said. "You have to go in."

Which means we'll have no way of knowing what we're walking into, Kate thought. At least, it seemed like her thought. It was hard to tell at this point.

"Let's not keep Caprice and Ethan waiting any longer," she said.

She stepped off the elevator, and Haksaw came after her, pushing the cart. She feared she was making a horrible mistake, one that might result in the death of reality itself, but she could see no other choice. Not for her. She approached the doorway and without hesitation stepped into the darkness.

Haksaw had been right. The instant she was through, she could see inside the Repository. Glowing shapes swirled around the chamber, so many that it was almost as bright as day there. Caprice stood next to Ethan, and Lee knelt on the floor next to them, wrists and ankles enclosed in leather restraints, a ball gag in their mouth. Several of the Lord's parts were laid out on the floor — the head, the left arm, and both legs. The head had no eyes, and the top of its skull was missing, no brain inside.

"Hello, my dear," Caprice said, smiling. "It's so nice to see you again."

Kate hadn't seen her great-aunt in a decade, and Tressa had owned no photos of her. *Why would I ever want to look at that bitch's face?* she'd once said. So Kate's memories of Caprice were hazy, and she hadn't known what to expect when she saw her. But this woman — who looked younger than Caprice should've — wearing an all-white suit jacket and skirt, wasn't it.

"You look like a TV evangelist," Kate said.

Caprice's smile fell away, but Ethan grinned.

"And you look like a young lady who's going to watch her boyfriend...girlfriend...whatever die if she doesn't hand over what I need."

Kate gave Haksaw a nod and he wheeled the cart over to Ethan.

"Step back," Caprice ordered, and Haksaw did so.

Caprice went to the cart, removed the cardboard, and tossed it onto the chamber's stone floor. She then took out *The Book of Depravity*, held it up to her face, closed her eyes, and inhaled.

"There's nothing like the smell of an old book, is there?" she said.

Kate thought she might gag. "You do know what that thing's probably made out of, right?"

"Of course," Caprice said. "That's *why* it smells so good."

LORD OF THE FEAST • 273

She nodded to Ethan, and he walked to the cart, limping on his left leg. Kate wondered what had happened to him. Whatever it was, judging by the way he winced with each step, it hurt like hell. *Good. Serves the fucker right.* Ethan, moving slowly due to his injury, unloaded the rest of the items from the cart and put them in their proper places on the floor. Soon the Lord's pieces were all laid out – head, arms, torso, and legs. Ethan then opened the jar, took out one eye at a time, and held it over the Lord's empty sockets. The eyes jerked out of his hand and entered the sockets with a pair of sickening *schlurps*.

"You've got what you wanted," Kate said. "Now let Lee go."

"I haven't got *everything* I want," Caprice said. "You may have noticed that one part is still missing."

"The brain," Ethan said. He placed the jar on the floor and hobbled over to rejoin Caprice.

She nodded. "Exactly."

"But we don't *have* the brain," Kate protested.

"Don't you?" Caprice said, a smile playing about her lips.

Kate intended to deny it once more, but then she realized: the voice in her head, the one that she'd come to suspect wasn't hers.

"No," she whispered.

"Oh yes," Caprice said. "After the first Incarnation failed, the family had quite the argument about who would get what part of the Lord to protect. We all wanted the brain – it was the most powerful of the parts, naturally, as it contained the Lord's intelligence. Its soul, if you will. If something artificially created can be said to have such a thing. The family worried that the brain was too powerful for any one member to have. If one of us learned how to tap into that power.... Well, it would put the others at quite a disadvantage. And we couldn't have that. Tressa was the one who came up with the solution, and I have to admit it was brilliant. The Lord's parts could not be destroyed, but that didn't mean they couldn't be separated even further than they already were – and a brain is two hemispheres connected by the corpus callosum. It took some power and even more skill, but Tressa managed to split the Lord's brain in two, and then we hid the halves where no one could ever get at them. You possess the right hemisphere, Kate, the one that's methodical and analytical." She turned to Ethan. "And you have the left hemisphere, the artistic, creative half."

Ethan looked as stunned as Kate felt. For the last ten years, she'd had part of a god's brain in her skull, and she'd had no idea. That explained the voice in her head. She'd started hearing it after her first exposure to the Lord's eyes – another part of its body. The pain she'd felt then was the half-brain trying to reunite with the eyes. It had literally wanted to break free of her head and go to another part of itself. The pain had subsided after a while, maybe because the half-brain had woken up enough to realize it just couldn't jump out of her skull, and maybe because it came to understand that this moment would come, when it would finally rejoin the rest of its body.

"Don't worry," Caprice said. "We didn't use surgery to cut you open and jam an extra half of a brain into your heads. We used magic to transport the hemispheres into you and merge them with your own brain. Technically, this means you each possess a brain-and-a-half. Bet you didn't know you were so smart, eh?"

"That's why you really wanted to have me around," Ethan said, "wasn't it? You wanted to keep half of the Lord's brain nearby at all times."

"That's one of the reasons," Caprice admitted. "But you demonstrated such an aptitude for killing that I decided to train you in the death-dealing arts. Plus, I never had children of my own. It was...nice having you in the House with me."

She reached out to touch his cheek, but he took a step back before her fingers connected with his skin. The hurt this caused her showed plainly on her face, but she quickly concealed it behind a mask of icy indifference. She turned to Kate.

"That's why Tressa took *you* in – to guard the other half of the brain."

"Maybe that's partly why she did it, but Tressa loved me. I know she did."

Caprice sniffed. "The bitch always was too sentimental for her own good. Enough talk. The Omniverse isn't going to end itself you know." She held out the book to Ethan. "If you'll do the honors...."

Ethan looked at Caprice, but he didn't reach out to take the book.

"No need to hesitate, child. I've taught you how to read the language, and you know as much about the rite as I do. It's time to take your place as the new head of the family."

He hesitated a moment longer before taking *The Book of Depravity* from Caprice. It opened by itself to the appropriate page, and he began reading aloud. The instant the first word left his mouth, pain erupted in Kate's skull. She cried out and pressed her hands to her head, as if to keep it from exploding.

You need to let me out, the voice inside her said. Its tone was cold now, taunting. *If you don't release me willingly, I'll be taken from you by force. Trust me, you don't want that to happen.*

"No...." She could barely get the word out.

It's going to happen either way. Your only choice is how much pain you experience in the process.

"No," she said again. "No, no, no, no, no, no, no!"

The ceiling vanished, and an incomprehensively vast darkness encircled by swirling light appeared in its place.

Kate screamed and collapsed to the floor.

NOW

Ethan ignored the Gyre's sudden appearance, fearing that if he looked up at it, he might lose his already tenuous grip on sanity. If he hadn't been so close to finishing the rite, he might not have been able to resist. The Gathered swirled around him like an unearthly storm, the wraiths' power surrounding him like crackling electricity. Then they broke away, streaked toward the Lord's body parts, and entered them. The parts writhed for a moment then joined together, merging seamlessly, and the patchwork creature opened its eyes.

The Lord of the Feast lived again.

Ethan watched with a mixture of awe and horror as the Lord of the Feast rose to its mismatched feet. Caprice laughed, equal parts triumph and madness in the sound. He could feel power emanating from the god, waves of force so strong that he feared they might sweep him away.

You shall not be harmed, a voice inside him said. *Not yet, anyway.*

Now that the rite had been completed, *The Book of Depravity* slammed shut. It tore itself from his hands and fell to the floor, its role in this drama over. Ethan barely noticed. As impressive as the god was, it was nothing compared to the unimaginably gigantic thing that swirled above them. The Repository's ceiling was gone, replaced by endless nothingness, and within that vast emptiness was a circle of light slowly rotating around a dark circle. This was the Gyre, the great hunger that lay at the center of all reality. Looking at it hurt like hell — his eyes burned and his head felt like a thousand hot spikes had been driven through it — but he *was* able to look upon it, and as near as he could tell, his sanity remained intact.

You conducted the rite, and of course you have me inside you. If neither of these things were true, you might well be a gibbering lunatic right now.

The Gyre was at once the most beautiful and most terrifying thing he had ever seen, magnificent and appalling in equal measure. This was the true god his family had worked so hard to serve, the god Ethan had worshipped with every life he'd taken in the House of Red Tears. And now that he saw it for what it was, he had one thought: *I've been feeding a gigantic garbage disposal.* The Gyre had no mind of its own, was only an insatiable hunger that devoured everything and gave nothing in return. The Omniverse had only one purpose – to be processed into nonexistence – and the Gyre was just another cog in that machine. The biggest, most important cog to be sure, but a cog just the same. He felt more than a little let down by this insight.

Never come face to face with your gods, the voice inside him said. *We're always bound to disappoint you.*

Ethan realized then that he was a cog too. An infinitely smaller and less important one than the Gyre, but in the end just another part in the machine. *This* was what Caprice had groomed him to become over the last ten years. He wasn't a fearsome killer, heir to a family of powerful dark magicians, midwife to a being that would bring about the end of all existence. He was just a fucking pawn in someone else's game, and that's all he ever had been, all Kate had ever been as well.

You shouldn't think such things, the voice said. *I mean, they're true, but you still shouldn't* think *them.* The voice giggled inside Ethan's mind.

He looked away from the Gyre to see what the others were doing. The Gathered were gone, the spirits absorbed by the Lord's body. Their unearthly glow no longer lit the chamber, but the light from the Gyre's swirling ring provided more than enough illumination to see by. Caprice gazed upon the Lord with adoration, continuing to laugh with crazed delight. Lee was bleeding from the ears and nose, eyes glazed over, in shock. Ethan kind of wished he could go into shock right now too, let his mind drift away into la-la land so he didn't have to deal with all this anymore.

Look on the bright side, the voice inside him said. *After the Lord tears your half of its brain from your head, you'll never have to deal with anything ever again.*

The currently mindless thing that was the Lord of the Feast let out an unearthly high-pitched shriek and then started toward Kate. She lay on the ground, writhing in pain. He could sense a battle was taking place inside her between herself and the half of the Lord's brain that she hosted. It wanted out, and she was determined to deny it its freedom. He wondered why he wasn't caught in the same struggle.

You haven't tried to resist me yet.

Haksaw was on his knees, hands clasped before him as if in prayer. He looked upon the Lord with the childlike awe of a young boy who had just discovered that Santa Claus was real. He also bled from the nose and ears, but he didn't seem to notice, and if he did, he didn't care.

The patchwork monstrosity that was the Lord of the Feast staggered toward Kate on uneven legs, lurching from side to side as it went. It had no brain to direct its actions, but it possessed a certain animal instinct, one that impelled it toward Kate and the portion of its brain hidden within her. Ethan didn't want to watch his cousin die – which, considering the amount of death he'd dealt today, was rather ludicrous – but he didn't know what he could do to stop the Lord. If he went too near the creature, it would most likely go for the half of the brain he hosted, and while Caprice had said she and the other adults had used magic to implant the half-brains into his and Kate's heads, that didn't mean the procedure for extracting them would be painless, or survivable. Still, he had to try.

He took a step forward and nearly fell as pain radiated from his injured knee. He grimaced but forced himself to take a second step, then a third.

You're making this easy for us, you know that, right?

"Shut up," he muttered. A fourth step.

He realized that the unearthly speed he'd demonstrated in High Strangeness, when he'd been able to deflect bullets with knife blades, had been granted to him by the half of the Lord's mind that he hosted, probably in order to protect itself. Too bad he didn't have access to that speed now. He could've used it.

Haksaw stood as the Lord came near him, and he hurried over to stand between it and Kate. At first Ethan thought the old murderer was attempting to protect her, but then he reached out and placed his hand on the Lord's chest.

"Are you there, love? Are you happy now?"

The Lord's eyes focused on Haksaw, and a soft whisper escaped its lips.

"*Yesssssssss....*"

Then, moving with inhuman speed, the Lord took hold of Haksaw's head with both hands, twisted, and pulled it free from his body. Blood gushed from both ends, and the Lord placed a hand on Haksaw's shoulder to keep his body from falling over, then raised his head high and drank from the ragged wound at its base, just as it had done with the head of Kate's mother a decade ago. When it finished, it tossed the head aside and leaned down to drink from the open neck. It made sense, Ethan thought. Weren't all newborns hungry?

The Lord lifted its head from Haksaw's body, shoved it aside, and continued walking toward Kate. Its mouth and chin were slick with blood, and rivulets of red streaked its body. Given the circumstances, Ethan thought it looked appropriately nightmarish. If you were going to be a monster, he thought, you should go all the way. He started toward Kate once more, but before he could take more than two steps, Caprice caught hold of his arm and stopped him.

"Do not interfere," she said. She kept her gaze fixed on her god as she spoke. "This is what must happen."

"Elisha told me the purpose of life is to suffer. Is that why you want everything to end? Because *you're* afraid to suffer?"

"The people of the Omniverse..." she began.

"Maybe they'd *like* to keep suffering. Has anyone asked them?"

"I...." For an instant, Ethan saw doubt in his great-aunt's eyes. But then she shook her head as if to clear it. She gripped his wounded shoulder with surprising strength, and the resulting pain was so intense, he nearly passed out. She pushed him down and forced him to kneel. When his injured knee came in contact with the ground, he did black out, just for a second, but then the pain vanished. It seemed the half of the Lord's brain he hosted wasn't going to allow him the kindness of unconsciousness.

"Watch what happens to your cousin," Caprice said. "It'll be your turn next."

The Lord had nearly reached Kate. Ethan mentally urged her to get up and flee, but she continued to lie on the ground, rolling back and forth, hands pressed against her head. It was no use. The Lord was going to take what it needed from her, and then it was going to come for him.

There was a loud *crack*, and the Lord's head snapped backward.

"What the *fuck* is that thing?"

Ethan looked toward the chamber's entrance and saw Mrs. No standing there, gun in hand and aimed at the Lord. Next to her crouched some kind of beast-man, and surrounding the two of them were a dozen wavering shapes that slowly took on distinct forms and came into focus. They were people, he thought, but they were transparent, as if only partially present. Not people – *ghosts* – and ones he recognized. His parents and Kate's, Tressa, Delmar, Reyna, Weston, Lissette, Victorina, Elisha.... Mr. Yes was there too. The only family member missing was Felton, and Ethan guessed that's who the beast-man was.

Things just got a lot more interesting.

★   ★   ★

The sound of the gunshot cut through Kate's pain. She looked up to see the Lord practically standing over her. Its head had been knocked back, and when it straightened, she saw there was now a large hole in the middle of its forehead. *Nice shot,* she thought. Too bad the Lord didn't have any brains inside its skull yet, otherwise Mrs. No might've succeeded in killing it.

"Is *that* the god you were trying to make, Caprice?" Mrs. No said, incredulous. "Your family is sick."

Now that the Lord was so close, information flooded into Kate's mind. People's names, details about their lives, their hopes, fears, pain…. She understood that these were the people from whom Tressa and Delmar had harvested the parts that made up the Lord of the Feast. Tressa had used her powers to search for people whose lives were dark and suffused with negative energy, and it was this darkness which provided the spark that gave the Lord its mockery of life. The half-brain inside her had once belonged to a woman named Whitney Harmon, who as a young girl learned to lie in order to survive abusive parents. She became so good at deception that she even believed her own lies, at least on the surface. Lying became a way of life for her, so natural that it was as easy as breathing. Certainly easier than telling the truth. She lied to her teachers through elementary school, middle school, high school, and college. She lied to get boyfriends and to get rid of them, lied to obtain jobs, hold on to them, and give false reasons why she wanted to quit them. Eventually she faked a pregnancy to get a boyfriend to marry her, then after the wedding she pretended to have a miscarriage. It was harder to maintain her lies living with someone day in and day out, and eventually her husband caught on. They began to fight about her habit of 'exaggerating', as she put it, and during one of these fights, she admitted what she'd done to trap him into marriage. Furious, he grabbed her throat and started squeezing. He didn't think he was hurting her, not really, and when she pounded on his arms to make him let go, he thought she was merely being overdramatic. He was wrong, but he didn't realize this until after Whitney was dead.

That was *me*, the voice inside her said. *But I'm the Lord of the Feast now, and I've got a reality to disassemble, so if you wouldn't mind letting me out….*

Kate ignored the voice and rose to her feet. Her head still hurt like hell, but she thought she could manage the pain. She had to.

The Lord was no longer looking at her. It had turned its attention to Mrs. No. She fired at it again, this time shooting until she'd emptied the gun's clip. The Lord's chest and abdomen were dotted with bullet wounds, all of which bled freely, but the god took no notice of them. It started toward Mrs. No, moving surprisingly fast on its mismatched legs. No ejected the spent clip but as fast as the Lord was moving, Kate knew

282 • TIM WAGGONER

the woman wouldn't be able to reload and fire before the god reached her – especially with only one fully functional hand.

But then something sleek and dark-furred rushed toward the Lord, leaped upon it, and began furiously raking its flesh with long curved claws, sending blood flying in all directions. Now that the Lord was alive, it could be harmed like any other physical being, and without its brain, it was nowhere near its full strength. Kate hoped the beast-thing that had been Uncle Felton would be able to do some serious damage to the god, maybe enough to cause it to lose cohesion and collapse into its component parts once more. She caught more movement from the corner of her eye and turned to see a group of people running toward her. No, not toward *her* – toward Caprice and Ethan. And these weren't just people; they were her family. Or rather, her family's spirits.

Tressa broke off from the others and came to her, a sad expression on her transparent face.

You know what you have to do, child. The book told you. And I'm so sorry for how we used you. You deserved better from us…better from me.

Then she rushed off to rejoin the others, gliding several inches above the chamber's stone floor. As stunned as Kate was to see her family, she forgot about them as her attention focused on Lee. They were also kneeling, expression blank, blood running from their ears and nostrils. They were looking up at the Gyre – the thing that Kate didn't want to see – and she knew that if Lee didn't look away soon, it would swallow their mind. She thrust all other thoughts aside and ran to help her partner.

CHAPTER EIGHTEEN

No finally managed to reload her gun despite having only one usable hand, but considering the amount of damage her furry friend was doing to the god, that wasn't necessarily a bad thing. She preferred to do her own killing, but in this case, she was more than willing to accept some help. Yes drifted over to her, and she saw that he'd now taken on the shape he'd worn in life. He looked good as a ghost, she thought. He was spooky, but still cute. She wondered if she could touch him or if her hand would pass through him as if he was no more substantial than mist. She was tempted to try, but restrained herself. She didn't want to embarrass him in front of everyone, especially the other ghosts.

"Do you think he can kill it?" she asked.

Before Yes could answer, the Lord of the Feast pulled the beast-man off of it and then, with seemingly no effort whatsoever, tore him in two. The half-human, half-animal howled in agony as blood and internal organs spilled out of both its halves. The Lord gazed hungrily at the glistening treasures, but then it hurled the two halves of the beast's body away and continued coming for her.

A headshot hadn't worked, and the other rounds she'd put in it hadn't even slowed it down. Maybe if she hit the heart dead on....

Fear not, my love.

Yes floated toward the Lord with the obvious intent of protecting her. It was a sweet gesture, but Yes was a ghost. What the hell could he do to a god?

Not much, as it turned out.

When he was close to the Lord, the creature drew in a massive breath. Yes was sucked toward its mouth as if the Lord was an industrial-strength vacuum and he nothing more than a clump of dust and dirt.

Yes looked at her one last time, expression unreadable, and then he was gone, slurped up like the last strand of spaghetti on a plate. No had come to the House of Red Tears with the express purpose of killing Kate to avenge her dead love. But now Yes was doubly dead, and his killer was the monstrous conglomeration that stood before her. She forgot about Kate and began firing at the Lord, advancing with each shot. The god's body jerked with the impact of each round, but it didn't go down. When the clip was spent, No dropped the gun and drew the nightstick. She ran to the creature and swung the stick, striking the creature on the sides of the head, on the abdomen, on the cock and balls, but these blows weren't any more effective than her bullets had been.

The Lord's right hand shot out and grabbed her by the throat. With its left hand, it yanked the nightstick from her grip, and rammed it into her right eye socket, shoving it in as far as it would go. No's body spasmed as if she was a short-circuiting machine, and then it went still. The Lord tossed her corpse aside, and when her ghost began to emerge, like a butterfly from its chrysalis, he inhaled it into himself just as he had done with Yes's spirit. Wherever they went, whatever their state of being – if any – at least No and Yes were together again.

⋆   ⋆   ⋆

This is going well, Caprice thought.

Not only was the Lord alive and ambulatory, it was drawing power from the Gyre itself. Now all that was necessary for the Incarnation to be complete was for the Lord to reclaim the two halves of its brain from Kate and Ethan. Lee had fulfilled their function by luring Kate here and was no longer a factor in the proceedings, but bound and helpless, they were no threat, and Caprice decided to let them live long enough to witness the Lord come into its full glory.

While the stated goal of the Quintessence was to end the Omniverse's suffering, Caprice had to admit – if only to herself – that she found the prospect of the destruction itself exciting. And it wouldn't happen all at once. The Lord might be a god, in many ways an avatar of the

Gyre itself, but it was still a physical being. It would take time for it to break down the entire Omniverse. Centuries, perhaps millennia. A swift process on a cosmic scale, but she wouldn't get to see it. Once the Lord was whole, it would finish off Kate and Ethan, then it would come for Lee, then her. Having the Lord take her life was the greatest honor she could imagine. Still, it would've been nice to stay around for a while longer and witness the culmination of her life's work. She imagined herself as the Lord's herald, announcing its coming to those who were about to die. Ah well. Some dreams weren't meant to be. At least she would see the Lord become complete before her death. That would have to be enough.

She'd been surprised by the arrival of her dead family members, but it was only fitting that they be here at the end. In life they may have argued with her over whether or not to risk a second attempt at the Incarnation, but now that they were present, they could see that her unwavering faith had been rewarded. Yes, the road to success had been long and difficult — and not without its casualties — but surely they were as filled with joy as she was. It was good that they were all together again, united in a single purpose, as it was meant to be. Because after all that had occurred, good and bad, weren't they still family?

Her dead relatives had assumed facsimiles of their earthly forms, and while they were only semi-visible, she could make out the expressions on their faces. None of them were smiling. They came at her then, rushing across the Repository, forms phasing in and out of their barely visible state, as if they were no longer concerned with maintaining the illusion of physical bodies. Tressa was in the lead of course, one instant appearing as herself, the next as wavering distortions in the air. The traitorous bitch led the others — which now included Felton's spirit — in their attack, and the hatred she saw in their faces struck her like a physical blow. Even after everything that had happened, that she had *caused* to happen, she had thought her family would come around to her side in the end. But she couldn't have been more wrong.

She raised her hands, mentally preparing a spell to defend herself, but she was too late. The spirits abandoned all pretense of human appearance and fused into a single mass of rippling energy. It came at her like a wall of solid force, and when it hit her, it knocked her back several steps. She could feel them inside her, roiling and seething, building pressure, as if they were steam and she was a thin-walled metal container.

Then her body exploded.

The pain was excruciating, but it was over in an instant. She looked around, saw her blood, bones, and organs spread outward from where she stood, only how could she see this if she no longer possessed eyes?

Welcome to the afterlife, Tressa said.

Caprice turned and saw her family standing behind her – Tressa, Delmar, Victorina, Elisha, Nila, Dalton, Lissette, Felton, Delora, Cordell, Reyna, and Weston. They no longer looked like phantoms, but appeared as solid, fully fleshed versions of themselves.

Tressa reached out and took hold of Caprice's arm, her grip firm.

Time to go.

No! Caprice protested. *I want to see, I want to see!*

The others came forward, the forms flickering, becoming pure energy once more. She felt herself entering the same state, and then they all merged as before, only this time she was part of them. She tried to pull free of the mass, but the others held her, and there was nothing she could do. As one, they began to rise toward the Gyre. They moved slowly at first, but then the great nothingness caught hold of them and pulled them toward the vast void of its mouth. They accelerated, moving faster than Caprice imagined was possible.

I want to see, Caprice pleaded. *Just a little more....*

But then the Gyre claimed them, and the Shardlows and Lintons were no more.

With two exceptions.

★   ★   ★

Kate watched as the ghosts of her family destroyed Caprice's body and then carried her spirit up to the Gyre. She felt them saying goodbye to her – her parents, Reyna and Weston, Tressa and Delmar, and the others – felt their love, their regret, their shame over what they had helped set in motion ten years ago – and then they were gone.

Now it was just her, Ethan, Lee, and the Lord of the Feast.

You're going to submit, the voice inside her said. *You have no other choice.*

If she got down on her hands and knees, she could slam her head against the stone floor repeatedly, dash out her brains, and maybe destroy her half of the Lord's brain in the process. It was a desperate ploy, but it was the only one she had left. But when she tried to lower herself to the floor, she found she couldn't move.

*Nice try, but I'm in your head too, and I'm not about to let you damage yourself like that. Just let go, Kate. If you cooperate, the extraction process will be noninvasive and painless. Well…*relatively *painless. No harm will come to you or Ethan. If you don't cooperate, I'll take what I need by force, and that would be most unpleasant for you.*

The Lord of the Feast – or at least its patchwork body – stood in front of her. None of its pieces matched, with the exception of the eyes, and they moved independently of each other, acting more lizard-like than human. The top of its head was missing, the cavity inside empty and waiting for what she and Ethan had unknowingly kept custody of in their own heads for the last decade. *This* was a god? This…this *thing*? The thought was so ludicrous, she almost laughed.

Ethan hurried over to Lee and began working on undoing their restraints.

"I checked *The Book of Depravity*," she called out to her cousin, "and I found a way to destroy the Lord."

Ethan stopped what he was doing and looked at her, hope on his face.

"Was it a rite or spell? Do we need some kind of special mystic object?"

She shook her head.

"Nothing like that. The book said only this: 'Give the Lord what it requires.'"

"That's it?" Ethan said.

"Yes."

Lee still had the ball gag in their mouth, but they shook their head vigorously, indicating they thought this was an extraordinarily bad idea.

288 • TIM WAGGONER

Ethan looked at Kate for a moment, and she could tell he was mulling over her words, trying to understand what they might mean. Finally, he shrugged. "Fuck it. Let's do it."

All right, Kate thought to the alien presence inside her mind. *You can go.*

The voice had told her it wouldn't hurt if she did it willingly, but she expected to feel *something* dramatic. After all, she'd hosted half of a supernatural being's mind in her own for over half her life, and relinquishing it should come as a major shock. But all she felt was a lightening, as if a weight had been lifted from her, one she had gotten so used to carrying that she'd come to think of it as a normal part of herself. There was a sense of loss as well, a melancholy feeling that she was no longer whole, but that was it. The voice had told her the truth – it hadn't hurt. There was no sign on Ethan's face to indicate whether he experienced the same sensations, but she thought he did.

As Kate watched, brain tissue swelled like a balloon to fill the cavity of the Lord's skull. The god drew in a deep breath, and its eyes ceased their independent movements and began working in unison. Its mouth stretched into a broad smile, and for the first time since it had risen to its feet, it spoke in a full voice.

"Now *this* is what I'm talking about!"

It reached up with both hands and gingerly touched its brain.

"It tickles! I guess I'm going to have to find a scalp somewhere. Maybe I'll take one of yours. Or maybe Lee's. I really like their hair. I'd say it was fun getting to know the two of you over the last decade, but I'd rather not start off my new life with a lie. Your heads were prisons to me, and I can't tell you how good it feels to finally be free of your small minds and their even smaller concerns."

"Just shut up and kill us already, would you?" Ethan said. "I'd rather die than listen to any more of your bullshit."

The Lord grinned. "As you wish. Since I'm closest to Kate, she'll have the honor of being the next to die. You'll have to settle for following her, Ethan."

"I'll do my best to contain my disappointment," Ethan said.

Still grinning, the Lord reached for Kate…but it stopped before it could touch her. It frowned, and a distant look came into its eyes, as if it were thinking of something. Or perhaps remembering.

"*This* is a god?" it whispered. "This…this *thing*?"

It held out its hands, examined them, looked down at its body, noted the seams where its mismatched parts joined.

"The people whose bodies I'm made from…. They weren't avatars of great darkness. They were ordinary humans who committed ordinary, even banal, sins." The Lord looked up at the Gyre swirling above them, at once too close and so far away. "I'm not really anything, am I? Certainly not compared to *that*. I'm a joke, a parody, a mockery. I'm not a god, I'm…." Its voice grew small. "I'm nothing."

The Lord's left arm shook, and then it detached from the torso and flew upward toward the Gyre. Within seconds, it was lost from sight. The same happened for its right arm, and then its legs. The Lord fell to the floor and lay on its back, gazing up at the Gyre. The torso began to quiver, and Kate knew that any second it would rise, likely taking the head with it, and it too would enter the Gyre and be no more.

"You don't have to die," Kate said. "Not unless you want to. You've had a home for the last ten years. Two of them, actually. You can come back to us if you want."

She looked at Ethan, and after a moment's thought, he nodded his agreement.

"Come home," she said.

The Lord's brain began to wither in its skull, losing mass and substance. Kate felt a weight settle on her once more, but she didn't mind it. It felt good, in fact, like it belonged there.

The head and torso lifted off the floor, splitting apart as they did so, and they flew upward toward the Gyre. Within seconds, the parts had been devoured, and without the Lord's presence connecting it to the earthly plane, the Gyre winked out, taking the light with it and plunging the Repository into darkness. A muffled cry came from Lee, and Kate didn't have to be able to read their mind to understand the message – *Someone get this goddamned gag off me!*

★   ★   ★

Lee rubbed their wrists as the three of them stepped off the elevator.

They worked their tongue around in their mouth a couple times, then grimaced.

"I don't want to ever taste leather again."

Kate laughed and reached out to take their hand. They exchanged smiles, and then she turned to Ethan.

"With Caprice gone, I suppose this place is yours now. What will you do with it?"

"I suppose I could keep the business going, but honestly, I think I've had my fill of killing people – for the time being, at least. Maybe I'll sell the House. Maybe I'll just walk away. This is the Cannery. Someone or something will move into it eventually. Or maybe I'll burn the fucker down, just like what happened to Tressa and Delmar's mansion when—"

He stopped. His right hand was now wreathed in crimson flame.

"Oh my god, does that hurt?" Kate asked.

"Not at all," Ethan said. "It feels good, actually. Warm and soothing."

"It's the same color as the fire that burned down Tressa and Delmar's house," Kate said. "Do you think it's coming from the part of the Lord inside you?"

"Maybe? Probably? Now that we're aware we each host half of the Lord's brain, who knows what power we can tap into?" He gazed at the flames flickering around his flesh for a moment, and then he pressed his hand to the wall. Crimson fire spread outward in all directions and raced up and down the wall. Intense heat blasted from the flames, but when Ethan pulled his hand away from the wall, not only was the fire gone from his flesh, the skin was undamaged.

"We should get out of here," Lee said. "Fast."

CHAPTER NINETEEN

They stood on the sidewalk across the street and watched the House of Red Tears burn. The mystic flames had spread rapidly, just as they had when they destroyed the Shardlow mansion, and the majority of the building was engulfed. No firefighters had arrived yet, and if they didn't get here quickly, the House would soon be a smoking ruin. Not that there was anything mere humans could do to stop a fire like this.

Lee's phone rang. They removed it from their pocket and checked the display to see who was calling.

"It's the Court," they said. "I'm sure they want me to report in. This shouldn't take long."

They walked down the sidewalk a bit, answered the phone, and began talking.

"How did the Court know it was over?" Kate asked.

Ethan gestured at the people that had gathered on the sidewalks to watch the House of Red Tears burn.

"Any of them could be Monitors for the Court," he said. "Hell, maybe *most* of them are." He paused, then in a softer voice asked, "Are you okay?"

"Okay is a relative concept. My life has completely changed in the last twelve hours, and it's going to take me some time to process everything that's happened."

It was strange, talking with Ethan like this – relaxed, even companionable – after all he'd done. Maybe it was because they both carried part of the Lord in them, or maybe Kate had more Shardlow in her than she'd thought. Or maybe she was just too goddamned tired.

"Look, about Tressa and Delmar—" Ethan began, but Kate held up a hand to stop him.

"Now that we're, well, I guess you could say *closer* to the Lord, I know what our grandparents did to harvest the parts to create it. They were hardly saints. No one in our family was." She smiled. "Or is."

"I guess not." He held up an index finger and a tiny crimson flame flickered to life at the tip. He blew on it and the flame extinguished. "Do you think you have any powers?"

"I don't know. I don't feel any different physically than I did before, but who can say? I'm not sure I want any, but if they're there, they'll probably manifest in time."

She hoped she never developed any strange abilities, certainly none as strong as Ethan's. What if she couldn't control them? She might end up becoming as much of a threat to others as the Lord of the Feast.

She looked over at Lee. They finished their call and put their phone back in their pocket. They stood there for a moment, then walked over to a public trash receptacle. They reached inside and withdrew a folded newspaper. They unfolded it enough to check inside, then refolded it, tucked it beneath an arm, and returned to Kate and Ethan.

Kate was careful not to look at the newspaper.

"How did the call go?" she asked.

Lee didn't answer right away. They watched the fire and refused to meet Kate's gaze. They continued watching the House burn when they finally began speaking.

"The Unbroken Court doesn't operate the way a normal court does. They gather a great deal of data in real time, and the Judges review it as it comes in. Because of this, they can deliberate and come to a verdict quickly."

"And what's their verdict in our case?" Ethan asked. His voice sounded casual, but there was wariness in his eyes.

"They're glad the second Incarnation didn't succeed, of course, and since the rest of your family is dead, there's no need to punish them."

"*We're* not dead," Kate said.

"True, but because you both helped defeat the Lord, I argued that you should be shown mercy."

"And did the Court agree?" Ethan asked.

"The Court is concerned that you each possess half of the Lord's mind. They fear that as long as the two halves of the Lord's brain remain intact, there's a chance a third Incarnation could be attempted."

"We don't have *The Book of Depravity*," Kate said. They hadn't been able to find it when they searched the Repository after the Lord's defeat. Maybe it had somehow been destroyed when the Lord awakened or, its work done, had returned to Tainted Pages under its own power. Either way, she was glad to be rid of the damned thing.

"The book may be one of a kind, but it's easier to find if you know how. There are Tainted Pages all over the world. Or I should say that the one store with the same proprietor can be accessed from nearly any city on Earth or even a good-sized small town. It's part of the store's magic. You could travel anywhere in the world and still find the book. And now that you're both in communication with the parts of the Lord that dwell inside you…well, you could cause some serious trouble if you had a mind to."

Now Kate dropped her gaze to the newspaper still tucked beneath their arm.

"Did they leave that for you?" she asked.

"Yes."

"Is it a gun?" Ethan asked.

"Yes."

"They want you to kill us."

"Yes. They think you're too much of a danger to let run around loose."

"And what do *you* think?" Ethan asked.

Anguish showed on Lee's face, but they didn't answer the question.

"You don't have to do what the Court tells you to," Kate said. "Ethan, me, and even the Lord learned that today. We're free to become whoever and whatever we want to be. You could be free with us."

A tear ran down the side of Lee's face.

"I took a vow…."

"Fuck your vow," Ethan said. He raised his hands and crimson fire blazed forth from his palms.

Lee pulled a gun from inside the newspaper, raised it, and aimed at Ethan. The discarded paper was carried away by the breeze.

"I'm so sorry," Lee said. They kept their gaze focused on Ethan, but they addressed Kate next. "I really do love you. That's what's going to make this so hard."

Lee began to squeeze the trigger....

Kate wished there was something she could do to stop Lee, and with that thought a black circle opened up in the air behind them, one wreathed with swirling bright light. Lee turned and gazed with horror on the mini-Gyre. They started to move away from it, but the Gyre pulled at them, and they were yanked off their feet as if shoved by hurricane-force winds. Lee was sucked into the Gyre, and when they were gone, the portal closed and vanished.

Kate stared at the spot where the mini-Gyre had been. She didn't know if she'd summoned the actual Gyre, created a passage to it, or if what had appeared had been her own creation. The details didn't matter, though. All that mattered was that Lee was gone.

She felt Ethan put a hand on her shoulder.

"I'm sorry, but Lee could never have accepted you for what you are."

She supposed she could understand Lee choosing duty over love, but that didn't make it hurt any less.

"And what am I? A monster?"

Ethan smiled. "You're my cousin."

Kate smiled back. They turned to watch the House burn some more, and they soon heard the sound of fire engines approaching in the distance.

ACKNOWLEDGMENTS

Thanks to my editor extraordinaire – and good friend – Don D'Auria. (This is our twelfth book together since 2005. Can you believe it?) Thanks to Mike Valsted, whose insightful comments helped make this a better novel, and thanks to all the good folks at Flame Tree who helped bring *Lord of the Feast* to you. And of course, thanks to my fantastic agent, Cherry Weiner, tireless champion of my work, stalwart guide through the tangled jungle that is publishing, and my friend.

FLAME TREE PRESS
FICTION WITHOUT FRONTIERS
Award-Winning Authors & Original Voices

Flame Tree Press is the trade fiction imprint of Flame Tree Publishing, focusing on excellent writing in horror and the supernatural, crime and mystery, science fiction and fantasy. Our aim is to explore beyond the boundaries of the everyday, with tales from both award-winning authors and original voices.

•

Also by Tim Waggoner:
The Mouth of the Dark
They Kill
The Forever House
Your Turn to Suffer
We Will Rise
A Hunter Called Night

You may also enjoy:
The Hungry Moon by Ramsey Campbell
The Influence by Ramsey Campbell
The Wise Friend by Ramsey Campbell
Somebody's Voice by Ramsey Campbell
Fellstones by Ramsey Campbell
The Lonely Lands by Ramsey Campbell
The Namelesss by Ramsey Campbell
The Haunting of Henderson Close by Catherine Cavendish
The Garden of Bewitchment by Catherine Cavendish
The Toy Thief by D.W. Gillespie
One By One by D.W. Gillespie
Black Wings by Megan Hart
The Playing Card Killer by Russell James
The Sorrows by Jonathan Janz
Will Haunt You by Brian Kirk
We Are Monsters by Brian Kirk
Hearthstone Cottage by Frazer Lee
Those Who Came Before by J.H. Moncrieff
Stoker's Wilde by Steven Hopstaken & Melissa Prusi
Ghost Mine by Hunter Shea
Slash by Hunter Shea

•

Join our mailing list for free short stories, new release details, news about our authors and special promotions:

flametreepress.com